Robert Ackroyd - Relate cha

# AMERICAN
## Short Stories

# AMERICAN
# *Short Stories*

*American Short Stories*

Previously published as part of
*The Masterpiece Library of Short Stories, Volume XV, American,*
issued by Allied Newspapers Ltd., in association with
The Educational Book Company Ltd, London.

This edition published in 1995 by Senate, an imprint of
Studio Editions Ltd, Princess House, 50 Eastcastle Street,
London W1N 7AP, England

Copyright © this edition Studio Editions Ltd 1995

All rights reserved. This publication may not be reproduced,
stored in a retrieval system or transmitted, in any form or
by any means, electronic, mechanical, photocopying
or otherwise, without the prior written permission
of the publishers.

ISBN 1 85958 115 3
Printed and bound in Guernsey by
The Guernsey Press Co. Ltd

# Contents

*George William Curtis (1824-92)*
Titbottom's Spectacles ................................................................. 17
*Bayard Taylor (1825-78)*
Who was She? ................................................................................ 35
*John W. De Forest (1826-1906)*
An Inspired Lobbyist .................................................................... 49
*John T. Trowbridge (1827-1916)*
The Man who Stole a Meeting House ....................................... 62
*William James Stillman (1828-1901)*
Billy and Hans ................................................................................ 76
*Thomas A. Burke (b. 1828)*
Polly Peablossom's Wedding ....................................................... 88
'Doing' a Sheriff ............................................................................. 95
*Jonathan F. Kelly (c. 1830)*
A Desperate Race ........................................................................... 98
*Fitz-James O'Brien (1828-62)*
The Diamond Lens ...................................................................... 103
*Noah Brooks (1830-1903)*
Lost in the Fog ............................................................................. 123
*Samuel Davis (c. 1830)*
The First Piano in Camp ............................................................ 136
*Rebecca Harding Davis (1831-1910)*
Balacchi Brothers ......................................................................... 142
*Frank R. Stockton (1834-1902)*
Mr. Tolman .................................................................................... 156
The Transferred Ghost ............................................................... 173
The Lady, or the Tiger? .............................................................. 182
*Harriet P. Spofford (1835-1921)*
The Mount of Sorrow ................................................................. 188

# CONTENTS

### Mark Twain
The Celebrated Jumping Frog of Calaveras County ................... 201
The Man who put up at Gadsby's ................................................. 206

### Thomas Bailey Aldrich
Marjorie Daw ................................................................................ 210
Mademoiselle Olympe Zabriski .................................................. 225
Our New Neighbours at Ponkapog ............................................. 234

### Francis Bret Harte
Tennessee's Partner ...................................................................... 239
Miggles .......................................................................................... 246
The Luck of Roaring Camp ........................................................ 255
The Outcasts of Poker Flat ......................................................... 263
The Idyl of Red Gulch ................................................................ 272

### George Brooke
How Angels got Religion ............................................................ 280

### W. H. H. Murray
A Ride with a Mad Horse in a Freight-Car ............................... 285

### Louise Stockton
Kirby's Coals of Fire .................................................................... 297

### Max Adeler
A Desperate Adventure ............................................................... 304

### George Alfred Townsend
Crutch, the Page .......................................................................... 311

### Ambrose Bierce
The Man and the Snake .............................................................. 327
The Damned Thing ..................................................................... 332
My Favourite Murder .................................................................. 339
An Occurrence at Owl Creek Bridge ......................................... 345
The Affair at Coulter's Notch .................................................... 353
A Watcher by the Dead .............................................................. 360

### Henry James
The Tree of Knowledge ............................................................... 369

# GEORGE WM. CURTIS
## 1824–1892

# TITBOTTOM'S SPECTACLES

*In my mind's eye, Horatio.—Hamlet.*

PRUE and I do not entertain much; our means forbid it. In truth, other people entertain for us. We enjoy that hospitality of which no account is made. We see the show, and hear the music, and smell the flowers, of great festivities, tasting, as it were, the drippings from rich dishes.

Our own dinner service is remarkably plain, our dinners, even on state occasions, are strictly in keeping, and almost our only guest is Titbottom. I buy a handful of roses as I come up from the office, perhaps, and Prue arranges them so prettily in a glass dish for the centre of the table, that even when I have hurried out to see Aurelia step into her carriage to go out to dine, I have thought that the bouquet she carried was not more beautiful because it was more costly.

I grant that it was more harmonious with her superb beauty and her rich attire. And I have no doubt that if Aurelia knew the old man, whom she must have seen so often watching her, and his wife, who ornaments her sex with as much sweetness, although with less splendour, than Aurelia herself, she would also acknowledge that the nosegay of roses was as fine and fit upon their table as her own sumptuous bouquet is for herself. I have so much faith in the perception of that lovely lady.

It is my habit—I hope I may say, my nature—to believe the best of people, rather than the worst. If I thought that all this sparkling setting of beauty—this fine fashion—these blazing jewels, and lustrous silks, and airy gauzes, embellished with gold-threaded embroidery and wrought in a thousand exquisite elaborations, so that I cannot see one of those lovely girls pass me by without thanking God for the vision—if I thought that this was all, and that, underneath her lace flounces and diamond bracelets, Aurelia was a sullen, selfish woman, then I should turn sadly homeward, for I should see that her jewels were flashing scorn upon the object they adorned, that her laces were of a more exquisite loveliness than the woman whom they merely touched with a superficial grace.

It would be like a gaily decorated mausoleum—bright to see, but silent and dark within.

"Great excellences, my dear Prue," I sometimes allow myself to say, "lie concealed in the depths of character, like pearls at the bottom of the sea. Under the laughing, glancing surface, how little they are suspected! Perhaps love is nothing else than the sight of them by one person. Hence every man's mistress is apt to be an enigma to everybody else.

"I have no doubt that, when Aurelia is engaged, people will say she is a most admirable girl, certainly; but they cannot understand why any man should be in love with her. As if it were at all necessary that they should! And her lover, like a boy who finds a pearl in the public street, and wonders as much that others did not see it as that he did, will tremble until he knows his passion is returned; feeling, of course, that the whole world must be in love with this paragon, who cannot possibly smile upon anything so unworthy as he.

"I hope, therefore, my dear Mrs. Prue," I continue, and my wife looks up, with pleased pride, from her work, as if I were such an irresistible humourist, "you will allow me to believe that the depth may be calm although the surface is dancing. If you tell me that Aurelia is but a giddy girl, I shall believe that you think so. But I shall know, all the while, what profound dignity, and sweetness, and peace lie at the foundation of her character."

I say such things to Titbottom during the dull season at the office. And I have known him sometimes to reply, with a kind of dry, sad humour, not as if he enjoyed the joke, but as if the joke must be made, that he saw no reason why I should be dull because the season was so.

"And what do I know of Aurelia, or any other girl?" he says to me with that abstracted air; "I, whose Aurelias were of another century and another zone."

Then he falls into a silence which it seems quite profane to interrupt. But as we sit upon our high stools at the desk, opposite each other, I leaning upon my elbows and looking at him, he, with sidelong face, glancing out of the window, as if it commanded a boundless landscape, instead of a dim, dingy office court, I cannot refrain from saying:

"Well!"

He turns slowly and I go chatting on—a little too loquacious perhaps, about those young girls. But I know that Titbottom regards such an excess as venial, for his sadness is so sweet that you could believe it the reflection of a smile from long, long years ago.

One day, after I had been talking for a long time, and we had put up our books and were preparing to leave, he stood for some time by the window, gazing with a drooping intentness, as if he really saw something more than the dark court, and said slowly:

"Perhaps you would have different impressions of things if you saw them through my spectacles."

There was no change in his expression. He still looked from the window, and I said:

"Titbottom, I did not know that you used glasses. I have never seen you wearing spectacles."

"No; I don't often wear them. I am not very fond of looking through them. But sometimes an irresistible necessity compels me to put them on, and I cannot help seeing."

Titbottom sighed.

"Is it so grievous a fate to see?" inquired I.

"Yes; through my spectacles," he said, turning slowly, and looking at me with wan solemnity.

It grew dark as we stood in the office talking, and, taking our hats, we went out together. The narrow street of business was deserted. The heavy iron shutters were gloomily closed over the windows. From one or two offices struggled the dim gleam of an early candle, by whose light some perplexed accountant sat belated, and hunting for his error. A careless clerk passed, whistling. But the great tide of life had ebbed. We heard its roar far away, and the sound stole into that silent street like the murmur of the ocean into an inland dell.

"You will come and dine with us, Titbottom?"

He assented by continuing to walk with me, and I think we were both glad when we reached the house and Prue came to meet us, saying:

"Do you know I hoped you would bring Mr. Titbottom to dine?"

Titbottom smiled gently, and answered:

"He might have brought his spectacles with him, and have been a happier man for it."

Prue looked a little puzzled.

"My dear," I said, "you must know that our friend, Mr. Titbottom, is the happy possessor of a pair of wonderful spectacles. I have never see them, indeed; and, from what he says, I should be rather afraid of being seen by them. Most short-sighted persons are very glad to have the help of glasses; but Mr. Titbottom seems to find very little pleasure in his."

"It is because they make him too far-sighted, perhaps," interrupted Prue quietly, as she took the silver soup-ladle from the sideboard.

We sipped our wine after dinner, and Prue took her work. Can a man be too far-sighted? I did not ask the question aloud. The very tone in which Prue had spoken, convinced me that he might.

"At least," I said, "Mr. Titbottom will not refuse to tell us the history of his mysterious spectacles. I have known plenty of magic in eyes" (and I glanced at the tender blue eyes of Prue), "but I have not heard of any enchanted glasses."

"Yet you must have seen the glass in which your wife looks every morning, and, I take it, that glass must be daily enchanted." said Titbottom, with a bow of quaint respect to my wife.

I do not think I have seen such a blush upon Prue's cheek since—well, since a great many years ago.

"I will gladly tell you the history of my spectacles," began Titbottom. "It is very simple; and I am not at all sure that a great many other people have not a pair of the same kind. I have never, indeed, heard of them by the gross, like those of our young friend, Moses, the son of the Vicar of Wakefield. In fact, I think a gross would be quite enough to supply the world. It is a kind of article for which the demand does not increase with use. If we should all wear spectacles like mine we should never smile any more. Or—I am not quite sure—we should all be very happy."

"A very important difference," said Prue, counting her stitches.

"You know my grandfather Titbottom was a West Indian. A large proprietor, and an easy man, he basked in the tropical sun, leading his quiet, luxurious life. He lived much alone, and was what people call eccentric—by which I understand that he was very much himself, and, refusing the influence of other people, they had their revenges, and called him names. It is a habit not exclusively tropical. I think I have seen the same thing even in this city.

"But he was greatly beloved—my bland and bountiful grandfather. He was so large-hearted and open-handed. He was so friendly, and thoughtful, and genial, that even his jokes had the air of graceful benedictions. He did not seem to grow old, and he was one of those who never appear to have been very young. He flourished in a perennial maturity, an immortal middle-age.

"My grandfather lived upon one of the small islands—St. Kitts, perhaps—and his domain extended to the sea. His house, a rambling West Indian mansion, was surrounded with deep, spacious piazzas, covered with luxurious lounges, among which one capacious chair was his peculiar seat. They tell me he used sometimes to sit there for the whole day, his great, soft, brown eyes fastened upon the sea, watching the specks of sails that flashed upon the horizon, while the evanescent expressions chased each other over his placid face, as if it reflected the calm and changing sea before him.

"His morning costume was an ample dressing-gown of gorgeously-flowered silk, and his morning was very apt to last all day. He rarely read; but he would pace the great piazza for hours, with his hands buried in the pockets of his dressing-gown, and an air of sweet reverie, which any book must be a very entertaining one to produce.

"Society, of course, he saw little. There was some slight apprehension that, if he were bidden to social entertainments, he might forget his coat, or arrive without some other essential part of his dress; and there is a sly tradition in the Titbottom family, that once, having been invited to a ball in honour of a new governor of the island, my grandfather Titbottom sauntered into the hall towards midnight, wrapped in the gorgeous flowers of his dressing-gown, and with his hands buried in the pockets, as usual. There was great excitement among the guests and immense deprecation of gubernatorial ire. Fortunately, it happened that the Governor and my grandfather were old friends, and there was no offence. But as they were conversing together, one of the distressed managers cast indignant glances at the brilliant costume of my grandfather, who summoned him, and asked courteously :

"' Did you invite me, or my coat ? '

"' You, in a proper coat,' replied the manager.

"The Governor smiled approvingly, and looked at my grandfather.

"' My friend,' said he to the manager, ' I beg your pardon, I forgot.'

"The next day, my grandfather was seen promenading in full ball dress along the streets of the little town.

"' They ought to know,' said he, ' that I have a proper coat, and that not contempt, nor poverty, but forgetfulness, sent me to a ball in my dressing-gown.'

"He did not much frequent social festivals after this failure, but he always told the story with satisfaction and a quiet smile.

"To a stranger, life upon those little islands is uniform even to weariness. But the old native dons, like my grandfather, ripen in the prolonged sunshine, like the turtle upon the Bahama banks, nor know of existence more desirable. Life in the tropics I take to be a placid torpidity.

"During the long, warm mornings of nearly half a century, my grandfather Titbottom had sat in his dressing-gown and gazed at the sea. But one calm June day, as he slowly paced the piazza after breakfast, his dreamy glance was arrested by a little vessel, evidently nearing the shore. He called for his spyglass, and, surveying the craft, saw that she came from the neighbouring island. She glided smoothly, slowly, over the summer sea. The warm morning air was sweet with perfumes and silent with heat. The sea sparkled languidly and the brilliant blue sky hung cloudlessly over. Scores of little island vessels had my grandfather seen coming over the horizon and cast anchor in the port. Hundreds of summer mornings had the white sails flashed and faded, like vague faces through forgotten dreams. But this time he laid down the spyglass, and leaned against a column of the piazza, and watched the vessel with an intentness that he could not explain. She came nearer and nearer, a graceful spectre in the dazzling morning.

"' Decidedly I must step down and see about that vessel,' said my grandfather Titbottom.

"He gathered his ample dressing-gown about him, and stepped from the piazza with no other protection from the sun than the little smoking-cap upon his head. His face wore a calm, beaming smile, as if he loved the whole world. He was not an old man; but there was almost a patriarchal pathos in his expression as he sauntered along in the sunshine towards the shore. A group of idle gazers was collected to watch the arrival. The little vessel furled her sails and drifted slowly landward, and as she was of very light draft, she came close to the shelving shore. A long plank was put out from her side, and the debarkation commenced.

"My grandfather Titbottom stood looking on, to see the passengers as they passed. There were but a few of them, and mostly traders from the neighbouring island. But suddenly the face of a young girl appeared over the side of the vessel, and she stepped upon the plank to descend. My grandfather Titbottom instantly advanced, and, moving briskly, reached the top of the plank at the same moment, and with the old tassel of his cap flashing in the sun, and one hand in the pocket of his dressing-gown, with the other he handed the young lady carefully down the plank. That young lady was afterwards my grandmother Titbottom.

"For, over the gleaming sea which he had watched so long, and which seemed thus to reward his patient gaze, came his bride that sunny morning.

"'Of course we are happy,' he used to say to her, after they were married: 'for you are the gift of the sun I have loved so long and so well.' And my grandfather Titbottom would lay his hand so tenderly upon the golden hair of his young bride, that you could fancy him a devout Parsee, caressing sunbeams.

"There were endless festivities upon occasion of the marriage; and my grandfather did not go to one of them in his dressing-gown. The gentle sweetness of his wife melted every heart into love and sympathy. He was much older than she, without doubt. But age, as he used to say with a smile of immortal youth, is a matter of feeling, not of years.

"And if, sometimes, as she sat by his side on the piazza, her fancy looked through her eyes upon that summer sea, and saw a younger lover, perhaps some one of those graceful and glowing heroes who occupy the foreground of all young maidens' visions by the sea, yet she could not find one more generous and gracious, nor fancy one more worthy and loving than my grandfather Titbottom.

"And if, in the moonlit midnight, while he lay calmly sleeping, she leaned out of the window, and sank into vague reveries of sweet possibility, and watched the gleaming path of the moonlight upon the water, until the dawn glided over it—it was only that mood of nameless regret and longing which underlies all human happiness; or it was the vision of that life of cities and the world which she had never seen, but of which she had often read, and which looked very fair and alluring across the sea to a girlish imagination, which knew that it should never see that reality.

"These West Indian years were the great days of the family." said Titbottom, with an air of majestic and regal regret, pausing, and musing, in our little parlour, like a late Stuart in exile, remembering England.

Prue raised her eyes from her work and looked at him with subdued admiration; for I have observed that, like the rest of her sex, she has a singular sympathy with the representative of a reduced family.

Perhaps it is their finer perception, which leads these tender-hearted women to recognise the divine right of social superiority so much more readily than we; and yet, much as Titbottom was enhanced in my wife's admiration by the discovery that his dusky sadness of nature and expression was, as it were, the expiring gleam and late twilight of ancestral splendours, I doubt if Mr. Bourne would have preferred him for book-keeper a moment sooner upon that account. In truth, I have observed, down town, that the fact of your ancestors doing nothing is not considered good proof that you can do anything.

But Prue and her sex regard sentiment more than action, and I understand easily enough why she is never tired of hearing me read of Prince Charlie. If Titbottom had been only a little younger a little handsomer, a little more gallantly dressed—in fact, a little more of a Prince Charlie, I am sure her eyes would not have fallen again upon her work so tranquilly, as he resumed his story.

"I can remember my grandfather Titbottom, although I was a very young child and he was a very old man. My young mother and my young grandmother are very distinct figures in my memory, ministering to the old gentleman, wrapped in his dressing-gown, and seated upon the piazza. I remember his white hair and his calm smile, and how, not long before he died, he called me to him, and laying his hand upon my head, said to me:

"'My child, the world is not this great sunny piazza, nor life the fairy stories which the women tell you here, as you sit in their laps. I shall soon be gone, but I want to leave with you some memento of my love for you, and I know of nothing more valuable than these spectacles, which your grandmother brought from her native island, when she arrived here one fine summer morning, long ago. I cannot tell whether, when you grow older, you will regard them as a gift of the greatest value, or as something that you had been happier never to have possessed.'

"'But, grandpapa, I am not short-sighted.'

"'My son, are you not human?' said the old gentleman; and how shall I ever forget the thoughtful sadness with which, at the same time, he handed me the spectacles?

"Instinctively I put them on, and looked at my grandfather.

But I saw no grandfather, no piazza, no flowered dressing-gown; I saw only a luxuriant palm-tree, waving broadly over a tranquil landscape; pleasant homes clustered around it; gardens teeming with fruit and flowers; flocks quietly feeding; birds wheeling and chirping. I heard children's voices, and the low lullaby of happy mothers. The sound of cheerful singing came wafted from distant fields upon the light breeze. Golden harvest glistened out of sight, and I caught their rustling whispers of prosperity. A warm, mellow atmosphere bathed the whole.

"I have seen copies of the landscapes of the Italian painter Claude, which seemed to me faint reminiscences of that calm and happy vision. But all this peace and prosperity seemed to flow from the spreading palm as from a fountain.

"I do not know how long I looked, but I had, apparently, no power, as I had no will, to remove the spectacles. What a wonderful island must Nevis be, thought I, if people carry such pictures in their pockets only by buying a pair of spectacles! What wonder that my dear grandmother Titbottom has lived such a placid life, and has blessed us all with her sunny temper, when she has lived surrounded by such images of peace!

"My grandfather died. But still, in the warm morning sunshine upon the piazza, I felt his placid presence, and as I crawled into his great chair, and drifted on in reverie through the still, tropical day, it was as if his soft, dreamy eye had passed into my soul. My grandmother cherished his memory with tender regret. A violent passion of grief for his loss was no more possible than for the pensive decay of the year.

"We have no portrait of him, but I see always, when I remember him, that peaceful and luxuriant palm. And I think that to have known one good old man—one man who, through the chances and rubs of a long life, has carried his heart in his hand, like a palm branch, waving all discords into peace—helps our faith in God, in ourselves, and in each other more than many sermons. I hardly know whether to be grateful to my grandfather for the spectacles; and yet when I remember that it is to them I owe the pleasant image of him which I cherish, I seem to myself sadly ungrateful.

"Madam," said Titbottom to Prue solemnly, "my memory is a long and gloomy gallery, and only remotely, at its farther end, do I see the glimmer of soft sunshine, and only there are the pleasant pictures hung. They seem to me very happy along whose gallery the sunlight streams to their very feet, striking all the pictured walls into unfading splendour."

Prue had laid her work in her lap, and as Titbottom paused a moment, and I turned towards her, I found her mild eyes fastened upon my face, and glistening with many tears. I knew that the tears meant that she felt herself to be one of those who seemed to Titbottom very happy.

"Misfortunes of many kinds came heavily upon the family after the head was gone. The great house was relinquished. My parents were both dead, and my grandmother had entire charge of me. But from the moment that I received the gift of the spectacles I could not resist their fascination, and I withdrew into myself and became a solitary boy. There were not many companions for me of my own age, and they gradually left me, or, at least, had not a hearty sympathy with me; for, if they teased me, I pulled out my spectacles and surveyed them so seriously that they acquired a kind of awe of me, and evidently regarded my gradfather's gift as a concealed magical weapon which might be dangerously drawn upon them at any moment. Whenever in our games there were quarrels and high words, and I began to feel about my dress and to wear a grave look, they all took the alarm, and shouted, 'Look out for Titbottom's spectacles,' and scattered like a flock of scared sheep.

"Nor could I wonder at it. For, at first, before they took the alarm, I saw strange sights when I looked at them through the glasses.

"If two were quarrelling about a marble or a ball I had only to go behind a tree where I was concealed and look at them leisurely. Then the scene changed, and it was no longer a green meadow with boys playing, but a spot which I did not recognise, and forms that made me shudder, or smile. It was not a big boy bullying a little one, but a young wolf with glistening teeth and a lamb cowering before him; or it was a dog faithful and famishing —or a star going slowly into eclipse—or a rainbow fading—or a flower blooming—or a sun rising—or a waning moon.

"The revelations of the spectacles determined my feeling for the boys, and for all whom I saw through them. No shyness, nor awkwardness, nor silence could separate me from those who looked lovely as lilies to my illuminated eyes. But the visions made me afraid. If I felt myself warmly drawn to any one, I struggled with the fierce desire of seeing him through the spectacles, for I feared to find him something else than I fancied. I longed to enjoy the luxury of ignorant feeling, to love without knowing, to float like a leaf upon the eddies of life, drifted now to a sunny point, now to a solemn shade—now over glittering ripples, now over gleaming calms—and not to determined ports, a trim vessel with an inexorable rudder.

"But sometimes, mastered after long struggles, as if the unavoidable condition of owning the spectacles were using them, I seized them and sauntered into the little town. Putting them to my eyes I peered into the houses and at the people who passed me. Here sat a family at breakfast, and I stood at the window looking in. O motley meal! fantastic vision! The good mother saw her lord sitting opposite, a grave, respectable being, eating muffins.

But I saw only a bank-bill, more or less crumpled and tattered, marked with a larger or lesser figure. If a sharp wind blew suddenly, I saw it tremble and flutter; it was thin, flat, impalpable. I removed my glasses and looked with my eyes at the wife. I could have smiled to see the humid tenderness with which she regarded her strange *vis-à-vis*. Is life only a game of blindman's buff? of droll cross purposes?

"Or I put them on again, and then looked at the wives. How many stout trees I saw—how many tender flowers—how many placid pools; yes, and how many little streams winding out of sight shrinking before the large, hard, round eyes opposite and slipping off into solitude and shade, with a low, inner song for their own solace.

"In many houses I thought to see angels, nymphs, or, at least, women, and could only find broomsticks, mops, or kettles, hurrying about, rattling and tinkling, in a state of shrill activity. I made calls upon elegant ladies, and after I had enjoyed the gloss of silk, and the delicacy of lace, and the glitter of jewels, I slipped on my spectacles, and saw a peacock's feather, flounced, and furbelowed and fluttering; or an iron rod, thin, sharp, and hard; nor could I possibly mistake the movement of the drapery for any flexibility of the thing draped.

"Or, mysteriously chilled, I saw a statue of perfect form, or flowing movement, it might be alabaster, or bronze, or marble—but sadly often it was ice; and I knew that after it had shone a little, and frozen a few eyes with its despairing perfection, it could not be put away in the niches of palaces for ornament and proud family tradition, like the alabaster, or bronze, or marble statues, but would melt, and shrink, and fall coldly away in colourless and useless water, be absorbed in the earth and utterly forgotten.

"But the true sadness was rather in seeing those who, not having the spectacles, thought that the iron rod was flexible, and the ice statue warm. I saw many a gallant heart, which seemed to me brave and loyal as the crusaders, pursuing, through days and nights, and a long life of devotion, the hope of lighting at least a smile in the cold eyes, if not a fire in the icy heart. I watched the earnest, enthusiastic sacrifice. I saw the pure resolve, the generous faith, the fine scorn of doubt, the impatience of suspicion. I watched the grace, the ardour, the glory of devotion. Through those strange spectacles how often I saw the noblest heart renouncing all other hope, all other ambition, all other life, than the possible love of some one of those statues.

"Ah me! it was terrible, but they had not the love to give. The face was so polished and smooth, because there was no sorrow in the heart—and drearily, often, no heart to be touched. I could not wonder that the noble heart of devotion was broken, for it had dashed itself against a stone. I wept, until my spectacles were dimmed, for those hopeless lovers; but there was a pang beyond tears for those icy statues.

"Still a boy, I was thus too much a man in knowledge—I did not comprehend the sights I was compelled to see. I used to tear my glasses away from my eyes and, frightened at myself, run to escape my own consciousness. Reaching the small house where we then lived, I plunged into my grandmother's room, and, throwing myself upon the floor, buried my face in her lap, and sobbed myself to sleep with premature grief.

"But when I awakened, and felt her cool hand upon my hot forehead, and heard the low sweet song, or the gentle story, or the tenderly told parable from the Bible, with which she tried to soothe me, I could not resist the mystic fascination that lured me, as I lay in her lap, to steal a glance at her through the spectacles.

"Pictures of the Madonna have not her rare and pensive beauty. Upon the tranquil little islands her life had been eventless, and all the fine possibilities of her nature were like flowers that never bloomed. Placid were all her years; yet I have read of no heroine, of no woman great in sudden crises, that it did not seem to me she might have been. The wife and widow of a man who loved his home better than the homes of others, I have yet heard of no queen, no belle, no imperial beauty, whom in grace, and brilliancy, and persuasive courtesy she might not have surpassed.

"Madam," said Titbottom to my wife, whose heart hung upon his story, "your husband's young friend, Aurelia, wears sometimes a camellia in her hair, and no diamond in the ballroom seems so costly as that perfect flower, which women envy, and for whose least and withered petal men sigh; yet, in the tropical solitudes of Brazil, how many a camellia bud drops from the bush that no eye has ever seen, which, had it flowered and been noticed, would have gilded all hearts with its memory.

"When I stole these furtive glances at my grandmother, half fearing that they were wrong, I saw only a calm lake, whose shores were low, and over which the sun hung unbroken, so that the least star was clearly reflected. It had an atmosphere of solemn twilight tranquillity, and so completely did its unruffled surface blend with the cloudless, star-studded sky that, when I looked through my spectacles at my grandmother, the vision seemed to me all heaven and stars.

"Yet, as I gazed and gazed, I felt what stately cities might well have been built upon those shores, and have flashed prosperity over the calm, like coruscations of pearls. I dreamed of gorgeous fleets, silken-sailed, and blown by perfumed winds, drifting over those depthless waters and through those spacious skies. I gazed upon the twilight, the inscrutable silence, like a God-fearing discoverer upon a new and vast sea bursting upon him through forest glooms, and in the fervour of whose impassioned gaze a millennial and poetic world arises, and man need no longer die to be happy.

"My companions naturally deserted me for I had grown wearily grave and abstracted: and, unable to resist the allurements of my spectacles, I was constantly lost in the world of which those companions were part, yet of which they knew nothing.

"I grew cold and hard, almost morose; people seemed to me so blind and unreasonable. They did the wrong thing. They called green, yellow; and black, white. Young men said of a girl, 'What a lovely, simple creature!' I looked, and there was only a glistening wisp of straw, dry and hollow. Or they said 'What a cold, proud beauty!' I looked, and lo! a Madonna, whose heart held the world. Or they said, 'What a wild, giddy girl!' and I saw a glancing, dancing mountain stream, pure as the virgin snows whence it flowed, singing through sun and shade, over pearls and gold dust, slipping along unstained by weed or rain, or heavy foot of cattle, touching the flowers with a dewy kiss—a beam of grace, a happy song, a line of light, in the dim and troubled landscape.

"My grandmother sent me to school, but I looked at the master and saw that he was a smooth, round ferule, or an improper noun, or a vulgar fraction, and refused to obey him. Or he was a piece of string, a rag, a willow-wand, and I had a contemptuous pity. But one was a well of cool, deep water, and looking suddenly in one day I saw the stars.

"That one gave me all my schooling. With him I used to walk by the sea, and, as we strolled and the waves plunged in long legions before us, I looked at him through the spectacles, and as his eyes dilated with the boundless view, and his chest heaved with an impossible desire, I saw Xerxes and his army, tossed and glittering, rank upon rank, multitude upon multitude, out of sight, but ever regularly advancing, and, with confused roar of ceaseless music, prostrating themselves in abject homage. Or, as with arms outstretched and hair streaming on the wind, he chanted full lines of the resounding *Iliad*, I saw Homer pacing the Ægean sands in the Greek sunsets of forgotten times.

"My grandmother died, and I was thrown into the world without resources, and with no capital but my spectacles. I tried to find employment, but everybody was shy of me. There was a vague suspicion that I was either a little crazed, or a good deal in league with the prince of darkness. My companions, who would persist in calling a piece of painted muslin a fair and fragrant flower, had no difficulty; success waited for them around every corner, and arrived in every ship.

"I tried to teach, for I loved children. But if anything excited a suspicion of my pupils, and putting on my spectacles I saw that I was fondling a snake, or smelling at a bud with a worm in it, I sprang up in horror and ran away; or if it seemed to me through the glasses that a cherub smiled upon me, or a rose was blooming in my buttonhole, then I felt myself imperfect and impure, not fit to be leading and training what was so essentially superior to myself, and I kissed the children and left them weeping and wondering.

"In despair I went to a great merchant on the island, and asked him to employ me.

"'My dear young friend,' said he, 'I understand that you have some singular secret, some charm, or spell, or amulet, or something, I don't know what, of which people are afraid. Now you know, my dear,' said the merchant, swelling up, and apparently prouder of his great stomach than of his large fortune, 'I am not cf that kind. I am not easily frightened. You may spare yourself the pain of trying to impose upon me. People who propose to come to time before I arrive are accustomed to arise very early in the morning,' said he, thrusting his thumbs in the armholes of his waistcoat, and spreading the fingers, like two fans, upon his bosom. 'I think I have heard something of your secret. You have a pair of spectacles, I believe, that you value very much, because your grandmother brought them as a marriage portion to your grandfather. Now if you think fit to sell me those spectacles I will pay you the largest market price for them. What do you say?'

"I told him I had not the slightest idea of selling my spectacles.

"'My young friend means to eat them, I suppose,' said he, with a contemptuous smile.

"I made no reply, but was turning to leave the office when the merchant called after me:

"'My young friend, poor people should never suffer themselves to get into pets. Anger is an expensive luxury in which only men of a certain income can indulge. A pair of spectacles and a hot temper are not the most promising capital for success in life, Master Titbottom.'

"I said nothing, but put my hand upon the door to go out when the merchant said, more respectfully:

"'Well, you foolish boy, if you will not sell your spectacles, perhaps you will agree to sell the use of them to me. That is, you shall only put them on when I direct you, and for my purposes. Hallo! you little fool!' cried he impatiently, as he saw that I intended to make no reply.

"But I had pulled out my spectacles and put them on for my own purposes, and against his wish and desire. I looked at him, and saw a huge, bald-headed wild boar, with gross chaps and a leering eye—only the more ridiculous for the high-arched, gold bowed spectacles, that straddled his nose. One of his forehoofs was thrust into the safe, where his bills receivable were hived, and the other into his pocket, among the loose change and bills there. His ears were pricked forward with a brisk, sensitive smartness. In a world where prize pork was the best excellence he would have carried off all the premiums.

"I stepped into the next office in the street, and a mild-faced, genial man, also a large and opulent merchant, asked me my business in such a tone that I instantly looked through my spectacles and saw a land flowing with milk and honey. There I pitched my tent, and stayed till the good man died and his business was discontinued.

"But while there," said Titbottom, and his voice trembled away into a sigh, "I first saw Preciosa. Despite the spectacles, I saw Preciosa. For days, for weeks, for months, I did not take my spectacles with me. I ran away from them, I threw them up on high shelves, I tried to make up my mind to throw them into the sea, or down the well. I could not, I would not, I dared not, look at Preciosa through the spectacles. It was not possible for me deliberately to destroy them; but I awoke in the night, and could almost have cursed my dear old grandfather for his gift.

"I sometimes escaped from the office, and sat for whole days with Preciosa. I told her the strange things I had seen with my mystic glasses. The hours were not enough for the wild romances which I raved in her ear. She listened, astonished and appalled. Her blue eyes turned upon me with sweet deprecation. She clung to me, and then withdrew, and fled fearfully from the room.

"But she could not stay away. She could not resist my voice, in whose tones burnt all the love that filled my heart and brain. The very effort to resist the desire of seeing her as I saw everybody else gave a frenzy and an unnatural tension to my feeling and my manner. I sat by her side, looking into her eyes, smoothing her hair, folding her to my heart, which was sunken deep and deep—why not for ever?—in that dream of peace. I ran from her presence, and shouted, and leaped with joy, and sat the whole night through, thrilled into happiness by the thought of her love and loveliness, like a wind-harp, tightly strung, and answering the airiest sigh of the breeze with music.

"Then came calmer days—the conviction of deep love settled upon our lives—as after the hurrying, heaving days of spring, comes the bland and benignant summer.

"'It is no dream, then, after all, and we are happy,' I said to her one day; and there came no answer, for happiness is speechless.

"'We are happy, then,' I said to myself, 'there is no excitement now. How glad I am that I can now look at her through my spectacles.'

"I feared lest some instinct should warn me to beware. I escaped from her arms, and ran home and seized the glasses, and bounded back again to Preciosa. As I entered the room I was heated, my head was swimming with confused apprehensions, my eyes must have glared. Preciosa was frightened, and, rising from her seat, stood with an inquiring glance of surprise in her eyes.

"But I was bent with frenzy upon my purpose. I was merely aware that she was in the room. I saw nothing else. I heard nothing.

I cared for nothing but to see her through that magic glass, and feel at once all the fulness of blissful perfection which that would reveal. Preciosa stood before the mirror, but alarmed at my wild and eager movements, unable to distinguish what I had in my hands, and seeing me raise them suddenly to my face, she shrieked with terror, and fell fainting upon the floor, at the very moment that I placed the glasses before my eyes, and beheld—*myself*, reflected in the mirror, before which she had been standing.

"Dear madam," cried Titbottom to my wife, springing up and falling back again in his chair, pale and trembling, while Prue ran to him and took his hand, and I poured out a glass of water—" I saw myself."

There was silence for many minutes. Prue laid her hand gently upon the head of our guest, whose eyes were closed, and who breathed softly like an infant in sleeping. Perhaps, in all the long years of anguish since that hour, no tender hand had touched his brow, nor wiped away the damps of a bitter sorrow. Perhaps the tender, maternal fingers of my wife soothed his weary head with the conviction that he felt the hand of his mother playing with the long hair of her boy in the soft West India morning. Perhaps it was only the natural relief of expressing a pent-up sorrow.

When he spoke again, it was with the old subdued tone, and the air of quaint solemnity.

"These things were matters of long, long ago, and I came to this country soon after. I brought with me premature age, a past of melancholy memories, and the magic spectacles. I had become their slave. I had nothing more to fear. Having seen myself, I was compelled to see others, properly to understand my relations to them. The lights that cheer the future of other men had gone out for me ; my eyes were those of an exile turned backwards upon the receding shore, and not forwards with hope upon the ocean.

"I mingled with men, but with little pleasure. There are but many varieties of a few types. I did not find those I came to clearer-sighted than those I had left behind. I heard men called shrewd and wise, and report said they were highly intelligent and successful. My finest sense detected no aroma of purity and principle ; but I saw only a fungus that had fattened and spread in a night. They went to the theatres to see actors upon the stage. I went to see actors in the boxes, so consummately cunning that others did not know they were acting, and they did not suspect it themselves.

"Perhaps you wonder it did not make me misanthropical. My dear friends, do not forget that I had seen myself. That made me compassionate, not cynical.

"Of course, I could not value highly the ordinary standards of success and excellence. When I went to church and saw a thin, blue, artificial flower, or a great sleepy cushion expounding the beauty of holiness to pews full of eagles, half-eagles, and threepences, however adroitly concealed they might be in broadcloth and boots : or saw an onion in an Easter bonnet weeping over the sins of Magdalen, I did not feel as they felt who saw in all this not only propriety but piety.

"Or when at public meetings an eel stood up on end, and wriggled and squirmed lithely in every direction, and declared that, for his part, he went in for rainbows and hot water—how could I help seeing that he was still black and loved a slimy pool ?

"I could not grow misanthropical when I saw in the eyes of so many who were called old the gushing fountains of eternal youth, and the light of an immortal dawn, or when I saw those who were esteemed unsuccessful and aimless, ruling a fair realm of peace and plenty, either in their own hearts, or in another's—a realm and princely possession for which they had well renounced a hopeless search and a belated triumph.

"I knew one man who had been for years a byword for having sought the philosopher's stone. But I looked at him through the spectacles and saw a satisfaction in concentrated energies, and a tenacity arising from devotion to a noble dream which was not apparent in the youths who pitied him in the aimless effeminacy of clubs, nor in the clever gentlemen who cracked their thin jokes upon him over a gossiping dinner.

"And there was your neighbour over the way, who passes for a woman who has failed in her career because she is an old maid. People wag solemn heads of pity, and say that she made so great a mistake in not marrying the brilliant and famous man who was for long years her suitor. It is clear that no orange flower will ever bloom for her. The young people make their tender romances about her as they watch her, and think of her solitary hours of bitter regret and wasting longing, never to be satisfied.

"When I first came to town I shared this sympathy, and pleased my imagination with fancying her hard struggle with the conviction that she had lost all that made life beautiful. I supposed that if I had looked at her through my spectacles, I should see that it was only her radiant temper which so illuminated her dress, that we did not see it to be heavy sables.

"But when, one day, I did raise my glasses, and glanced at her, I did not see the old maid whom we all pitied for a secret sorrow, but a woman whose nature was a tropic, in which the sun shone, and birds sang, and flowers bloomed for ever. There were no regrets, no doubts and half wishes, but a calm sweetness, a transparent peace. I saw her blush when that old lover passed by, or paused to speak to her, but it was only the sign of delicate feminine consciousness. She knew his love, and honoured it, although she could not understand it nor return it. I looked closely at her, and I saw that although all the world had exclaimed at her indifference to such homage, and had declared it was astonishing she should lose so fine a match, she would only say simply and quietly :

"'If Shakespeare loved me and I did not love him, how could I marry him?'

"Could I be misanthropical when I saw such fidelity, and dignity, and simplicity?

"You may believe that I was especially curious to look at that old lover of hers, through my glasses. He was no longer young, you know, when I came, and his fame and fortune were secure. Certainly I have heard of few men more beloved, and of none more worthy to be loved. He had the easy manner of a man of the world, the sensitive grace of a poet, and the charitable judgment of a wide traveller. He was accounted the most successful and most unspoiled of men. Handsome, brilliant, wise, tender, graceful, accomplished, rich, and famous, I looked at him, without the spectacles, in surprise and admiration, and wondered how your neighbour over the way had been so entirely untouched by his homage. I watched their intercourse in society, I saw her gay smile, her cordial greeting; I marked his frank address, his lofty courtesy. Their manner told no tales. The eager world was baulked, and I pulled out my spectacles.

"I had seen her already, and now I saw him. He lived only in memory, and his memory was a spacious and stately palace. But he did not oftenest frequent the banqueting hall, where were endless hospitality and feasting; nor did he loiter much in the reception rooms, where a throng of new visitors was for ever swarming; nor did he feed his vanity by haunting the apartment in which were stored the trophies of his varied triumphs—nor dream much in the great gallery hung with pictures of his travels.

"From all these lofty halls of memory he constantly escaped to a remote and solitary chamber, into which no one had ever penetrated. But my fatal eyes, behind the glasses, followed and entered with him, and saw that the chamber was a chapel. It was dim, and silent, and sweet with perpetual incense that burned upon an altar before a picture for ever veiled. There, whenever I chanced to look, I saw him kneel and pray; and there, by day and by night, a funeral hymn was chanted.

"I do not believe you will be surprised that I have been content to remain a deputy book-keeper. My spectacles regulated my ambition, and I early learned that there were better gods than Plutus. The glasses have lost much of their fascination now, and I do not often use them. But sometimes the desire is irresistible. Whenever I am greatly interested, I am compelled to take them out and see what it is that I admire.

"And yet—and yet," said Titbottom, after a pause, "I am not sure that I thank my grandfather."

Prue had long since laid away her work, and had heard every word of the story. I saw that the dear woman had yet one question to ask, and had been earnestly hoping to hear something that would spare her the necessity of asking. But Titbottom had resumed his usual tone, after the momentary excitement, and made no further allusion to himself. We all sat silently; Titbottom's eyes fastened musingly upon the carpet, Prue looking wistfully at him, and I regarding both.

It was past midnight, and our guest arose to go. He shook hands quietly, made his grave Spanish bow to Prue, and, taking his hat, went towards the front door. Prue and I accompanied him. I saw in her eyes that she would ask her question. And as Titbottom opened the door, I heard the low words:

"And Preciosa?"

Titbottom paused. He had just opened the door, and the moonlight streamed over him as he stood, turning back to us.

"I have seen her but once since. It was in church, and she was kneeling, with her eyes closed, so that she did not see me. But I rubbed the glasses well, and looked at her, and saw a white lily, whose stem was broken, but which was fresh, and luminous, and fragrant still."

"That was a miracle," interrupted Prue.

"Madam, it was a miracle," replied Titbottom, "and for that one sight I am devoutly grateful for my grandfather's gift. I saw that although a flower may have lost its hold upon earthly moisture, it may still bloom as sweetly, fed by the dews of heaven."

The door closed and he was gone. But as Prue put her arm in mine, and we went upstairs together, she whispered in my ear:

"How glad I am that you don't wear spectacles."

# BAYARD TAYLOR
### 1825-1878

## WHO WAS SHE?

COME, now, there may as well be an end of this! Every time I meet your eyes squarely I detect the question just slipping out of them. If you had spoken it, or even boldly looked it; if you had shown in your motions the least sign of a fussy or fidgety concern on my account; if this were not the evening of my birthday, and you the only friend who remembered it; if confession were not good for the soul, though harder than sin to some people, of whom I am one—well, if all reasons were not at this instant converged into a focus, and burning me rather violently, in that region where the seat of emotion is supposed to lie, I should keep my trouble to myself.

Yes, I have fifty times had it on my mind to tell you the whole story. But who can be certain that his best friend will not smile—or, what is worse, cherish a kind of charitable pity ever afterward—when the external forms of a very serious kind of passion seem trivial, fantastic, foolish? And the worst of all is that the heroic part which I imagined I was playing proves to have been almost the reverse. The only comfort which I can find in my humiliation is that I am capable of feeling it. There isn't a bit of a paradox in this, as you will see; but I only mention it now to prepare you for, maybe, a little morbid sensitiveness of my moral nerves.

The documents are all in this portfolio under my elbow. I had just read them again completely through when you were announced. You may examine them as you like afterward: for the present, fill your glass, take another Cabaña, and keep silent until my " ghastly tale " has reached its most lamentable conclusion.

The beginning of it was at Wampsocket Springs three years ago last summer. I suppose most unmarried men who have reached, or passed, the age of thirty—and I was then thirty-three—experience a milder return of their adolescent warmth, a kind of fainter second spring, since the first has not fulfilled its promise. Of course I wasn't clearly conscious of this at the time: who is? But I had had my youthful passion and my tragic disappointment as you know: I had looked far enough into what Thackeray used to call the cryptic mysteries to save me from the Scylla of dissipation and yet preserved enough of natural nature to keep me out of the Pharisaic Charybdis. My devotion to my legal studies had already brought me a mild distinction; the paternal legacy was a good nest-egg for the incubation of wealth—in short, I was a fair, respectable " party," desirable to the humbler mammas, and not to be despised by the haughty exclusives.

The fashionable hotel at the Springs holds three hundred, and it was packed. I had meant to lounge there for a fortnight and then finish my holidays at Long Branch; but eighty, at least, out of the three hundred were young and moved lightly in muslin. With my years and experience I felt so safe that to walk, talk, or dance with them became simply a luxury such as I had never—at least so freely—possessed before. My name and standing, known to some families, were agreeably exaggerated to the others, and I enjoyed that supreme satisfaction which a man always feels when he discovers, or imagines, that he is popular in society. There is a kind of premonitory apology implied in my saying this, I am aware. You must remember that I am culprit and culprit's counsel at the same time.

You have never been at Wampsocket? Well, the hills sweep around in a crescent on the northern side, and four or five radiating glens descending from them unite just above the village. The central one, leading to a waterfall (called " Minne-hehe " by the irreverent young people because there is so little of it), is the fashionable drive and promenade; but the second ravine on the left, steep, crooked, and cumbered with boulders which have tumbled from somewhere and lodged in the most extraordinary groupings, became my favourite walk of a morning. There was a footpath in it, well trodden at first, but gradually fading out as it became more like a ladder than a path, and I soon discovered that no other city feet than mine were likely to scale a certain rough slope which seemed the end of the ravine. With the aid of the tough laurel-stems I climbed to the top, passed through a cleft as narrow as a doorway, and presently found myself in a little upper dell, as wild and sweet and strange as one of the pictures that haunts us on the brink of sleep.

There was a pond—no, rather a bowl—of water in the centre; hardly twenty yards across, yet the sky in it was so pure and far down that the circle of rocks and summer foliage enclosing it seemed like a little planetary ring floating off alone through space. I can't explain the charm of the spot, nor the selfishness which instantly suggested that I should keep the discovery to myself. Ten years earlier I should have looked around for some fair spirit to be my " minister," but now—

One forenoon—I think it was the third or fourth time I had visited the place—I was startled to find the dent of a heel in the

earth, halfway up the slope. There had been rain during the night
and the earth was still moist and soft. It was the mark of a woman's
boot, only to be distinguished from that of a walking-stick by its
semicircular form. A little higher, I found the outline of a foot,
not so small as to awake an ecstasy, but with a suggestion of light-
ness, elasticity, and grace. If hands were thrust through holes
in a board-fence, and nothing of the attached bodies seen, I can
easily imagine that some would attract and others repel us : with
footprints the impression is weaker, of course, but we cannot escape
it. I am not sure whether I wanted to find the unknown wearer
of the boot within my precious personal solitude : I was afraid
I should see her while passing through the rocky crevice, and yet was
disappointed when I found no one.

But on the flat, warm rock overhanging the tarn—my special
throne—lay some withering wild flowers and a book ! I looked up
and down, right and left : there was not the slightest sign of another
human life than mine. Then I lay down for a quarter of an hour,
and listened : there were only the noises of bird and squirrel, as
before. At last, I took up the book, the flat breadth of which
suggested only sketches. There were, indeed, some tolerable
studies of rocks and trees on the first pages ; a few not very striking
caricatures, which seemed to have been commenced as portraits,
but recalled no faces I knew ; then a number of fragmentary notes,
written in pencil. I found no name, from first to last ; only, under
the sketches, a monogram so complicated and laborious that the
initials could hardly be discovered unless one already knew them.

The writing was a woman's, but it had surely taken its character
from certain features of her own : it was clear, firm, individual.
It had nothing of that air of general debility which usually marks
the manuscript of young ladies, yet its firmness was far removed
from the stiff, conventional slope which all Englishwomen seem to
acquire in youth and retain through life. I don't see how any man
in my situation could have helped reading a few lines—if only for
the sake of restoring lost property. But I was drawn on, and on,
and finished by reading all : thence, since no further harm could
be done, I reread, pondering over certain passages until they stayed
with me. Here they are, as I set them down, that evening, on the
back of a legal blank :

" It makes a great deal of difference whether we wear social forms
as bracelets or handcuffs."

" Can we not still be wholly our independent selves, even while
doing, in the main, as others do ? I know two who are so ; but
they are married."

" The men who admire these bold, dashing young girls treat
them like weaker copies of themselves. And yet they boast of
what they call ' experience ' ! "

" I wonder if any one felt the exquisite beauty of the noon as I did to-day? A faint appreciation of sunsets and storms is taught us in youth, and kept alive by novels and flirtations; but the broad, imperial splendour of this summer noon!—and myself standing alone in it—yes, utterly alone!"

"The men I seek *must* exist: where are they? How make an acquaintance, when one obsequiously bows himself away, as I advance? The fault is surely not all on my side."

There was much more, intimate enough to inspire me with a keen interest in the writer, yet not sufficiently so to make my perusal a painful indiscretion. I yielded to the impulse of the moment, took out my pencil, and wrote a dozen lines on one of the blank pages. They ran something in this wise:

"IGNOTUS IGNOTÆ!—You have bestowed without intending it, and I have taken without your knowledge. Do not regret the accident which has enriched another. This concealed idyl of the hills was mine, as I supposed, but I acknowledge your equal right to it. Shall we share the possession, or will you banish me?"

There was a frank advance, tempered by a proper caution, I fancied, in the words I wrote. It was evident that she was unmarried, but outside of that certainty there lay a vast range of possibilities, some of them alarming enough. However, if any nearer acquaintance should arise out of the incident, the next step must be taken by her. Was I one of the men she sought? I almost imagined so—certainly hoped so.

I laid the book on the rock, as I had found it, bestowed another keen scrutiny on the lonely landscape, and then descended the ravine. That evening, I went early to the ladies' parlour, chatted more than usual with the various damsels whom I knew, and watched with a new interest those whom I knew not. My mind, involuntarily, had already created a picture of the unknown. She might be twenty-five, I thought; a reflective habit of mind would hardly be developed before that age. Tall and stately, of course; distinctly proud in her bearing, and somewhat reserved in her manners. Why she should have large dark eyes, with long dark lashes, I could not tell; but so I seemed to see her. Quite forgetting that I was (or had meant to be) *Ignotus*, I found myself staring rather significantly at one or the other of the young ladies, in whom I discovered some slight general resemblance to the imaginary character. My fancies, I must confess, played strange pranks with me. They had been kept in a coop so many years that now, when I suddenly turned them loose, their rickety attempts at flight quite bewildered me.

No! there was no use in expecting a sudden discovery. I went to the glen betimes, next morning: the book was gone and so were the faded flowers, but some of the latter were scattered over the top of another rock, a few yards from mine. Ha! this means that I am not to withdraw, I said to myself: she makes room for me!

But how to surprise her?—for by this time I was fully resolved to make her acquaintance, even though she might turn out to be forty, scraggy, and sandy-haired.

I knew no other way so likely as that of visiting the glen at all times of the day. I even went so far as to write a line of greeting, with a regret that our visits had not yet coincided, and laid it under a stone on the top of *her* rock. The note disappeared, but there was no answer in its place. Then I suddenly remembered her fondness for the noon hours, at which time she was "utterly alone." The hotel *table d'hôte* was at one o'clock: her family, doubtless, dined later, in their own rooms. Why, this gave me, at least, her place in society! The question of age, to be sure, remained unsettled; but all else was safe.

The next day I took a late and large breakfast, and sacrificed my dinner. Before noon the guests had all straggled back to the hotel from glen and grove and lane, so bright and hot was the sunshine. Indeed, I could hardly have supported the reverberation of heat from the sides of the ravine, but for a fixed belief that I should be successful. While crossing the narrow meadow upon which it opened, I caught a glimpse of something white among the thickets higher up. A moment later it had vanished, and I quickened my pace, feeling the beginning of an absurd nervous excitement in my limbs. At the next turn, there it was again! but only for another moment. I paused, exulting, and wiped my drenched forehead. "She cannot escape me!" I murmured between the deep draughts of cooler air I inhaled in the shadow of a rock.

A few hundred steps more brought me to the foot of the steep ascent, where I had counted on overtaking her. I was too late for that, but the dry, baked soil had surely been crumbled and dislodged, here and there, by a rapid foot. I followed, in reckless haste, snatching at the laurel branches right and left, and paying little heed to my footing. About one-third of the way up I slipped, fell, caught a bush which snapped at the root, slid, whirled over, and before I fairly knew what had happened, I was lying doubled up at the bottom of the slope.

I rose, made two steps forward, and then sat down with a groan of pain; my left ankle was badly sprained, in addition to various minor scratches and bruises. There was a revulsion of feeling, of course—instant, complete, and hideous. I fairly hated the Unknown. "Fool that I was!" I exclaimed, in the theatrical manner, dashing the palm of my hand softly against my brow: "lured to this by the fair traitress! But no!—not fair: she shows the artfulness of faded, desperate spinsterhood; she is all compact of enamel, 'liquid bloom of youth' and hair dye!"

There was a fierce comfort in this thought, but it couldn't help me out of the scrape. I dared not sit still, lest a sunstroke should be added, and there was no resource but to hop or crawl down the rugged path, in the hope of finding a forked sapling from which I could extemporise a crutch. With endless pain and trouble I reached a thicket, and was feebly working on a branch with my penknife, when the sound of a heavy footstep surprised me.

A brown harvest-hand, in straw hat and shirt-sleeves, presently appeared. He grinned when he saw me, and the thick snub of his nose would have seemed like a sneer at any other time.

"Are you the gentleman that got hurt?" he asked. "Is it pretty tolerable bad?"

"Who said I was hurt?" I cried in astonishment.

"One of your town-women from the hotel—I reckon she was. I was binding oats, in the field over the ridge; but I haven't lost no time in comin' here."

While I was stupidly staring at this announcement, he whipped out a big clasp-knife, and in a few minutes fashioned me a practicable crutch. Then, taking me by the other arm, he set me in motion toward the village.

Grateful as I was for the man's help, he aggravated me by his ignorance. When I asked if he knew the lady, he answered: "It's more'n likely *you* know her better." But where did she come from? Down from the hill, he guessed, but it might ha' been up the road. How did she look? was she old or young? what was the colour of her eyes? of her hair? There, now, I was too much for him. When a woman kept one o' them speckled veils over her face, turned her head away, and held her parasol between, how were you to know her from Adam? I declare to you, I couldn't arrive at one positive particular. Even when he affirmed that she was tall, he added, the next instant: "Now I come to think on it, she stepped mighty quick; so I guess she must ha' been short."

By the time we reached the hotel, I was in a state of fever; opiates and lotions had their will of me for the rest of the day. I was glad to escape the worry of questions, and the conventional sympathy expressed in inflections of the voice which are meant to soothe, and only exasperate. The next morning, as I lay upon my sofa, restful, patient, and properly cheerful, the waiter entered with a bouquet of wild flowers.

"Who sent them?" I asked.

"I found them outside your door, sir. Maybe there's a card; yes, here's a bit o' paper."

I opened the twisted slip he handed me, and read: "From your dell—and mine." I took the flowers; among them were two or three rare and beautiful varieties which I had only found in that one spot. Fool, again! I noiselessly kissed, while pretending to smell them, had them placed on a stand within reach, and fell into a state of quiet and agreeable contemplation.

Tell me yourself whether any male human being is ever too old for sentiment, provided that it strikes him at the right time and in the right way! What did that bunch of wild flowers betoken? Knowledge, first; then, sympathy; and finally, encouragement, at least. Of course she had seen my accident, from above; of course she had sent the harvest labourer to aid me home. It was quite natural she should imagine some special, romantic interest in the lonely dell, on my part, and the gift took additional value from her conjecture.

Four days afterwards, there was a hop in the large dining-room of the hotel. Early in the morning, a fresh bouquet had been left at my door. I was tired of my enforced idleness, eager to discover the fair unknown (she was again fair, to my fancy!), and I determined to go down, believing that a cane and a crimson velvet slipper on the left foot would provoke a glance of sympathy from certain eyes, and thus enable me to detect them.

The fact was, the sympathy was much too general and effusive. Everybody, it seemed, came to me with kindly greetings; seats were vacated at my approach, even fat Mrs. Huxter insisting on my taking her warm place, at the head of the room. But Bob Leroy—you know him—as gallant a gentleman as ever lived, put me down at the right point, and kept me there. He only meant to divert me, yet gave me the only place where I could quietly inspect all the younger ladies, as dance or supper brought them near.

One of the dances was an old-fashioned cotillon, and one of the figures, the "coquette," brought every one, in turn, before me. I received a pleasant word or two from those whom I knew, and a long, kind, silent glance from Miss May Danvers. Where had been my eyes? She was tall, stately, twenty-five, had large dark eyes, and long dark lashes! Again the changes of the dance brought her near me; I threw (or strove to throw) unutterable meanings into my eyes, and cast them upon hers. She seemed startled, looked suddenly away, looked back to me, and—blushed. I knew her for what is called "a nice girl"—that is, tolerably frank, gently feminine, and not dangerously intelligent. Was it possible that I had overlooked so much character and intellect?

As the cotillon closed, she was again in my neighbourhood, and her partner led her in my direction. I was rising painfully from my chair, when Bob Leroy pushed me down again, whisked another seat from somewhere, planted it at my side, and there she was!

She knew who was her neighbour, I plainly saw; but instead of turning toward me, she began to fan herself in a nervous way and to fidget with the buttons of her gloves. I grew impatient.

"Miss Danvers!" I said at last.

"Oh!" was all her answer, as she looked at me for a moment.

"Where are your thoughts?" I asked.

Then she turned, with wide, astonished eyes, colouring softly up to the roots of her hair. My heart gave a sudden leap.

"How can you tell, if I cannot?" she asked.

"May I guess?"

She made a slight inclination of the head, saying nothing. I was then quite sure.

"The second ravine to the left of the main drive?"

This time she actually started; her colour became deeper, and a leaf of the ivory fan snapped between her fingers.

"Let there be no more a secret!" I exclaimed. "Your flowers have brought me your messages; I knew I should find you——"

Full of certainty, I was speaking in a low, impassioned voice. She cut me short by rising from her seat; I felt that she was both angry and alarmed. Fisher, of Philadelphia, jostling right and left in his haste, made his way toward her. She fairly snatched his arm, clung to it with a warmth I had never seen expressed in a ballroom. and began to whisper in his ear. It was not five minutes before he came to me, alone, with a very stern face, bent down, and said:

"If you have discovered our secret, you will keep silent. You are certainly a gentleman."

I bowed, coldly and savagely. There was a draught from the open window; my ankle became suddenly weary and painful, and I went to bed. Can you believe that I didn't guess, immediately, what it all meant? In a vague way, I fancied that I had been premature in my attempt to drop our mutual incognito, and that Fisher, a rival lover, was jealous of me. This was rather flattering than otherwise; but when I limped down to the ladies' parlour, the next day no Miss Danvers was to be seen. I did not venture to ask for her; it might seem importunate, and a woman of so much hidden capacity was evidently not to be wooed in the ordinary way.

So another night passed by; and then, with the morning, came a letter which made me feel, at the same instant, like a fool and a hero. It had been dropped in the Wampsocket post office, was legibly addressed to me and delivered with some other letters which had arrived by the night mail. Here it is; listen!

"NOTO IGNOTA!—Haste is not a gift of the gods, and you have been impatient, with the usual result. I was almost prepared for this, and thus am not wholly disappointed. In a day or two more you will discover your mistake, which, so far as I can learn, has done no particular harm. If you wish to find *me*, there is only one way to seek me; should I tell you what it is, I should run the risk of losing you—that is, I should preclude the manifestation of a certain quality which I hope to find in the man who may—or, rather, must—be my friend. This sounds enigmatical, yet you have read enough of my nature, as written in those random notes in my sketch-book, to guess, at least, how much I require. Only this let me add: mere guessing is useless.

"Being unknown, I can write freely. If you find me, I shall be justified; if not, I shall hardly need to blush, even to myself, over a futile experiment.

"It is possible for me to learn enough of your life, henceforth, to direct my relation toward you. This may be the end; if so, I shall know it soon. I shall also know whether you continue to seek me. Trusting in your honour as a man, I must ask you to trust in mine, as a woman."

I *did* discover my mistake, as the Unknown promised. There had been a secret betrothal between Fisher and Miss Danvers, and, singularly enough, the momentous question and answer had been given in the very ravine leading to my upper dell! The two meant to keep the matter to themselves; but therein, it seems, I thwarted them; there was a little opposition on the part of their respective families, but all was amicably settled before I left Wampsocket.

The letter made a very deep impression upon me. What was the one way to find her? What could it be but the triumph that follows ambitious toil—the manifestation of all my best qualities as a man? Be she old or young, plain or beautiful, I reflected, hers is surely a nature worth knowing, and its candid intelligence conceals no hazards for me. I have sought her rashly, blundered, betrayed that I set her lower, in my thoughts, than her actual self: let me now adopt the opposite course, seek her openly no longer, go back to my tasks, and, following my own aims vigorously and cheerfully, restore that respect which she seemed to be on the point of losing. For, consciously or not, she had communicated to me a doubt, implied in the very expression of her own strength and pride. She had meant to address me as an equal, yet, despite herself, took a stand a little above that which she accorded to me.

I came back to New York earlier than usual, worked steadily at my profession and with increasing success, and began to accept opportunities (which I had previously declined) of making myself personally known to the great, impressible, fickle, tyrannical public. One or two of my speeches in the hall of the Cooper Institute, on various occasions—as you may perhaps remember—gave me a good headway with the party, and were the chief cause of my nomination for the State office which I still hold. (There, on the table lies a resignation, written to-day, but not yet signed. We'll talk of it afterward.) Several months passed by, and no further letter reached me. I gave up much of my time to society, moved familiarly in more than one province of the kingdom here, and vastly extended my acquaintance, especially among the women; but not one of them betrayed the mysterious something or other—really I can't explain precisely what it was!—which I was looking for. In fact, the more I endeavoured quietly to study the sex, the more confused I became.

At last I was subjected to the usual onslaught from the strong-minded. A small but formidable committee entered my office one morning and demanded a categorical declaration of my principles. What my views on the subject were I knew very well; they were clear and decided; and yet I hesitated to declare them! It wasn't a temptation of Saint Anthony—that is, turned the other way—and the belligerent attitude of the dames did not alarm me in the least; but *she*! What was *her* position? How could I best please her? It flashed upon my mind, while Mrs. —— was making her formal speech, that I had taken no step for months without a vague, secret reference to *her*. So I strove to be courteous, friendly, and agreeably non-committal; begged for further documents, and promised to reply by letter in a few days.

I was hardly surprised to find the well-known hand on the envelope of a letter shortly afterward. I held it for a minute in my palm, with an absurd hope that I might sympathetically feel its character before breaking the seal. Then I read it with a great sense of relief.

"I have never assumed to guide a man, except toward the full exercise of his powers. It is not opinion in action, but opinion in a state of idleness or indifference, which repels me. I am deeply glad that you have gained so much since you left the country. If, in shaping your course, you have thought of me, I will frankly say that *to that extent*, you have drawn nearer. Am I mistaken in conjecturing that you wish to know my relation to the movement concerning which you were recently interrogated? In this, as in other instances which may come, I must beg you to consider me only as a spectator. The more my own views may seem likely to sway your action, the less I shall be inclined to declare them. If you find this cold or unwomanly, remember that it is not easy!"

Yes! I felt that I had certainly drawn much nearer to her. And from this time on, her imaginary face and form became other than they were. She was twenty-eight—three years older; a very little above the middle height, but not tall; serene, rather than stately, in her movements; with a calm, almost grave face, relieved by the sweetness of the full, firm lips; and finally eyes of pure, limpid grey, such as we fancy belonged to the Venus of Milo. I found her thus much more attractive than with the dark eyes and lashes —but she did not make her appearance in the circles which I frequented.

Another year slipped away. As an official personage, my importance increased, but I was careful not to exaggerate it to myself. Many have wondered (perhaps you among the rest) at my success, seeing that I possess no remarkable abilities. If I have any secret, it is simply this—doing faithfully, with all my might, whatever I undertake. Nine-tenths of our politicians become inflated and careless, after the first few years, and are easily forgotten when they once lose place.

I am a little surprised now that I had so much patience with the Unknown. I was too important, at least, to be played with; too mature to be subjected to a longer test; too earnest, as I had proved, to be doubted, or thrown aside without a further explanation.

Growing tired, at last, of silent waiting, I bethought me of advertising. A carefully written "Personal," in which *Ignotus* informed *Ignota* of the necessity of his communicating with her, appeared simultaneously in the *Tribune, Herald, World,* and *Times.* I renewed the advertisement as the time expired without an answer, and I think it was about the end of the third week before one came, through the post, as before.

Ah, yes! I had forgotten. See! my advertisement is pasted on the note, as a heading or motto for the manuscript lines. I don't know why the printed slip should give me a particular feeling of humiliation as I look at it, but such is the fact. What she wrote is all I need read to you:

"I could not, at first, be certain that this was meant for me. If I were to explain to you why I have not written for so long a time, I might give you one of the few clues which I insist on keeping in my own hands. In your public capacity, you have been (so far as a woman may judge) upright, independent, wholly manly: in your relations with other men I learn nothing of you that is not honourable: toward women you are kind, chivalrous, no doubt, overflowing with the *usual* social refinements, but—— Here, again, I run hard upon the absolute necessity of silence. The way to me, if you care to traverse it, is so simple, so very simple! Yet, after what I have written, I cannot even wave my hand in the direction of it, without certain self-contempt. When I feel free to tell you, we shall draw apart and remain unknown for ever.

"You desire to write? I do not prohibit it. I have heretofore made no arrangement for hearing from you, in turn, because I could not discover that any advantage would accrue from it. But it seems only fair, I confess, and you dare not think me capricious. So, three days hence, at six o'clock in the evening, a trusty messenger of mine will call at your door. If you have anything to give her for me, the act of giving it must be the sign of a compact on your part that you will allow her to leave immediately, unquestioned and unfollowed."

You look puzzled, I see: you don't catch the real drift of her words? Well, that's a melancholy encouragement. Neither did I, at the time: it was plain that I had disappointed her in some way, and my intercourse with or manner toward women had something to do with it. In vain I ran over as much of my later social life as I could recall. There had been no special attention, nothing to mislead a susceptible heart ; on the other side, certainly no rudeness, no want of " chivalrous " (she used the word !) respect and attention. What, in the name of all the gods, was the matter ?

In spite of all my efforts to grow clearer, I was obliged to write my letter in a rather muddled state of mind. I had *so* much to say ! sixteen folio pages, I was sure, would only suffice for an introduction to the case ; yet, when the creamy vellum lay before me and the moist pen drew my fingers towards it, I sat stock dumb for half an hour. I wrote, finally, in a half-desperate mood, without regard to coherency or logic. Here's a rough draft of a part of the letter, and a single passage from it will be enough :

" I can conceive of no simpler way to you than the knowledge of your name and address. I have drawn airy images of you, but they do not become incarnate, and I am not sure that I should recognise you in the brief moment of passing. Your nature is not of those which are instantly legible. As an abstract power, it has wrought in my life and it continually moves my heart with desires which are unsatisfactory because so vague and ignorant. Let me offer you, personally, my gratitude, my earnest friendship : you would laugh if I were *now* to offer more."

Stay ! here is another fragment, more reckless in tone :

" I want to find the woman whom I can love—who can love me. But this is a masquerade where the features are hidden, the voice disguised, even the hands grotesquely gloved. Come ! I will venture more than I ever thought it was possible to me. You shall know my deepest nature as I myself seem to know it. Then, give me the commonest chance of learning yours, through an intercourse which shall leave both free, should we not feel the closing of the inevitable bond ! "

After I had written that, the pages filled rapidly. When the appointed hour arrived, a bulky epistle, in a strong linen envelope, sealed with five wax seals, was waiting on my table. Precisely at six there was an announcement : the door opened, and a little outside, in the shadow, I saw an old woman, in a threadbare dress of rusty black.

" Come in ! " I said.

" The letter ! " answered a husky voice. She stretched out a bony hand, without moving a step.

" It is for a lady—very important business," said I, taking up the letter ; " are you sure that there is no mistake ? "

She drew her hand under the shawl, turned without a word, and moved toward the hall door.

" Stop ! " I cried : " I beg a thousand pardons ! Take it—take it !

You are the right messenger!"

She clutched it, and was instantly gone.

Several days passed, and I gradually became so nervous and uneasy that I was on the point of inserting another " Personal " in the daily papers, when the answer arrived. It was brief and mysterious; you shall hear the whole of it:

"I thank you. Your letter is a sacred confidence which I pray you never to regret. Your nature is sound and good. You ask no more than is reasonable, and I have no real right to refuse. In the one respect which I have hinted, I may have been unskilful or too narrowly cautious: I must have the certainty of this. Therefore, as a generous favour, give me six months more! At the end of that time I will write to you again. Have patience with these brief lines: another word might be a word too much."

You notice the change in her tone? The letter gave me the strongest impression of a new, warm, almost anxious interest on her part. My fancies, as first at Wampsocket, began to play all sorts of singular pranks: sometimes she was rich and of an old family, sometimes moderately poor and obscure, but always the same calm reposeful face and clear grey eyes. I ceased looking for her in society, quite sure that I should not find her, and nursed a wild expectation of suddenly meeting her, face to face, in the most unlikely places and under startling circumstances. However, the end of it all was patience—patience for six months.

There's not much more to tell; but this last letter is hard for me to read. It came punctually, to a day. I knew it would, and at the last I began to dread the time, as if a heavy note were falling due, and I had no funds to meet it. My head was in a whirl when I broke the seal. The fact in it stared at me blankly, at once, but it was a long time before the words and sentences became intelligible.

"The stipulated time has come, and our hidden romance is at an end. Had I taken this resolution a year ago, it would have saved me many vain hopes, and you, perhaps, a little uncertainty. Forgive me, first, if you can, and then hear the explanation:

"You wished for a personal interview: *you have had, not one, but many*. We have met, in society, talked face to face, discussed the weather, the opera, toilettes, Queechy, Aurora Floyd, Long Branch and Newport, and exchanged a weary amount of fashionable gossip; and you never guessed that I was governed by any deeper interest! I have purposely uttered ridiculous platitudes, and you were as smilingly courteous as if you enjoyed them: I have let fall remarks whose hollowness and selfishness could not have escaped you, and have waited in vain for a word of sharp, honest, manly reproof. Your manner to me was unexceptionable, as it was to all other women : but there lies the source of my disappointment, of—yes—of my sorrow!

"You appreciate, I cannot doubt, the qualities in woman which men value in one another—culture, independence of thought, a high and earnest apprehension of life; but you know not how to seek them. It is not true that a mature and unperverted woman is flattered by receiving only the general obsequiousness which most men give to the whole sex. In the man who contradicts and strives with her, she discovers a truer interest, a nobler respect. The empty-headed, spindle-shanked youths who dance admirably, understand something of billiards, much less of horses, and still less of navigation, soon grow inexpressibly wearisome to us; but the men who adopt their social courtesy, never seeking to arouse, uplift, instruct us, are a bitter disappointment.

"What would have been the end, had you really found me? Certainly a sincere, satisfying friendship. No mysterious magnetic force has drawn you to me or held you near me, nor has my experiment inspired me with an interest which cannot be given up without a personal pang. I am grieved, for the sake of all men and all women. Yet, understand me! I mean no slightest reproach. I esteem and honour you for what you are. Farewell!"

There! Nothing could be kinder in tone, nothing more humiliating in substance. I was sore and offended for a few days; but I soon began to see, and ever more and more clearly, that she was wholly right. I was sure, also, that any further attempt to correspond with her would be in vain. It all comes of taking society just as we find it, and supposing that conventional courtesy is the only safe ground on which men and women can meet.

The fact is—there's no use in hiding it from myself (and I see, by your face, that the letter cuts into your own conscience)—she is a free, courageous, independent character, and—I am not.

But who *was* she?

## JOHN W. DE FOREST
1826–1906

# AN INSPIRED LOBBYIST

A CERTAIN fallen angel (politeness toward his numerous and influential friends forbids me to mention his name abruptly) lately entered into the body of Mr. Ananias Pullwool, of Washington D.C.

As the said body was a capacious one, having been greatly enlarged circumferentially since it acquired its full longitude, there was accommodation in it for both the soul of Pullwool himself (it was a very little one) and for his distinguished visitant. Indeed, there was so much room in it that they never crowded each other, and that Pullwool hardly knew, if he even so much as mistrusted, that there was a chap in with him. But other people must have been aware of this double tenantry, or at least must have been shrewdly suspicious of it, for it soon became quite common to hear fellows say, " Pullwool has got the Devil in him."

There was, indeed, a remarkable change—a change not so much moral as physical and mental—in this gentleman's ways of deporting and behaving himself. From being loggy in movement and slow if not absolutely dull in mind, he became wonderfully agile and energetic. He had been a lobbyist, and he remained a lobbyist still, but such a different one, so much more vigorous, eager, clever, and impudent, that his best friends (if he could be said to have any friends) scarcely knew him for the same Pullwool. His fat fingers were in the buttonholes of Congressmen from the time when they put those buttonholes on in the morning to the time when they took them off at night. He seemed to be at one and the same moment treating some honourable member in the bar-room of the Arlington and running another honourable member to cover in the committee-rooms of the Capitol. He log-rolled bills which nobody else believed could be log-rolled, and he pocketed fees which absolutely and point-blank refused to go into other people's pockets. During this short period of his life he was the most successful and famous lobbyist in Washington, and the most sought after by the most rascally and desperate claimants of unlawful millions.

But, like many another man who has the Devil in him, Mr. Pullwool ran his luck until he ran himself into trouble. An investigating committee pounced upon him ; he was put in confinement for refusing to answer questions; his filchings were held up to the execration of the envious by both virtuous members and a virtuous press; and when he at last got out of durance he found it good to quit the District of Columbia for a season. Thus it happened that Mr. Pullwool and his eminent lodger took the cars and went to and fro upon the earth seeking what they might devour.

In the course of their travels they arrived in a little State, which may have been Rhode Island, or may have been Connecticut, or may have been one of the Pleiades, but which at all events had two capitals. Without regard to Morse's *Gazetteer*, or to whatever other Gazetteer may now be in currency, we shall affirm that one of these capitals was called Slowburg and the other Fastburg. For some hundreds of years (let us say five hundred, in order to be sure and get it high enough) Slowburg and Fastburg had shared between them, turn and turn about, year on and year off, all the gubernatorial and legislative pomps and emoluments that the said State had to bestow. On the 1st of April of every odd year the governor, preceded by citizen soldiers, straddling or curvetting through the mud—the governor, followed by twenty barouches full of eminent citizens, who were not known to be eminent at any other time, but who made a rush for a ride on this occasion as certain old ladies do at funerals— the governor, taking off his hat to pavements full of citizens of all ages, sizes, and colours, who did not pretend to be eminent—the governor, catching a fresh cold at every corner, and wishing the whole thing were passing at the equator—the governor triumphantly entered Slowburg—observe, Slowburg—read his always enormously long message there, and convened the legislature there. On the 1st of April of every even year the same governor, or a better one who had succeeded him, went through the same ceremonies in Fastburg. Each of these capitals boasted, or rather blushed over, a shabby old barn of a State-House, and each of them maintained a company of foot-guards and ditto of horse-guards, the latter very loose in their saddles. In each the hotels and boarding-houses had a full year and a lean year, according as the legislature sat in the one or in the other. In each there was a loud call for fresh shad and stewed oysters, or a comparatively feeble call for fresh shad and stewed oysters, under the same biennial conditions.

Such was the oscillation of grandeur and power between the two cities. It was an old-time arrangement, and like many other old-fashioned things, as, for instance, wood fires in open fireplaces, it had not only its substantial merits but its superficial inconveniences. Every year certain ancient officials were obliged to pack up hundreds of public documents and expedite them from Fastburg to Slowburg, or from Slowburg back to Fastburg. Every year there was an expense of a few dollars on this account, which the State treasurer figured up with agonies of terror, and which the opposition roared at as if the administration could have helped it. The State-Houses were

## AN INSPIRED LOBBYIST

two mere deformities of patched plaster and leprous whitewash; they were such shapeless, graceless, dilapidated wigwams, that no sensitive patriot could look at them without wanting to fly to the uttermost parts of the earth; and yet it was not possible to build new ones, and hardly possible to obtain appropriations enough to shingle out the weather; for Fastburg would vote no money to adorn Slowburg, and Slowburg was equally niggardly toward Fastburg. The same jealousy produced the same frugality in the management of other public institutions, so that the patients of the lunatic asylum were not much better lodged and fed than the average sane citizen, and the gallows-birds in the State's prison were brought down to a temperance which caused admirers of that species of fowl to tremble with indignation. In short, the two capitals were as much at odds as the two poles of a magnet, and the results of this repulsion were not all of them worthy of hysterical admiration.

But advantages seesawed with disadvantages. In this double-ender of a State political jobbery was at fault, because it had no headquarters. It could not get together a ring; it could not raise a corps of lobbyists. Such few axe-grinders as there were had to dodge back and forth between the Fastburg grindstone and the Slowburg grindstone, without ever fairly getting their tools sharpened. Legislature here and legislature there; it was like guessing at a pea between two thimbles; you could hardly ever put your finger on the right one. Then what one capital favoured the other disfavoured, and between them appropriations were kicked and hustled under the table, the grandest of railroad schemes shrunk into waste-paper baskets; in short, the public treasury was next door to the unapproachable. Such, indeed, was the desperate condition of lobbyists in this State, that, had it contained a single philanthropist of the advanced radical stripe, he would surely have brought in a bill for their relief and encouragement.

Into the midst of this happily divided community dropped Mr. Ananias Pullwool with the Devil in him. It remains to be seen whether this pair could figure up anything worth pocketing out of the problem of two capitals.

It was one of the even years, and the legislature met in Fastburg, and the little city was brimful. Mr Pullwool with difficulty found a place for himself without causing the population to slop over. Of course he went to an hotel, for he needed to make as many acquaintances as possible, and he knew that a bar was a perfect hot-house for ripening such friendships as he cared for. He took the best room he could get; and as soon as chance favoured he took a better one, with parlour attached; and on the sideboard in the parlour he always had cigars and decanters. The result was that in a week or so he was on jovial terms with several senators, numerous members of the lower house, and all the members of the "third house." But lobbying did not work in Fastburg as Mr. Pullwool

had found it to work in other capitals. He exhibited the most
dazzling double-edged axes, but nobody would grind them; he
pointed out the most attractive and convenient of logs for rolling,
but nobody would put a lever to them.

"What the doose does this mean?" he at last inquired of Mr.
Josiah Dicker, a member who had smoked dozens of his cigars and
drunk quarts out of his decanters. "I don't understand this little
old legislature at all, Mr. Dicker. Nobody wants to make any money;
at least, nobody has the spirit to try to make any. And yet the
State is full; never been bled a drop; full as a tick. What does it
mean?"

Mr. Dicker looked disconsolate. Perhaps it may be worth a
moment's time to explain that he could not well look otherwise.
Broken in fortune and broken in health, he was a failure and knew
it. His large forehead showed power, and he was, in fact, a lawyer
of some ability; and still he could not support his family, could not
keep a mould of mortgages from creeping all over his house-lot, and
had so many creditors that he could not walk the streets comfortably.
The trouble lay in hard drinking, with its resultant waste of time,
infidelity to trust, and impatience of application. Thin, haggard,
duskily pallid, deeply wrinkled at forty, his black eyes watery and
set in baggy circles of a dull brown, his lean dark hands shaky and
dirty, his linen wrinkled and buttonless, his clothing frayed and un-
brushed, he was an impersonation of failure. He had gone into the
legislature with a desperate hope of somehow finding money in it,
and as yet he had discovered nothing more than his beggarly three
dollars a day, and he felt himself more than ever a failure. No
wonder that he wore an air of profound depression, approaching
to absolute wretchedness and threatening suicide.

He looked the more cast down by contrast with the successful
Mr. Pullwool, gaudily alight with satin and jewellery, and shining
with conceit. Pullwool, by the way, although a dandy (that is,
such a dandy as one sees in gambling-saloons and behind liquor-
bars), was far from being a thing of beauty. He was so obnoxiously
gross and shapeless, that it seemed as if he did it on purpose and to
be irritating. His fat head was big enough to make a dwarf of,
hunchback and all. His mottled cheeks were vast and pendulous
to that degree that they inspired the imaginative beholder with
terror, as reminding him of avalanches and landslides which might
slip their hold at the slightest shock and plunge downward in a
path of destruction. One puffy eyelid drooped in a sinister way;
obviously that was the eye that the Devil had selected for his own;
he kept it well curtained for purposes of concealment. Looking
out of this peep-hole, the Satanic badger could see a short, thick
nose, and by leaning forward a little he could get a glimpse of a
broad chin of several stories. Another unpleasing feature was a
full set of false teeth, which grinned in a ravenous fashion that was,

truly disquieting, as if they were capable of devouring the whole internal revenue. Finally, this continent of physiognomy was diversified by a gigantic hairy wart, which sprouted defiantly from the temple nearest the game eye, as though Lucifer had accidentally poked one of his horns through. Mr. Dicker, who was a sensitive, squeamish man (as drunkards sometimes are, through bad digestion and shaky nerves), could hardly endure the sight of this wart, and always wanted to ask Pullwool why he didn't cut it off.

"What's the meaning of it all?" persisted the Washington wire-puller, surveying the Fastburg wire-puller with bland superiority, much as the city mouse may have surveyed the country mouse.

"Two capitals," responded Dicker, withdrawing his nervous glance from the wart, and locking his hands over one knee to quiet their trembling.

Mr. Pullwool, having the Old Harry in him, and being consequently full of all malice and subtlety, perceived at once the full scope and force of the explanation.

"I see," he said, dropping gently back into his arm-chair, with the plethoric, soft movement of a subsiding pillow. The puckers of his cumbrous eyelids drew a little closer together; his bilious eyes peered out cautiously between them like sallow assassins watching through curtained windows; for a minute or so he kept up what might without hyperbole be called a devil of a thinking.

"I've got it," he broke out at last. "Dicker, I want you to bring in a bill to make Fastburg the only capital."

"What is the use?" asked the legislator, looking more disconsolate, more hopless than ever. "Slowburg will oppose it and beat it."

"Never you mind," persisted Mr. Pullwool. "You bring in your little bill and stand up for it like a man. There's money in it. You don't see it? Well, I do; I'm used to seeing money in things, and in this case I see it plain. As sure as whisky is whisky, there's money in it."

Mr. Pullwool's usually dull and, so to speak, extinct countenance was fairly alight and aflame with exultation. It was almost a wonder that his tallowy person did not gutter beneath the blaze, like an over-fat candle under the flaring of a wick too large for it.

"Well, I'll bring in the bill," agreed Mr. Dicker, catching the enthusiasn of his counsellor and shaking off his lethargy. He perceived a dim promise of fees, and at the sight his load of despondency dropped away from him, as Christian's burden loosened in presence of the Cross. He looked a little like the confident, resolute Tom Dicker who twenty years before had graduated from college the brightest, bravest, most eloquent fellow in his class, and the one who seemed to have before him the finest future.

"Snacks!" said Mr. Pullwool.

At this brazen word Mr. Dicker's countenance fell again; he was ashamed to talk so frankly about plundering his fellow-citizens: "a little grain of conscience turned him sour."

"I will take pay for whatever I can do as a lawyer," he stammered.

"Get out!" laughed the Satanic one. "You just take all there is a-going! You need it bad enough. I know when a man's hard up. I know the signs. I've been as bad off as you; had to look all ways for five dollars; had to play second fiddle and say thanky. But what I offer you ain't a second fiddle. It's as good a chance as my own. Even divides. One half to you and one half to me. You know the people and I know the ropes. It's a fair bargain. What do you say?"

Mr. Dicker thought of his decayed practice and his unpaid bills, and flipping overboard his little grain of conscience, he said, "Snacks."

"All right," grinned Pullwool, his teeth gleaming alarmingly. "Word of a gentleman," he added, extending his pulpy hand, loaded with ostentatious rings, and grasping Dicker's recoiling fingers. "Harness up your little bill as quick as you can, and drive it like Jehu. Fastburg to be the only capital. Slowburg no claims at all, historical, geographical, or economic. The old arrangement a humbug; as inconvenient as a fifth wheel of a coach; cost the State thousands of greenbacks every year. Figure it all up statistically and dab it over with your shiniest rhetoric and make a big thing of it every way. That's what you've got to do; that's your little biz. I'll tend to the rest."

"I don't quite see where the money is to come from," observed Mr. Dicker.

"Leave that to me," said the veteran of the lobbies; "my name is Pullwool, and I know how to pull the wool over men's eyes, and then I know how to get at their breeches-pockets. You bring in your bill and make your speech. Will you do it?"

"Yes," answered Dicker, bolting all scruples in another half tumbler of brandy.

He kept his word. As promptly as parliamentary forms and mysteries would allow, there was a bill under the astonished noses of honourable law-givers, removing the seat of legislation from Slowburg and centring it in Fastburg. This bill Mr. Thomas Dicker supported with that fluency and fiery enthusiasm of oratory which had for a time enabled him to show as the foremost man of his State. Great was the excitement, great the rejoicing and anger. The press of Fastburg sent forth shrieks of exultation, and the press of Slowburg responded with growlings of disgust. The two capitals and the two geographical sections which they represented were ready to fire Parrott guns at each other, without regard to life and property in the adjoining regions of the earth. If there was a citizen of the little Commonwealth who did not hear of this bill and did not talk of it, it was because that citizen was as deaf as a post and as dumb as an oyster. Ordinary political distinctions were forgotten, and the old party-whips could not manage their very wheel-horses, who went snorting and kicking over the traces in all directions. In short, both in the legislature and out of it, nothing was thought of but the question of the removal of the capital.

Among the loudest of the agitators was Mr. Pullwool; not that he cared one straw whether the capital went to Fastburg, or to Slowburg, or to Ballyhack; but for the money which he thought he saw in the agitation he did care mightily, and to get that money he laboured with a zeal which was not of this world alone. At the table of his hotel, and in the bar-room of the same institution, and in the lobbies of the legislative hall, and in editorial sanctums and barber's shops, and all other nooks of gossip, he trumpeted the claims of Fastburg as if that little city were the New Jerusalem and deserved to be the metropolis of the sidereal universe. All sorts of trickeries, too: he sent spurious telegrams and got fictitious items into the newspapers; he lied through every medium known to the highest civilisation. Great surely was his success, for the row which he raised was tremendous. But a row alone was not enough; it was the mere breeze upon the surface of the waters; the treasure-ship below was still to be drawn up and gutted.

"It will cost money," he whispered confidentially to capitalists and land-owners. "We must have the sinews of war, or we can't carry it on. There's your city lots goin' to double in value if this bill goes through. What per cent. will you pay on the advance? That's the question. Put your hands in your pockets and pull 'em out full, and put back ten times as much. It's a sure investment; warranted to yield a hundred per cent.; the safest and biggest thing a-going."

Capitalists and land owners and merchants hearkened and believed and subscribed. The slyest old hunks in Fastburg put a faltering forefinger into his long pocket-book, touched a greenback which had been laid away there as neatly as a corpse in its coffin, and resurrected it for the use of Mr. Pullwool. By tens, by twenties, by fifties, and by hundreds the dollars of the ambitious citizens of the little metropolis were charmed into the portemonnaie of this rattlesnake of a lobbyist.

"I never saw a greener set," chuckled Pullwool. "By jiminy, I believe they'd shell out for a bill to make their town a seaport, if it was a hundred miles from a drop of water."

But he was not content with individual subscriptions, and conscientiously scorned himself until he had got at the city treasury.

"The corporation must pony up," he insisted, with the mayor. "This bill is just shaking in the wind for lack of money Fastburg must come down with the dust. You ought to see to it. What are you chief magistrate for ? Ain't it to tend to the welfare of the city ? Look here, now ; you call the common council together—secret session, you understand. You call 'em together and let me talk to 'em. I want to make the loons comprehend that it's their duty to vote something handsome for this measure."

The mayor hummed and hawed one way, and then he hawed and hummed the other way, and the result was that he granted the request. There was a secret session in the council-room, with his honour at the top of the long green table, with a row of more or less respectable functionaries on either side of it, and with Mr. Pullwool and the Devil at the bottom. Of course it is not to be supposed that this last-named personage was visible to the others, or that they had more than a vague suspicion of his presence. Had he fully revealed himself, had he plainly exhibited his horns and hoofs, or even so much as uncorked his perfume-bottle of brimstone, it is more than probable that the city authorities would have been exceedingly scandalised, and they might have adjourned the session. As it was, seeing nothing more disagreeable than the obese form of the lobbyist, they listened calmly while he unfolded his project.

Mr. Pullwool spoke at length, and to Fastburg ears eloquently. Fastburg must be the sole capital ; it had every claim, historical, geographical, and commercial, to that distinction ; it ought, could, would, and should be the sole capital ; that was about the substance of his exordium.

"But, gentlemen, it will cost," he went on. "There is an unscrupulous and furious opposition to the measure. The other side —those fellows from Slowburg and vicinity—are putting their hands into their breeches-pockets. You must put your hands into yours. The thing will be worth millions to Fastburg. But it will cost thousands. Are you ready to fork over ? *Are* you ready ? "

"What's the figure ? " asked one of the councilmen. "What do you estimate ? "

"Gentlemen, I shall astonish *some* of you," answered Mr. Pullwool cunningly. It was well put ; it was as much as to say, " I shall astonish the green ones ; of course the really strong heads among you won't be in the least bothered." " I estimate," he continued, " that the city treasury will have to put up a good round sum, say a hundred thousand dollars, be it more or less."

A murmur of surprise, of chagrin, and of something like indignation ran along the line of official mustaches. "Nonsense," "The dickens," "Can't be done," "We can't think of it," broke out several councilmen, in a distinctly unparliamentary manner.

"Gentlemen, one moment," pleaded Pullwool, passing his greasy smile around the company, as though it were some kind of refreshment. "Look at the whole job ; it's a big job. We must have lawyers ; we must have newspapers in all parts of the State ; we must have writers to work up the historical claims of the city ; we must have fellows to buttonhole honourable members; we must have fees for honourable members themselves. How can you do it for less?"

Then he showed a schedule; so much to this wire-puller and that and the other; so much apiece to so many able editors; so much for eminent legal counsel; finally, a trifle for himself. And one hundred thousand dollars or thereabouts was what the schedule footed up, turn it whichever way you would.

Of course this common council of Fastburg did not dare to vote such a sum for such a purpose. Mr. Pullwool had not expected that it would; all that he had hoped for was the half of it; but that half he got.

"Did they do it?" breathlessly inquired Tom Dicker of him, when he returned to the hotel.

"They done it," calmly, yet triumphantly, responded Mr. Pullwool.

"Thunder!" exclaimed the amazed Dicker. "You are the most extraordinary man! You must have the very Devil in you!"

Instead of being startled by this alarming supposition, Mr. Pullwool looked gratified. People thus possessed generally do look gratified when the possession is alluded to.

But the inspired lobbyist did not pass his time in wearing an aspect of satisfaction. When there was money to get and to spend he could run his fat off almost as fast as if he were pouring it into candle-moulds. The ring—the famous capital ring of Fastburg—must be seen to, its fingers greased, and its energy quickened. Before he rolled his apple-dumpling of a figure into bed that night he had interviewed Smith and Brown the editors, Jones and Robinson the lawyers, Smooth and Slow the literary characters, various lobbyists, and various law-givers.

"Work, gentlemen, and capitalise Fastburg and get your dividends," was his inspiring message to one and all. He promised Smith and Brown ten dollars for every editorial, and five dollars for every humbugging telegram, and two dollars for every telling item; Jones and Robinson were to have five hundred dollars apiece for concurrent legal statements of the claim of the city; Smooth and Slow, as being merely authors and so not accustomed to obtain much for their labour, got a hundred dollars between them for working up the case historically. To the lobbyists and members Pullwool was munificent; it seemed as if those gentlemen could not be paid enough for their "influence"; as if they alone had that kind of time which is money. Only, while dealing liberally with them, the inspired one did not forget himself. A thousand for Mr. Sly; yes, Mr. Sly was to receipt for a thousand; but he must let half of it stick to the Pullwool fingers. The same arrangement was made with Mr. Green and Mr. Sharp and Mr. Bummer and Mr. Pickpurse and Mr. Buncombe. It was a game of snacks, half to you and half to me;

and sometimes it was more than snacks—a thousand for you two and a thousand for me too.

With such a greasing of the wheels, you may imagine that the machinery of the ring worked to a charm. In the city and in the legislature and throughout the State there was the liveliest buzzing and humming and clicking of political wheels and cranks and cogs that had ever been known in those hitherto pastoral localities. The case of Fastburg against Slowburg was put in a hundred ways, and proved as sure as it was put. It really seemed to the eager burghers as if they already heard the clink of hammers on a new State-House and beheld a perpetual legislature sitting on their fences and curb-stones until the edifice should be finished. The great wire-puller and his gang of stipendiaries were the objects of popular gratitude and adoration. The landlord of the hotel which Mr. Pullwool patronised actually would not take pay for that gentleman's board.

" No, sir ! " declared this simple Boniface, turning crimson with enthusiasm. " You are going to put thousands of dollars into my purse, and I'll take nothing out of yours. And any little thing in the way of cigars and whisky that you want, sir, why, call for it. It's my treat, sir."

" Thank you, sir," kindly smiled the great man. " That's what I call the square thing. Mr. Boniface, you are a gentleman and a scholar, and I'll mention your admirable house to my friends. By the way, I shall have to leave you for a few days."

" Going to leave us ! " exclaimed Mr. Boniface, aghast. " I hope not till this job is put through."

" I must run about a bit," muttered Pullwool confidentially. " A little turn through the State, you understand, to stir up the country districts. Some of the members ain't as hot as they should be, and I want to set their constituents after them. Nothing like getting on a few deputations."

" Oh, exactly ! " chuckled Mr. Boniface, ramming his hands into his pockets and cheerfully jingling a bunch of keys and a penknife for lack of silver. It was strange indeed that he should actually see the Devil in Mr. Pullwool's eye and should not have a suspicion that he was in danger of being humbugged by him. " And your rooms ? " he suggested. " How about them ? "

" I keep them," replied the lobbyist grandly, as if blaspheming the expense—to Boniface. " Our friends must have a little hole to meet in. And while you are about it, Mr. Boniface, see that they get something to drink and smoke, and we'll settle it between us."

" Pre—cisely ! " laughed the landlord, as much as to say, " My treat ! " And so Mr. Pullwool, that Pericles and Lorenzo de'Medici rolled in one, departed for a season from the city which he ruled and blessed. Did he run about the State and preach and crusade in behalf of Fastburg, and stir up the bucolic populations to stir up their representatives in its favour ? Not a bit of it ; the place that he went to, and the only place that he went to, was Slowburg ; yes, covering up his tracks in his usual careful style, he made direct for the rival of Fastburg. What did he propose to do there ? Oh, how can we reveal the whole duplicity and turpitude of Ananias Pullwool ? The subject is too vast for a merely human pen ; it requires the literary ability of a recording angel. Well, we must get our feeble lever under this boulder of wickedness as we can, and do our faint best to expose all the reptiles and slimy things beneath it. The first person whom this apostle of lobbyism called upon in Slowburg was the mayor of that tottering capital.

"My name is Pullwool," he said to the official, and he said it with an almost enviable ease of impudence, for he was used to introducing himself to people who despised and detested him. "I want to see you confidentially about this capital ring which is making so much trouble."

"I thought you were in it," replied the mayor, turning very red in the face, for he had heard of Mr. Pullwool as the leader of said ring ; and being an iracund man, he was ready to knock his head off.

"In it!" exclaimed the possessed one. "I wish I was. It's a fat thing. More than fifty thousand dollars paid out already!"

"Good gracious!" exclaimed the mayor in despair.

"By the way, this is between ourselves," added Pullwool. "You take it so, I hope. Word of honour, eh ?"

"Why, if you have anything to communicate that will help us, why, of course, I promise secrecy," stammered the mayor. "Yes, certainly ; word of honour."

"Well, I've been looking about among those fellows a little," continued Ananias. "I've kept my eyes and ears open. It's a way I have. And I've learned a thing or two that it will be to your advantage to know. Yes, sir! fifty thousand dollars !—the city has voted it and paid it, and the ring has got it. That's why they are all working so. And depend upon it, they'll carry the legislature and turn Slowburg out to grass unless you wake up and do something."

"By heavens!" exclaimed the iracund mayor, turning red again. "It's a piece of confounded rascality. It ought to be exposed."

"No, don't expose it," put in Mr. Pullwool, somewhat alarmed. "That game never works. Of course they'd deny it and swear you down, for bribing witnesses is as easy as bribing members. I'll tell you what to do. Beat them at their own weapons. Raise a purse that will swamp theirs. That's the way the world goes. It's an auction. The highest bidder gets the article."

Well, the result of it all was that the city magnates of Slowburg did just what had been done by the city magnates of Fastburg, only, instead of voting fifty thousand dollars into the pockets of the ring, they voted sixty thousand. With a portion of this money about him, and with authority to draw for the rest on proper vouchers,

Mr. Pullwool, his tongue in his cheek, bade farewell to his new allies. As a further proof of the ready wit and solid impudence of this sublime politician and model of American statesman, let me here introduce a brief anecdote. Leaving Slowburg by the cars, he encountered a gentleman from Fastburg, who saluted him with tokens of amazement, and said, "What are you doing here, Mr. Pullwool?"

"Oh, just breaking up these fellows a little," whispered the man with the Devil in him. "They were making too strong a fight. I had to *see* some of them," putting one hand behind his back and rubbing his fingers together, to signify that there had been a taking of bribes. "But be shady about it. For the sake of the good cause, keep quiet. Mum's the word."

The reader can imagine how briskly the fight between the two capitals reopened when Mr. Pullwool re-entered the lobby. Slowburg now had its adherents, and they struggled like men who saw money in their warfare, and they struggled not in vain. To cut a very long story very short, to sum the whole of an exciting drama in one sentence, the legislature kicked overboard the bill to make Fastburg the sole seat of government. Nothing had come of the whole row, except that a pair of simple little cities had spent over one hundred thousand dollars, and that the capital ring, fighting on both sides and drawing pay from both sides, had lined its pockets, while the great creator of the ring had crammed his to bursting.

"What does this mean, Mr. Pullwool?" demanded the partially honest and entirely puzzled Tom Dicker, when he had discovered by an unofficial count of noses how things were going. "Fastburg has spent all its money for nothing. It won't be sole capital, after all."

"I never expected it would be," replied Pullwool, so tickled by the Devil that was in him that he could not help laughing. "I never wanted it to be. Why, it would spoil the little game. This is a trick that can be played every year."

"Oh!" exclaimed Mr. Dicker, and was dumb with astonishment for a minute.

"Didn't you see through it before?" grinned the grand master of all guile and subtlety.

"I did not," confessed Mr. Dicker, with a mixture of shame and abhorrence. "Well," he presently added, recovering himself, "shall we settle?"

"Oh, certainly, if you are ready," smiled Pullwool, with the air of a man who has something coming to him.

"And what, exactly, will be my share?" asked Dicker humbly.

"What do you mean?" stared Pullwool, apparently in the extremity of amazement.

"You said *snacks*, didn't you?" urged Dicker, trembling violently.

"Well, *snacks* it is, replied Pullwool. "Haven't you had a thousand?"

"Yes," admitted Dicker.

"Then you owe me five hundred?" Mr. Dicker did not faint, though he came very near it, but he staggered out of the room as white as a sheet, for he was utterly crushed by this diabolical impudence.

That very day Mr. Pullwool left for Washington, and the Devil for *his* place, each of them sure to find the other when he wanted him, if indeed their roads lay apart.

# JOHN TOWNSEND TROWBRIDGE
1827–1916

## THE MAN WHO STOLE A MEETING-HOUSE

ON a recent journey to the Pennsylvania oil regions, I stopped one evening with a fellow-traveller at a village which had just been thrown into a turmoil of excitement by the exploits of a horse-thief. As we sat around the tavern hearth, after supper, we heard the particulars of the rogue's capture and escape fully discussed; then followed many another tale of theft and robbery, told amid curling puffs of tobacco-smoke; until, at the close of an exciting story, one of the natives turned to my travelling acquaintance, and, with a broad laugh, said, " Kin you beat that, stranger ? "

"Well, I don't know—maybe I could if I should try. I never happened to fall in with any such tall horse-stealing as you tell of, but I knew a man who stole a meeting-house once."

"Stole a meetin'-house! That goes a little beyant anything yit," remarked another of the honest villagers. "Ye don't mean he stole it and carried it away?"

"Stole it and carried it away," repeated my travelling companion seriously, crossing his legs, and resting his arm on the back of his chair. "And, more than all that, I helped him."

"How happened that?—for you don't look much like a thief yourself."

All eyes were now turned upon my friend, a plain New England farmer, whose honest homespun appearance and candid speech commanded respect.

"I was his hired man, and I acted under orders. His name was Jedwort—Old Jedwort the boys called him, although he wasn't above fifty when the crooked little circumstance happened, which I'll make as straight a story of as I can, if the company would like to hear it."

"Sartin, stranger! sartin! about stealin' the meetin'-house," chimed in two or three voices.

My friend cleared his throat, put his hair behind his ears, and with a grave, smooth face, but with a merry twinkle in his shrewd grey eye, began as follows:—

"Jedwort, I said his name was; and I shall never forget how he looked one particular morning. He stood leaning on the front gate —or rather on the post, for the gate itself was such a shackling concern a child couldn't have leaned on't without breaking it down. And Jedwort was no child. Think of a stoutish, stooping, duck-legged man, with a mountainous back, strongly suggestive of a bag of grist under his shirt—and you have him. That imaginary grist had been growing heavier and heavier, and he more and more bent under it, for the last fifteen years and more, until his head and neck just came forward out from between his shoulders like a turtle's from its shell. His arms hung, as he walked, almost to the ground. Being curved with the elbows outward, he looked for all the world, in a front view, like a waddling interrogation-point enclosed in a parenthesis.

"If man was ever a quadruped, as I've heard some folks tell, and rose gradually from four legs to two, there must have been a time, very early in his history, when he went about like Old Jedwort.

"The gate had been a very good gate in its day. It had even been a genteel gate when Jedwort came into possession of the place by marrying his wife, who inherited it from her uncle. That was some twenty years before, and everything had been going to rack and ruin ever since.

"Jedwort himself had been going to rack and ruin, morally speaking. He was a middling decent sort of man when I first knew him; and I judge there must have been something about him more than common, or he never could have got such a wife. But then women do marry sometimes unaccountably.

"I speak with feeling on this subject, for I had an opportunity of seeing what Mrs. Jedwort had to put up with from a man no woman of her stamp could do anything but detest. She was the patientest creature you ever saw. She was even too patient. If I had been tied to such a cub, I think I should have cultivated the beautiful and benignant qualities of a wild cat; there would have been one good fight, and one of us would have been living, and the other would have been dead, and that would have been the end of it.

"But Mrs. Jedwort bore and bore untold miseries, and a large number of children. She had had nine of these, and three were under the sod and six above it when Jedwort ran off with the meeting-house in the way I am going on to tell you. There was Maria, the oldest girl, a perfect picture of what her mother had been at nineteen. Then there were the two boys, Dave and Dan, fine young fellows, spite of their father. Then came Lottie and Susie, and then Willie, a little four-year-old.

"It was amazing to see what the mother would do to keep her family looking decent with the little means she had. For Jedwort was the tightest screw ever you saw. It was avarice that had spoiled him, and came so near turning him into a beast. The boys used to say he grew so bent looking in the dirt for pennies. That was true of his mind, if not of his body. He was a poor man, and a pretty respectable man, when he married his wife; but he had no sooner come into possession of a little property than he grew crazy for more.

"There are a good many men in the world, that nobody looks upon as monomaniacs, who are crazy in just that sort of way. They are all for laying up money, depriving themselves of comforts, and their families of the advantages of society and education, just to add a few dollars to their hoard every year; and so they keep on till they die and leave it to their children, who would be much better off if a little more had been invested in the cultivation of their minds and manners, and less in stocks and bonds.

"Jedwort was just one of that class of men, although perhaps he carried the fault I speak of a little to excess. A dollar looked so big to him, and he held it so close, that at last he couldn't see much of anything else. By degrees he lost all regard for decency and his neighbour's opinions. His children went barefoot, even after they got to be great boys and girls, because he was too mean to buy them shoes. It was pitiful to see a nice, interesting girl like Maria go about looking as she did, while her father was piling his money into the bank. She wanted to go to school and learn music, and be somebody; but he wouldn't keep a hired girl, and so she was obliged to stay at home and do housework; and she could no more have got a dollar out of him to pay for clothes and tuition than you could squeeze sap out of a hoe-handle.

"The only way his wife could ever get anything new for the family was by stealing butter from her own dairy, and selling it behind his back. 'You needn't say anything to Mr. Jedwort about this batch of butter,' she would hint to the storekeeper; 'but you may hand the money to me, or I will take my pay in goods.' In this way a new gown, or a piece of cloth for the boy's coats, or something else the family needed, would be smuggled into the house, with fear and trembling lest old Jedwort should make a row and find where the money came from.

"The house inside was kept neat as a pin; but everything around it looked terribly shiftless. It was built originally in an ambitious style, and painted white. It had four tall front pillars, supporting the portion of the roof that came over the porch—lifting up the eyebrows of the house, if I may so express myself, and making it look as if it was going to sneeze. Half the blinds were off their hinges, and the rest flapped in the wind. The front-door step had rotted away. The porch had once a good floor, but for years Jedwort had been in the habit of going to it whenever he wanted a board for the pig-pen, until not a bit of floor was left.

"But I began to tell about Jedwort leaning on the gate that morning. We had all noticed him; and as Dave and I brought in the milk, his mother asked, 'What is your father planning now?

Half the time he stands there, looking up the road; or else he's walking up that way in a brown study.'

"'He's got his eye on the old meeting-house,' says Dave, setting down his pail. 'He has been watching it and walking round it, off and on, for a week.'

"That was the first intimation I had of what the old fellow was up to. But after breakfast he followed me out of the house, as if he had something on his mind to say to me.

"'Stark,' says he at last, 'you've always insisted on't that I wasn't an enterprisin' man.'

"'I insist on't still,' says I; for I was in the habit of talking mighty plain to him, and joking him pretty hard sometimes. 'If I had this farm, I'd show you enterprise. You wouldn't see the hogs in the garden half the time, just for want of a good fence to keep 'em out. You wouldn't see the very best strip of land lying waste, just for want of a ditch. You wouldn't see that stone wall by the road tumbling down year after year, till by and by you won't be able to see it for the weeds and thistles.'

"'Yes,' says he sarcastically, 'ye'd lay out ten times as much money on the place as ye'd ever git back agin, I've no doubt. But I believe in economy.'

"That provoked me a little, and I said, 'Economy! you're one of the kind of men that'll skin a flint for sixpence and spoil a jack-knife worth a shilling. You waste fodder and grain enough every three years to pay for a bigger barn—to say nothing of the inconvenience.'

"'Wal, Stark,' says he, grinning and scratching his head, 'I've made up my mind to have a bigger barn, if I have to steal one.'

"'That won't be the first thing you've stole neither,' says I.

"He flared up at that. 'Stole?' says he. 'What did I ever steal?'

"'Well, for one thing, the rails the freshet last spring drifted off from Talcott's land onto yours, and you grabbed: what was that but stealing?'

"'That was luck. He couldn't swear to his rails. By the way, they'll jest come in play now.'

"'They've come in play already,' says I. 'They've gone on to the old fences all over the farm, and I could use a thousand more without making much show.'

"'That's 'cause you're so dumbed extravagant with rails, as you are with everything else. A few loads can be spread from the fences here and there, as well as not. Harness up the team, boys, and git together enough to make about ten rods o' zigzag, two rails high.'

"'Two rails?' says Dave, who had a healthy contempt for the old man's narrow, contracted way of doing things. 'What's the good of such a fence as that?'

"'It'll be,' says I, 'like the single bar in music. When our old singing-master asked his class once what a single bar was, Bill Wilkins spoke up and said, "It's a bar that horses and cattle jump over, and pigs and sheep run under." What do you expect to keep out with two rails?'

"'The *law*, boys, the *law*,' says Jedwort. I know what I'm about. I'll make a fence the *law* can't run under nor jump over; and I don't care a cuss for the cattle and pigs. You git the rails, and I'll rip some boards off'n the pig-pen to make stakes.'

"'Boards a'n't good for nothin' for stakes,' says Dave. 'Besides, none can't be spared from the pig-pen.'

"'I'll have boards enough in a day or two for forty pig-pens,' says Jedwort. 'Bring along the rails, and dump 'em out in the road for the present, and say nothin' to nobody.'

"We got the rails, and he made his stakes; and right away after dinner he called us out. 'Come, boys,' says he, 'now we'll astonish the natives.'

"The wagon stood in the road, with the last jag of rails still on it. Jedwort piled on his stakes, and threw on the crowbar and axe, while we were hitching up the team.

"'Now, drive on, Stark,' says he.

"'Yes; but where shall I drive to?'

"'To the old meetin'-house,' says Jedwort, trudging on ahead.

"The old meeting-house stood on an open common, at the northeast corner of his farm. A couple of cross-roads bounded it on two sides; and it was bounded on the other two by Jedwort's overgrown stone wall. It was a square, old-fashioned building, with a low steeple, that had a belfry, but no bell in it, and with a high square pulpit and high straight-backed pews inside. It was now some time since meetings had been held there; the old society that used to meet there having separated, one division of it building a fashionable chapel in the North Village, and the other a fine new church at the Centre.

"Now, the peculiarity about the old church property was, that nobody had any legal title to it. A log meeting-house had been built there when the country was first settled and land was of no account. In the course of time that was torn down, and a good framed house put up in its place. As it belonged to the whole community, no title, either to the house or land, was ever recorded; and it wasn't until after the society dissolved that the question came up as to how the property was to be disposed of. While the old deacons were carefully thinking it over, Jedwort was on hand to settle it by putting in his claim.

"'Now, boys,' says he, 'ye see what I'm up to.'

"'Yes,' says I, provoked as I could be at the mean trick, 'and I knew it was some such mischief all along. You never show any enterprise, as you call it, unless it is to get the start of a neighbour.'

"'But what *are* you up to, pa?' says Dan, who didn't see the trick yet.

"The old man says, 'I'm goin' to fence in the rest part of my farm.'

"'What rest part?'

"'This part that never was fenced; the old meetin'-house common.'

"'But, pa,' says Dave, disgusted as I was, 'you've no claim on that.'

"'Wal, if I ha'n't, I'll make a claim. Give me the crowbar. Now, here's the corner, nigh as I can squint'; and he stuck the bar into the ground. 'Make a fence to here from the wall, both sides. Now work spry, for there comes Deacon Talcott.'

"'Wal, wal!' says the Deacon, coming up, puffing with excitement; 'what ye doin' to the old meetin'-house?'

"'Wal,' says Jedwort, driving away at his stakes, and never looking up, 'I've been considerin' some time what I should do with 't, and I've concluded to make a barn on 't.'

"'Make a barn! make a barn!' cries the Deacon. 'Who give ye liberty to make a barn of the house of God?'

"'Nobody; I take the liberty. Why shouldn't I do what I please with my own prop'ty?'

"'Your own property—what do ye mean? 'Ta'n't your meetin'-house.'

"'Whose is't, if 't a'n't mine?' says Jedwort, lifting his turtle's head from between his horizontal shoulders, and grinning in the Deacon's face.

"'It belongs to the society,' says the Deacon.

"'But the s'ciety's pulled up stakes and gone off.'

"'It belongs to individooals of the society—to individooals.'

"'Wal, I'm an individooal,' says Jedwort.

"'You! you never went to meetin' here a dozen times in your life!'

"'I never did have my share of the old meetin'-house, that's a fact,' says Jedwort; 'but I'll make it up now.'

"'But what are ye fencin' up the common for?' says the Deacon.

"'It'll make a good calf-pastur'. I've never had my share o' the vally o' that either. I've let my neighbours' pigs and critters run on't long enough; and now I'm jest goin' to take possession o' my own.'

"'Your own!' says the Deacon in perfect consternation. 'You've no deed on't.'

"'Wal, have you?'

"'No—but—the society——'

"'The s'ciety, I tell ye,' says Jedwort, holding his head up longer than I ever knew him to hold it up at a time, and grinning all the while in Talcott's face—'the s'ciety is split to pieces. There a'n't no s'ciety now, any more'n a pig's a pig arter you've butchered and e't it. You've e't the pig amongst ye, and left me the pen. The s'ciety never had a deed o' this 'ere prop'ty, and no man never had a deed o' this 'ere prop'ty. My wife's gran'daddy, when he took up the land here, was a good-natered sort of man, and he allowed a corner on't for his neighbours to put up a temp'rary meetin'-house. That was finally used up—the kind o' preachin' they had them days was enough to use up in a little time any house that wa'n't fireproof; and when that was preached to pieces they put up another shelter in its place. This is it. And now't the land a'n't used no more for the purpose 'twas lent for it goes back nat'rally to the estate 'twas took from, and the buildin's along with it.'

"'That's all a sheer fabrication,' says the Deacon. 'This land was never a part of what's now your farm any more than it was a part of mine.'

"'Wal,' says Jedwort, 'I look at it in my way, and you've a perfect right to look at it in your way. But I'm goin' to make sure o' my way by puttin' a fence round the hull concern.'

"'And you're usin' some of my rails for to do it with!' says the Deacon.

"'Can you swear 't they're your rails?'

"'Yes, I can; they're rails the freshet carried off from my farm last spring and landed on to yourn.'

"'So I've heard ye say. But can you swear to the partic'lar rails? Can you swear, for instance, 't this 'ere is your rail? or this 'ere one?'

"'No; I can't swear to precisely them two—but——'

"'Can you swear to these two? or to any one or two?' says Jedwort. 'No, ye can't. Ye can swear to the lot in general, but you can't swear to any partic'lar rail, and that kind o' swearin' won't stand law, Deacon Talcott. I don't boast of bein' an edicated man, but I know suthin' o' what law is, and when I know it I dror a line there, and I toe that line, and I make my neighbours toe that line, Deacon Talcott. Nine p'ints of the law is possession, and I'll have possession o' this 'ere house and land by fencin' on't in; and though every man 't comes along should say these 'ere rails belong to them, I'll fence it in with these 'ere very rails.'

" Jedwort said this, wagging his obstinate old head, and grinning with his face turned up pugnaciously at the Deacon; then went to work again as if he had settled the question, and didn't wish to discuss it any further.

" As for Talcott, he was too full of wrath and boiling indignation to answer such a speech. He knew that Jedwort had managed to get the start of him with regard to the rails by mixing a few of his own with those he had stolen, so that nobody could tell 'em apart; and he saw at once that the meeting-house was in danger of going the same way, just for want of an owner to swear out a clear title to the property. He did just the wisest thing when he swallowed his vexation, and hurried off to alarm the leading men of the two societies, and to consult a lawyer. . . . The common was fenced in by sundown; and the next day Jedwort had over a house-mover from the North Village to look and see what could be done with the building. 'Can ye snake it over and drop it back of my house?' says he.

"'It'll be a hard job,' says old Bob, 'without you tear down the steeple fust.'

"But Jedwort said, 'What's a meetin'-house 'thout a steeple? I've got my heart kind o' set on that steeple, and I'm bound to go the hull hog on this 'ere concern now I've began.'

"'I vow,' says Bob, examining the timbers, 'I won't warrant but what the old thing'll all tumble down.'

"'I'll resk it.'

"'Yes; but who'll resk the lives of me and my men?'

"'Oh, you'll see if it's re'ly goin' to tumble and look out. I'll engage 't me and my boys 'll do the most dangerous part of the work. Dumbed if I wouldn't agree to ride in the steeple and ring the bell, if there was one.'

"It wasn't many days before Bob came over again, bringing with him this time his screws and ropes and rollers, his men and timbers, horse and capstan; and at last the old house might have been seen on its travels.

"It was an exciting time all around. The societies found that Jedwort's fence gave him the first claim to house and land, unless a regular siege of the law was gone through to beat him off—and then it might turn out that he would beat them. Some said fight him; some said let him be—the thing a'n't worth going to law for; and so, as the leading men couldn't agree as to what should be done, nothing was done. That was just what Jedwort had expected, and he laughed in his sleeve while Bob and his boys screwed up the old meeting-house, and got their beams under it, and set it on rollers, and slued it around, and slid it on the timbers laid for it across into Jedwort's field, steeple foremost, like a locomotive on a track.

"It was a trying time for the women-folks at home. Maria had declared that if her father did persist in stealing the meeting-house, she would not stay a single day after it, but would follow Dave, who had already gone away.

"That touched me pretty close, for, to tell the truth, it was rather more Maria than her mother that kept me at work for the old man. 'If you go,' says I, 'then there is no object for me to stay; I shall go too.'

"'That's what I supposed,' says she; 'for there's no reason in the world why you should stay. But then Dan will go; and who'll be left to take sides with mother? That's what troubles me. Oh, if she could only go too! But she won't, and she couldn't if she would, with the other children depending on her. Dear, dear! what shall we do?'

"The poor girl put her head on my shoulder and cried; and if I should own up to the truth, I suppose I cried a little too. For where's the man that can hold a sweet woman's head on his shoulder, while she sobs out her trouble, and he hasn't any power to help her—who, I say, can do any less, in such circumstances, than drop a tear or two for company?

"'Never mind; don't hurry,' says Mrs. Jedwort. 'Be patient, and wait awhile, and it'll all turn out right, I'm sure.'

"'Yes, you always say, "Be patient, and wait!"' says Maria, brushing back her hair. 'But, for my part, I'm tired of waiting, and my patience has given out long ago. We can't always live in this way, and we may as well make a change now as ever. But I can't bear the thought of going and leaving you.'

"Here the two younger girls came in, and seeing that crying was the order of the day, they began to cry; and when they heard Maria talk of going, they declared they would go; and even little Willie, the four-year-old, began to howl.

"'There, there! Maria! Lottie! Susie!' said Mrs. Jedwort in her calm way; 'Willie, hush up! I don't know what we are to do; but I feel that something is going to happen that will show us the right way, and we are to wait. Now go and wash the dishes, and set the cheese.'

"That was just after breakfast, the second day of the moving; and sure enough, something like what she prophesied did happen before another sun.

"The old frame held together pretty well till along toward night, when the steeple showed signs of seceding. 'There she goes! She's falling now!' sung out the boys, who had been hanging around all day in hopes of seeing the thing tumble.

"The house was then within a few rods of where Jedwort wanted it; but Bob stopped right there, and said it wasn't safe to haul it another inch. 'That steeple's bound to come down, if we do,' says he.

"'Not by a dumbed sight, it a'n't,' says Jedwort. 'Them cracks a'n't nothin'; the j'ints is all firm yit.' He wanted Bob to go up and examine; but Bob shook his head—the concern looked too shaky. Then he told me to go up, but I said I hadn't lived quite long enough, and had a little rather be smoking my pipe on *terra firma*. Then the boys began to hoot. 'Dumbed if ye a'n't all a set of cowards,' says he. 'I'll go up myself.'

"We waited outside while he climbed up inside. The boys jumped on the ground to jar the steeple and make it fall. One of them blew a horn—as he said, to bring down the old Jericho—and another thought he'd help things along by starting up the horse and giving the building a little wrench. But Bob put a stop to that; and finally out came a head from the belfry window. It was Jedwort, who shouted down to us: 'There a'n't a j'int or brace gin out. Start the hoss, and I'll ride. *Pass me up that 'ere horn, and——*'

"Just then there came a cracking and loosening of timbers, and we that stood nearest had only time to jump out of the way, when down came the steeple crashing to the ground, with Jedwort in it."

"I hope it killed the cuss," said one of the village story-tellers.

"Worse than that," replied my friend; "it just cracked his skull —not enough to put an end to his miserable life, but only to take away what little sense he had. We got the doctors to him, and they patched up his broken head; and by George it made me mad to see the fuss the women-folks made over him. It would have been my way to let him die; but they were as anxious and attentive to him as if he had been the kindest husband and most indulgent father that ever lived; for that's women's style: they're unreasoning creatures.

"Along towards morning we persuaded Mrs. Jedwort, who had been up all night, to lie down a spell and catch a little rest, while Maria and I sat up and watched with the old man. All was still except our whispers and his heavy breathing; there was a lamp burning in the next room; when all of a sudden a light shone into the windows, and about the same time we heard a roaring and crackling sound. We looked out, and saw the night all lighted up as if by some great fire. As it appeared to be on the other side of the house, we ran to the door, and there what did we see but the old meeting-house all in flames. Some fellows had set fire to it to spite Jedwort. It must have been burning some time inside, for when we looked out the flames had burst through the roof.

"As the night was perfectly still, except a light wind blowing away from the other buildings on the place, we raised no alarm, but just stood in the door and saw it burn. And a glad sight it was to us, you may be sure. I just held Maria close to my side, and told her that all was well—it was the best thing that could happen. 'Oh yes,' says she, 'it seems to me as though a kind Providence was burning up his sin and shame out of our sight.'

"I had never yet said anything to her about marriage—for the time to come at that had never seemed to arrive; but there's nothing like a little excitement to bring things to a focus. You've seen water in a tumbler just at the freezing-point, but not exactly able to make up its mind to freeze, when a little jar will set the crystals forming, and in a minute what was liquid is ice. It was the shock of events that night that touched my life into crystals—not of ice, gentlemen, by any manner of means.

"After the fire had got along so far that the meeting-house was a gone case, an alarm was given, probably by the very fellows that set it, and a hundred people were on the spot before the thing had done burning.

"Of course these circumstances put an end to the breaking up of the family. Dave was sent for, and came home. Then as soon as we saw that the old man's brain was injured so that he wasn't likely to recover his mind, the boys and I went to work and put that farm through a course of improvement it would have done your eyes good to see. The children were sent to school, and Mrs. Jedwort had all the money she wanted now to clothe them, and to provide the house with comforts, without stealing her own butter. Jedwort was a burden; but, in spite of him, that was just about the happiest family for the next four years that ever lived on this planet.

"Jedwort soon got his bodily health, but I don't think he knew one of us again after his hurt. As near as I could get at his state of mind, he thought he had been changed into some sort of animal. He seemed inclined to take me for a master, and for four years he followed me around like a dog. During that time he never spoke, but only whined and growled. When I said, 'Lie down,' he'd lie down; and when I whistled he'd come.

"I used sometimes to make him work; and certain simple things he would do very well as long as I was by. One day I had a jag of hay to get in; and, as the boys were away, I thought I'd have him load it. I pitched it on to the waggon about where it ought to lie, and looked to him only to pack it down. There turned out to be a bigger load than I had expected, and the higher it got the worse the shape of it, till finally, as I was starting it towards the barn, off it rolled, and the old man with it, head foremost.

"He struck a stone heap, and for a moment I thought he was killed. But he jumped up and spoke for the first time. '*I'll blow it*,' says he, finishing the sentence he had begun four years before, when he called for the horn to be passed up to him.

"I couldn't have been much more astonished if one of the horses had spoken. But I saw at once that there was an expression in Jedwort's face that hadn't been there since his tumble in the belfry; and I knew that, as his wits had been knocked out of him by one blow on the head, so another blow had knocked 'em in again.

"'Where's Bob?' says he, looking all around.

"'Bob?' says I, not thinking at first who he meant. 'Oh, Bob is dead—he has been dead these three years.'

"Without noticing my reply, he exclaimed, 'Where did all that hay come from? Where's the old meetin'-house?'

"'Don't you know?' says I. 'Some rogues set fire to it the night after you got hurt, and burned it up.'

"He seemed then just beginning to realise that something extraordinary had happened.

"'Stark,' says he, 'what's the matter with ye? You're changed.'

"'Yes,' says I, 'I wear my beard now, and I've grown older!'

"'Dumbed if 't a'n't odd!' says he. 'Stark, what in thunder's the matter with *me*?'

"'You've had meeting-house on the brain for the past four years,' says I; 'that's what's the matter.'

"It was some time before I could make him understand that he had been out of his head, and that so long a time had been a blank to him.

"Then he said, 'Is this my farm?'

"'Don't you know it?' says I.

"'It looks more slicked up than ever it used to,' says he.

"'Yes,' says I; 'and you'll find everything else on the place slicked up in about the same way.'

"'Where's Dave?' says he.

"'Dave has gone to town to see about selling the wool.'

"'Where's Dan?'

"'Dan's in college. He takes a great notion to medicine, and we're going to make a doctor of him.'

"'Whose house is that?' says he, as I was taking him home.

"'No wonder you don't know it,' says I. 'It has been painted, and shingled, and had new blinds put on; the gates and fences are all in prime condition; and that's a new barn we put up a couple of years ago.'

"'Where does the money come from to make all these improvements?'

"'It comes off the place,' says I. 'We haven't run in debt the first cent for anything, but we've made the farm more profitable than it ever was before.'

"'That *my* house?' he repeated wonderingly as we approached it. 'What sound is that?'

"'That's Lottie practising her lesson on the piano.'

"'A pianer in my house?' he muttered. 'I can't stand that!' He listened. 'It sounds pooty though!'

"'Yes, it does sound pretty, and I guess you'll like it. How does the place suit you?'

"'It *looks* pooty.' He started. 'What young lady is that?'

"It was Lottie, who had left her music and stood by the window.

"'My dahter! ye don't say! Dumbed if she a'n't a mighty nice gal.'

"'Yes,' says I; 'she takes after her mother.'

"'Just then Susie, who heard talking, ran to the door.

"'Who's that agin?' says Jedwort.

"I told him.

"'Wal, *she's* a mighty nice-lookin' gal!'

"'Yes,' says I; '*she* takes after her mother.'

"Little Willie, now eight years old, came out of the wood-shed with a bow and arrow in his hand, and stared like an owl, hearing his father talk.

"'What boy is that? says Jedwort. And when I told him, he muttered, 'He's an ugly-looking brat!'

"' He's more like his father,' says I.

"The truth is, Willie was such a fine boy the old man was afraid to praise him for fear I'd say of him, as I'd said of the girls, that he favoured his mother.

"Susie ran back and gave the alarm, and then out came mother, and Maria with her baby in her arms—for I forgot to tell you that we had been married now nigh on to two years.

"Well, the women-folks were as much astonished as I had been when Jedwort first spoke, and a good deal more delighted. They drew him into the house, and I am bound to say he behaved remarkably well. He kept looking at his wife, and his children, and his grandchild, and the new paper on the walls, and the new furniture, and now and then asking a question or making a remark.

"' It all comes back to me now,' says he at last. ' I thought I was living in the moon, with a superior race of human bein's, and this is the place and you are the people.'

"It wasn't more than a couple of days before he began to pry around, and find fault, and grumble at the expense; and I saw there was danger of things relapsing into something like their former condition. So I took him one side and talked to him.

"' Jedwort,' says I, ' you're like a man raised from the grave. You was the same as buried to your neighbours, and now they come and look at you as they would at a dead man come to life. To you it's like coming into a new world; and I'll leave it to you now if you don't rather like the change from the old state of things to what you see around you to-day. You've seen how the family affairs go on—how pleasant everything is, and how we all enjoy ourselves. You hear the piano and like it; you see your children sought after and respected—your wife in finer health and spirits than you've ever known her since the day she was married; you see industry and neatness everywhere on the premises; and you're a beast if you don't like all that. In short, you see that our management is a great deal better than yours; and that we beat you even in the matter of economy. Now, what I want to know is this: whether you think you'd like to fall into our way of living, or return like a hog to your wallow?'

"' I don't say but what I like your way of livin' very well,' he grumbled.

"' Then,' says I, ' you must just let us go ahead as we have been going ahead. Now's the time for you to turn about and be a respectable man like your neighbours. Just own up and say you've not only been out of your head the past four years, but that you've been more or less out of your head the last four-and-twenty years. But say you're in your right mind now, and prove it by acting like a man in his right mind. Do that, and I'm with you—we're all with you. But go back to your old dirty ways, and you go alone. Now I sha'n't let you off till you tell me what you mean to do.'

"He hesitated some time, then said, 'Maybe you're about right, Stark; you and Dave and the old woman seem to be doin' pooty well, and I guess I'll let you go on.'"

Here my friend paused, as if his story was done; when one of the villagers asked, "About the land where the old meetin'-house stood—whatever was done with that?"

"That was appropriated for a new school-house, and there my little shavers go to school."

"And old Jedwort, is he alive yet?"

"Both Jedwort and his wife have gone to that country where meanness and dishonesty have a mighty poor chance—where the only investments worth much are those recorded in the Book of Life. Mrs. Jedwort was rich in that kind of stock; and Jedwort's account, I guess, will compare favourably with that of some respectable people, such as we all know. I tell ye, my friends," continued my fellow-traveller, "there's many a man, both in the higher and lower ranks of life, that 'twould do a deal of good, say nothing of the mercy 'twould be to their families, just to knock 'em on the head, and make Nebuchadnezzars of 'em—then, after they'd been turned out to grass a few years, let 'em come back again, and see how happy folks have been, and how well they have got along without 'em.

"I carry on the old place now," he added. "The younger girls are married off; Dan's a doctor in the North Village; and as for Dave, he and I have struck ile. I'm going out to look at our property now."

# WILLIAM JAMES STILLMAN
1828–1901

# BILLY AND HANS

IN my favourite summer resort at the lower edge of the Black Forest, the quaint old town of Laufenburg, a farmer's boy one day brought me a young squirrel for sale. He was a tiny creature, probably not yet weaned, a variation on the ordinary type of the European squirrel, dark grey instead of the usual red, and with black tail and ears, so that at first, as he contented himself with drinking his milk and sleeping, I was not sure that he was not a dormouse. But examination of the paws, with their delicate anatomy, so marvellously like the human hand in their flexibility and handiness, and the graceful curl of his tail, settled the question of genus; and mindful of my boyhood and a beloved pet of the American species of his genus, I bought him and named him Billy. From the first moment that he became my companion he gave me his entire confidence, and accepted his domestication without the least indication that he considered it captivity. There is generally a short stage of mute rebellion in wild creatures before they come to accept us entirely as their friends—a longing for freedom which makes precautions against escape necessary. This never appeared in Billy; he came to me for his bread and milk, and slept in my pocket, from the first, and enjoyed being caressed as completely as if he had been born under my roof. No other animal is so clean in its personal habits as the squirrel, when in health; and Billy soon left the basket which cradled his infancy, and habitually slept under a fold of my bedcover, sometimes making his way to my pillow and sleeping by my cheek; and he never knew what a cage was except when travelling, and even then for the most part he slept in my pocket, in which he went with me to the *table d'hôte*, and when invited out sat on the edge of the table and ate his bit of bread with a decorum that made him the admiration of all the children in the hotel, so that he accompanied me in all my journeys. He acquired a passion for tea, sweet and warm, and to my indulgence of this taste I fear I owe his early loss. He would, when placed on the breakfast table, rush to my cup and plunge his nose in when it was hot enough to scald him. This peculiar taste I could never account for. He had full liberty to roam in my room; but his favourite resort was my work-table when I was at work ; and when his diet became nuts he used to hide them among my books, and then come to hunt them out again, like a child with its toys. I sometimes found my typewriter stopped, and discovered a hazel nut in the works. And when tired of his hide-and-seek he would come to the edge of the table and nod to me, to indicate that he wished to go into my pocket or be put down to run about the room ; and he soon made a gesture-language of movements of his head to tell me his few wants—food, drink, to sleep, or to take a climb on the highest piece of furniture in the room. He was from the beginning devoted to me, and naturally became like a spoiled child. If I gave him an uncracked nut, he rammed it back into my hand to be cracked for him with irresistible persistence. I did as many parents do, and indulged him, to his harm and to my own later grief. I could not resist that coaxing nodding, and gave him what he wished—tea when I had mine, and cracked his nuts, to the injury of his teeth, I was told.[1] In short, I made him as happy as I knew how.

Early in my possession of him I cast about if I might find in the neighbourhood a companion of the other sex for him ; and when finally I heard that in a village just across the Rhine there was a captive squirrel for sale, I sent my son with orders to buy it if a female. It turned out to be a male, but Michael bought it just the same—a bright, active, and quite unwilling prisoner, two months older than Billy, of the orthodox red, just tamed enough to take his food from the hand, but accustomed to be kept with his neck in a collar to which there was attached a fathom of light dog-chain. He refused with his utmost energy to be handled ; and as it was not possible to keep the little creature in the torture of that chain—for I refuse to keep a caged creature—I cut the collar and turned him loose in my chamber, where he kept reluctant company with Billy. The imprisonment of the half-tamed but wholly unreconciled animal was perhaps more painful to me than to him, and my first impulse was to turn him out into his native forest to take his chances of life ; but I considered that he was already too far compromised with Mother Nature for this to be prudent ; for having learned to take his food from a man, the first attack of hunger was sure to drive him to seek it where he had been accustomed to find it, and the probable consequence was being knocked on the head by a village boy, or at best recognised to a worse captivity than mine. He had no mother, and he was still little more than a baby, so I decided to keep him and make him as happy as he would let me. His name was Hans. Had I released him as I thought to do, I had

[1] This idea that a squirrel's teeth grow too long from not gnawing hard food is, I think, a mistake, as Billy's never grew beyond their proper form, nor did Hans's. Billy used to sharpen his teeth by grinding them together. I have often heard the process going on as he lay by my ear on my pillow at night. The cases known of long teeth requiring cutting off were probably due to the breaking of the opposing tooth.

saved myself one sorrow, and this history had lost its interest.

After a little strangeness the companionship between the two became as perfect as the utterly diverse nature of their squirrelships would permit. Billy was social and as friendly as a little dog, Hans always a little morose and not overready to accept familiarities; Billy always making friendly advances to his companion, which were at first unnoticed, and afterwards only submitted to with equanimity. It was as if Billy had assumed the position of the spoiled child of the family, and Hans reluctantly taken that of an elder brother who is always expected to make way for the pet and baby of the house. Billy was full of fun, and delighted to tease Hans when he was sleeping, by nibbling at his toes and ears, biting him playfully anywhere he could get at him; and Hans, after a little indignant bark, used to bolt away and find another place to sleep in. As they both had the freedom of my large bedroom—the door of which was carefully guarded, as Hans was always on the look-out for a chance to bolt out into the unknown—they had plenty of room for climbing, and comparative freedom; and after a little time Hans adopted Billy's habit of passing the night in the fold of my bed-rug, and even of nestling with Billy near my head. Billy was from the beginning a bad sleeper, probably owing to the tea, and in his waking moments his standing amusement was nibbling at Hans, who would finally break out of his sleep and go to the foot of the bed to lie—but never for long, for he always worked his way back to Billy and nestled down again. When I gave Hans a nut, Billy would wait for him to crack it, and deliberately take it out of his jaws and eat it, an aggression to which Hans submitted without a fight, or a snarl even, though at first he held to the nut a little; but the good humour and caressing ways of Billy were as irresistible with Hans as with us, and I never knew him to retaliate in any way.

No two animals of the most domesticated species could have differed in disposition more than these. During the first phase of Hans's life he never lost his repugnance to being handled, while Billy delighted in being fondled. The European squirrel is by nature one of the most timid of animals, even more so than the hare, being equalled in this respect only by the exquisite flying-squirrel of America; and when it is frightened, as, for instance, when held fast in any way, or in a manner that alarms it, it will generally bite even the most familiar hand, the feeling being apparently that it is necessary to gnaw away the ligature which holds it. Of course, considering the irreconcilability of Hans to captivity, I was obliged, much against my will, to get a cage for him to travel in; and I made a little dark chamber in the upper part of a wire bird-cage in which the two squirrels were put for travelling. During the first journeys the motion of the carriage or railway train made Hans quite frantic, while Billy took it with absolute unconcern. On stopping at a hotel, they were invariably released in my room, where they raced about at will, climbing the highest pieces of furniture and the window-curtain, but always coming to sleep in the familiar fur railway-rug which was my bedcover. At this stage of his career Hans was perfectly familiarised—came to me for his food and drink, and climbed on me, getting on my hand when held out to him ; but always resisting being grasped round the body, and always watching diligently for a door left ajar.

Arriving at Rome, I fitted up a deep window recess for their home ; but they always had the run of the study, and Hans, while watching the chance-opened door, and often escaping into the adjoining rooms, made himself apparently happy in his new quarters, climbing the high curtains, racing along the curtain-poles, and at intervals making excursions to the top of the bookcase, though to both the table at which I was at work soon became the favourite resort, and their antics there were as amusing as those of a monkey. Toward the end of the year Billy developed an indolent habit, which I now can trace to the disease that finally took him from us ; but he never lost his love for my writing-table, where he used to lie and watch me at my work by the hour. Hans soon learned to climb down from their window-bench, and up my legs and arms to the writing-table, and down again by the same road when he was tired of his exercises with the pencils or penholders he found there, or of hunting out the nuts which he had hidden the day before among the books and papers ; but I never could induce him to stay in my pocket with Billy, who on cold days preferred sleeping there, as the warmth of my body was more agreeable than that of their fur-lined nest. There was something uncanny in Billy—a preternatural animal intelligence which one sees generally only in animals that have had training and heredity to work on. He used his little gesture-language with great volubility and on every occasion, insisting imperiously on my obeying his summons ; and one of the things which will never fade from my memory was the pretty way in which he used to come to the edge of the window-bench and nod his head to me to show that he wished to be taken ; for he soon learned that it was easier to call to me and be taken than it was to climb down the curtain and run across the room to me. He nodded and wagged his head until I went to him, and his flexible nose wrinkled into the grotesque semblance of a smile—he used all the seductive entreaty an animal could show ; so that we learned to understand each other so well that I rarely mistook his want, were it water or food, or to climb, or to get on my table, or rest in my pocket. Notwithstanding all the forbearance which Hans showed for his mischievous ways, and the real attachment he had for Billy, Billy clearly preferred me to his companion ; and when during the following winter I was attacked by bronchitis, and was kept in my bedroom for several days, my wife, going into the study after a day of my absence, found him in an extraordinary state of excitement, which she said resembled hysterics, and he insisted on being taken. It occurred to her that he wanted me, and she brought him upstairs to my bedroom, when he immediately pointed with his nose to be taken to me ; and as she was curious to see what he would do, and stopped at the threshold, he bit her hand gently to spur her forward to the bed. When put on the bed, he nestled down in the fur of my bedcover perfectly contented. As long as I kept my room he was brought up every day, and passed the day on my bed. At other times the two slept together in an open box lined with fur, or, what they seemed greatly to delight in, a wisp of fragrant new-mown hay, or the bend of the window-curtain, so nestled together that it was hard to distinguish whether they were one or two. The attitudes they took in their sleep were so pretty that my daughter made many attempts to draw them in their sleep, but we found that even then they were in perpetual motion, and never in one pose long enough to get even a satisfactory sketch. Their restlessness in sleep was only interrupted when in my bedcover, and not always then.

Some instincts of the woods they were long losing the use of, as the habit of changing often their sleeping-places. I provided them with several, of which the ultimate favourite was the bag of the window-curtain ; but sometimes, when Billy was missing, he was found in my waste-paper basket, and even in the drawer of my typewriter desk, asleep. In their native forests these squirrels have this habit of changing their nests, and the mother will carry her little ones from one tree to another to hide their resting-place, as if she suspected the mischievous plans of the boys to hunt them ; and probably she does. But the nest I made my squirrels in their travelling carriage— of hard cardboard well lined with fur—suited the hiding and secluding ways of Hans for a long time best of all, and he abandoned it entirely only when he grew so familiar as not to care to hide. They also lost the habit of hiding their surplus food when they found food never wanting.

When the large cones of the stone-pine came into the market late in the autumn, I got some, to give them a taste of fresh nuts ; and the frantic delight with which Hans recognised the relation to his national fir-cones, far away and slight as it was, was touching. He raced around the huge and impenetrable cone, tried it from every side, gnawed at the stem and then at the apex, but in vain. Yet he persisted. The odour of the pine seemed an intoxication to him, and the eager satisfaction with which he split the nuts, once taken out for him—even when Billy was watching him to confiscate them when open—was very interesting ; for he had never seen the fruit of the stone-pine, and knew only the little seeds which the fir of the Northern Forest bears ; and to extricate the pine-nuts from their strong and hard cones was impossible to his tiny teeth, and I had to extract them for him. As for Billy, he was content to sit and look on while Hans gnawed, and to take the kernel from him when he had split the shell; and the charming *bonhomie* with which he appropriated it, and with which Hans submitted to the piracy, was a study.

The friendship between the two was very interesting, for while Billy generally preferred being with me to remaining on his window-bench with Hans, he had intervals when he insisted on being with Hans, while the latter seemed to care for nothing but Billy, and would not willingly remain away from him as long as Billy lived. When the summer came again, being unable to leave them with servants or the housekeeper, I put them in their cage once more, and took them back to Laufenburg for my vacation. Hans still retained his impatience at the confinement even of my large chamber, and with a curious diligence watched the door for a crack to escape by, though in all other respects he seemed happy and at home, and perfectly familiar; and though always in this period of his life shy with strangers, he climbed over me with perfect *nonchalance*. Billy, on the contrary, refused freedom, and when I took him out into his native woods he ran about a little, and came back to find his place in my pocket as naturally as if it had been his birth-nest. But the apparent yearning of Hans for liberty was to me an exquisite pain. He would get up on the window-bench, looking out one way on the rushing Rhine, and the other on the stretching pine forest, and stand with one paw on the sash and the other laid across his breast, and turn his bright black eyes from one to the other view incessantly, and with a look of passionate eagerness which made my heart ache. If I could have found a friendly park where he could have been turned loose in security from hunger, the danger of hunting boys, and the snares which beset a wild life, I would have released him at once. I never so felt the wrong and mutual pain of imprisonment of God's free creatures as then with poor Hans, whose independent spirit had always made him the favourite of the two with my wife; and now that the little drama of their lives is over, and Nature has taken them both to herself again, I can never think of this pretty little creature, with his eager outlook over the Rhineland, without tears. But in the Rhineland, under the pretext that they eat off the top twigs of the pine-trees, and so spoil their growth, they hunt the poor things with a malignancy that makes it a wonder that there is one left to be captured, and Hans's chance of life in those regions was the very least a creature could have. We have seen that the poor little creatures, when famished, will eat the young twigs of trees; but in my opinion the accusation is that of the wolf who wants an excuse to eat the lamb. Hans and Billy were both fond of roses and lettuce; but nothing else in the way of vegetation other than nuts and a very little fruit would they eat.

The evolutionists tell us that we are descended from some common ancestor of the monkey and the man. It may be so; and if, as has been conjectured by one scientist, that ancestor was the lemur, which

is the link between the monkey and the squirrel, I should not object;
but I hope that we branched off at the *Sciurus*, for I would willingly
be the near cousin of my little pets.

But before leaving Rome for my summer vacation at Laufenburg,
the artificial habits of life, and my ignorance of the condition of
squirrel health, had begun to work on Billy their usual consequences.
He had begun to droop, and symptoms of some organic malady
appeared. Though he grew more and more devoted to me, his
ambition to climb and disport himself diminished, and it was clear
that his civilised life had done for him what it does for many of us—
shortened his existence. He never showed signs of pain, but grew
more sluggish, and would come to me and rest, licking my hand like
a little dog, and was as happy as his nature could show. They both
hailed again with greedy enthusiasm the first nuts, fresh and crisp,
and the first peaches, which I went to Bâsle to purchase for them,
and of which they ate small morsels; and what the position permitted me I supplied them with, with a guilty feeling that I could
never atone for what they lost with freedom. I tried to make them
happy in any way in my limited abilities, and, the vacation over,
we went back to Rome and the fresh pine-cones and their window
niche.

But there Billy grew rapidly worse, and I realised that a crisis
had come to our little *ménage*. He grew apathetic, and would lie
with his great black eyes looking into space, as if in a dream. It
became a tragedy for me, for the symptoms were the same as those
of a dear little fellow who had first rejoiced my father's heart in the
years gone by, and who lies in an old English churchyard; whose
last hours I watched lapsing painlessly into the eternity beyond,
and he, thank God! understanding nothing of the great change.
When he could no longer speak, he beckoned me to lay my head on
the same pillow. He died of blood-poisoning, as I found after
Billy's death that he also did; and the identity of the symptoms
(of the cause of which I then understood nothing) brought back the
memory of that last solitary night when my boy passed from under
my care, and his eyes, large and dark like Billy's, grew dim and
vacant like his. Billy, too, clung the closer to me as his end
approached; and when the apathy left him almost no recognition
of things around, he would grasp one of my fingers with his two
paws, and lick it till he tired. It was clear that death was at hand,
and on the last afternoon I took him out into the grounds of the
Villa Borghese to lie in the sunshine, and get perhaps a moment of
return to Mother Nature; but when I put him on the grass in the
warm light he only looked away into vacancy and lay still, and
after a little dreamily indicated to me to take him up again; and I
remembered that on the day before his death I had carried Russie
into the green fields, hoping they would revive him for one breathing-space, for I knew that death was on him; and he lay and looked off

beyond the fields and flowers, and now he almost seemed to be looking out of dear little Billy's eyes. Billy signed to go into my pocket, and lay there, still, even in his apathy grasping my forefinger with his paws, and licking it as if in his approaching dissolution he still wished to show his love for me.

I went out to walk early the next morning, and when I returned I found Billy dead, still warm, and sitting up in his box of fresh hay in the attitude of making his toilet ; for to the last he would wash his face and paws, and comb out his tail, even when his strength no longer sufficed for more than the mere form of it. I am not ashamed to say that I wept like a child.

The dear little creature had been to me not merely a pet to amuse my vacant hours, though many of those most vacant which the tired brain passes in its sleepless nights had been diverted by his pretty ways as he shared my bed, and by his singular devotion to me ; but he had been as a door open into the world of God's lesser creatures, an apostle of pity and tenderness for all living things, and his memory stands on the eternal threshold, nodding and beckoning to me to enter in and make part of the creation I had ignored till he taught it to me, so that while life lasts I can no longer idly inflict pain upon the least of God's creatures. If it be true that " to win the secret of a plain weed's heart " gives the winner a clue to the hidden things of the spiritual life, how much more the conscient and reciprocal love which Billy and I bore—and I could gladly say still bear—each other, must widen the sphere of spiritual sympathy which, widening still, reaches at last the eternal source of all life and love, and finds indeed that one touch of nature makes all things kin. To me this fine contact with a subtle mute nature, and the intense sympathy between us, was the touching of a hitherto hidden vein of life which runs through the universe—it was as if a little fact had revealed to me, as the fall of the apple had to Newton the law of gravity, the great law of love which binds the God of our reverence to the last and lowest of His creatures, and makes Creation but one great fabric of spiritual affinities of which He is the weaver, and over the furthest threads of which come to Him the appeals of all His creatures :

> That thread of the all-sustaining beauty
> Which runs through all, and does all unite,

and through which we are conscious of the Divinity in and around us. Then I felt how it is that no sparrow falls without His knowledge, and how Billy and I were only two links of the same chain in which this eternal love bound us both to union in a common existence, if not a common destiny. There flashed on me, like a vision, the mighty truth, that this Love is the common life of all that lives. Living and dying, Billy has opened to me a window into the universe, of the existence of which I had no suspicion ;

his little history has added a chamber to that eternal mansion into which my constant and humble faith assures me that I shall some time enter: he has helped me to a higher life. If love could confer immortality, he would share eternity with me, and I would thank the Creator for the companionship; and if I have any conception of the conditions of immortality, the love of my squirrel will no more leave me than that of my own children. And who knows? Thousands of human beings to whom we dare not deny the possession of immortal souls have not half Billy's claim to live for ever. May not the Indian philosopher, with his transmigration of souls, have had some glimpses of a truth?

But my history is only half told, for the revelation which Billy brought me was completed by Hans, by the finer touch of their mutual love. When I found the little creature dead, and laid him down in an attitude befitting death, Hans came to him, and making a careful and curious study of him, seemed to realise that something strange had come, and stretched himself out at full length on the body, evidently trying to warm it into life again, or feeling that something was wanting which he might impart, and this failing, began licking the body. When he found that all this was of no avail, and he seemed to realise—what must be strange even to us at our first acquaintance with it—that this was death—the last parting—and that Billy would no more respond to his brotherly love, he went away into the remotest corner of his window niche, refusing to lie any longer in their common bed, or stay where they had been in the habit of staying together. All day he would touch neither food nor drink, and for days following he took no interest in anything, hardly touching his food. Fearing that he would starve himself to death, I took him out on the large open terrace of my house, where, owing to his old persistent desire to escape, I had never dared trust him, and turned him loose among the plants. He wandered a few steps as if bewildered; looked all about him, and then came deliberately to me, climbed my leg, and went voluntarily into the pocket Billy loved to lie in, and in which, even in Billy's company, I had never been able to make Hans stay for more than a minute or so. The whole nature of the creature became changed. He reconciled himself to life, but never again became what he had been before. His gaiety was gone, his wandering ambitions were forgotten, and his favourite place was my pocket—Billy's pocket. From that time he lost all desire to escape; even when I took him out into the fields or woods he had no desire to leave me, but after a little turn and a half-attempt to climb a tree, would come back voluntarily to me, and soon grew as fond of being caressed and stroked as Bill had been. It was as if the love he bore Billy had changed him to Billy's likeness. He never became as demonstrative as Billy was, and to my wife, who was fond of teasing him, he always showed a little pique, and even if buried in his curtain nest or in the fold of my rug, and asleep, he would scold if she approached within several yards of him; but to me he behaved as if he had consciously taken Billy's place. I sent to Turin to get him a companion, and the merchant sent me one guaranteed young and a female; but I found it a male, which died of old age within a few weeks of his arrival. Hans had hardly become familiarised with him when he died. The night before his death I came home late in the evening, and having occasion to go into my study, I was surprised, when I opened the door, to find Hans on the threshold, nodding to me to be taken, with no attempt to escape. I took him up, wondering what had disturbed him at an hour when he was never accustomed to be afoot, put him back in his bed, and went to mine. But thinking over the strange occurrence, I got up, dressed myself, and went down to see if anything was wrong, and found the new squirrel hanging under the curtain in which the two had been sleeping, with his hind claws entangled in the stuff, head down, and evidently very ill. He had probably felt death coming, and tried to get down and find a hiding-place, but got his claws entangled, and could not extricate them. He died the next day, and I took Hans to sleep in his old place in the fold of my bedcover, where, with a few days' interruption, he slept as long as he lived. He insisted, in fact, on being taken when his sleeping-time came; he would come to the edge of his shelf and nod to me till I took him, or if I delayed he would climb down the curtain and come to me. One night I was out late, and on reaching home I went to take him, and not finding him in his place, alarmed the house to look for him. After long search I found him sitting quietly under the chair I always occupied in the study. He got very impatient if I delayed for even a moment putting him to bed, and, like Billy, he used to nip my hand to indicate his discontent, gently at first, but harder and harder till I attended to him. When he saw that we were going upstairs to the bedroom he became quiet.

Whether from artificial conditions of life, or, as I am now convinced by greater experience of his kind, because he suffered from the loss of Billy (after whose death he never recovered his spirits), his hind legs became partially paralysed. He now ran with difficulty; but his eyes were as bright and his intelligence was as quick as ever, and his fore feet were as dexterous. His attachment to me increased as the malady progressed, and though from habit he always scolded a little when my wife approached him, he showed a great deal of affection for her toward the end, which was clearly approaching. Vacation had come again, and I took him once more with me to the Black Forest, hoping that his mysterious intelligence might find some consolation in his native air. He was evidently growing weak, and occasionally showed impatience as if in pain; but for the most of the time he rested quietly in my pocket, and

was most happy when I gave him my hand for a pillow, and at
night he would seek out the hand, and lay his head on it with a
curious persistence which showed a distinct pleasure in the contact,
sometimes, though rarely, licking the fingers, for he was even
then far more reserved in all his expressions of feeling than Billy.
At times he would sit on the window-bench, and scan the landscape with something of the old eagerness that used to give me so
much pain, snuffing the mountain air eagerly for a half-hour, and
then nod to go into my pocket again ; and at other times, as if
restless, would insist, in the way he had made me understand, that,
like a baby, he wanted motion, and when I walked about with him
he grew quiet and content again. At home he had been very fond
of a dish of dried rose-leaves, in which he would wallow and burrow,
and my wife sent him from Rome a little bag of them, which he
enjoyed weakly for a little. But in his last days the time was
spent by day mostly in my pocket, and by night on my bed with
his head on my hand. It was only the morning before his death
that he seemed really to suffer, and then a great restlessness came
on him, and a disposition to bite convulsively whatever was near
him, so that when the spasm was on him I gave him a little chloro-
form to inhale till it had passed, and then he lay quietly in my hand
until another spasm came on, and when he breathed his last in
my pocket I knew that he was dead only by my hand on his heart.
I buried him, as I had wished, in his native forest, in his bed of
rose-leaves, digging a grave for him under a great granite boulder.
He had survived his companion little more than six months, and
if the readers of my little history are disposed to think me weak
when I say that his death was to me a great and lasting grief,
I am not concerned to dispute their judgment. I have known
grief in all its most blinding and varied forms, and I thank God
that He constituted me loving enough to have kept a tender place
in my heart " even for the least of these," the little companions
of two years ; and but for my having perhaps shortened their
innocent lives, I thank Him for having known and loved them as
I have. I cannot to this day decide if I wronged them even
unintentionally in depriving them of their liberty and introducing
them to an artificial life. I possibly shortened their lives, but
probably made them in the main happier than a wild and hunted
life could have made them. Billy lived without care or unsatisfied
desire, and died without pain. He loved me above all things, and
who knows what love might have been to his little heart ? Hans
I rescued from a far more bitter form of imprisonment, and I would
fain believe that the intensity of his life with me and Billy—the
freedom from that fear which haunts the lives of all hunted creatures
—compensated him for what he lost in the wild wood. And I
will hope that this history will awaken in some sympathetic hearts
a tenderness to the wild creatures, which shall, in the great balance

of gain and loss, weigh down the little loss of one poor beastie, sacrificed, not intentionally, to the good of his fellows. And this is, after all, the noblest and even of our human lives—to die that others may live.

# THOMAS A. BURKE
B. 1828

# POLLY PEABLOSSOM'S WEDDING

"My stars! that parson is *powerful* slow a-coming! I reckon he wa'n't so tedious gitting to his own wedding as he is coming here," said one of the bridesmaids of Miss Polly Peablossom, as she bit her lips to make them rosy, and peeped into a small looking-glass for the twentieth time.

"He preaches enough about the shortness of a lifetime," remarked another pouting miss, "and how we ought to improve our opportunities, not to be creeping along like a snail, when a whole wedding-party is waiting for him and the waffles are getting cold, and the chickens burning to a crisp."

"Have patience, girls. Maybe the man's lost his spurs, and can't get along any faster," was the consolatory appeal of an arch-looking damsel, as she finished the last of a bunch of grapes.

"Or perhaps his old fox-eared horse has jumped out of the pasture, and the old gentleman has to take it afoot," surmised the fourth bridesmaid.

The bride used industrious efforts to appear patient and rather indifferent amid the general restiveness of her aids, and would occasionally affect extreme merriment; but her shrewd attendants charged her with being fidgety and rather more uneasy than she wanted folks to believe.

"Helloo, Floyd!" shouted old Captain Peablossom, out of doors, to his copperas-trousered son, who was entertaining the young beaux of the neighbourhood with feats of agility in jumping with weights—"Floyd, throw down them rocks, and put the bridle on old Snip, and ride down the road and see if you can't see Parson Gympsey, and tell him hurry along: we are all waiting for him. He must think weddings are like his meetings, that can be put off to the 'Sunday after the fourth Saturday in next month,' after the crowd's all gathered and ready to hear the preaching. If you don't meet him, go clean to his house. I 'spect he's heard that Bushy Creek Ned's here with his fiddle, and taken a scare."

As the night was wearing on, and no parson had come yet to

unite the destinies of George Washington Hodgkins and "the amiable and accomplished" Miss Polly Peablossom, the former individual intimated to his intended the propriety of passing off the time by having a dance.

Polly asked her ma, and her ma, after arguing that it was not the fashion in her time, in North Car'lina, to dance before the ceremony, at last consented.

The artist from Bushy Creek was called in, and, after much tuning and spitting on the screws, he struck up "Money Musk"; and away went the country-dance, Polly Peablossom at the head, with Thomas Jefferson Hodgkins as her partner, and George Washington Hodgkins next, with Polly's sister Luvisa for his partner. Polly danced to every gentleman, and Thomas Jefferson danced to every lady; then up and down in the middle, and hands all round. Next came George Washington and his partner, who underwent the same process; and "so on through the whole," as *Daboll's Arithmetic* says.

The yard was lit up by three or four large light-wood fires, which gave a picturesque appearance to the groups outside. On one side of the house was Daniel Newman Peablossom and a bevy of youngsters, who either could not or did not desire to get into the dance—probably the former—and who amused themselves by jumping and wrestling. On the other side, a group of matrons sat under the trees, in chairs, and discoursed of the mysteries of making butter, curing chickens of the pip and children of the croup, besides lamenting the misfortunes of some neighbour, or the indiscretion of some neighbour's daughter who had run away and married a circus-rider. A few pensive couples, eschewing the "giddy dance," promenaded the yard and admired the moon, or "wondered if all them little stars were worlds like this." Perhaps they may have sighed sentimentally at the folly of the mosquitoes and bugs which were attracted round the fires to get their pretty little wings scorched and lose their precious lives; or they may have talked of "true love," and plighted their vows, for aught we know.

Old Captain Peablossom and his pipe, during the while, were the centre of a circle in front of the house, who had gathered around the old man's arm-chair to listen to his "twice-told tales" of "hair-breadth 'scapes," of "the battles and sieges he had passed"; for, you must know, the captain was no "summer soldier and sunshine patriot": he had burned gunpowder in defence of his beloved country.

At the especial request of Squire Tompkins, the captain narrated the perilous adventures of Newnan's little band among the Seminoles: how "bold Newnan" and his men lived on alligator-flesh and parched corn and marched barefooted through saw-palmetto; how they met Bowlegs and his warriors near Paine's Prairie, and what fighting was there. The amusing incident of

Bill Cone and the terrapin-shell raised shouts of laughter among the young brood, who had flocked around to hear of the wars. Bill (the "Camden Bard," peace to his ashes!), as the captain familiarly called him, was sitting one day against the logs of the breastwork, drinking soup out of a terrapin-shell, when a random shot from the enemy broke the shell and spilt his soup, whereupon he raised his head over the breastwork and sung out, "Oh you villain! you couldn't do that again if you tried forty times." Then the captain, after repeated importunities, laid down his pipe, cleared his throat, and sung:

> We marchèd on to our next station,
> The Injens on before did hide,
> They shot and killed Bold Newnan's nigger,
> And two other white men by his side.

The remainder of the epic we have forgotten.

After calling out for a chunk of fire and relighting his pipe, he dashed at once over into Alabama, in General Floyd's army, and fought the battles of Calebee and Otassee over again in detail. The artillery from Baldwin County blazed away, and made the little boys aforesaid think they could hear thunder, almost, and the rifles from Putnam made their patriotic young spirits long to revenge that gallant corps. And the squire was astonished at the narrow escape his friend had of falling into the hands of Weatherford and his savages, when he was miraculously rescued by Timpoochie Barnard, the Uchee chief.

At this stage of affairs, Floyd (not the general, but the ambassador) rode up, with a mysterious look on his countenance. The dancers left off in the middle of a set, and assembled around the messenger, to hear the news of the parson. The old ladies crowded up too, and the captain and the squire were eager to hear. But Floyd felt the importance of his situation, and was in no hurry to divest himself of the momentary dignity.

"Well, as I rode on down to Boggy Gut, I saw——"

"Who cares what the devil you saw?" exclaimed the impatient captain. "Tell us if the parson is coming first, and you may take all night to tell the balance, if you like, afterwards."

"I saw——" continued Floyd pertinaciously.

"Well, my dear, what did you see?" asked Mrs. Peablossom.

"I saw that some one had tooken away some of the rails on the cross-way, or they had washed away, or somehow——"

"Did anybody ever hear the like?" said the captain.

"And so I got down," continued Floyd, "and hunted some more, and fixed over the boggy place——"

Here Polly laid her hand on his arm and requested, with a beseeching look, to know if the parson was on the way.

"I'll tell you all about it presently, Polly. And when I got to the run of the creek, then——"

"Oh, the devil!" ejaculated Captain Peablossom. "Stalled again!"

"Be still, honey; let the child tell it in his own way. He always would have his way, you know, since we had to humour him so when he had the measles," interposed the old lady.

Daniel Newnan Peablossom, at this juncture, facetiously lay down on the ground, with the root of an old oak for his pillow, and called out yawningly to his pa to "wake him when brother Floyd had crossed over the run of the creek and arrived safely at the parson's." This caused loud laughter.

Floyd simply noticed it by observing to his brother, "Yes, you think you're mighty smart before all these folks!" and resumed his tedious route to Parson Gympsey's, with as little prospect of reaching the end of his story as ever.

Mrs. Peablossom tried to coax him to "jest" say if the parson was coming or not. Polly begged him, and all the bridesmaids implored. But Floyd "went on his way rejoicing," "When I came to the Piney Flat," he continued, "old Snip seed something white over in the baygall, and shied clean out o' the road, and——" Where he would have stopped would be hard to say, if the impatient captain had not interfered.

That gentleman, with a peculiar glint of the eye, remarked, "Well, there's one way I can bring him to a showing," as he took a large horn from between the logs, and rung a "wood-note wild," that set a pack of hounds to yelping. A few more notes, as loud as those that issued from "Roland's horn at Roncesvalles," was sufficient invitation to every hound, foist, and "cur of low degree," that followed the guests, to join in the chorus. The captain was a man of good lungs, and "the way he *did* blow was the way," as Squire Tompkins afterwards very happily describe it; and, as there were in the canine choir some thirty voices of every key, the music may be imagined better than described. Miss Tabitha Tidwell, the first bridesmaid, put her hands to her ears and cried out, "My stars! we shall all git blowed away!"

The desired effect of abbreviating the messenger's story was produced, as that prolix personage in copperas pants was seen to take Polly aside and whisper something in her ear.

"Oh Floyd, you are joking! you oughtn't to serve me so. An't you joking, bud?" asked Polly, with a look that seemed to beg he would say yes.

"It's true as preaching," he replied: "the cake's all dough!"

Polly whispered something to her mother, who threw up her hands, and exclaimed, "Oh my!" and then whispered the secret to some other lady, and away it went. Such whispering and throwing up of hands and eyes is rarely seen at a Quaker meeting. Consternation was in every face. Poor Polly was a very personification of "Patience on a monument, smiling at green and yellow Melancholy."

The captain, discovering that something was the matter, drove off the dogs, and inquired what had happened to cause such confusion. "What the devil's the matter now?" he said. "You all look as down in the mouth as we did on the Santafee when the quartermaster said the provisions had all give out. What's the matter? Won't somebody tell me? Old 'oman, has the dogs got into the kitchen and eat up all the supper? or what else has come to pass? Out with it!"

"Ah, old man, bad news!" said the wife, with a sigh.

"Well, what is it? You are all getting as bad as Floyd, terrifying a fellow to death."

"Parson Gympsey was digging a new horse-trough, and cut his leg to the bone with a foot-adze and can't come. Oh, dear!"

"I wish he had taken a fancy to 'a' done it a week ago, so we mout 'a' got another parson; or, as long as no other time would suit but to-day, I wish he had cut his derned eternal head off!"

"Oh, my! husband!" exclaimed Mrs. Peablossom. Bushy Creek Ned, standing in the piazza with his fiddle, struck up the old tune of

> We'll dance all night, till broad daylight,
> And go home with the gals in the morning.

Ned's hint caused a movement towards the dancing-room among the young people, when the captain, as if waking from a reverie, exclaimed, in a loud voice, "Oh, the devel! what are we all thinking of? Why, here's Squire Tompkins; he can perform the ceremony. If a man can't marry folks, what's the use of being squire at all?"

Manna did not come in better time to the children of Israel in the wilderness than did this discovery of the worthy captain to the company assembled. It was as vivifying as a shower of rain on corn that is about to shoot and tassel, especially to G. W. Hodgkins and his lady-love.

Squire Tompkins was a newly-elected magistrate, and somewhat diffident of his abilities in this untried department. He expressed a hint of the sort, which the captain only noticed with the exclamation, "Hoot, toot!"

Mrs. Peablossom insinuated to her husband that in her day the "quality," or better sort of people, in North Car'lina, had a prejudice ag'in' being married by a magistrate; to which the old gentleman replied, "None of your nonsense, old lady; none of your Duplin County aristocracy about here now. The better sort of people, I think you say! Now, you know North Car'lina ain't the best State in the Union, no how, and Duplin's the poorest county in the State. Better sort of people, is it? Quality, eh? Who the devil's better than we are? Ain't we honest? Ain't we raised our children decent, and learned them how to read, write, and cipher ? Ain't I fou't under Newnan and Floyd for the country ? Why, darn it ! we are the very best sort of people. Stuff ! nonsense ! The wedding shall go on ; Polly shall have a husband."

Mrs. P.'s eyes lit up, her cheek flushed, as she heard " the old North State " spoken of so disparagingly ; but she was a woman of good sense, and reserved the castigation for a future curtain lecture.

Things were soon arranged for the wedding ; and as the old wooden clock on the mantelpiece struck one, the bridal party were duly arranged on the floor, and the crowd gathered round, eager to observe every twinkle of the bridegroom's eye and every blush of the blooming bride.

The bridesmaids and their male attendants were arranged in couples, as in a cotillon, to form a hollow square, in the centre of which were the squire and betrothing parties. Each of the attendants bore a candle ; Miss Tabitha held hers in a long brass candlestick which had belonged to Polly's grandmother, in shape and length somewhat resembling Cleopatra's Needle ; Miss Luvisa bore a flat tin one ; the third attendant bore such an article as is usually suspended on a nail against the wall ; and the fourth had a curiously-devised something cut out of wood with a pocket-knife. For want of a further supply of candlesticks, the male attendants held naked candles in their hands. Polly was dressed in white, and wore a bay flower with its green leaves in her hair, and the whisper went round, " Now *don't* she look pretty ? " George Washington Hodgkins rejoiced in a white satin stock and a vest and pantaloons of orange colour ; the vest was straight-collared, like a Continental officer's in the Revolution, and had eagle buttons on it. They were a fine-looking couple.

When everything was ready, a pause ensued, and all eyes were turned on the squire, who seemed to be undergoing a mental agony such as Fourth-of-July orators feel when they forget their speeches, or a boy at an exhibition when he has to be prompted from behind the scenes. The truth was, Squire Tompkins was a man of forms, but had always taken them from form-books, and never trusted his memory. On this occasion he had no " Georgia Justice " or any other book from which to read the marriage ceremony, and was at a loss how to proceed. He thought over everything he had ever learned " by heart," even to

> Thirty days hath the month of September ;
> The same may be said of June, April, November.

but all in vain ; he could recollect nothing that suited such an occasion. A suppressed titter all over the room admonished him that he must proceed with something, and, in the agony of desperation, he began :

" Know all men by these presents that I——" Here he paused,

and looked up to the ceiling, while an audible voice in a corner of the room was heard to say, "He's drawing up a deed to a tract of land," and they all laughed.

"In the name of God, Amen!" he began a second time, only to hear another voice, in a loud whisper, say, "He's making his will, now. I thought he couldn't live long, he looks so powerful bad."

"Now I lay me down to sleep,
I pray the Lord——"

was the next essay, when some erudite gentleman remarked, "He is not dead, but sleepeth."

"O yes! O yes!" continued the squire. One voice replied, "Oh, no! oh, no! don't let's"; another whispered, "No bail!" Some person out of doors sang out, "Come into court!" and the laughter was general. The bridesmaids spilt the tallow from their candles all over the floor, in the vain attempt to look serious. One of them had a red mark on her lip for a month afterwards, where she had bit it. The bridegroom put his hands in his pockets, and took them out again; the bride looked as if she would faint; and so did the squire.

But the squire was an indefatigable man, and kept trying. His next effort was:

"To all and singular the sher——" "Let's run! he's going to level on us," said two or three at once.

Here a gleam of light flashed across the face of Squire Tompkins. That dignitary looked around all at once, with as much satisfaction as Archimedes could have felt when he discovered the method of ascertaining the specific gravity of bodies. In a grave and dignified manner, he said, "Mr. Hodgkins, hold up your right hand." George Washington obeyed, and held up his hand. "Miss Polly, hold up yours." Polly in confusion held up her left hand. "The other hand, Miss Peablossom." And the squire proceeded, in a loud and composed manner, to qualify them: "You and each of you do solemnly swear, in the presence of Almighty God and the present company, that you will perform toward each other all and singular the functions of husband and wife, as the case may be, to the best of your knowledge and ability, so help you God!"

"Good as wheat!" said Captain Peablossom. "Polly, my gal, come and kiss your old father: I never felt so happy since the day I was discharged from the army and set out homeward to see your mother."

# "DOING" A SHERIFF

Thomas A. Burke

Many persons in the county of Hall, State of Georgia, recollect a queer old customer who used to visit the county site regularly on " general muster " days and court week. His name was Joseph Johnson, but he was universally known as Uncle Josey. The old man, like many others of that and the present day, loved his dram, and was apt, when he got among " the boys " in town, to take more than he could conveniently carry. His inseparable companion on all occasions was a black pony, who rejoiced in the name of " General Jackson," and whose diminutiveness and sagacity were alike remarkable.

One day, while court was in session in the little village of Gainesville, the attention of the judge and bar was attracted by a rather unusual noise at the door. Looking towards that aperture, " his honour " discovered the aforesaid pony and rider deliberately entering the hall of justice. This, owing to the fact that the floor of the courthouse was nearly on a level with the ground, was not difficult.

" Mr. Sheriff," said the judge, " see who is creating such a disturbance of this court."

" It's only Uncle Josey and Gin'ral Jackson, judge," said the intruder, looking up with a drunken leer—" jest me an' the Gin'ral come to see how you an' the boys is gettin' along."

" Well, Mr. Sheriff," said the judge, totally regardless of the interest manifested in his own and the lawyers' behalf by Uncle Josey, " you will please collect a fine of ten dollars from Uncle Josey and the General, for contempt of court."

" Look a-here, judge, old feller," continued Uncle Josey, as he stroked the " Gin'ral's " mane, " you don't mean to say it, now, do yer ? This child hain't had that much money in a coon's age ; and as for the Gin'ral here, I know he don't deal in no kind of quine, which he hain't done, 'cept fodder and corn, for these many years."

" Very well, then, Mr. Sheriff," continued his honour, " in default of the payment of the fine, you will convey the body of Joseph Johnson to the county gaol, there to be retained for the space of twenty-four hours."

" Now, judge, you ain't in right down good yearnest, is you ? Uncle Josey hain't never been put into that there boardin'-house yet, which he don't want to be, neither," appealed the old man, who was apparently too drunk to know whether it was a joke or not.

"The sheriff will do his duty immediately," was the judge's stern reply, who began to tire of the old man's drunken insolence. Accordingly, Uncle Josey and the "Gin'ral" were marched off towards the county prison, which stood in a retired part of the village. Arriving at the door, the prisoner was commanded by the sheriff to "light."

"Look a-here, Jess, horse-fly, you ain't a-gwine to put yer old uncle Josey in there, is yer?"

"'Bliged to do it, Uncle Josey," replied the sheriff. "Ef I don't, the old man [the judge] will give me *goss* when I go back. I hate it powerful, but I must do it."

"But, Jess, couldn't you manage to let the old man git away? Thar ain't nobody here to see you. Now, do, Jess. You know how I *fit* for you in that last run you had 'longer Jim Smith, what like to 'a' beat you for sheriff, which he would 'a' done it, if it hadn't been for yer uncle Josey's influence."

"I know that, Uncle Josey, but thar ain't no chance. My oath is very p'inted against allowin' anybody to escape. So you must go in, 'cos thar ain't no other chance."

"I tell you what it is, Jess: I'm afeard to go in thar. Looks too dark and dismal."

"Thar ain't nothing in thar to hurt you, Uncle Josey, which thar hain't been for nigh about six months."

"Yes, thar is, Jess. You can't fool me that a-way. I know thar is somethin' in thar to ketch the old man."

"No, thar ain't; I pledge you my honour thar ain't."

"Well, Jess, if thar ain't, you jest go in and see, and show Uncle Josey that you ain't afeard."

"Certainly. I ain't afeard to go in."

Saying which, the sheriff opened the door, leaving the key in the lock. "Now, Uncle Josey, what did I tell you? I knowed thar wa'n't nothin' in thar."

"Maybe thar ain't whar you are standin'; but jest le's see you go up into that dark place in the corner."

"Well, Uncle Josey," said the unsuspecting sheriff, "I'll satisfy you thar ain't nothin' thar either." And he walked towards the "dark corner." As he did so, the old man dexterously closed the door and locked it.

"Hello, thar!" yelled the frightened officer; "none o' yer tricks, Uncle Josey. This is carryin' the joke a cussed sight too far."

"Joke! I ain't a-jokin', Jess: never was more in yearnest in my life. Thar ain't nothin' in thar to hurt you, though; that's one consolation. Jest hold on a little while, and I'll send some of the boys down to let you out."

And, before the "sucked-in" sheriff had recovered from his

astonishment, the pony and his master were out of hearing.

Uncle Josey, who was not as drunk as he appeared, stopped at the grocery, took a drink, again mounted the " Gin'ral," and called the keeper of the grocery to him, at the same time drawing the key of the gaol from his pocket. " Here, Jeems, take this 'ere key, and ef the old man or any them boys up thar at the court-house inquires after Jess Runion, the sheriff, jest you give 'em this key and my compliments and tell 'em Jess is safe. Ketch 'em takin' in old Uncle Josey, will yer ? Git up, Gin'ral : these boys here won't do to trust ; so we'll go into the country, whar people's honest, if they *is* poor."

The sheriff, after an hour's imprisonment, was released, and severely reprimanded by the judge, but the sentence of Uncle Josey was never executed, as he never troubled the court again, and the judge thought it useless to imprison him with any hope of its effecting the slightest reform.

# JONATHAN F. KELLY
circa 1830

# A DESPERATE RACE

SOME years ago, I was one of a convivial party that met in the principal hotel in the town of Columbus, Ohio, the seat of government of the Buckeye State.

It was a winter's evening, when all without was bleak and stormy and all within were blithe and gay—when song and story made the circuit of the festive board, filling up the chasms of life with mirth and laughter.

We had met for the express purpose of making a night of it, and the pious intention was duly and most religiously carried out. The Legislature was in session in that town, and not a few of the worthy legislators were present upon this occasion.

One of these worthies I will name, as he not only took a big swath in the evening's entertainment, but he was a man *more* generally known than our worthy President, James K. Polk. That man was the famous Captain Riley, whose "Narrative" of suffering and adventures is pretty generally known all over the civilised world. Captain Riley was a fine, fat, good-humoured joker, who at the period of my story was the representative of the Dayton district, and lived near that little city when at home. Well, Captain Riley had amused the company with many of his far-famed and singular adventures, which, being mostly told before and read by millions of people that have seen his book, I will not attempt to repeat.

Many were the stories and adventures told by the company, when it came to the turn of a well-known gentleman who represented the Cincinnati district. As Mr. —— is yet among the living, and perhaps not disposed to be the subject of joke or story, I do not feel at liberty to give his name. Mr. —— was a slow believer of other men's adventures, and, at the same time, much disposed to magnify himself into a marvellous hero whenever the opportunity offered. As Captain Riley wound up one of his truthful though really marvellous adventures, Mr. —— coolly remarked that the captain's story was all very *well*, but it did not begin to compare with an adventure that he had, "once upon a time," on the Ohio, below the present city of Cincinnati.

"Let's have it!"—"Let's have it!" resounded from all hands.

"Well, gentlemen," said the Senator, clearing his voice for action and knocking the ashes from his cigar against the arm of his chair,—" gentlemen, I am not in the habit of spinning yarns of marvellous or fictitious matters; and therefore it is scarcely necessary to affirm upon the responsibility of my reputation, gentlemen, that what I am about to tell you I most solemnly proclaim to be truth, and—— "

"Oh, never mind that: go on, Mr. ——," chimed the party.

"Well, gentlemen, in 18— I came down the Ohio River, and settled at Losanti, now called Cincinnati. It was at that time but a little settlement of some twenty or thirty log and frame cabins, and where now stand the Broadway Hotel and blocks of stores and dwelling-houses, was the cottage and corn-patch of old Mr. ——, the tailor, who, by the bye, bought that land for the making of a coat for one of the settlers. Well, I put up my cabin, with the aid of my neighbours, and put in a patch of corn and potatoes, about where the Fly Market now stands, and set about improving my lot, house, etc.

"Occasionally I took up my rifle and started off with my dog down the river, to look up a little deer, or *bar* meat, then very plenty along the river. The blasted red-skins were lurking about and hovering around the settlement, and every once in a while picked off some of our neighbours or stole our cattle or horses. I hated the red demons, and made no bones of peppering the blasted sarpents whenever I got a sight at them. In fact, the red rascals had a dread of me, and had laid a good many traps to get my scalp, but I wasn't to be catched napping. No, no, gentlemen, I was too well up to 'em for that.

"Well, I started off one morning, pretty early, to take a hunt, and travelled a long way down the river, over the bottoms and hills, but couldn't find no *bar* nor deer. About four o'clock in the afternoon I made tracks for the settlement again. By and by I sees a buck just ahead of me, walking leisurely down the river. I slipped up, with my faithful old dog close in my rear, to within clever shooting-distance, and just as the buck stuck his nose in the drink I drew a bead upon his top-knot, and over he tumbled, and splurged and bounded awhile, when I came up and relieved him by cutting his wizen——"

"Well, but what has that to do with an *adventure*?" said Riley.

"Hold on a bit, if you please, gentlemen; by Jove, it had a great deal to do with it. For while I was busy skinning the hind-quarters of the buck, and stowing away the kidney-fat in my hunting-shirt, I heard a noise like the breaking of brush under a moccasin up 'the bottom.' My dog heard it, and started up to reconnoitre, and I lost no time in reloading my rifle. I had hardly got my priming out before my dog raised a howl and broke through the brush towards me with his tail down, as he was not used to doing unless there were wolves, painters [panthers], or Injins about.

"I picked up my knife, and took up my line of march in a skulking trot up the river. The frequent gullies on the lower bank made it tedious travelling there, so I scrabbled up to the upper bank, which was pretty well covered with buckeye and sycamore, and very little underbrush. One peep below discovered to me three as big and strapping red rascals, gentlemen, as you ever clapped your eyes on! Yes, there they came, not above six hundred yards in my rear, shouting and yelling like hounds, and coming after me like all possessed."

"Well," said an old woodsman, sitting at the table, "you took a tree, of course."

"Did I? No, gentlemen, I took no tree just then, but I took to my heels like sixty, and it was just as much as my old dog could do to keep up with me. I ran until the whoops of my red-skins grew fainter and fainter behind me, and, clean out of wind, I ventured to look behind me, and there came one single red whelp, puffing and blowing, not three hundred yards in my rear. He had got on to a piece of bottom where the trees were small and scarce. 'Now,' thinks I, 'old fellow, I'll have you.' So I trotted off at a pace sufficient to let my follower gain on me, and when he had got just about near enough I wheeled and fired, and down I brought him, dead as a door-nail, at a hundred and twenty yards!"

"Then you skelp'd [scalped] him immediately?" said the back-woodsman.

"Very clear of it, gentlemen; for by the time I got my rifle loaded, here came the other two red-skins, shouting and whooping close on me, and away I broke again like a quarter-horse. I was now about five miles from the settlement, and it was getting towards sunset. I ran till my wind began to be pretty short, when I took a look back, and there they came, snorting like mad buffaloes, one about two or three hundred yards ahead of the other: so I acted possum again until the foremost Injin got pretty well up, and I wheeled and fired at the very moment he was 'drawing a bead' on me: he fell head over stomach into the dirt, and up came the last one!"

"So you laid for him, and——" gasped several.

"No," continued the "member," "I didn't lay for him, I hadn't time to load, so I laid my *legs* to ground and started again. I heard every bound he made after me. I ran and ran until the fire flew out of my eyes, and the old dog's tongue hung out of his mouth a quarter of a yard long!"

"Phe-e-e-e-w!" whistled somebody.

"Fact, gentlemen. Well, what I was to do I didn't know: rifle empty, no big trees about, and a murdering red Indian not three hundred yards in my rear; and what was worse, just then it occurred to me that I was not a great ways from a big creek (now called Mill Creek), and there I should be pinned at last.

"Just at this juncture, I struck my toe against a root, and down I tumbled, and my old dog over me. Before I could scrabble up——"

"The Indian fired!" gasped the old woodsman.

"He did, gentlemen, and I felt the ball strike me under the shoulder; but that didn't seem to put any embargo upon my locomotion, for as soon as I got up I took off again, quite freshened by my fall! I heard the red-skin close behind me coming booming on, and every minute I expected to have his tomahawk dashed into my head or shoulders.

"Something kind of cool began to trickle down my legs into my boots——"

"Blood, eh? for the shot the varmint gin you," said the old woodsman, in a great state of excitement.

"I thought so," said the Senator; "but what do you think it was?"

Not being blood, we were all puzzled to know what the blazes it could be; when Riley observed—

"I suppose you had——"

"Melted the deer-fat which I had stuck in the breast of my hunting-shirt, and the grease was running down my legs until my feet got so greasy that my heavy boots flew off, and one, hitting the dog, nearly knocked his brains out."

We all grinned, which the "member" noticing, observed—

"I hope, gentlemen, no man here will presume to think I'm exaggerating?"

"Oh, certainly not! Go on, Mr. ——," we all chimed in.

"Well, the ground under my feet was soft, and, being relieved of my heavy boots, I put off with double-quick time, and, seeing the creek about half a mile off, I ventured to look over my shoulder to see what kind of chance there was to hold up and load. The red-skin was coming jogging along, pretty well blowed out, about five hundred yards in the rear. Thinks I 'Here goes to load, anyhow.' So at it I went: in went the powder, and, putting on my patch, down went the ball about half-way, and off snapped my ramrod!"

"Thunder and lightning!" shouted the old woodsman, who was worked up to the top-notch in the "member's" story.

"Good gracious! wasn't I in a pickle! There was the red whelp within two hundred yards of me, pacing along and *loading up his rifle as he came*! I jerked out the broken ramrod, dashed it away, and started on, priming up as I cantered off, determined to turn and give the red-skin a blast, anyhow, as soon as I reached the creek.

"I was now within a hundred yards of the creek, could see the smoke from the settlement chimneys. A few more jumps, and I was by the creek. The Indian was close upon me: he gave a whoop, and I raised my rifle: on he came, knowing that I had broken my ramrod and my load not down: another whoop! whoop! and he was within fifty yards of me. I pulled trigger, and——"

" And killed *him* ? " chuckled Riley.

" No, *sir* ! I missed fire ! "

" And the red-skin——" shouted the old woodsman, in a frenzy of excitement.

" *Fired and killed me !* "

The screams and shouts that followed this finale brought landlord Noble, servants, and hostlers running upstairs to see if the house was on fire!

## FITZ-JAMES O'BRIEN
### 1828–1862

# THE DIAMOND LENS

### I

FROM a very early period of my life the entire bent of my inclinations had been toward microscopic investigations. When I was not more than ten years old, a distant relative of our family, hoping to astonish my inexperience, constructed a simple microscope for me by drilling in a disk of copper a small hole in which a drop of pure water was sustained by capillary attraction. This very primitive apparatus, magnifying some fifty diameters, presented, it is true, only indistinct and imperfect forms, but still sufficiently wonderful to work up my imagination to a preternatural state of excitement.

Seeing me so interested in this rude instrument, my cousin explained to me all that he knew about the principles of the microscope, related to me a few of the wonders which had been accomplished through its agency, and ended by promising to send me one regularly constructed, immediately on his return to the city. I counted the days, the hours, the minutes that intervened between that promise and his departure.

Meantime I was not idle. Every transparent substance that bore the remotest resemblance to a lens I eagerly seized upon, and employed in vain attempts to realise that instrument the theory of whose construction I as yet only vaguely comprehended. All panes of glass containing those oblate spheroidal knots familiarly known as " bull's-eyes " were ruthlessly destroyed in the hope of obtaining lenses of marvellous power. I even went so far as to extract the crystalline humour from the eyes of fishes and animals, and endeavoured to press it into the microscopic service. I plead guilty to having stolen the glasses from my Aunt Agatha's spectacles, with a dim idea of grinding them into lenses of wondrous magnifying properties—in which attempt it is scarcely necessary to say that I totally failed.

At last the promised instrument came. It was of that order known as Field's simple microscope, and had cost perhaps about fifteen dollars. As far as educational purposes went, a better apparatus could not have been selected. Accompanying it was a small treatise on the microscope—its history, uses, and discoveries. I comprehended then for the first time the *Arabian Nights' Entertainments*. The dull veil of ordinary existence that hung across the world seemed suddenly to roll away, and to lay bare a land of enchantments. I felt toward my companions as the seer might feel toward the ordinary masses of men. I held conversations with Nature in a tongue which they could not understand. I was in daily communication with living wonders such as they never imagined in their wildest visions. I penetrated beyond the external portal of things and roamed through the sanctuaries. Where they beheld only a drop of rain slowly rolling down the window-glass, I saw a universe of beings animated with all the passions common to physical life, and convulsing their minute sphere with struggles as fierce and protracted as those of men. In the common spots of mould, which my mother, good housekeeper that she was, fiercely scooped away from her jam-pots, there abode for me, under the name of mildew, enchanted gardens, filled with dells and avenues of the densest foliage and most astonishing verdure, while from the fantastic boughs of these microscopic forests hung strange fruits glittering with green and silver and gold.

It was no scientific thirst that at this time filled my mind. It was the pure enjoyment of a poet to whom a world of wonders has been disclosed. I talked of my solitary pleasures to none. Alone with my microscope, I dimmed my sight, day after day and night after night, poring over the marvels which it unfolded to me. I was like one who, having discovered the ancient Eden still existing in all its primitive glory, should resolve to enjoy it in solitude, and never betray to mortal the secret of its locality. The rod of my life was bent at this moment. I destined myself to be a microscopist.

Of course, like every novice, I fancied myself a discoverer. I was ignorant at the time of the thousands of acute intellects engaged in the same pursuit as myself, and with the advantage of instruments a thousand times more powerful than mine. The names of Leeuwenhoek, Williamson, Spencer, Ehrenberg, Schultz, Dujardin, Schact, and Schleiden were then entirely unknown to me, or, if known, I was ignorant of their patient and wonderful researches. In every fresh specimen of cryptogamia which I placed beneath my instrument I believed that I discovered wonders of which the world was as yet ignorant. I remember well the thrill of delight and admiration that shot through me the first time that I discovered the common wheel animalcule (*Rotifera vulgaris*) expanding and contracting its flexible spokes and seemingly rotating through the water. Alas, as I grew older, and obtained some works treating of my favourite study, I found that I was only on the threshold of a science to the investigation of which some of the greatest men of the age were devoting their lives and intellects!

As I grew up, my parents, who saw but little likelihood of anything practical resulting from the examination of bits of moss and drops of water through a brass tube and a piece of glass, were anxious that I should choose a profession. It was their desire that I should enter the counting-house of my uncle, Ethan Blake, a prosperous merchant, who carried on business in New York. This suggestion I decisively combated. I had no taste for trade ; I should only make a failure ; in short, I refused to become a merchant.

But it was necessary for me to select some pursuit. My parents were staid New England people, who insisted on the necessity of labour, and therefore, although, thanks to the bequest of my poor Aunt Agatha, I should, on coming of age, inherit a small fortune sufficient to place me above want, it was decided that, instead of waiting for this, I should act the nobler part, and employ the intervening years in rendering myself independent.

After much cogitation I complied with the wishes of my family, and selected a profession. I determined to study medicine at the New York Academy. This disposition of my future suited me. A removal from my relatives would enable me to dispose of my time as I pleased without fear of detection. As long as I paid my Academy fees I might shirk attending the lectures if I chose ; and as I never had the remotest intention of standing an examination, there was no danger of my being " plucked." Besides, a metropolis was the place for me. There I could obtain excellent instruments, the newest publications, intimacy with men of pursuits kindred with my own —in short, all things necessary to ensure a profitable devotion of my life to my beloved science. I had an abundance of money, few desires that were not bounded by my illuminating mirror on one side and my object-glass on the other ; what, therefore, was to prevent my becoming an illustrious investigator of the veiled worlds ? It was with the most buoyant hope that I left my New England home and established myself in New York.

II

My first step, of course, was to find suitable apartments. These I obtained, after a couple of days' search, in Fourth Avenue ; a very pretty second floor, unfurnished, containing sitting-room, bedroom, and a smaller apartment which I intended to fit up as a laboratory. I furnished my lodgings simply, but rather elegantly, and then devoted all my energies to the adornment of the temple of my worship. I visited Pike, the celebrated optician, and passed in review his splendid collection of microscopes—Field's Compound, Hingham's, Spencer's, Nachet's Binocular (that founded on the principles of the stereoscope), and at length fixed upon that form known as Spencer's Trunnion Microscope, as combining the greatest number of improvements with an almost perfect freedom from tremor. Along with this I purchased every possible accessory—draw-tubes, micrometers, a *camera lucida*, lever-stage, achromatic condensers, white cloud illuminators, prisms, parabolic condensers, polarising apparatus, forceps, aquatic boxes, fishing-tubes, with a host of other articles, all of which would have been useful in the hands of an experienced microscopist, but, as I afterward discovered, were not of the slightest present value to me. It takes years of practice to know how to use a complicated microscope. The optician looked suspiciously at me as I made these valuable purchases. He evidently was uncertain whether to set me down as some scientific celebrity or a madman. I think he was inclined to the latter belief. I suppose I was mad. Every great genius is mad upon the subject in which he is greatest. The unsuccessful madman is disgraced and called a lunatic.

Mad or not, I set myself to work with a zeal which few scientific students have ever equalled. I had everything to learn relative to the delicate study upon which I had embarked—a study involving he most earnest patience, the most rigid analytic powers, the steadiest hand, the most untiring eye, the most refined and subtle manipulation.

For a long time half my apparatus lay inactively on the shelves of my laboratory, which was now most amply furnished with every possible contrivance for facilitating my investigations. The fact was that I did not know how to use some of my scientific implements—never having been taught microscopics—and those whose use I understood theoretically were of little avail until by practice I could attain the necessary delicacy of handling. Still, such was the fury of my ambition, such the untiring perseverance of my experiments, that, difficult of credit as it may be, in the course of one year I became theoretically and practically an accomplished microscopist.

During this period of my labours, in which I submitted specimens of every substance that came under my observation to the action of my lenses, I became a discoverer—in a small way, it is true, for I was very young, but still a discoverer. It was I who destroyed Ehrenberg's theory that the *Volvox globator* was an animal, and proved that his " monads " with stomachs and eyes were merely phases of the formation of a vegetable cell, and were, when they reached their mature state, incapable of the act of conjugation, or any true generative act, without which no organism rising to any stage of life higher than vegetable can be said to be complete. It was I who resolved the singular problem of rotation in the cells and hairs of plants into ciliary attraction, in spite of the assertions of Wenham and others that my explanation was the result of an optical illusion.

But notwithstanding these discoveries, laboriously and painfully made as they were, I felt horribly dissatisfied. At every step I found myself stopped by the imperfections of my instruments. Like all active microscopists, I gave my imagination full play. Indeed, it is a common complaint against many such that they supply the defects of their instruments with the creations of their brains. I imagined depths beyond depths in nature which the limited power of my lenses prohibited me from exploring. I lay awake at night constructing imaginary microscopes of immeasurable power, with which I seemed to pierce through all the envelopes of matter down to its original atom. How I cursed those imperfect mediums which necessity through ignorance compelled me to use! How I longed to discover the secret of some perfect lens, whose magnifying power should be limited only by the resolvability of the object, and which at the same time should be free from spherical and chromatic aberrations—in short, from all the obstacles over which the poor microscopist finds himself continually stumbling! I felt convinced that the simple microscope, composed of a single lens of such vast yet perfect power, was possible of construction. To attempt to bring the compound miscroscope up to such a pitch would have been commencing at the wrong end; this latter being simply a partially successful endeavour to remedy those very defects of the simplest instrument which, if conquered, would leave nothing to be desired.

It was in this mood of mind that I became a constructive microscopist. After another year passed in this new pursuit, experimenting on every imaginable substance—glass, gems, flints, crystals, artificial crystals formed of the alloy of various vitreous materials—in short, having constructed as many varieties of lenses as Argus had eyes—I found myself precisely where I started, with nothing gained save an extensive knowledge of glass-making. I was almost dead with despair. My parents were surprised at my apparent want of progress in my medical studies (I had not attended one lecture since my arrival in the city), and the expenses of my mad pursuit had been so great as to embarrass me very seriously.

I was in this frame of mind one day, experimenting in my laboratory on a small diamond—that stone, from its great refracting power, having always occupied my attention more than any other —when a young Frenchman who lived on the floor above me, and who was in the habit of occasionally visiting me, entered the room.

I think that Jules Simon was a Jew. He had many traits of the Hebrew character: a love of jewellery, of dress, and of good living. There was something mysterious about him. He always had something to sell, and yet went into excellent society. When I say sell, I should perhaps have said peddle; for his operations were generally confined to the disposal of single articles—a picture, for instance, or a rare carving in ivory, or a pair of duelling-pistols, or the dress of a Mexican *caballero*. When I was first furnishing my rooms, he paid me a visit, which ended in my purchasing an antique silver lamp, which he assured me was a Cellini—it was handsome enough even for that—and some other knick-knacks for my sitting-room. Why Simon should pursue this petty trade I never could imagine. He apparently had plenty of money, and had the *entrée* of the best houses in the city —taking care, however, I suppose, to drive no bargains within the enchanted circle of the Upper Ten. I came at length to the conclusion that this peddling was but a mask to cover some greater object, and even went so far as to believe my young acquaintance to be implicated in the slave-trade. That, however, was none of my affair.

On the present occasion, Simon entered my room in a state of considerable excitement.

"*Ah! mon ami!*" he cried, before I could even offer him the ordinary salutation, " it has occurred to me to be the witness of the most astonishing things in the world. I promenade myself to the house of Madame—— How does the little animal—*le renard*—name himself in the Latin ? "

"Vulpes," I answered.

" Ah ! yes—Vulpes. I promenade myself to the house of Madame Vulpes."

" The spirit medium ? "

" Yes, the great medium. Great heavens ! what a woman ! I write on a slip of paper many of questions concerning affairs of the most secret—affairs that conceal themselves in the abysses of my heart the most profound ; and behold, by example, what occurs ? This devil of a woman makes me replies the most truthful to all of them. She talks to me of things that I do not love to talk of to myself. What am I to think ? I am fixed to the earth ! "

" Am I to understand you, M. Simon, that this Mrs. Vulpes replied to questions secretly written by you, which questions related to events known only to yourself ? "

" Ah ! more than that, more than that," he answered, with an air of some alarm. " She related to me things—— But," he added after a pause, and suddenly changing his manner, " why occupy ourselves with these follies ? It was all the biology, without doubt. It goes without saying that it has not my credence. But why are we here, *mon ami* ? It has occurred to me to discover the most beautiful thing as you can imagine—a vase with green lizards on it, composed by the great Bernard Palissy. It is in my apartment ; let us mount. I go to show it to you."

I followed Simon mechanically ; but my thoughts were far from Palissy and his enamelled ware, although I, like him, was seeking in the dark a great discovery. This casual mention of the spiritualist, Madame Vulpes, set me on a new track. What if, through communication with more subtle organisms than my own, I could reach at a single bound the goal which perhaps a life of agonizing mental toil would never enable me to attain ?

While purchasing the Palissy vase from my friend Simon, I was mentally arranging a visit to Madame Vulpes.

III

Two evenings after this, thanks to an arrangement by letter and the promise of an ample fee, I found Madame Vulpes awaiting me at her residence alone. She was a coarse-featured woman, with keen and rather cruel dark eyes, and an exceedingly sensual expression about her mouth and under jaw. She received me in perfect silence, in an apartment on the ground floor, very sparely furnished. In the centre of the room, close to where Mrs. Vulpes sat, there was a common round mahogany table. If I had come for the purpose of sweeping her chimney, the woman could not have looked more indifferent to my appearance. There was no attempt to inspire the visitor with awe. Everything bore a simple and practical aspect. This intercourse with the spiritual world was evidently as familiar an occupation with Mrs. Vulpes as eating her dinner or riding in an omnibus.

" You come for a communication, Mr. Linley ? " said the medium, in a dry, businesslike tone of voice.

" By appointment—yes."

" What sort of communication do you want—a written one ? "

" Yes, I wish for a written one."

" From any particular spirit ? "

" Yes."

" Have you ever known this spirit on this earth ? "

" Never. He died long before I was born. I wish merely to obtain from him some information which he ought to be able to give better than any other."

" Will you seat yourself at the table, Mr. Linley," said the medium, " and place your hands upon it ? "

I obeyed, Mrs. Vulpes being seated opposite to me, with her hands also on the table. We remained thus for about a minute and a half, when a violent succession of raps came on the table, on the back of my chair, on the floor immediately under my feet, and even on the window-panes. Mrs. Vulpes smiled composedly.

" They are very strong to-night," she remarked. " You are fortunate." She then continued, " Will the spirits communicate with this gentleman ? "

Vigorous affirmative.

" Will the particular spirit he desires to speak with communicate ? "

A very confused rapping followed this question.

" I know what they mean," said Mrs. Vulpes, addressing herself to me ; " they wish you to write down the name of the particular spirit that you desire to converse with. Is that so ? " she added, speaking to her invisible guests.

That it was so was evident from the numerous affirmatory responses. While this was going on, I tore a slip from my pocket-book and scribbled a name under the table.

" Will this spirit communicate in writing with this gentleman ? " asked the medium once more.

After a moment's pause her hand seemed to be seized with a

violent tremor, shaking so forcibly that the table vibrated. She said that a spirit had seized her hand and would write. I handed her some sheets of paper that were on the table and a pencil. The latter she held loosely in her hand, which presently began to move over the paper with a singular and seemingly involuntary motion. After a few moments had elapsed she handed me the paper, on which I found written, in a large, uncultivated hand, the words, "He is not here, but has been sent for." A pause of a minute or so ensued, during which Mrs. Vulpes remained perfectly silent, but the raps continued at regular intervals. When the short period I mention had elapsed, the hand of the medium was again seized with its convulsive tremor, and she wrote, under this strange influence, a few words on the paper, which she handed to me. They were as follows:

"I am here. Question me.

"LEEUWENHOEK."

I was astounded. The name was identical with that I had written beneath the table, and carefully kept concealed. Neither was it at all probable that an uncultivated woman like Mrs. Vulpes should know even the name of the great father of microscopics. It may have been biology; but this theory was soon doomed to be destroyed. I wrote on my slip—still concealing it from Mrs. Vulpes—a series of questions which, to avoid tediousness, I shall place with the responses, in the order in which they occurred:

*I.*—Can the microscope be brought to perfection?
*Spirit.*—Yes.
*I.*—Am I destined to accomplish this great task?
*Spirit.*—You are.
*I.*—I wish to know how to proceed to attain this end. For the love which you bear to science, help me!
*Spirit.*—A diamond of one hundred and forty carats, submitted to electro-magnetic currents for a long period, will experience a rearrangement of its atoms *inter se*, and from that stone you will form the universal lens.
*I.*—Will great discoveries result from the use of such a lens?
*Spirit.*—So great that all that has gone before is as nothing.
*I.*—But the refractive power of the diamond is so immense that the image will be formed within the lens. How is that difficulty to be surmounted?
*Spirit.*—Pierce the lens through its axis, and the difficulty is obviated. The image will be formed in the pierced space, which will itself serve as a tube to look through. Now I am called. Good-night.

I cannot at all describe the effect that these extraordinary communications had upon me. I felt completely bewildered. No biological theory could account for the *discovery* of the lens. The medium might, by means of biological *rapport* with my mind, have gone so far as to read my questions and reply to them coherently. But biology could not enable her to discover that magnetic currents would so alter the crystals of the diamond as to remedy its previous defects and admit of its being polished into a perfect lens. Some such theory may have passed through my head, it is true; but if so, I had forgotten it. In my excited condition of mind there was no course left but to become a convert, and it was in a state of the most painful nervous exaltation that I left the medium's house that evening. She accompanied me to the door, hoping that I was satisfied. The raps followed us as we went through the hall, sounding on the balusters, the flooring, and even the lintels of the door. I hastily expressed my satisfaction, and escaped hurriedly into the cool night air. I walked home with but one thought possessing me—how to obtain a diamond of the immense size required. My entire means multiplied a hundred times over would have been inadequate to its purchase. Besides, such stones are rare, and become historical. I could find such only in the regalia of Eastern or European monarchs.

## IV

There was a light in Simon's room as I entered my house. A vague impulse urged me to visit him. As I opened the door of his sitting-room unannounced, he was bending, with his back toward me, over a Carcel lamp, apparently engaged in minutely examining some object which he held in his hands. As I entered he started suddenly, thrust his hand into his breast pocket, and turned to me with a face crimson with confusion.

"What!" I cried, "pouring over the miniature of some fair lady? Well, don't blush so much; I won't ask to see it."

Simon laughed awkwardly enough, but made none of the negative protestations usual on such occasions. He asked me to take a seat.

"Simon," said I, "I have just come from Madame Vulpes."

This time Simon turned as white as a sheet, and seemed stupefied, as if a sudden electric shock had smitten him. He babbled some incoherent words, and went hastily to a small closet where he usually kept his liquors. Although astonished at his emotion, I was too preoccupied with my own idea to pay much attention to anything else.

"You say truly when you call Madame Vulpes a devil of a woman," I continued. "Simon, she told me wonderful things to-night, or rather was the means of telling me wonderful things. Ah! if I could only get a diamond that weighed one hundred and forty carats!"

Scarcely had the sigh with which I uttered this desire died upon my lips when Simon, with the aspect of a wild beast, glared at me savagely, and, rushing to the mantelpiece, where some foreign weapons hung on the wall, caught up a Malay creese, and brandished it furiously before him.

"No!" he cried in French, into which he always broke when excited. "No! you shall not have it! You are perfidious! You have consulted with that demon, and desire my treasure! But I will die first! Me, I am brave! You cannot make me fear!"

All this, uttered in a loud voice, trembling with excitement, astounded me. I saw at a glance that I had accidentally trodden upon the edges of Simon's secret, whatever it was. It was necessary to reassure him.

"My dear Simon," I said, "I am entirely at a loss to know what you mean. I went to Madame Vulpes to consult with her on a scientific problem, to the solution of which I discovered that a diamond of the size I just mentioned was necessary. You were never alluded to during the evening, nor, so far as I was concerned, even thought of. What can be the meaning of this outburst? If you happen to have a set of valuable diamonds in your possession, you need fear nothing from me. The diamond which I require you could not possess; or, if you did possess it, you would not be living here."

Something in my tone must have completely reassured him, for his expression immediately changed to a sort of constrained merriment, combined, however, with a certain suspicious attention to my movements. He laughed, and said that I must bear with him; that he was at certain moments subject to a species of vertigo, which betrayed itself in incoherent speeches, and that the attacks passed off as rapidly as they came. He put his weapon aside while making this explanation, and endeavoured, with some success, to assume a more cheerful air.

All this did not impose on me in the least. I was too much accustomed to analytical labours to be baffled by so flimsy a veil. I determined to probe the mystery to the bottom.

"Simon," I said gaily, "let us forget all this over a bottle of Burgundy. I have a case of Lausseure's *Clos Vougeot* downstairs, fragrant with the odours and ruddy with the sunlight of the Côte d'Or. Let us have up a couple of bottles. What say you?"

"With all my heart," answered Simon smilingly.

I produced the wine, and we seated ourselves to drink. It was of a famous vintage, that of 1848, a year when war and wine throve together, and its pure but powerful juice seemed to impart renewed vitality to the system. By the time we had half finished the second bottle, Simon's head, which I knew was a weak one, had begun to yield, while I remained calm as ever, only that every draught seemed to send a flush of vigour through my limbs. Simon's utterance became more and more indistinct. He took to singing French *chansons* of a not very moral tendency. I rose suddenly from the table just at the conclusion of one of those incoherent verses, and, fixing my eyes on him with a quiet smile, said, "Simon, I have deceived you. I learned your secret this evening. You may as well be frank with me. Mrs. Vulpes—or rather, one of her spirits—told me all."

He started with horror. His intoxication seemed for the moment to fade away, and he made a movement toward the weapon that he had a short time before laid down. I stopped him with my hand.

"Monster!" he cried passionately, "I am ruined! What shall I do? You shall never have it! I swear by my mother!"

"I don't want it," I said; "rest secure, but be frank with me. Tell me all about it."

The drunkenness began to return. He protested with maudlin earnestness that I was entirely mistaken—that I was intoxicated; then asked me to swear eternal secrecy, and promised to disclose the mystery to me. I pledged myself, of course, to all. With an uneasy look in his eyes, and hands unsteady with drink and nervousness, he drew a small case from his breast and opened it. Heavens! How the mild lamplight was shivered into a thousand prismatic arrows as it fell upon a vast rose-diamond that glittered in the case! I was no judge of diamonds, but I saw at a glance that this was a gem of rare size and purity. I looked at Simon with wonder and—must I confess it?—with envy. How could he have obtained this treasure? In reply to my questions, I could just gather from his drunken statements (of which, I fancy, half the incoherence was affected) that he had been superintending a gang of slaves engaged in diamond-washing in Brazil; that he had seen one of them secrete a diamond, but, instead of informing his employers, had quietly watched the negro until he saw him bury his treasure; that he had dug it up and fled with it, but that as yet he was afraid to attempt to dispose of it publicly—so valuable a gem being almost certain to attract too much attention to its owner's antecedents—and he had not been able to discover any of those obscure channels by which such matters are conveyed away safely. He added that, in accordance with oriental practice, he had named his diamond with the fanciful title of "The Eye of Morning."

While Simon was relating this to me, I regarded the great diamond attentively. Never had I beheld anything so beautiful. All the glories of light ever imagined or described seemed to pulsate in its crystalline chambers. Its weight, as I learned from Simon, was exactly one hundred and forty carats. Here was an amazing coincidence. The hand of destiny seemed in it. On the very evening when the spirit of Leeuwenhoek communicates to me the great secret of the microscope, the priceless means which he directs me to employ start up within my easy reach! I determined, with the most perfect deliberation, to possess myself of Simon's diamond.

I sat opposite to him while he nodded over his glass and calmly revolved the whole affair. I did not for an instant contemplate so foolish an act as a common theft, which would of course be discovered, or at least necessitate flight and concealment, all of which must interfere with my scientific plans. There was but one step to be taken—to kill Simon. After all, what was the life of a little peddling Jew in comparison with the interests of science? Human beings are taken every day from the condemned prisons to be experimented on by surgeons. This man, Simon, was by his own confession a criminal, a robber, and I believed on my soul a murderer. He deserved death quite as much as any felon condemned by the laws: why should I not, like government, contrive that his punishment should contribute to the progress of human knowledge?

The means for accomplishing everything I desired lay within my reach. There stood upon the mantelpiece a bottle half full of French laudanum. Simon was so occupied with his diamond, which I had just restored to him, that it was an affair of no difficulty to drug his glass. In a quarter of an hour he was in a profound sleep.

I now opened his waistcoat, took the diamond from the inner pocket in which he had placed it, and removed him to the bed, on which I laid him so that his feet hung down over the edge. I had possessed myself of the Malay creese, which I held in my right hand, while with the other I discovered as accurately as I could by pulsation the exact locality of the heart. It was essential that all the aspects of his death should lead to the surmise of self-murder. I calculated the exact angle at which it was probable that the weapon, if levelled by Simon's own hand, would enter his breast; then with one powerful blow I thrust it up to the hilt in the very spot which I desired to penetrate. A convulsive thrill ran through Simon's limbs. I heard a smothered sound issue from his throat, precisely like the bursting of a large air-bubble sent up by a diver when it reaches the surface of the water; he turned half round on his side, and, as if to assist my plans more effectually, his right hand, moved by some mere spasmodic impulse, clasped the handle of the creese, which it remained holding with extraordinary muscular tenacity. Beyond this there was no apparent struggle. The laudanum, I presume, paralyzed the usual nervous action. He must have died instantly.

There was yet something to be done. To make it certain that all suspicion of the act should be diverted from any inhabitant of the house to Simon himself, it was necessary that the door should be found in the morning *locked on the inside*. How to do this, and afterward escape myself? Not by the window; that was a physical impossibility. Besides, I was determined that the windows *also* should be found bolted. The solution was simple enough. I descended softly to my own room for a peculiar instrument which I had used for holding small slippery substances, such as minute spheres of glass, etc. This instrument was nothing more than a long, slender hand-vice, with a very powerful grip and a considerable leverage, which last was accidentally owing to the shape of the handle. Nothing was simpler than, when the key was in the lock to seize the end of its stem in this vice, through the keyhole, from the outside, and so lock the door. Previously, however, to doing this, I burned a number of papers on Simon's hearth. Suicides almost always burn papers before they destroy themselves. I also emptied some more laudanum into Simon's glass—having first removed from it all traces of wine—cleaned the other wine-glass, and brought the bottles away with me. If traces of two persons drinking had been found in the room, the question naturally would have arisen, Who was the second? Besides, the wine-bottles might have been identified as belonging to me. The laudanum I poured out to account for its presence in his stomach, in case of a *post-mortem* examination. The theory naturally would be that he first intended to poison himself, but, after swallowing a little of the drug, was either disgusted with its taste or changed his mind from other motives, and chose the dagger. These arrangements made, I walked out, leaving the gas burning, locked the door with my vice, and went to bed.

Simon's death was not discovered until nearly three in the afternoon. The servant, astonished at seeing the gas burning—the light streaming on the dark landing from under the door—peeped through the keyhole and saw Simon on the bed. She gave the alarm. The door was burst open, and the neighbourhood was in a fever of excitement.

Every one in the house was arrested, myself included. There was an inquest; but no clue to his death beyond that of suicide could be obtained. Curiously enough, he had made several speeches to his friends the preceding week that seemed to point to self-destruction. One gentleman swore that Simon had said in his presence that "he was tired of life." His landlord affirmed that Simon, when paying him his last month's rent, remarked that "he should not pay him rent much longer." All the other evidence corresponded—the door locked inside, the position of the corpse, the burned papers. As I anticipated, no one knew of the possession of the diamond by Simon, so that no motive was suggested for his murder. The jury, after a prolonged examination, brought in the usual verdict, and the neighbourhood once more settled down to its accustomed quiet.

## V

The three months succeeding Simon's catastrophe I devoted night and day to my diamond lens. I had constructed a vast galvanic battery, composed of nearly two thousand pairs of plates: a higher power I dared not use lest the diamond should be calcined. By means of this enormous engine I was enabled to send a powerful current of electricity continually through my great diamond, which it seemed to me gained in lustre every day. At the expiration of a month I commenced the grinding and polishing of the lens, a work of intense toil and exquisite delicacy. The great density of the stone, and the care required to be taken with the curvatures of the surfaces of the lens, rendered the labour the severest and most harassing that I had yet undergone.

At last the eventful moment came; the lens was completed. I stood trembling on the threshold of new worlds. I had the realisation of Alexander's famous wish before me. The lens lay on the table, ready to be placed upon its platform. My hand fairly shook as I enveloped a drop of water with a thin coating of oil of turpentine, preparatory to its examination, a process necessary in order to prevent the rapid evaporation of the water. I now placed the drop on a thin slip of glass under the lens, and throwing upon it, by the combined aid of a prism and a mirror, a powerful stream of light, I approached my eye to the minute hole drilled through the axis of the lens. For an instant I saw nothing save what seemed to be an illuminated chaos, a vast luminous abyss. A pure white light, cloudless and serene, and seemingly limitless as space itself, was my first impression. Gently, and with the greatest care, I depressed the lens a few hairbreadths. The wondrous illumination still continued, but as the lens approached the object a scene of indescribable beauty was unfolded to my view.

I seemed to gaze upon a vast space, the limits of which extended far beyond my vision. An atmosphere of magical luminousness permeated the entire field of view. I was amazed to see no trace of animalculous life. Not a living thing, apparently, inhabited that dazzling expanse. I comprehended instantly that, by the wondrous power of my lens, I had penetrated beyond the grosser particles of aqueous matter, beyond the realms of infusoria and protozoa, down to the original gaseous globule, into whose luminous interior I was gazing as into an almost boundless dome filled with a supernatural radiance.

It was, however, no brilliant void into which I looked. On every side I beheld beautiful inorganic forms, of unknown texture, and coloured with the most enchanting hues. These forms presented the appearance of what might be called, for want of a more specific definition, foliated clouds of the highest rarity—that is, they undulated and broke into vegetable formations, and were tinged with splendours compared with which the gilding of our autumn woodlands is as dross compared with gold. Far away into the illimitable distance stretched long avenues of these gaseous forests, dimly transparent, and painted with prismatic hues of unimaginable brilliancy. The pendent branches waved along the fluid glades until every vista seemed to break through half-lucent ranks of many-coloured drooping silken pennons. What seemed to be either fruits or flowers, pied with a thousand hues, lustrous and ever-varying, bubbled from the crowns of this fairy foliage. No hills, no lakes, no rivers, no forms animate or inanimate, were to be seen save those vast auroral copses that floated serenely in the luminous stillness, with leaves and fruits and flowers gleaming with unknown fires, unrealisable by mere imagination.

How strange, I thought, that this sphere should be thus condemned to solitude! I had hoped, at least, to discover some new form of animal life, perhaps of a lower class than any with which we are at present acquainted, but still some living organism. I found my newly discovered world, if I may so speak, a beautiful chromatic desert.

While I was speculating on the singular arrangements of the internal economy of Nature, with which she so frequently splinters into atoms our most compact theories, I thought I beheld a form moving slowly through the glades of one of the prismatic forests. I looked more attentively, and found that I was not mistaken. Words cannot depict the anxiety with which I awaited the nearer approach of this mysterious object. Was it merely some inanimate substance, held in suspense in the attenuated atmosphere of the globule, or was it an animal endowed with vitality and motion? It approached, flitting behind the gauzy, coloured veils of cloud-foliage, for seconds dimly revealed, then vanishing. At last the violent pennons that trailed nearest to me vibrated; they were gently pushed aside, and the form floated out into the broad light.

It was a female human shape. When I say human, I mean it possessed the outlines of humanity; but there the analogy ends. Its adorable beauty lifted it illimitable heights beyond the loveliest daughter of Adam.

I cannot, I dare not, attempt to inventory the charms of this divine revelation of perfect beauty. Those eyes of mystic violet, dewy and serene, evade my words. Her long, lustrous hair following her glorious head in a golden wake, like the track sown in heaven by a falling star, seems to quench my most burning phrases with its splendours. If all the bees of Hybla nestled upon my lips, they would still sing but hoarsely the wondrous harmonies of outline that inclosed her form.

She swept out from between the rainbow-curtains of the cloud-trees into the broad sea of light that lay beyond. Her motions were those of some graceful naiad, cleaving, by a mere effort of her will, the clear, unruffled waters that fill the chambers of the sea. She floated forth with the serene grace of a frail bubble ascending through the still atmosphere of a June day. The perfect roundness

of her limbs formed suave and enchanting curves. It was like
listening to the most spiritual symphony of Beethoven the divine
to watch the harmonious flow of lines. This, indeed, was a pleasure
cheaply purchased at any price. What cared I if I had waded to
the portal of this wonder through another's blood. I would have
given my own to enjoy one such moment of intoxication and
delight.

Breathless with gazing on this lovely wonder, and forgetful for an
instant of everything save her presence, I withdrew my eye from
the microscope eagerly. Alas! as my gaze fell on the thin slide
that lay beneath my instrument, the bright light from mirror and
from prism sparkled on a colourless drop of water! There, in that
tiny bead of dew, this beautiful being was for ever imprisoned.
The planet Neptune was not more distant from me than she. I
hastened once more to apply my eye to the microscope.

Animula (let me now call her by that dear name which I subsequently bestowed on her) had changed her position. She had again
approached the wondrous forest, and was gazing earnestly upward.
Presently one of the trees—as I must call them—unfolded a long
ciliary process, with which it seized one of the gleaming fruits that
glittered on its summit, and sweeping slowly down, held it within
reach of Animula. The sylph took it in her delicate hand and
began to eat. My attention was so entirely absorbed by her that
I could not apply myself to the task of determining whether this
singular plant was or was not instinct with volition.

I watched her, as she made her repast, with the most profound
attention. The suppleness of her motions sent a thrill of delight
through my frame; my heart beat madly as she turned her beautiful
eyes in the direction of the spot in which I stood. What would I
not have given to have had the power to precipitate myself into
that luminous ocean and float with her through those groves of
purple and gold! While I was thus breathlessly following her every
movement, she suddenly started, seemed to listen for a moment,
and then cleaving the brilliant ether in which she was floating,
like a flash of light, pierced through the opaline forest and
disappeared.

Instantly a series of the most singular sensations attacked me.
It seemed as if I had suddenly gone blind. The luminous sphere was
still before me, but my daylight had vanished. What caused this
sudden disappearance? Had she a lover or a husband? Yes, that
was the solution! Some signal from a happy fellow-being had
vibrated through the avenues of the forest, and she had obeyed
the summons.

The agony of my sensations, as I arrived at this conclusion,
startled me. I tried to reject the conviction that my reason forced
upon me. I battled against the fatal conclusion—but in vain.
It was so. I had no escape from it. I loved an animalcule.

It is true that, thanks to the marvellous power of my microscope, she appeared of human proportions. Instead of presenting the revolting aspect of the coarser creatures, that live and struggle and die, in the more easily resolvable portions of the water-drop, she was fair and delicate and of surpassing beauty. But of what account was all that? Every time that my eye was withdrawn from the instrument it fell on a miserable drop of water, within which, I must be content to know, dwelt all that could make my life lovely.

Could she but see me once! Could I for one moment pierce the mystical walls that so inexorably rose to separate us, and whisper all that filled my soul, I might consent to be satisfied for the rest of my life with the knowledge of her remote sympathy. It would be something to have established even the faintest personal link to bind us together—to know that at times, when roaming through these enchanted glades, she might think of the wonderful stranger who had broken the monotony of her life with his presence and left a gentle memory in her heart!

But it could not be. No invention of which human intellect was capable could break down the barriers that nature had erected. I might feast my soul upon her wondrous beauty, yet she must always remain ignorant of the adoring eyes that day and night gazed upon her, and, even when closed, beheld her in dreams. With a bitter cry of anguish I fled from the room, and, flinging myself on my bed, sobbed myself to sleep like a child.

## VI

I arose the next morning almost at daybreak, and rushed to my microscope. I trembled as I sought the luminous world in miniature that contained my all. Animula was there. I had left the gas-lamp, surrounded by its moderators, burning when I went to bed the night before. I found the sylph bathing, as it were, with an expression of pleasure animating her features, in the brilliant light which surrounded her. She tossed her lustrous golden hair over her shoulders with innocent coquetry. She lay at full length in the transparent medium, in which she supported herself with ease, and gambolled with the enchanting grace that the nymph Salmacis might have exhibited when she sought to conquer the modest Hermaphroditus. I tried an experiment to satisfy myself if her powers of reflection were developed. I lessened the lamplight considerably. By the dim light that remained I could see an expression of pain flit across her face. She looked upward suddenly, and her brows contracted. I flooded the stage of the microscope again with a full stream of light, and her whole expression changed. She sprang forward like some substance deprived of all weight.

Her eyes sparkled and her lips moved. Ah! if science had only the means of conducting and reduplicating sounds, as it does rays of light, what carols of happiness would then have entranced my ears! what jubilant hymns to Adonais would have thrilled the illumined air!

I now comprehended how it was that the Count de Cabalis peopled his mystic world with sylphs—beautiful beings whose breath of life was lambent fire, and who sported for ever in regions of purest ether and purest light. The Rosicrucian had anticipated the wonder that I had practically realised.

How long this worship of my strange divinity went on thus I scarcely know. I lost all note of time. All day from early dawn, and far into the night, I was to be found peering through that wonderful lens. I saw no one, went nowhere, and scarce allowed myself sufficient time for my meals. My whole life was absorbed in contemplation as rapt as that of any of the Romish saints. Every hour that I gazed upon the divine form strengthened my passion—a passion that was always overshadowed by the maddening conviction that, although I could gaze on her at will, she never, never could behold me!

At length I grew so pale and emaciated, from want of rest and continual brooding over my insane love and its cruel conditions, that I determined to make some effort to wean myself from it. "Come," I said, " this is at best but a fantasy. Your imagination has bestowed on Animula charms which in reality she does not possess. Seclusion from female society has produced this morbid condition of mind. Compare her with the beautiful women of your own world, and this false enchantment will vanish."

I looked over the newspapers by chance. There I beheld the advertisement of a celebrated *danseuse* who appeared nightly at Niblo's. The Signorina Caradolce had the reputation of being the most beautiful as well as the most graceful woman in the world. I instantly dressed and went to the theatre.

The curtain drew up. The usual semicircle of fairies in white muslin were standing on the right toe around the enamelled flower-bank of green canvas, on which the belated prince was sleeping. Suddenly a flute is heard. The fairies start. The trees open, the fairies all stand on the left toe, and the queen enters. It was the Signorina. She bounded forward amid thunders of applause, and, lighting on one foot, remained poised in the air. Heavens! was this the great enchantress that had drawn monarchs at her chariot-wheels? Those heavy, muscular limbs, those thick ankles, those cavernous eyes, that stereotyped smile, those crudely painted cheeks! Where were the vermeil blooms, the liquid, expressive eyes, the harmonious limbs of Animula?

The Signorina danced. What gross, discordant movements! The play of her limbs was all false and artificial. Her bounds were painful athletic efforts; her poses were angular and distressed the eye. I could bear it no longer; with an exclamation of disgust that drew every eye upon me, I rose from my seat in the very middle of the Signorina's *pas de fascination* and abruptly quitted the house.

I hastened home to feast my eyes once more on the lovely form of my sylph. I felt that henceforth to combat this passion would be impossible. I applied my eyes to the lens. Animula was there— but what could have happened? Some terrible change seemed to have taken place during my absence. Some secret grief seemed to cloud the lovely features of her I gazed upon. Her face had grown thin and haggard; her limbs trailed heavily; the wondrous lustre of her golden hair had faded. She was ill—ill, and I could not assist her! I believe at that moment I would have forfeited all claims to my human birthright if I could only have been dwarfed to the size of an animalcule, and permitted to console her from whom fate had for ever divided me.

I racked my brain for the solution of this mystery. What was it that afflicted the sylph? She seemed to suffer intense pain. Her features contracted, and she even writhed, as if with some internal agony. The wondrous forests appeared also to have lost half their beauty. Their hues were dim and in some places faded away altogether. I watched Animula for hours with a breaking heart, and she seemed absolutely to wither away under my very eye. Suddenly I remembered that I had not looked at the water-drop for several days. In fact, I hated to see it; for it reminded me of the natural barrier between Animula and myself. I hurriedly looked down on the stage of the microscope. The slide was still there—but, great heavens, the water-drop had vanished! The awful truth burst upon me; it had evaporated, until it had become so minute as to be invisible to the naked eye; I had been gazing on its last atom, the one that contained Animula—and she was dying!

I rushed again to the front of the lens and looked through. Alas! the last agony had seized her. The rainbow-hued forests had all melted away, and Animula lay struggling feebly in what seemed to be a spot of dim light. Ah! the sight was horrible: the limbs once so round and lovely shrivelling up into nothing; the eyes—those eyes that shone like heaven—being quenched into black dust; the lustrous golden hair now lank and discoloured. The last throe came. I beheld that final struggle of the blackening form—and I fainted.

When I awoke out of a trance of many hours, I found myself lying amid the wreck of my instrument, myself as shattered in mind and body as it. I crawled feebly to my bed, from which I did not rise for many months.

They say now that I am mad; but they are mistaken. I am poor, for I have neither the heart nor the will to work; all my money is spent, and I live on charity. Young men's associations that love a joke invite me to lecture on optics before them, for which they pay me, and laugh at me while I lecture. "Linley, the mad microscopist," is the name I go by. I suppose that I talk incoherently while I lecture. Who could talk sense when his brain is haunted by such ghastly memories, while ever and anon among the shapes of death I behold the radiant form of my lost Animula!

# NOAH BROOKS
### 1830–1903

## LOST IN THE FOG

"Down with your helm! you'll have us hard and fast aground!"

My acquaintance with Captain Booden was at that time somewhat limited, and if possible I knew less of the difficult and narrow exit from Bolinas Bay than I did of Captain Booden. So with great trepidation I jammed the helm hard down, and the obedient little *Lively Polly* fell off easily, and we were over the bar and gliding gently along under the steep bluff of the Mesa, whose rocky edge, rising sheer from the beach and crowned with dry grass, rose far above the pennon of the little schooner. I did not intend to deceive Captain Booden, but being anxious to work my way down to San Francisco, I had shipped as "able seaman" on the *Lively Polly*, though it was a long day since I had handled a foresheet or anything bigger than the little plungers which hover about Bolinas Bay, and latterly I had been ranching it at Point Reyes, so what could I know about the bar and the shoals of the harbour, I would like to know? We had glided out of the narrow channel which is skirted on one side by a long sandspit that curves around and makes the southern and western shelter of the bay, and on the other side by a huge elevated tongue of tableland, called by the inhabitants thereabouts the Mesa. High, precipitous, perpendicular, level, and dotted with farmhouses, this singular bit of land stretches several miles out southward to sea, bordered with a rocky beach, and tapered off into the wide ocean with Duxbury Ree—a dangerous rocky reef, curving down to the southward and almost always white with foam, save when the sea is calm, and then the great lazy green waves eddy noiselessly over the half-hidden rocks, or slip like oil over the dreadful dangers which they hide.

Behind us was the lovely bay of Bolinas, blue and sparkling in the summer afternoon sun, its borders dotted with thrifty ranches, and the woody ravines and bristling Tamalpais Range rising over all. The tide was running out, and only a peaceful swash whispered along the level sandy beach on our left, where the busy sandpiper chased the playful wave as it softly rose and fell along the shore. On the higher centre of the sandspit which shuts in the bay on that side, a row of ashy-coloured gulls sunned themselves, and blinked at us sleepily as we drifted slowly out of the channel, our breeze cut off by the Mesa that hemmed us in on the right. I have told you that I did not much pretend to seamanship, but I was not sorry that I had taken passage on the *Lively Polly*. for there is always something novel and fascinating to me in coasting a region which I have heretofore known only by its hills, cañons, and sea-beaches. The trip is usually made from Bolinas Bay to San Francisco in five or six hours, when wind and tide favour; and I could bear being knocked about by Captain Booden for that length of time, especially as there was one other hand on board—" Lanky " he was called—but whether a foremast hand or landsman I do not know. He had been teaching school at Jaybird Cañon, and was a little more awkward with the running rigging of the *Lively Polly* than I was. Captain Booden was, therefore, the main reliance of the little twenty-ton schooner, and if her deck-load of firewood and cargo of butter and eggs ever reached a market, the skilful and profane skipper should have all the credit thereof.

The wind died away, and the sea, before ruffled with a wholesale breeze, grew as calm as a sheet of billowy glass, heaving only in long, gentle undulations on which the sinking sun bestowed a green and golden glory, dimmed only by the white fog-bank that came drifting slowly up from the Farralones, now shut out from view by the lovely haze. Captain Booden gazed morosely on the western horizon, and swore by a big round oath that we should not have a capful of wind if that fog-bank did not lift. But we were fairly out of the bay; the Mesa was lessening in the distance, and as we drifted slowly southward the red-roofed buildings on its level rim grew to look like toy-houses, and we heard the dull moan of the ebb-tide on Duxbury Reef on our starboard bow. The sea grew dead calm and the wind fell quite away, but still we drifted southward, passing Rocky Point and peering curiously into Pilot Boat Cove, which looked so strangely unfamiliar to me from the sea, though I had fished in its trout-brooks many a day, and had hauled driftwood from the rocky beach to Johnson's ranch in times gone by. The tide turned after sundown, and Captain Booden thought we ought to get a bit of wind then; but it did not come, and the fog crept up and up the glassy sea, rolling in huge wreaths of mist, shutting out the surface of the water, and finally the grey rocks of North Heads were hidden, and little by little the shore was curtained from our view and we were becalmed in the fog.

To say that the skipper swore would hardly describe his case. He cursed his luck, his stars, his foretop, his main hatch, his blasted foolishness, his lubberly crew—Lanky and I—and a variety of other persons and things; but all to no avail. Night came on, and the light on North Heads gleamed at us with a sickly eye through the deepening fog. We had a bit of luncheon with us, but no fire, and were fain to content ourselves with cold meat, bread, and water, hoping that a warm breakfast in San Francisco would make some amends for our present short rations. But the night wore on, and we were still tumbling about in the rising sea without wind enough to fill our sails, a rayless sky overhead, and with breakers continually under our lee. Once we saw lights on shore, and heard the sullen thud of rollers that smote against the rocks; it was aggravating, as the fog lifted for a space, to see the cheerful windows of the Cliff House, and almost hear the merry calls of pleasure-seekers as they muffled themselves in their wraps and drove gaily up the hill, reckless of the poor homeless mariners who were drifting comfortlessly about so near the shore they could not reach. We got out the sweeps and rowed lustily for several hours, steering by the compass and taking our bearings from the cliff.

But we lost our bearings in the maze of currents in which we soon found ourselves, and the dim shore melted away in the thickening fog. To add to our difficulties, Captain Booden put his head most frequently into the cuddy; and when it emerged, he smelt dreadfully of gin. Lanky and I held a secret council, in which we agreed, in case he became intoxicated, we would rise up in mutiny and work the vessel on our own account. He shortly "lost his head," as Lanky phrased it; and slipping down on the deck, went quietly into the sleep of the gin-drunken. At four o'clock in the morning the grey fog grew greyer with the early dawning; and as I gazed with weary eyes into the vague unknown that shut us in, Booden roused him from his booze, and seizing the tiller from my hand, bawled: "'Bout ship, you swab! we're on the Farralones!" And sure enough, there loomed right under our starboard quarter a group of conical rocks, steeply rising from the restless blue sea. Their wild white sides were crowded with chattering sea-fowl; and far above, like a faint nimbus in the sky, shone the feeble rays of the lighthouse lantern, now almost quenched by the dull gleam of day that crept up from the water. The helm was jammed hard down. There was no time to get out sweeps; but still drifting helplessly, we barely grazed the bare rocks of the islet, and swung clear, slinking once more into the gloom.

Our scanty stock of provisions and water was gone; but there was no danger of starvation, for the generous product of the henneries and dairies of Bolinas filled the vessel's hold—albeit raw eggs and butter without bread might only serve as a barrier against famine. So we drifted and tumbled about—still no wind and no sign of the lifting of the fog. Once in a while it would roll upward and show a long, flat expanse of water, tempting us to believe that the blessed sky was coming out at last; but soon the veil fell again, and we aimlessly wondered where we were and whither we were drifting. There is something awful and mysterious in the shadowy nothingness that surrounds one in a fog at sea. You fancy that out of that impenetrable mist may suddenly burst some great disaster or danger.

Strange shapes appear to be forming themselves in the obscurity out of which they emerge, and the eye is wearied beyond expression with looking into a vacuity which continually promises to evolve into something, but never does.

Thus idly drifting, we heard, first, the creaking of a block, then a faint wash of sea; and out of the white depths of the fog came the bulky hull of a full-rigged ship. Her sails were set, but she made scarcely steerage way. Her rusty sides and general look bespoke a long voyage just concluding; and we found on hailing her that she was the British ship *Marathon*, from Calcutta for San Francisco. We boarded the *Marathon*, though almost in sight of our own port, with something of the feeling that shipwrecked seamen may have when they reach land. It was odd that we, lost and wandering as we were, should be thus encountered in the vast unknown where we were drifting by a strange ship; and though scarcely two hours' sail from home, should be supplied with bread and water by a Britisher from the Indies. We gave them all the information we had about the pilots, whom we wanted so much to meet ourselves; and after following slowly for a few hours by the huge side of our strange friend, parted company—the black hull and huge spars of the Indiaman gradually lessening in the mist that shut her from our view. We had touched a chord that bound us to our fellow-men, but it was drawn from our hands, and the unfathomable abyss in which we floated had swallowed up each human trace, except what was comprised on the contracted deck of the *Lively Polly*, where Captain Booden sat glumly whittling, and Lanky meditatively peered after the disappeared *Marathon*, as though his soul and all his hopes had gone with her. The deck, with its load of cord-wood; the sails and rigging; the sliding-hutch of the little cuddy; and all the features of the *Lively Polly*, but yesterday so unfamiliar were now as odiously wearisome as though I had known them for a century. It seemed as if I had never known any other place.

All that day we floated aimlessly along, moved only by the sluggish currents, which shifted occasionally, but generally bore us westward and southward; not a breath of wind arose, and our sails were as useless as though we had been on dry land. Night came on again, and found us still entirely without reckoning and as completely "at sea" as ever before. To add to our discomfort, a drizzling rain, unusual for the season of the year, set in, and we cowered on the wet deck-load, more than ever disgusted with each other and the world. During the night a big ocean steamer came plunging and crashing through the darkness, her lights gleaming redly through the dense medium as she cautiously felt her way past us, falling off a few points as she heard our hail. We lay right in her path, but with tin horns and a wild Indian yell from the versatile Lanky managed to make ourselves heard, and the mysterious stranger disappeared in the fog as suddenly as she had come, and we were once more alone in the darkness.

The night wore slowly away, and we made out to catch a few hours' sleep, standing "watch and watch" with each other of our slender crew. Day dawned again, and we broke our fast with the last of the *Marathon's* biscuit, having "broken cargo" to eke out our cold repast with some of the Bolinas butter and eggs which we were taking to a most unexpected market.

Suddenly, about six o'clock in the morning, we heard the sound of breakers ahead, and above the sullen roar of the surf I distinctly heard the tinklings of a bell. We got out our sweeps and had commenced to row wearily once more when the fog lifted and before us lay the blessed land. A high range of sparsely wooded hills, crowned with rocky ledges, and with abrupt slopes covered with dry brown grass, running to the water's edge, formed the background of the picture. Nearer, a tongue of high land, brushy and rocky, made out from the main shore, and, curving southward, formed a shelter to what seemed a harbour within. Against the precipitous point the sea broke with a heavy blow, and a few ugly peaks of rock lifted their heads above the heaving green of the sea. High up above the sky-line rose one tall sharp, blue peak, yet veiled in the floating mist, but its base melted away into a mass of verdure that stretched from the shore far up the mountain-side. Our sweeps were now used to bring us around the point, and cautiously pulling in, we opened a lovely bay bordered with orchards and vineyards, in the midst of which was a neat village, glittering white in the sunshine, and clustered around an old-fashioned mission church, whose quaint gable and tower reminded us of the buildings of the early Spanish settlers of the country. As we neared the shore (there was no landing-place) we could see an unwonted commotion in the clean streets, and a flag was run up to the top of a white staff that stood in the midst of a plaza. Captain Booden returned the compliment by hoisting the Stars and Stripes at our mainmast head, but was sorely bothered with the mingled dyes of the flag on shore. A puff of air blew out its folds, and to our surprise disclosed the Mexican national standard.

"Blast them greasers," said the patriotic skipper, "if they ain't gone and histed a Mexican cactus flag, then I'm blowed." He seriously thought of hauling down his beloved national colours again, resenting the insult of hoisting a foreign flag on American soil. He pocketed the affront, however, remarking that "they probably knew that a Bolinas butter-boat was not much of a fightist anyway."

We dropped anchor gladly, Captain Booden being wholly at a loss as to our whereabouts. We judged that we were somewhere south of the Golden Gate, but what town this was that slept so tranquilly in the summer sun, and what hills were these that

walled in the peaceful scene from the rest of the world, we could
not tell. The village seemed awakening from its serene sleepiness,
and one by one the windows of the adobe cottages swung open as
if the people rubbed their long-closed eyes at some unwonted sight ;
and the doors gradually opened as though their dumb lips would
hail us and ask who were these strangers that vexed the quiet
waters of their bay. But two small fishing-boats lay at anchor,
and these Booden said reminded him of Christopher Columbus or
Noah's Ark, they were so clumsy and antique in build.

We hauled our boat up alongside, and all hands got in and went
ashore. As we landed, a little shudder seemed to go through the
sleepy old place, as if it had been rudely disturbed from its comfortable nap, and a sudden sob of sea air swept through the quiet
streets as though the insensate houses had actually breathed the
weary sigh of awaking. The buildings were low and white, with
dark-skinned children basking in the doors, and grass hammocks
swinging beneath open verandahs. There were no stores, no sign
of business, and no sound of vehicles or labour ; all was as decorous
and quiet, to use the skipper's description, " as if the people had
slicked up their door-yards, whitewashed their houses, and gone to
bed." It was just like a New England Sabbath in a Mexican
village.

And this fancy was further coloured by a strange procession
which now met us as we went up from the narrow beach, having
first made fast our boat. A lean Mexican priest, with an enormous
shovel hat and particularly shabby cassock, came towards us,
followed by a motley crowd of Mexicans, prominent among whom
was a pompous old man clad in a seedy Mexican uniform and
wearing a trailing rapier at his side. The rest of the procession
was brought up with a crowd of shy women, dark-eyed and tawny
and all poorly clad, though otherwise comfortable enough in condition. These hung back and wonderingly looked at the strange
faces, as though they had never seen the like before. The old
padre lifted his skinny hands, and said something in Spanish which
I did not understand.

" Why, the old mummy is slinging his popish blessings at us ! "
This was Lanky's interpretation of the kindly priest's paternal
salutation. And, sure enough, he was welcoming us to the shore
of San Ildefonso with holy fervour and religious phrase.

" I say," said Booden, a little testily, " what did you say was the
name of this place, and where away does it lay from ' Frisco ? "
In very choice Castilian, as Lanky declared, the priest rejoined
that he did not understand the language in which Booden was
speaking. " Then bring on somebody that does," rejoined that
irreverent mariner, when due interpretation had been made. The
padre protested that no one in the village understood the English
tongue. The skipper gave a long low whistle of suppressed astonish-

ment, and wondered if we had drifted to Lower California in two days and nights, and had struck a Mexican settlement. The colours on the flagstaff and the absence of any Americans gave some show of reason to this startling conclusion; and Lanky, who was now the interpreter of the party, asked the name of the place, and was again told that it was San Ildefonso; but when he asked what country it was in and how far it was to San Francisco, he was met with a polite "I do not understand you, Señor." Here was a puzzle: becalmed in a strange port only two days' drift from the city of San Francisco; a town which the schoolmaster declared was not laid down on any map; a population that spoke only Spanish and did not know English when they heard it; a Mexican flag flying over the town, and an educated priest who did not know what we meant when we asked how far it was to San Francisco. Were we bewitched?

Accepting a hospitable invitation from the padre, we sauntered up to the plaza, where we were ushered into a long, low room, which might once have been a military barrack-room. It was neatly whitewashed and had a hard clay floor, and along the walls were a few ancient firelocks and a venerable picture of "His Excellency, General Santa Aña, President of the Republic of Mexico," as a legend beneath it set forth. Breakfast of chickens, vegetables, bread, and an excellent sort of country wine (this last being served in a big earthen bottle) was served up to us on the long unpainted table that stood in the middle of the room. During the repast our host, the priest, sat with folded hands intently regarding us, while the rest of the people clustered around the door and open windows, eyeing us with indescribable and incomprehensible curiosity. If we had been visitors from the moon we could not have attracted more attention. Even the stolid Indians, a few of whom strolled lazily about, came and gazed at us until the pompous old man in faded Mexican uniform drove them noisily away from the window, where they shut out the light and the pleasant morning air, perfumed with heliotropes, verbenas, and sweet herbs that grew luxuriantly about the houses.

The padre had restrained his curiosity out of rigid politeness until we had eaten, when he began by asking, "Did our galleon come from Manila?" We told him that we only came from Bolinas; whereat he said once more, with a puzzled look of pain, "I do not understand you, Señor." Then pointing through the open doorway to where the *Lively Polly* peacefully floated at anchor, he asked what ensign was that which floated at her masthead. Lanky proudly, but with some astonishment, replied: "That's the American flag, Señor." At this the seedy old man in uniform eagerly said: "Americanos! Americanos! why, I saw some of those people and that flag at Monterey." Lanky asked him if Monterey was not full of Americans, and did not have plenty of flags. The Ancient replied that he did not know; it was a long time since he had been there. Lanky observed that perhaps he had never been there. "I was there in 1835," said the Ancient. This curious speech being interpreted to Captain Booden, that worthy remarked that he did not believe that he had seen a white man since.

After an ineffectual effort to explain to the company where Bolinas was, we rose and went out for a view of the town. It was beautifully situated on a gentle rise which swelled up from the water's edge and fell rapidly off in the rear of the town into a deep ravine, where a brawling mountain stream supplied a little flouring-mill with motive power. Beyond the ravine were small fields of grain, beans and lentils on the rolling slopes, and back of these rose the dark, dense vegetation of low hills, while over all were the rough and ragged ridges of mountains closing in all the scene. The town itself, as I have said, was white and clean; the houses were low-browed, with windows secured by wooden shutters, only a few glazed sashes being seen anywhere. Out of these openings in the thick adobe walls of the humble homes of the villagers flashed the curious, the abashed glances of many a dark-eyed senorita, who fled, laughing, as we approached. The old church was on the plaza, and in its odd-shaped turret tinkled the little bell whose notes had sounded the morning angelus when we were knocking about in the fog outside. High up on its quaintly arched gable was inscribed in antique letters "1796." In reply to a sceptical remark from Lanky, Booden declared that "the old shell looked as though it might have been built in the time of Ferdinand and Isabella, for that matter." The worthy skipper had a misty idea that all old Spanish buildings were built in the days of these famous sovereigns.

Hearing the names of Ferdinand and Isabella, the padre gravely and reverentially asked: "And is the health of His Excellency, General Santa Aña, whom God protect, still continued to him?" With great amazement, Lanky replied: "Santa Aña! why, the last heard of him was that he was keeping a cockpit in Havana; some of the newspapers published an obituary of him about six months ago, but I believe he is alive yet somewhere."

A little flush of indignation mantled the old man's cheek, and with a tinge of severity in his voice he said: "I have heard that shameful scandal about our noble President once before, but you must excuse me if I ask you not to repeat it. It is true he took away our Pious Fund some years since, but he is still our revered President, and I would not hear him ill-spoken of any more than our puissant and mighty Ferdinand, of whom you just spoke— may he rest in glory!" and here the good priest crossed himself devoutly.

"What is the old priest jabbering about?" asked Captain

Booden impatiently; for he was in haste to "get his bearings" and be off. When Lanky replied, he burst out: "Tell him that Santa Aña is not President of Mexico any more than I am, and that he hasn't amounted to a row of pins since California was part of the United States."

Lanky faithfully interpreted this fling at the ex-President, whereupon the padre, motioning to the Ancient to put up his rapier, which had leaped out of its rusty scabbard, said: "Nay, Señor, you would insult an old man. We have never been told yet by our government that the Province of California was alienated from the great Republic of Mexico, and we owe allegiance to none save the nation whose flag we love so well"; and the old man turned his tear-dimmed eyes toward the ragged standard of Mexico that drooped from the staff in the plaza. Continuing, he said: "Our noble country has strangely forgotten us, and though we watch the harbour entrance year after year, no tidings ever come. The galleon that was to bring us stores has never been seen on the horizon yet, and we seem lost in the fog."

The schoolmaster of Jaybird Cañon managed to tell us what the priest had said, and then asked when he had last heard of the outside world. "It was in 1837," said he sadly, "when we sent a courier to the Mission del Carmelo, at Monterey, for tidings from New Spain. He never came back, and the great earthquake which shook the country hereabout opened a huge chasm across the country just back of the Sierra yonder, and none dared to cross over to the mainland. The saints have defended us in peace, and it is the will of Heaven that we shall stay here by ourselves until the Holy Virgin, in answer to our prayers, shall send us deliverance."

Here was a new revelation. This was an old Spanish Catholic mission, settled in 1796, called San Ildefonso, which had evidently been overlooked for nearly forty years, and had quietly slept in an unknown solitude while the country had been transferred to the United States from the flag that still idly waved over it. Lost in the fog! Here was a whole town lost in a fog of years. Empires and dynasties had risen and fallen; the world had repeatedly been shaken to its centre, and this people had heeded it not; a great civil war had ravaged the country to which they now belonged, and they knew not of it; poor Mexico herself had been torn with dissensions and had been insulted with an empire, and these peaceful and weary watchers for tidings from "New Spain" had recked nothing of all these things. All around them the busy State of California was scarred with the eager pick of gold-seekers or the shining share of the husbandman; towns and cities had sprung up where these patriarchs had only known of vast cattle ranges or sleepy missions of the Roman Catholic Fathers. They knew nothing of the great city of San Francisco, with its busy marts and crowded harbour; and thought of its broad bay—if they thought of it at all—as the lovely shore of Yerba Buena, bounded by bleak hills and almost unvexed by any keel. The political storms of forty years had gone hurtless over their heads, and in a certain sort of dreamless sleep San Ildefonso had still remained true to the red, white, and green flag that had long since disappeared from every part of the State save here, where it was still loved and revered as the banner of the soil.

The social and political framework of the town had been kept up through all these years. There had been no connection with the fountain of political power, but the town was ruled by the legally elected Ayuntamiento, or Common Council, of which the Ancient, Señor Apolonario Maldonado, was President or Alcade. They were daily looking for advices from Don José Castro, Governor of the loyal province of California; and so they had been looking daily for forty years. We asked if they had not heard from any of the prying Yankees who crowd the country. Father Ignacio—for that was the padre's name—replied: "Yes; five years ago, when the winter rains had just set in, a tall, spare man, who talked some French and some Spanish came down over the mountains with a pack containing pocket-knives, razors, soap, perfumery, laces, and other curious wares, and besought our people to purchase. We have not much coin, but were disposed to treat him Christianly, until he did declare that President General Santa Aña, whom may the saints defend! was a thief and gambler, and had gambled away the Province of California to the United States; whereupon we drave him hence, the Ayuntamiento sending a trusty guard to see him two leagues from the borders of the Pueblo. But months after we discovered his pack and such of his poor bones as the wild beasts of prey had not carried off at the base of a precipice where he had fallen. His few remains and his goods were together buried on the mountain-side, and I lamented that we had been so hard with him. But the saints forbid that he should go back and tell where the people of San Ildefonso were waiting to hear from their own neglectful country, which may Heaven defend, bless, and prosper."

The little town took on a new interest to us cold outsiders after hearing its strange and almost improbable story. We could have scarcely believed that San Ildefonso had actually been overlooked in the transfer of the country from Mexico to the United States, and had for nearly forty years been hidden away between the Sierra and the sea; but if we were disposed to doubt the word of the good father, here was intrinsic evidence of the truth of his narrative. There were no Americans here: only the remnants of the old Mexican occupation and the civilised Indians. No traces of later civilisation could be found; but the simple dresses, tools, implements of husbandry, and household utensils were such as I have seen in the half-civilised wilds of Central America. The old mill in the cañon behind the town was a curiosity of clumsiness, and nine-tenths of the water-power of the arroya that supplied it were wasted. Besides, until now, who ever heard of such a town in California as San Ildefonso? Upon what map can any such headland and bay be traced? and where are the historic records of the pueblo whose well-defined boundaries lay palpably before us? I have dwelt upon this point, about which I naturally have some feeling, because of the sceptical criticism which my narrative has since provoked. There are some people in the world who never will believe anything that they have not seen, touched, or tasted for themselves; California has her share of such.

Captain Booden was disposed to reject Father Ignacio's story, until I called his attention to the fact that this was a tolerable harbour for small craft, and yet had never before been heard of; that he never knew of such a town, and that if any of his numerous associates in the marine profession knew of the town or harbour of San Ildefonso, he surely would have heard of it from them. He restrained his impatience to be off long enough to allow Father Ignacio to gather from us a few chapters of the world's history for forty years past. The discovery of gold in California, the settlement of the country and the Pacific Railroad were not so much account to him, somehow, as the condition of Europe, the Church of Mexico, and what had become of the Pious Fund; this last I discovered had been a worrisome subject to the good Father. I did not know what it was myself, but I believe it was the alienation from the Church of certain moneys and incomes which were transferred to speculators by the Mexican Congress years and years ago.

I was glad to find that we were more readily believed by Father Ignacio and the old Don than our Yankee predecessor had been; perhaps we were believed more on his corroborative evidence. The priest, however, politely declined to believe all we said—that was evident; and the Don steadily refused to believe that California had been transferred to the United States. It was a little touching to see Father Ignacio's doubt and hopes struggle in his withered face as he heard in a few brief sentences the history of his beloved land and Church for forty years past. His eye kindled or it was bedewed with tears as he listened, and an occasional flash of resentment flushed his cheek when he heard something that shook his ancient faith in the established order of things. To a proposition to take a passage with us to San Francisco, he replied warmly that he would on no account leave his flock, nor attempt to thwart the manifest will of Heaven that the town should remain unheard of until delivered from its long sleep by the same agencies that had cut it off from the rest of the world. Neither would he allow any of the people to come with us.

And so we parted. We went out with the turn of the tide, Father Ignacio and the Ancient accompanying us to the beach, followed by a crowd of the townsfolk, who carried for us water and provisions for a longer voyage than ours promised to be. The venerable priest raised his hands in parting blessing as we shoved off, and I saw two big tears roll down the furrowed face of Señor Maldonado, who looked after us as a stalwart old warrior might look at the departure of a band of hopeful comrades leaving him to fret in monkish solitude while they were off to the wars again. Wind and tide served, and in a few minutes the *Lively Polly* rounded the point, and looking back, I saw the yellow haze of the afternoon sun sifted sleepily over all the place; the knots of white-clad people standing statuesque and motionless as they gazed; the flag of Mexico faintly waving in the air; and with a sigh of relief a slumbrous veil seemed to fall over all the scene; and as our boat met the roll of the current outside the headland, the grey rocks of the point shut out the fading view, and we saw the last of San Ildefonso.

Captain Booden had gathered enough from the people to know that we were somewhere south of San Francisco (the *Lively Polly* had no chart or nautical instrument on board of course), and so he determined to coast cautiously along northward, marking the shore line in order to be able to guide other navigators to the harbour. But a light mist crept down the coast, shutting out the view of the headlands, and by midnight we had stretched out to sea again, and we were once more out of our reckoning. At daybreak, however, the fog lifted, and we found ourselves in sight of land, and a brisk breeze blowing, we soon made Pigeon Point, and before noon were inside the Golden Gate, and ended our long and adventurous cruise from Bolinas Bay by hauling into the wharf of San Francisco.

I have little left to tell. Of the shameful way in which our report was received, every newspaper reader knows. At first there were some persons, men of science and reading, who were disposed to believe what we said. I printed in one of the daily newspapers an account of what we had discovered, giving a full history of San Ildefonso as Father Ignacio had given it to us. Of course, as I find is usual in such cases, the other newspapers pooh-poohed the story their contemporary had published to their exclusion, and made themselves very merry over what they were pleased to term "The Great San Ildefonso Sell." I prevailed on Captain Booden to make a short voyage down the coast in search of the lost port. But we never saw the headland, the ridge beyond the town, nor anything that looked like these landmarks, though we went down as far as San Pedro Bay and back twice or three times. It actually did seem that the whole locality had been swallowed up, or had vanished into air. In vain did I bring the matter to the notice of the merchants and scientific men of San Francisco. Nobody would fit out an exploring expedition by land or sea; those who listened at first finally inquired "if there was any money in it?" I could not give an affirmative answer, and they turned away with the discouraging remark that the California Academy of Natural Science and the Society of Pioneers were the only bodies interested in the fate of our lost city. Even Captain Booden somehow lost all interest in the enterprise, and returned to his Bolinas coasting with the most stolid indifference. I combated the attacks of the newspaper with facts and depositions of my fellow-voyagers as long as I could, until one day the editor of the *Daily Trumpeter* (I suppress the real name of the sheet) coldly told me that the public were tired of the story of San Ildefonso. It was plain that his mind had been soured by the sarcasms of his contemporaries, and he no longer believed in me.

The newspaper controversy died away and was forgotten, but I have never relinquished the hope of proving the verity of my statements. At one time I expected to establish the truth, having heard that one Zedekiah Murch had known a Yankee peddler who had gone over the mountains of Santa Cruz and never was heard of more. But Zedekiah's memory was feeble, and he only knew that such a story prevailed long ago ; so that clue was soon lost again, and the little fire of enthusiasm which it had kindled among a few persons died out. I have not yet lost all hope ; and when I think of the regretful conviction that will force itself upon the mind of good Father Ignacio, that we were, after all, impostors, I cannot bear to reflect that I may die and visit the lost town of San Ildefonso no more.

## SAMUEL DAVIS
*circa* 1830

# THE FIRST PIANO IN CAMP

In 1858—it might have been five years earlier or later; this is not the history for the public schools—there was a little camp about ten miles from Pioche, occupied by upward of three hundred miners, every one of whom might have packed his prospecting implements and left for more inviting fields any time before sunset.

When the day was over, these men did not rest from their labours, like honest New England agriculturists, but sang, danced, gambled, and shot each other, as the mood seized them.

One evening the report spread along the main street (which was the only street) that three men had been killed at Silver Reef and that the bodies were coming in. Presently a lumbering old conveyance laboured up the hill, drawn by a couple of horses, well worn out with their pull. The cart contained a good-sized box, and no sooner did its outlines become visible, through the glimmer of a stray light, than it began to affect the idlers.

Death always enforces respect, and even though no one had caught sight of the remains, the crowd gradually became subdued, and when the horses came to a standstill the cart was immediately surrounded. The driver, however, was not in the least impressed with the solemnity of his commission.

" All there ? " asked one.

" Haven't examined. Guess so."

The driver filled his pipe, and lit it as he continued :

"Wish the bones and load had gone over the grade ! "

A man who had been looking on stepped up to the man at once.

" I don't know who you have in that box, but if they happen to be any friends of mine I'll lay you alongside."

" We can mighty soon see," said the teamster coolly. " Just burst the lid off, and if they happen to be the men you want, I'm here."

The two looked at each other for a moment, and then the crowd gathered a little closer, anticipating trouble.

" I believe that dead men are entitled to good treatment, and when you talk about hoping to see corpses go over a bank, all I

## THE FIRST PIANO IN CAMP

have to say is, that it will be better for you if the late lamented ain't my friends."

"We'll open the box. I don't take back what I've said, and if my language don't suit your ways of thinking, I guess I can stand it."

With these words the teamster began to pry up the lid. He got a board off, and then pulled out some rags. A strip of something dark, like rosewood, presented itself.

"Eastern coffins, by thunder!" said several, and the crowd looked quite astonished.

Some more boards flew up, and the man who was ready to defend his friend's memory shifted his weapon a little. The cool manner of the teamster had so irritated him that he had made up his mind to pull his weapon at the first sight of the dead, even if the deceased was his worst and oldest enemy. Presently the whole of the box-cover was off, and the teamster, clearing away the packing revealed to the astonished group the top of something which puzzled all alike.

"Boys," said he, "this is a pianner."

A general shout of laughter went up, and the man who had been so anxious to enforce respect for the dead muttered something about feeling dry, and the keeper of the nearest bar was several ounces better off by the time the boys had given the joke all the attention it called for.

Had a dozen dead men been in the box their presence in the camp could not have occasioned half the excitement that the arrival of that lonely piano caused. But the next morning it was known that the instrument was to grace a hurdy-gurdy saloon, owned by Tom Goskin, the leading gambler in the place. It took nearly a week to get this wonder on its legs, and the owner was the proudest individual in the State. It rose gradually from a recumbent to an upright position amid a confusion of tongues, after the manner of the Tower of Babel.

Of course everybody knew just how such an instrument should be put up. One knew where the "off hind leg" should go, and another was posted on the "front piece."

Scores of men came to the place every day to assist.

"I'll put the bones in good order."

"If you want the wires tuned up, I'm the boy."

"I've got music to feed it for a month."

Another brought a pair of blankets for a cover, and all took the liveliest interest in it. It was at last in a condition for business.

"It's been showin' its teeth all the week. We'd like to have it spit out something."

Alas! there wasn't a man to be found who could play upon the instrument. Goskin began to realise that he had a losing speculation on his hands. He had a fiddler, and a Mexican who thrummed a guitar. A pianist would have made his orchestra complete. One day a three-card monte player told a friend confidentially that he could "knock any amount of music out of the piano, if he only had it alone a few hours to get his hand in." This report spread about the camp, but on being questioned he vowed that he didn't know a note of music. It was noted, however, as a suspicious circumstance, that he often hung about the instrument and looked upon it longingly, like a hungry man gloating over a beef-steak in a restaurant window. There was no doubt but that this man had music in his soul, perhaps in his finger-ends, but did not dare to make trial of his strength after the rules of harmony had suffered so many years of neglect. So the fiddler kept on with his jigs, and the greasy Mexican pawed his discordant guitar, but no man had the nerve to touch the piano. There were doubtless scores of men in the camp who would have given ten ounces of gold-dust to have been half-an-hour alone with it, but every man's nerve shrank from the jeers which the crowd would shower upon him should his first attempt prove a failure. It got to be generally understood that the hand which first essayed to draw music from the keys must not slouch its work.

It was Christmas eve, and Goskin, according to his custom, had decorated his gambling-hell with sprigs of mountain cedar and a shrub whose crimson berries did not seem a bad imitation of English holly. The piano was covered with evergreens, and all that was wanting to completely fill the cup of Goskin's contentment was a man to play the instrument.

"Christmas night, and no piano-pounder," he said. "This is a nice country for a Christian to live in."

Getting a piece of paper, he scrawled the words:

$20 REWARD
TO A COMPETENT PIANO PLAYER

This he stuck up on the music-rack, and, though the inscription glared at the frequenters of the room until midnight, it failed to draw any musician from his shell.

So the merrymaking went on; the hilarity grew apace. Men danced and sang to the music of the squeaky fiddle and worn-out guitar as the jolly crowd within tried to drown the howling of the storm without. Suddenly they became aware of the presence of a white-haired man, crouching near the fireplace. His garments—such as were left—were wet with melting snow, and he had a half-starved, half-crazed expression. He held his thin, trembling hands toward the fire, and the light of the blazing wood made them almost transparent. He looked about him once in a while as if in search

## THE FIRST PIANO IN CAMP

of something, and his presence cast such a chill over the place that gradually the sound of the revelry was hushed, and it seemed that this waif of the storm had brought in with it all the gloom and coldness of the warring elements. Goskin, mixing up a cup of hot egg-nog, advanced and remarked cheerily:

"Here, stranger, brace up! This is the real stuff."

The man drained the cup, smacked his lips, and seemed more at home.

"Been prospecting, eh? Out in the mountains—caught in the storm? Lively night, this!"

"Pretty bad," said the man.

"Must feel pretty dry?"

The man looked at his streaming clothes and laughed, as if Goskin's remark was a sarcasm.

"How long out?"

"Four days."

"Hungry?"

The man rose up, and, walking over to the lunch-counter, fell to work upon some roast bear, devouring it like any wild animal would have done. As meat and drink and warmth began to permeate the stranger, he seemed to expand and lighten up. His features lost their pallor, and he grew more and more content with the idea that he was not in the grave. As he underwent these changes, the people about him got merrier and happier, and threw off the temporary feeling of depression which he had laid upon them.

"Do you always have your place decorated like this?" he finally asked of Goskin.

"This is Christmas Eve," was the reply.

The stranger was startled.

"December 24th, sure enough."

"That's the way I put it up, pard."

"When I was in England I always kept Christmas. But I had forgotten that this was the night. I've been wandering about in the mountains until I've lost track of the feasts of the Church."

Presently his eye fell upon the piano.

"Where's the player?" he asked.

"Never had any," said Goskin, blushing at the expression.

"I used to play when I was young."

Goskin almost fainted at the admission.

"Stranger, do tackle it, and give us a tune! Nary man in this camp ever had the nerve to wrestle with that music-box." His pulse beat faster, for he feared that the man would refuse.

"I'll do the best I can," he said.

There was no stool, but seizing a candle-box, he drew it up and seated himself before the instrument. It only required a few seconds for a hush to come over the room.

"That old coon is going to give the thing a rattle."

The sight of a man at the piano was something so unusual that even the faro-dealer, who was about to take in a fifty-dollar bet on the tray, paused and did not reach for the money. Men stopped drinking, with the glasses at their lips. Conversation appeared to have been struck with a sort of paralysis, and cards were no longer shuffled.

The old man brushed back his long white locks, looked up to the ceiling, half closed his eyes, and in a mystic sort of reverie passed his fingers over the keys. He touched but a single note, yet the sound thrilled the room. It was the key to his improvisation, and as he wove his chords together the music laid its spell upon every ear and heart. He felt his way along the keys like a man treading uncertain paths, but he gained confidence as he progressed, and presently bent to his work like a master. The instrument was not in exact tune, but the ears of his audience did not detect anything radically wrong. They heard a succession of grand chords, a suggestion of paradise, melodies here and there, and it was enough.

"See him counter with his left!" said an old rough enraptured.

"He calls the turn every time on the upper end of the board," responded a man with a stack of chips in his hand.

The player wandered off into the old ballads they had heard at home. All the sad and melancholy and touching songs, that came up like dreams of childhood, this unknown player drew from the keys. His hands kneaded their hearts like dough and squeezed out tears as from a wet sponge.

As the strains flowed one upon the other, the listeners saw their homes of the long-ago reared again; they were playing once more where the apple-blossoms sank through the soft air to join the violets on the green turf of the old New England States; they saw the glories of the Wisconsin maples and the haze of the Indian summer blending their hues together; they recalled the heather of Scottish hills, the white cliffs of Britain, and heard the sullen roar of the sea, as it beat upon their memories, vaguely. Then came all the old Christmas carols, such as they had sung in church thirty years before; the subtle music that brings up the glimmer of wax tapers, the solemn shrines, the evergreen, holly, mistletoe, and surpliced choirs. Then the remorseless performer planted his final stab in every heart with "Home, Sweet Home."

When the player ceased the crowd slunk away from him. There was no more revelry and devilment left in his audience. Each man wanted to sneak off to his cabin and write the old folks a letter. The day was breaking as the last man left the place, and the player, with his head on the piano, fell asleep.

"I say, pard," said Goskin, "don't you want a little rest?"

"I feel tired," the old man said. "Perhaps you'll let me rest here for the matter of a day or so."

He walked behind the bar, where some old blankets were lying, and stretched himself upon them.

"I feel pretty sick. I guess I won't last long. I've got a brother down in the ravine—his name's Driscoll. He don't know I'm here. Can you get him before morning? I'd like to see his face once before I die."

Goskin started up at the mention of the name. He knew Driscoll well.

"He your brother? I'll have him here in half an hour."

As Goskin dashed out into the storm the musician pressed his hand to his side and groaned. Goskin heard the word "Hurry!" and sped down the ravine to Driscoll's cabin. It was quite light in the room when the two men returned. Driscoll was pale as death.

"My God! I hope he's alive! I wronged him when we lived in England twenty years ago."

They saw the old man had drawn the blankets over his face. The two stood a moment, awed by the thought that he might be dead. Goskin lifted the blanket and pulled it down, astonished. There was no one there!

"Gone!" cried Driscoll wildly.

"Gone!" echoed Goskin, pulling out his cash-drawer. "Ten thousand dollars in the sack, and the Lord knows how much loose change in the drawer!"

The next day the boys got out, followed a horse's track through the snow, and lost them in the trail leading toward Pioche.

There was a man missing from the camp. It was the three-card monte man, who used to deny point-blank that he could play the scale. One day they found a wig of white hair, and called to mind when the "stranger" had pushed those locks back when he looked toward the ceiling for inspiration on the night of December 24, 1858.

# REBECCA HARDING DAVIS
1831–1910

## BALACCHI BROTHERS

"THERE'S a man, now, that has been famous in his time," said Davidge as we passed the mill, glancing in at the sunny gap in the side of the building.

I paused incredulously: Phil's lion so often turned out to be Snug the joiner. Phil was my chum at college, and in inviting me home to spend the vacation with him I thought he had fancied the resources of his village larger than they proved. In the two days since we came we had examined the old doctor's cabinet, listened superciliously to a debate in the literary club upon the Evils of the Stage, and passed two solid afternoons in the circle about the stove in the drug-shop, where the squire and the Methodist parson, and even the mild, white-cravated young rector of St. Mark's, were wont to sharpen their wits by friction. What more was left? I was positive that I knew the mental gauge of every man in the village.

A little earlier or later in life a gun or fishing-rod would have satisfied me. The sleepy, sunny little market-town was shut in by the bronzed autumn meadows, that sent their long groping fingers of grass or parti-coloured weeds drowsily up into the very streets: there were ranges of hills and heavy stretches of oak and beech woods, too, through which crept glittering creeks full of trout. But I was just at that age when the soul disdains all aimless pleasures: my game was Man. I was busy in philosophically testing, weighing, labelling human nature.

"Famous, eh?" I said, looking after the pursy figure of the miller, in his floury canvas roundabout and corduroy trousers, trotting up and down among the bags.

"That is one of the Balacchi Brothers," Phil answered as we walked on. "You've heard of them when you were a boy?"

I had heard of them. The great acrobats were as noted in their line of art as Ellsler and Jenny Lind in theirs. But acrobats and danseuses had been alike brilliant, wicked impossibilities to my youth, for I had been reared a Covenanter of the Covenanters. In spite of the doubting philosophies with which I had clothed myself at college, that old Presbyterian training clung to me in everyday life close as my skin.

After that day I loitered about the mill, watching this man whose life had been spent in one godless theatre after another, very much as the Florentine peasants looked after Dante when they knew he had come back from hell. I was on the look-out for the taint, the abnormal signs, of vice. It was about that time that I was fevered with the missionary enthusiasm, and in Polynesia, where I meant to go (but where I never did go), I declared to Phil daily that I should find in every cannibal the half-effaced image of God, only waiting to be quickened into grace and virtue. That was quite conceivable. But that a flashy, God-defying actor could be the same man at heart as this fat, good-tempered, gossiping miller, who jogged to the butcher's every morning for his wife, a basket on one arm and a baby on the other, was not conceivable. He was a close dealer at the butcher's, too, though dribbling gossip there as everywhere; a regular attendant at St. Mark's, with his sandy-headed flock about him, among whom he slept comfortably enough, it is true, but with as pious dispositions as the rest of us.

I remember how I watched this man, week in and week out. It was a trivial matter, but it irritated me unendurably to find that this circus-rider had human blood precisely like my own: it outraged my early religion.

We talk a great deal of the rose-coloured illusions in which youth wraps the world, and the agony it suffers as they are stripped from its bare, hard face. But the fact is, that youth (aside from its narrow, passionate friendships) is usually apt to be acrid and watery and sour in its judgment and creeds—it has the quality of any other unripe fruit: it is middle age that is just and tolerant, that has found room enough in the world for itself and all human flies to buzz out their lives good-humouredly together. It is youth who can see a tangible devil at work in every party or sect opposed to its own, whose enemy is always a villain, and who finds treachery and falsehood in the friend who is occasionally bored or indifferent: it is middle age that has discovered the reasonable sweet *juste milieu* of human nature—who knows few saints perhaps, but is apt to find its friend and grocer and shoemaker agreeable and honest fellows. It is these vehement illusions, these inherited bigotries and prejudices, that tear and cripple a young man as they are taken from him one by one. He creeps out of them as a crab from the shell that has grown too small for him, but he thinks he has left his identity behind him.

It was such a reason as this that made me follow the miller assiduously, and cultivate a quasi intimacy with him, in the course of which I picked the following story from him. It was told at divers times, and with many interruptions and questions from me. But for obvious reasons I have made it continuous. It had its meaning to me, coarse and common though it was—the same which Christ taught in the divine beauty of His parables. Whether that meaning might not be found in the history of every human life, if we had eyes to read it, is matter for question.

Balacchi Brothers? And you've heard of them, eh? Well, well! (with a pleased nod, rubbing his hands on his knees.) Yes, sir. Fifteen years ago they were known as The Admirable Crichtons of the Ring. It was George who got up that name: I did not see the force of it. But no name could claim too much for us. Why, I could show you notices in the newspapers that—— I used to clip them out and stuff my pocket-book with them as we went along, but after I quit the business I pasted them in an old ledger, and I often now read them of nights. No doubt I lost a good many too.

Yes, sir: I was one of Balacchi Brothers. My name *is* Zack Loper. And it was then, of course.

You think we would have plenty of adventures? Well, no—not a great many. There's a good deal of monotony in the business. Towns seem always pretty much alike to me. And there was such a deal of rehearsing to be done by day and at night. I looked at nothing but the rope and George: the audience was nothing but a packed flat surface of upturned, staring eyes and half-open mouths. It was an odd sight, yes, when you come to think of it. I never was one for adventures. I was mostly set upon shaving close through the week, so that when Saturday night came I'd have something to lay by: I had this mill in my mind, you see. I was married, and had my wife and a baby that I'd never seen waiting for me at home. I was brought up to milling, but the trapeze paid better. I took to it naturally, as one might say.

But George!—he had adventures every week. And as for acquaintances! Why, before we'd be in a town two days he'd be hail-fellow-well-met with half the people in it. That fellow could scent a dance or a joke half-a-mile off. You never see such wide-awake men nowadays. People seem to me half dead or asleep when I think of him.

Oh, I thought you knew. My partner Balacchi. It was Balacchi on the bills: the actors called him Signor, and people like the manager, South, and we, who knew him well, George. I asked him his real name once or twice, but he joked it off. " How many names must a man be saddled with? " he said. I don't know it to this day, nor who he had been. They hinted there was something queer about his story, but I'll go my bail it was a clean one, whatever it was.

You never heard how " Balacchi Brothers " broke up? That was as near to an adventure as I ever had. Come over to this bench and I'll tell it to you. You don't dislike the dust of the mill? The sun's pleasanter on this side.

It was early in August of '56 when George and I came to an old town on the Ohio, half city, half village, to play an engagement. We were under contract with South then, who provided the rest of the troupe, three or four posture-girls, Stradi, the pianist, and a Madame Somebody, who gave readings and sang. "Concert" was the heading in large caps on the Bills, " Balacchi Brothers will give their aesthetic *tableaux vivants* in the interludes," in agate below.

"I've got to cover you fellows over with respectability here," South said. " Rope-dancing won't go down with these aristocratic church-goers."

I remember how George was irritated. "When I was my own agent," he said, " I only went to the cities. Educated people can appreciate what we do, but in these country towns we rank with circus-riders."

George had some queer notions about his business. He followed it for sheer love of it, as I did for money. I've seen all the great athletes since, but I never saw one with his wonderful skill and strength, and with the grace of a woman too, or a deer. Now that takes hard, steady work, but he never flinched from it as I did; and when night came, and the people and lights, and I thought of nothing but to get through, I used to think he had the pride of a thousand women in every one of his muscles and nerves: a little applause would fill him with a mad kind of fury of delight and triumph. South had a story that Geroge belonged to some old Knickerbocker family, and had run off from home years ago. I don't know. There was that wild restless blood in him that no home could have kept him.

We were to stay so long in this town that I found rooms for us with an old couple named Peters, who had but lately moved in from the country, and had half-a-dozen carpenters and masons boarding with them. It was cheaper than the hotel, and George preferred that kind of people to educated men, which made me doubt that story of his having been a gentleman. The old woman Peters was uneasy about taking us, and spoke out quite freely about it when we called, not knowing that George and I were Balacchi Brothers ourselves.

"The house has been respectable so far, gentlemen," she said. " I don't know what about taking in them half-naked, drunken play-actors. What do you say, Susy ? " to her grand-daughter.

"Wait till you see them, grandmother," the girl said gently. " I should think that men whose lives depended every night on their steady eyes and nerves would not dare to touch liquor."

"You are quite right—nor even tobacco," said George. It was such a prompt, sensible thing for the little girl to say that he looked at her attentively a minute, and then went up to the old lady, smiling : " We don't look like drinking men, do we, madam ? "

"No, no, sir. I did not know that you were the I-talians." She was quite flustered and frightened, and said cordially enough how glad she was to have us both. But it was George she shook hands with. There was something clean and strong and inspiring about that man that made most women friendly to him on sight.

Why, in two days you'd have thought he'd never had another home than the Peter's. He helped the old man milk, and had tinkered up the broken kitchen-table, and put in half-a-dozen window-panes, and was intimate with all the boarders; could give the masons the prices of job-work at the East, and put Stoll, the carpenter, on the idea of contract-houses, out of which he afterward made a fortune. It was nothing but jokes and fun and shouts of laughter when he was in the house: even the old man brightened up and told some capital stories. But from the first I noticed that George's eye followed Susy watchfully wherever she went, though he was as distant and respectful with her as he was with most women. He had a curious kind of respect for women, George had. Even the Slingsbys, that all the men in the theatre joked with, he used to pass by as though they were logs leaning against the wall. They were the posture-girls, and anything worse besides the name *I* never saw.

There was a thing happened once on that point which I often thought might have given me a clue to his history if I'd followed it up. We were playing in one of the best theatres in New York (they brought us into some opera), and the boxes were filled with fine ladies beautifully dressed, or, I might say, half dressed.

George was in one of the wings. "It's a pretty sight," I said to him.

"It's a shameful sight!" he said with an oath. "The Slingsbys do it for their living, but these women——"

I said they were ladies, and ought to be treated with respect. I was amazed at the heat he was in.

"I had a sister, Zack, and there's where I learned what a woman should be."

"I never heard of your sister, George," said I. I knew he would not have spoken of her but for the heat he was in.

"No. I'm as dead to her, being what I am, as if I were six feet under ground."

I turned and looked at him, and when I saw his face I said no more, and I never spoke of it again. It was something neither I nor any other man had any business with.

So when I saw how he was touched by Susy and drawn toward her, it raised her in my opinion, though I'd seen myself how pretty and sensible a little body she was. But I was sorry, for I knew 'twan't no use. The Peters were Methodists, and Susy more strict than any of them; and I saw she looked on the theatre as the gate of hell, and George and me swinging over it.

I don't think, though, that George saw how strong her feeling about it was, for after we'd been there a week or two he began to ask her to go and see us perform, if only for once. I believe he thought the girl would come to love him if she saw him at his best. I don't wonder at it, sir. I've seen those pictures and statues they've made of the old gods, and I reckon they put in them the best they thought a man could be; but I never knew what real manhood was until I saw my partner when he stood quiet on the stage waiting the signal to begin, the light full on his keen blue eyes, the gold-worked velvet tunic and his perfect figure.

He looked more like other men in his ordinary clothing. George liked a bit of flash, too, in his dress—a red necktie or gold chain stretched over his waistcoat.

Susy refused at first, steadily. At last, however, came our final night, when George was to produce his great leaping feat, never yet performed in public. We had been practising it for months, and South judged it best to try it first before a small, quiet audience, for the risk was horrible. Whether because it was to be the last night, and her kind heart disliked to hurt him by refusal, or whether she loved him better than either she or he knew, I could not tell, but I saw she was strongly tempted to go. She was an innocent little thing, and not used to hide what she felt. Her eyes were red that morning, as though she had been crying all the night. Perhaps, because I was a married man, and quieter than George, she acted more freely with me than him.

"I wish I knew what to do," she said, looking up to me with her eyes full of tears. There was nobody in the room but her grandmother.

"I couldn't advise you, Miss Susy," says I. "Your church discipline goes against our trade, I know."

"I know what's right myself: I don't need church discipline to teach me," she said sharply.

"I think I'd go, Susy," said her grandmother. "It is a concert, after all: it's not a play."

"The name don't alter it."

Seeing the temper she was in, I thought it best to say no more, but the old lady added, "It's Mr. George's last night. Dear, dear! how I'll miss him!"

Susy turned quickly to the window. "Why does he follow such godless ways then?" she cried. She stood still a good while, and when she turned about her pale little face made my heart ache. "I'll take home Mrs. Tyson's dress now, grandmother," she said, and went out of the room. I forgot to tell you Susy was a seamstress. Well, the bundle was large, and I offered to carry it for her, as the time for rehearsal did not come till noon. She crept alongside of me without a word, looking weak and done-out: she was always so busy and bright, it was the more noticeable. The house where the dress was to go was one of the largest in the town. The servant showed us into a back parlour, and took the dress up to her mistress. I looked around me a good deal, for I'd never been in such a house before; but very soon I caught sight of a lady who made me forget carpets and pictures. I only saw her in the mirror, for she was standing by the fireplace in the front room. The door was open between. It wasn't that she was especially pretty, but in her white morning-dress, with the lace about her throat and her hair drawn back from her face, I thought she was the delicatest, softest, finest thing of man or woman kind I ever saw.

"Look there, Susy! look there!" I whispered.

"It is a Mrs. Lloyd from New York. She is here on a visit. That is her husband"; and then she went down into her own gloomy thoughts again.

The husband was a grave, middle-aged man. He had had his paper up before his face, so that I had not seen him before.

"You will go for the tickets, then, Edward?" she said.

"If you make a point of it, yes," in an annoyed tone. "But I don't know why you make a point of it. The musical part of the performance is beneath contempt, I understand, and the real attraction is the exhibition of these mountebanks of trapezists, which will be simply disgusting to you. You would not encourage such people at home: why would you do it here?"

"They are not necessarily wicked." I noticed there was a curious unsteadiness in her voice, as though she was hurt and agitated. I thought perhaps she knew I was there.

"There is very little hope of any redeeming qualities in men who make a trade of twisting their bodies like apes," he said. "Contortionists and ballet-dancers and clowns and harlequins——" he rattled all the names over with a good deal of uncalled-for sharpness, I thought, calling them "dissolute and degraded, the very offal of humanity." I could not understand his heat until he added, "I never could comprehend your interest and sympathy for that especial class, Ellinor."

"No, you could not, Edward," she said quietly. "But I have it. I have never seen an exhibition of the kind. But I want to see this to-night, if you will gratify me. I have no reason," she added when he looked at her curiously. "The desire is unaccountable to myself."

The straightforward look of her blue eyes as she met his seemed strangely familiar and friendly to me.

At that moment Susy stood up to go. Her cheeks were burning and her eyes sparkling. "Dissolute and degraded!" she said again and again when we were outside. But I took no notice.

As we reached the house she stopped me when I turned off to go to rehearsal. "You'll get seats for grandmother and me, Mr. Balacchi?" she said.

"You're going, then, Susy?"

"Yes, I'm going."

Now the house in which we performed was a queer structure. A stock company, thinking there was a field for a theatre in the town, had taken a four-storey building, gutted the interior, and fitted it up with tiers of seats and scenery. The stock company was starved out, however, and left the town, and the theatre was used as a gymnasium, a concert-room or a church by turns. Its peculiarity was, that it was both exceedingly lofty and narrow, which suited our purpose exactly.

It was packed that night from dome to pit. George and I had rehearsed our new act both morning and afternoon, South watching us without intermission. South was terribly nervous and anxious, half disposed, at the last minute, to forbid it, although it had been announced on the bills for a week. But a feat which is successful in an empty house, with but one spectator, when your nerves are quiet and blood cool, is a different thing before an excited, terrified, noisy audience, your whole body at fever heat. However, George was cool as a cucumber, indeed almost indifferent about the act, but in a mad boyish glee all day about everything else. I suppose the reason was that Susy was going.

South had lighted the house brilliantly and brought in a band. And all classes of people poured into the theatre until it could hold no more. I saw Mrs. Peters in one of the side-seats, with Susy's blushing, frightened little face beside her. George, standing back among the scenes, saw her too: I think, indeed, it was all he did see.

There were the usual readings from Shakespeare at first.

While Madame was on, South came to us. "Boys," said he, "let this matter go over a few weeks. A little more practice will do you no harm. You can substitute some other trick, and these people will be none the wiser."

George shrugged his shoulders impatiently: "Nonsense! When did you grow so chicken-hearted, South? It is I who have to run the risk, I fancy."

I suppose South's uneasiness had infected me. "I am quite willing to put it off," I said. I had felt gloomy and superstitious all day. But I never ventured to oppose George more decidedly than that.

He only laughed by way of reply, and went off to dress. South looked after him, I remember, saying what a magnificently built fellow he was. If we could only have seen the end of that night's work!

As I went to my dressing-room I saw Mrs. Lloyd and her husband in one of the stage-boxes, with one or two other ladies and gentlemen. She was plainly and darkly dressed, but to my mind she looked like a princess among them all. I could not but wonder what interest she could have in such a rough set as we, although her husband, I confess, did judge us hardly.

After the readings came the concert part of the performance, and then what South chose to call the Moving Tableaux, which was really nothing in the world but ballet-dancing. George and I were left to crown the whole. I had some ordinary trapeze-work to do at first, but George was reserved for the new feat in order that his nerves might be perfectly unshaken. When I went out alone and bowed to the audience, I observed that Mrs. Lloyd was leaning eagerly forward, but at the first glance at my face she sank back with a look of relief, and turned away, that she might not see my exploits. It nettled me a little, I think, yet they were worth watching.

Well I finished, and then there was a song to give me time to cool. I went to the side-scenes, where I could be alone for that five minutes. I had no risk to run in the grand feat, you see, but I had George's life in my hands. I haven't told you yet—have I?—what it was he proposed to do.

A rope was suspended from the centre of the dome, the lower end of which I held, standing in the highest gallery opposite the stage. Above the stage hung the trapeze on which George and the two posture-girls were to be. At a certain signal I was to let the rope go, and George, springing from the trapeze across the full width of the dome, was to catch it in mid-air, a hundred feet above the heads of the people. You understand? The mistake of an instant of time on either his part or mine, and death was almost certain. The plan we had thought surest was for South to give the word, and then that both should count—One, Two, Three! At Three the rope fell and he leaped. We had practised so often that we thought we counted as one man.

When the song was over the men hung the rope and the trapeze. Jenny and Lou Slingsby swung themselves up to it, turned a few somersaults, and then were quiet. They were only meant to give effect to the scene in their gauzy dresses and spangles. Then South came forward and told the audience what we meant to do. It was a feat, he said, which had never been produced before in any theatre, and in which failure was death. No one but that most daring of all acrobats, Balacchi, would attempt it. Now, I knew South so well that I saw under all his confident, bragging tone he was more anxious and doubtful than he had ever been. He hesitated a moment, and then requested that after we took our places the audience should preserve absolute silence, and refrain from even the slightest movements until the feat was over. The merest trifle might distract the attention of the performers and render their eyes and hold unsteady, he said. He left the stage, and the music began.

I went round to take my place in the gallery. George had not yet left his room. As I passed I tapped at the door and called, " Good luck, old fellow ! "

" That's certain now, Zack," he answered with a joyous laugh. He was so exultant, you see, that Susy had come.

But the shadow of death seemed to have crept over me. When I took my stand in the lofty gallery, and looked down at the brilliant lights and the great mass of people, who followed my every motion as one man, and the two glittering, half-naked girls swinging in the distance, and heard the music rolling up thunders of sound, it was all ghastly and horrible to me, sir. Some men have such presentiments, they say : I never had before or since. South remained on the stage perfectly motionless, in order, I think, to maintain his control over the audience.

The trumpets sounded a call, and in the middle of a burst of triumphant music George came on the stage. There was a deafening outbreak of applause, and then a dead silence, but I think every man and woman felt a thrill of admiration of the noble figure. Poor George ! the new, tight-fitting dress of purple velvet that he had bought for this night set off his white skin, and his fine head was bare, with no covering but the short curls that Susy liked.

It was for Susy ! He gave one quick glance up at her, and a bright, boyish smile, as if telling her not to be afraid, which all the audience understood, and answered by an ivoluntary, long-drawn breath. I looked at Susy. The girl's colourless face was turned to George, and her hands were clasped as though she saw him already dead before her ; but she could be trusted I saw. *She* would utter no sound. I had only time to glance at her, and then turned to my work. George and I dared not take our eyes from each other.

There was a single bugle note, and then George swung himself up to the trapeze. The silence was like death as he steadied himself and slowly turned so as to front me. As he turned he faced the stage-box for the first time. He had reached the level of the posture-girls, who fluttered on either side, and stood on the swaying rod poised on one foot, his arms folded, when in the breathless stillness there came a sudden cry and the words, " Oh, Charley ! Charley ! "

Even at the distance where I stood I saw George start and a shiver pass over his body. He looked wildly about him.

" To me ! to me ! " I shouted.

He fixed his eye on mine and steadied himself. There was a terrible silent excitement in the people, in the very air.

There was the mistake. We should have stopped then, shaken as he was, but South, bewildered and terrified, lost control of himself : he gave the word.

I held the rope loose—held George with my eyes—One !

I saw his lips move : he was counting with me.

Two !

His eye wandered, turned to the stage-box.

Three!

Like a flash I saw the white upturned faces below me, the posture-girls' gestures of horror, the dark springing figure through the air, that wavered—and fell a shapeless mass on the floor.

There was a moment of deathlike silence, and then a wild outcry—women fainting, men cursing and crying out in that senseless, helpless way they have when there is sudden danger. By the time I had reached the floor they had straightened out his shattered limbs, and two or three doctors were fighting their way through the great crowd that was surging about him.

Well, sir, at that minute what did I hear but George's voice above all the rest, choked and hollow as it was, like a man calling out of the grave: "The women! Good God! don't you see the women?" he gasped.

Looking up then, I saw those miserable Slingsbys hanging on to the trapeze for life. What with the scare and shock, they'd lost what little sense they had, and there they hung helpless as limp rags high over our heads.

"Damn the Slingsbys!" said I. God forgive me! But I saw this battered wreck at my feet that had been George. Nobody seemed to have any mind left. Even South stared stupidly up at them and then back at George. The doctors were making ready to lift him, and half of the crowd were gaping in horror, and the rest yelling for ladders or ropes, and scrambling over each other, and there hung the poor flimsy wretches, their eyes starting out of their heads from horror, and their lean fingers losing their hold every minute. But, sir—I couldn't help it—I turned from them to watch George as the doctors lifted him.

"It's hardly worth while," whispered one.

But they raised him and, sir—the body went one way and the legs another.

I thought he was dead. I couldn't see that he breathed, when he opened his eyes and looked up for the slingsbys. "Put me down," he said, and the doctors obeyed him. There was that in his voice that they had to obey him, though it wasn't but a whisper.

"Ladders are of no use," he said. "Loper!"

"Yes, George."

"You can swing yourself up. Do it."

I went. I remember the queer stunned feeling I had: my joints moved like a machine.

When I reached the trapeze, he said, as cool as if he was calling the figures for a Virginia reel, "Support them, you—Loper. Now lower the trapeze, men—carefully!"

It was the only way their lives could be saved, and he was the only man to see it. He watched us until the girls touched the floor more dead than alive, and then his head fell back and the life seemed to go suddenly out of him like the flame out of a candle, leaving only the dead wick.

As they were carrying him out I noticed for the first time that a woman was holding his hand. It was that frail little wisp of a Susy, that used to blush and tremble if you spoke to her suddenly, and here she was quite quiet and steady in the midst of this great crowd.

"His sister, I suppose?" one of the doctors said to her.

"No, sir. If he lives I will be his wife." The old gentleman was very respectful to her after that I noticed.

Now the rest of my story is very muddled, you'll say, and confused. But the truth is, I don't understand it myself. I ran on ahead to Mrs. Peter's to prepare his bed for him, but they did not bring him to Peter's. After I waited an hour or two, I found George had been taken to the principal hotel in the place, and a bedroom and every comfort that money could buy were there for him. Susy came home sobbing late in the night, but she told me nothing, except that those who had a right to have charge of him had taken him. I found afterward the poor girl was driven from the door of his room, where she was waiting like a faithful dog. I went myself but I fared no better. What with surgeons and professional nurses, and the gentlemen that crowded about with their solemn looks of authority, I dared not ask to see him. Yet I believe still George would rather have had old Loper by him in his extremity than any of them. Once, when the door was opened, I thought I saw Mrs. Lloyd stooping over the bed between the lace curtains, and just then her husband came out talking to one of the surgeons.

He said: "It is certain there were here the finest elements of manhood. And I will do my part to rescue him from the abyss into which he has fallen."

"Will you tell me how George is, sir?" I asked, pushing up. "Balacchi? My partner?"

Mr. Lloyd turned away directly, but the surgeon told me civilly enough that if George's life could be saved, it must be with the loss of one or perhaps both of his legs.

"He'll never mount a trapeze again, then," I said, and I suppose I groaned; for to think of George helpless——

"God forbid!" cried Mr. Lloyd sharply. "Now look here my good man: you can be of no possible use to Mr.—Balacchi, as you call him. He is in the hands of his own people, and he will feel, as they do, that the kindest thing you can do is to let him alone."

There was nothing to be done after that but to touch my hat and go out, but as I went I heard him talking of "inexplicable madness and years of wasted opportunities."

Well, sir, I never went again: the words hurt like the cut of a whip, though 'twan't George that spoke them. But I quit business and hung around the town till I heard he was going to live, and I broke up my contract with South. I never went on a trapeze again. I felt as if the infernal thing was always dripping with his blood after that day. Anyhow, all the heart went out of the business for me with George. So I came back here and settled down to the milling, and by degrees I learned to think of George as a rich and fortunate man.

I've nearly done now—only a word or two more. About six years afterward there was a circus came to town, and I took the wife and children and went. I always did when I had the chance. It was the old Adam in me yet, likely.

Well, sir, among the attractions of the circus was the great and unrivalled Hercules, who could play with cannon-balls as other men would with dice. I don't know what made me restless and excited when I read about this man. It seemed as though the old spirit was coming back to me again. I could hardly keep still when the time drew near for him to appear. I don't know what I expected. But when he came out from behind the curtain I shouted out like a mad man, " Balacchi! George! George!"

He stopped short, looked about, and catching sight of me tossed up his cap with his old boyish shout : then he remembered himself, and went on with his performance.

He was lame—yes, in one leg. The other was gone altogether. He walked on crutches. Whether the strength had gone into his chest and arms, I don't know ; but there he stood tossing about the cannon-balls as I might marbles. So full of hearty good-humour too, joking with his audience, and so delighted when they gave him a round of applause.

After the performance I hurried around the tent, and you may be sure there was rejoicing that made the manager and other fellows laugh.

George haled me off with him down the street. He cleared the ground with that crutch and wooden leg like a steam-engine. "Come! come along!" he cried : "I've something to show you, Loper."

He took me to a quiet boarding-house, and there, in a cosy room was Susy with a four-year-old girl.

"We were married as soon as I could hobble about," he said, "and she goes with me and makes a home wherever I am."

Susy nodded and blushed and laughed. "Baby and I," she said. "Do you see Baby? She has her father's eyes, do you see?"

"She *is* her mother, Loper," said George—"just as innocent and pure and foolish—just as sure of the Father in heaven taking care of her. They've made a different man of me in some ways—a different man," bending his head reverently.

After a while I began, "You did not stay with—— ?"

But Balacchi frowned. "I knew where *I* belonged," he said.

Well, he's young yet. He's the best Hercules in the profession, and has laid up a snug sum. Why don't he invest it and retire? I doubt if he'll ever do that, sir. He may do it, but I doubt it. He can't change his blood, and there's that in Balacchi that makes me suspect he will die with the velvet and gilt on and in the height of good-humour and fun with his audience.

# FRANK R. STOCKTON
1834-1902

## MR. TOLMAN

MR. TOLMAN was a gentleman whose apparent age was of a varying character. At times, when deep in thought on business matters or other affairs, one might have thought him fifty-five or fifty-seven, or even sixty. Ordinarily, however, when things were running along in a satisfactory and commonplace way, he appeared to be about fifty years old, while upon some extraordinary occasions, when the world assumed an unusually attractive aspect, his age seemed to run down to forty-five or less.

He was the head of a business firm; in fact he was the only member of it. The firm was known as Pusey and Co.; but Pusey had long been dead, and the " Co.," of which Mr. Tolman had been a member, was dissolved. Our elderly hero having bought out the business, firm name and all, for many years had carried it on with success and profit. His counting-house was a small and quiet place, but a great deal of money had been made in it. Mr. Tolman was rich—very rich indeed.

And yet as he sat in his counting-room one winter evening he looked his oldest. He had on his hat and his overcoat, his gloves and his fur collar. Every one else in the establishment had gone home; and he, with the keys in his hand, was ready to lock up and leave also. He often stayed later than any one else, and left the keys with Mr. Canterfield, the head clerk, as he passed his house on his way home.

Mr. Tolman seemed in no hurry to go. He simply sat and thought, and increased his apparent age. The truth was he did not want to go home. He was tired of going home. This was not because his home was not a pleasant one. No single gentleman in the city had a handsomer or more comfortable suite of rooms. It was not because he felt lonely, or regretted that a wife and children did not brighten and enliven his home. He was perfectly satisfied to be a bachelor. The conditions suited him exactly. But, in spite of all this, he was tired of going home.

" I wish," said Mr. Tolman to himself, " that I could feel some interest in going home "; and then he rose and took a turn or two up and down the room; but as that did not seem to give him any more interest in the matter, he sat down again. " I wish it were necessary for me to go home," said he ; " but it isn't " ; and then he fell again to thinking. " What I need," he said after a while, " is to depend more upon myself—to feel that I am necessary to myself. Just now I'm not. I'll stop going home—at least in this way. Where's the sense in envying other men when I can have all that they have just as well as not ? And I'll have it too," said Mr. Tolman as he went out and locked the doors. Once in the streets, and walking rapidly, his ideas shaped themselves easily and readily into a plan which, by the time he reached the house of his head clerk, was quite matured. Mr. Canterfield was just going down to dinner as his employer rang the bell, so he opened the door himself. " I will detain you but a minute or two." said Mr. Tolman, handing the keys to Mr. Canterfield. " Shall we step into the parlour ? "

When his employer had gone, and Mr. Canterfield had joined his family at the dinner-table, his wife immediately asked him what Mr. Tolman wanted.

" Only to say that he is going away to-morrow, and that I am to attend to the business, and send his personal letters to——," naming a city not a hundred miles away.

" How long is he going to stay ? "

" He didn't say," answered Mr. Canterfield.

" I'll tell you what he ought to do," said the lady. " He ought to make you a partner in the firm, and then he could go away and stay as long as he pleased."

" He can do that now," returned her husband. " He has made a good many trips since I have been with him, and things have gone on very much in the same way as when he was here. He knows that."

" But still you'd like to be a partner ? "

" Oh yes," said Mr. Canterfield.

" And common gratitude ought to prompt him to make you one," said his wife.

Mr. Tolman went home and wrote a will. He left all his property, with the exception of a few legacies, to the richest and most powerful charitable organisation in the country.

" People will think I'm crazy," said he to himself ; " and if I should die while I am carrying out my plan, I'll leave the task of defending my sanity to people who are able to make a good fight for me." And before he went to bed he had his will signed and witnessed.

The next day he packed a trunk and left for the neighbouring city. His apartments were to be kept in readiness for his return at any time. If you had seen him walking over to the railroad depôt, you would have taken him for a man of forty-five.

When he arrived at his destination, Mr. Tolman established himself temporarily at an hotel, and spent the next three or four days in walking about the city looking for what he wanted. What he wanted was rather difficult to define, but the way in which he put the matter to himself was something like this—

"I'd like to find a snug little place where I can live and carry on some business which I can attend to myself, and which will bring me into contact with people of all sorts—people who will interest me. It must be a small business, because I don't want to have to work very hard, and it must be snug and comfortable, because I want to enjoy it. I would like a shop of some sort, because that brings a man face to face with his fellow-creatures."

The city in which he was walking about was one of the best places in the country in which to find the place of business he desired. It was full of independent little shops. But Mr. Tolman could not readily find one which resembled his ideal. A small dry-goods establishment seemed to presuppose a female proprietor. A grocery store would give him many interesting customers; but he did not know much about groceries, and the business did not appear to him to possess any aesthetic features. He was much pleased by a small shop belonging to a taxidermist. It was exceedingly cosy, and the business was probably not so great as to overwork any one. He might send the birds and beasts which were brought to be stuffed to some practical operator, and have him put them in proper condition for the customers. He might—But no; it would be very unsatisfactory to engage in a business of which he knew absolutely nothing. A taxidermist ought not to blush with ignorance when asked some simple questions about a little dead bird or a defunct fish. And so he tore himself from the window of this fascinating place, where, he fancied, had his education been differently managed, he could in time have shown the world the spectacle of a cheerful and unblighted Mr. Venus.

The shop which at last appeared to suit him best was one which he had passed and looked at several times before it struck him favourably. It was in a small brick house in a side street, but not far from one of the main business avenues of the city. The shop seemed devoted to articles of stationery and small notions of various kinds not easy to be classified. He had stopped to look at three penknives fastened to a card, which was propped up in the little show-window, supported on one side by a chess-board with "History of Asia" in gilt letters on the back, and on the other by a small violin labelled "1 dollar"; and as he gazed past these articles into the interior of the shop, which was now lighted up, it gradually dawned upon him that it was something like his ideal of an attractive and interesting business place. At any rate he would go in and look at it. He did not care for a violin, even at the low price marked on the one in the window, but a new pocket-knife might be useful; so he walked in and asked to look at pocket-knives.

The shop was in charge of a very pleasant old lady of about sixty, who sat sewing behind the little counter. While she went to the window, and very carefully reached over the articles displayed therein to get the card of penknives, Mr. Tolman looked about him. The shop was quite small, but there seemed to be a good deal in it. There were shelves behind the counter, and there were shelves on the opposite wall, and they all seemed well filled with something or other. In the corner near the old lady's chair was a little coal stove with a bright fire in it, and at the back of the shop, at the top of two steps, was a glass door partly open, through which he saw a small room, with a red carpet on the floor and a little table apparently set for a meal.

Mr. Tolman looked at the knives when the old lady showed them to him, and after a good deal of consideration he selected one which he thought would be a good knife to give a boy. Then he looked over some things in the way of paper-cutters, whist-markers, and such small matters, which were in a glass case on the counter; and while he looked at them he talked to the old lady.

She was a friendly, sociable body, and very glad to have any one to talk to, and so it was not at all difficult for Mr. Tolman, by some general remarks, to draw from her a great many points about herself and her shop. She was a widow, with a son who, from her remarks, must have been forty years old. He was connected with a mercantile establishment and they had lived here for a long time. While her son was a salesman and came home every evening, this was very pleasant; but after he became a commercial traveller and was away from the city for months at a time, she did not like it at all. It was very lonely for her.

Mr. Tolman's heart rose within him, but he did not interrupt her.

"If I could do it," said she, "I would give up this place and go and live with my sister in the country. It would be better for both of us, and Henry could come there just as well as here when he gets back from his trips."

"Why don't you sell out?" asked Mr. Tolman a little fearfully, for he began to think that all this was too easy sailing to be entirely safe.

"That would not be easy," said she with a smile. "It might be a long time before we could find any one who would want to take the place. We have a fair trade in the store, but it isn't what it used to be when times were better; and the library is falling off too. Most of the books are getting pretty old, and it don't pay to spend much money for new ones now."

"The library!" said Mr. Tolman. "Have you a library?"

"Oh yes," replied the old lady. "I've had a circulating library here for nearly fifteen years. There it is, on those two upper shelves behind you."

Mr. Tolman turned, and beheld two long rows of books in brown paper covers, with a short step-ladder standing near the door of the inner room, by which these shelves might be reached. This pleased him greatly. He had had no idea that there was a library here.

"I declare!" said he. "It must be very pleasant to manage a circulating library—a small one like this, I mean. I shouldn't mind going into a business of the kind myself."

The old lady looked up, surprised. Did he wish to go into business? She had not supposed that, just from looking at him.

Mr. Tolman explained his views to her. He did not tell what he had been doing in the way of business or what Mr. Canterfield was doing for him now. He merely stated his present wishes, and acknowledged to her that it was the attractiveness of her establishment that had led him to come in.

"Then you do not want the penknife?" she said quickly.

"Oh yes, I do," said he; "and I really believe, if we can come to terms, that I would like the two other knives, together with the rest of your stock in trade."

The old lady laughed a little nervously. She hoped very much indeed that they could come to terms. She brought a chair from the back room, and Mr. Tolman sat down with her by the stove to talk it over. Few customers came in to interrupt them and they talked the matter over very thoroughly. They both came to the conclusion that there would be no difficulty about terms, nor about Mr. Tolman's ability to carry on the business after a very little instruction from the present proprietress. When Mr. Tolman left, it was with the understanding that he was to call again in a couple of days, when the son Henry would be at home, and matters could be definitely arranged.

When the three met, the bargain was soon struck. As each party was so desirous of making it, few difficulties were interposed. The old lady, indeed, was in favour of some delay in the transfer of the establishment, as she would like to clean and dust every shelf and corner and every article in the place; but Mr. Tolman was in a hurry to take possession; and as the son Henry would have to start off on another trip in a short time, he wanted to see his mother moved and settled before he left. There was not much to move but trunks and bandboxes and some antiquated pieces of furniture of special value to the old lady, for Mr. Tolman insisted on buying everything in the house, just as it stood. The whole thing did not cost him, he said to himself, as much as some of his acquaintances would pay for a horse. The methodical son Henry took an account of stock, and Mr. Tolman took several lessons from the old lady, in which she explained to him how to find out the selling prices of the various articles from the marks on the little tags attached to them; and she particularly instructed him in the management of the circulating library. She informed him of the character of the books and, as far as possible, of the character of the regular patrons. She told him whom he might trust to take out a book without paying for the one brought in if they didn't happen to have the change with them, and she indicated with little crosses opposite their names those persons who should be required to pay cash down for what they had had before receiving further benefits.

It was astonishing to see what interest Mr. Tolman took in all this. He was really anxious to meet some of the people about whom the old lady discoursed. He tried, too, to remember a few of the many things she told him of her methods of buying and selling and the general management of her shop; and he probably did not forget more than three-fourths of what she told him.

Finally, everything was settled to the satisfaction of the two male parties to the bargain—although the old lady thought of a hundred things she would yet like to do—and one fine frosty afternoon a car-load of furniture and baggage left the door, the old lady and her son took leave of the old place, and Mr. Tolman was left sitting behind the little counter, the sole manager and proprietor of a circulating library and a stationery and notion shop. He laughed when he thought of it, but he rubbed his hands and felt very well satisfied.

"There is nothing really crazy about it," he said to himself. "If there is a thing that I think I would like, and I can afford to have it, and there's no harm in it, why not have it?"

There was nobody there to say anything against this; so Mr. Tolman rubbed his hands again before the fire, and rose to walk up and down his shop, and wonder who would be his first customer.

In the course of twenty minutes a little boy opened the door and came in. Mr. Tolman hastened behind the counter to receive his commands. The little boy wanted two sheets of note-paper and an envelope.

"Any particular kind?" asked Mr. Tolman.

The boy didn't know of any particular variety being desired. He thought the same kind he always got would do; and he looked very hard at Mr. Tolman, evidently wondering at the change in the shopkeeper, but asking no questions.

"You are a regular customer, I suppose," said Mr. Tolman, opening several boxes of paper which he had taken down from the shelves. "I have just begun business here and don't know what kind of paper you have been in the habit of buying. But I suppose this will do"; and he took out a couple of sheets of the best, with an envelope to match. These he carefully tied up in a piece of thin brown paper and gave to the boy, who handed him three cents. Mr. Tolman took them, smiled, and then having made a rapid calculation, he called to the boy, who was just opening the door, and gave him back one cent.

"You have paid me too much," he said.

The boy took the cent, looked at Mr. Tolman, and then got out of the store as quickly as he could.

"Such profits as that are enormous," said Mr. Tolman; "but I suppose the small sales balance them." This Mr. Tolman subsequently found to be the case.

One or two other customers came in in the course of the afternoon, and about dark the people who took out books began to arrive. These kept Mr. Tolman very busy. He not only had to do a good deal of entering and cancelling, but he had to answer a great many questions about the change in proprietorship, and the probability of his getting in some new books, with suggestions as to the quantity and character of these, mingled with a few dissatisfied remarks in regard to the volumes already on hand.

Every one seemed sorry that the old lady had gone away; but Mr. Tolman was so pleasant and anxious to please, and took such an interest in their selection of books, that only one of the subscribers appeared to take the change very much to heart. This was a young man who was forty-three cents in arrears. He was a long time selecting a book, and when at last he brought it to Mr. Tolman to be entered, he told him in a low voice that he hoped there would be no objection to letting his account run on for a little while longer. On the first of the month he would settle it, and then he hoped to be able to pay cash whenever he brought in a book.

Mr. Tolman looked for his name on the old lady's list, and finding no cross against it, told him that it was all right, and that the first of the month would do very well. The young man went away perfectly satisfied with the new librarian. Thus did Mr. Tolman begin to build up his popularity. As the evening grew on he found himself becoming very hungry; but he did not like to shut up the shop, for every now and then some one dropped in, sometimes to ask what time it was, and sometimes to make a little purchase, while there were still some library patrons coming in at intervals.

However, taking courage during a short rest from customers, he put up the shutters, locked the door, and hurried off to a hotel, where he partook of a meal such as few keepers of little shops even think of indulging in.

The next morning Mr. Tolman got his own breakfast. This was delightful. He had seen how cosily the old lady had spread her table in the little back room, where there was a stove suitable for any cooking he might wish to indulge in, and he longed for such a cosy meal. There were plenty of stock provisions in the house, which he had purchased with the rest of the goods; and he went out and bought himself a fresh loaf of bread. Then he broiled a piece of ham, made some good strong tea, boiled some eggs, and had a breakfast on the little round table, which, though plain enough, he enjoyed more than any breakfast at his club which he could remember. He had opened the shop, and sat facing the glass door, hoping, almost, that there would be some interruption to his meal. It would seem so much more proper in that sort of business if he had to get up and go and attend to a customer.

Before evening of that day Mr. Tolman became convinced that he would soon be obliged to employ a boy or some one to attend to the establishment during his absence. After breakfast, a woman recommended by the old lady came to make his bed and clean up generally, but when she had gone he was left alone with his shop. He determined not to allow this responsibility to injure his health, and so at one o'clock boldly locked the shop door and went out to his lunch.

He hoped that no one would call during his absence, but when he returned he found a little girl with a pitcher standing at the door. She came to borrow half a pint of milk.

"Milk!" exclaimed Mr. Tolman in surprise. "Why, my child, I have no milk. I don't even use it in my tea."

The little girl looked very much disappointed. "Is Mrs. Walker gone away for good?" said she.

"Yes," replied Mr. Tolman. "But I would be just as willing to lend you the milk as she would be if I had any. Is there any place near here where you can buy milk?"

"Oh yes," said the girl; "you can get it round in the market-house."

"How much would half a pint cost?" he asked.

"Three cents," replied the girl.

"Well, then," said Mr. Tolman, "here are three cents. You can go and buy the milk for me and then you can borrow it. Will that suit?"

The girl thought it would suit very well, and away she went.

Even this little incident pleased Mr. Tolman. It was so very novel. When he came back from his dinner in the evening, he found two circulating library subscribers stamping their feet on the door-step, and he afterwards heard that several others had called and gone away. It would certainly injure the library if he suspended business at meal-times. He could easily have his choice of a hundred boys if he chose to advertise for one, but he shrank from having a youngster in the place. It would interfere greatly with his cosiness and his experiences. He might possibly find a boy who went to school, and who would be willing to come at noon and in the evening if he were paid enough. But it would have to be a very steady and responsible boy. He would think it over before taking any steps.

He thought it over for a day or two, but he did not spend his whole time in doing so. When he had no customers, he sauntered about in the little parlour over the shop, with its odd old furniture, its quaint prints on the walls, and its absurd ornaments on the mantelpiece. The other little rooms seemed almost as funny to him, and he was sorry when the bell on the shop door called him down from their contemplation. It was pleasant to him to think that he owned all these odd things. The ownership of the varied goods in the shop also gave him an agreeable feeling which none of his other possessions had ever afforded him. It was all so odd and novel.

He liked much to look over the books in the library. Many of them were old novels, the names of which were familiar enough to him, but which he had never read. He determined to read some of them as soon as he felt fixed and settled.

In looking over the book in which the names and accounts of the subscribers were entered, he amused himself by wondering what sort of persons they were who had out certain books. Who, for instance, wanted to read *The Book of Cats*; and who could possibly care for *The Mysteries of Udolpho*? But the unknown person in regard to whom Mr. Tolman felt the greatest curiosity was the subscriber who now had in his possession a volume entitled *Dormstock's Logarithms of the Diapason*.

"How on earth," exclaimed Mr. Tolman, "did such a book get into this library; and where on earth did the person spring from who would want to take it out? And not only want to take it," he continued as he examined the entry regarding the volume, "but come and have it renewed one, two, three, four—nine times! He has had that book for eighteen weeks!"

Without exactly making up his mind to do so, Mr. Tolman deferred taking steps toward getting an assistant until P. Glascow, the person in question, should make an appearance, and it was nearly time for the book to be brought in again.

"If I get a boy now," thought Mr. Tolman, "Glascow will be sure to come and bring the book while I am out."

In almost exactly two weeks from the date of the last renewal of the book P. Glascow came in. It was the middle of the afternoon and Mr. Tolman was alone. This investigator of musical philosophy was a quiet young man of about thirty, wearing a light brown cloak, and carrying under one arm a large book.

P. Glascow was surprised when he heard of the change in the proprietorship of the library. Still he hoped that there would be no objection to his renewing the book which he had with him and which he had taken out some time ago.

"Oh no," said Mr. Tolman, "none in the world. In fact, I don't suppose there are any other subscribers who would want it. I have had the curiosity to look to see if it had ever been taken out before, and I find it has not."

The young man smiled quietly. "No," said he, "I suppose not. It is not every one who would care to study the higher mathematics of music, especially when treated as Dormstock treats the subject."

"He seems to go into it pretty deeply," remarked Mr. Tolman, who had taken up the book. "At least I should think so, judging from all these calculations, and problems, and squares, and cubes."

"Indeed he does," said Glascow; "and although I have had the book some months, and have more reading-time at my disposal than most persons, I have only reached the fifty-sixth page, and doubt if I shall not have to review some of that before I can feel that I thoroughly understand it."

"And there are three hundred and forty pages in all." said Mr. Tolman compassionately.

"Yes," replied the other; "but I am quite sure that the matter will grow easier as I proceed. I have found that out from what I have already done."

"You say you have a good deal of leisure?" remarked Mr. Tolman. "Is the musical business dull at present?"

"Oh, I'm not in the musical business," said Glascow. "I have a great love for music and wish thoroughly to understand it; but my business is quite different. I am a night druggist and that is the reason I have so much leisure for reading."

"A night druggist?" repeated Mr. Tolman inquiringly.

"Yes, sir," said the other. "I am in a large down town drug-store, which is kept open all night, and I go on duty after the day-clerks leave."

"And does that give you more leisure?" asked Mr. Tolman.

"It seems to," answered Glascow. "I sleep until about noon, and then I have the rest of the day, until seven o'clock, to myself. I think that people who work at night can make a more satisfactory use of their own time than those who work in the daytime. In the summer I can take a trip on the river, or go somewhere out of town, everyday if I like."

"Daylight is more available for many things, that is true," said Mr. Tolman. "But is it not dreadfully lonely sitting in a drug-store all night? There can't be many people to come to buy medicine at night. I thought there was generally a night-bell to drug stores by which a clerk could be awakened if anybody wanted anything."

"It's not very lonely in our store at night," said Glascow. "In fact it's often more lively then than in the daytime. You see, we are right down among the newspaper offices, and there's always somebody coming in for soda-water, or cigars, or something or other. The store is a bright, warm place for the night editors and reporters to meet together and talk and drink hot soda, and there's always a knot of 'em around the stove about the time the papers begin to go to press. And they're a lively set, I can tell you, sir. I've heard some of the best stories I ever heard in my life told in our place after three o'clock in the morning."

"A strange life!" said Mr. Tolman. "Do you know, I never thought that people amused themselves in that way. And night after night, I suppose."

"Yes, sir, night after night, Sundays and all."

The night druggist now took up his book.

"Going home to read?" asked Mr. Tolman.

"Well, no" said the other; "it's rather cold this afternoon to read. I think I'll take a brisk walk."

"Can't you leave your book until you return?" asked Mr. Tolman; "that is, if you will come back this way. It's an awkward book to carry about."

"Thank you, I will," said Glascow. "I shall come back this way."

When he had gone, Mr. Tolman took up the book and began to look over it more carefully than he had done before. But his examination did not last long.

"How anybody of common-sense can take any interest in this stuff is beyond my comprehension," said Mr. Tolman as he closed the book and put it on a little shelf behind the counter.

When Glascow came back, Mr. Tolman asked him to stay and warm himself; and then, after they had talked for a short time, Mr. Tolman began to feel hungry. He had his winter appetite and had lunched early. So said he to the night druggist, who had opened his "Dormstock," "How would you like to sit here and read awhile, while I go and get my dinner? I will light the gas and you can be very confortable here if you are not in a hurry."

P. Glascow was in no hurry at all and was very glad to have some quiet reading by a warm fire; and so Mr. Tolman left him, feeling perfectly confident that a man who had been allowed by the old lady to renew a book nine times must be perfectly trustworthy.

When Mr. Tolman returned, the two had some further conversation in the corner by the little stove.

"It must be rather annoying," said the night druggist, "not to be able to go out to your meals without shutting up your shop. If you like," said he rather hestitatingly, "I will step in about this time in the afternoon and stay here while you go to dinner. I'll be glad to do this until you get an assistant. I can easily attend to most people who come in and others can wait."

Mr. Tolman jumped at this proposition. It was exactly what he wanted.

So P. Glascow came every afternoon and read "Dormstock" while Mr. Tolman went to dinner; and before long he came at lunch-time also. It was just as convenient as not, he said. He had finished his breakfast and would like to read awhile. Mr. Tolman fancied that the night druggist's lodgings were, perhaps, not very well warmed, which idea explained the desire to walk rather than read on a cold afternoon. Glascow's name was entered on the free list, and he always took away the "Dormstock" at night, because he might have a chance of looking into it at the store when custom began to grow slack in the latter part of the early morning.

One afternoon there came into the shop a young lady, who brought back two books which she had had for more than a month. She made no excuses for keeping the books longer than the prescribed time, but simply handed them in and paid her fine. Mr. Tolman did not like to take this money, for it was the first of the kind he had received; but the young lady looked a if she was well able to afford the luxury of keeping books over their time, and business was business. So he gravely gave her her change. Then she said she would like to take out *Dormstock's Logarithms of the Diapason.*

Mr. Tolman stared at her. She was a bright, handsome young lady and looked as if she had very good sense. He could not understand it. But he told her the book was out.

"Out!" she said. "Why, it's always out. It seems strange to me that there should be such a demand for that book. I have been trying to get it for ever so long."

"It *is* strange," said Mr. Tolman; "but it is certainly in demand. Did Mrs. Walker ever make you any promises about it?"

"No," said she; "but I thought my turn would come around some time. And I particularly want the book just now."

Mr. Tolman felt somewhat troubled. He knew that the night druggist ought not to monopolise the volume, and yet he did not wish to disoblige one who was so useful to him and who took such an earnest interest in the book. And he could not temporise with the young lady and say that he thought the book would soon be in. He knew it would not. There were three hundred and forty pages of it. So he merely remarked that he was sorry.

"So am I," said the young lady, "very sorry. It so happens that just now I have a peculiar opportunity for studying that book which may not occur again."

There was something in Mr. Tolman's sympathetic face which seemed to invite her confidence, and she continued.

"I am a teacher," she said, "and on account of certain circumstances I have a holiday for a month, which I intended to give up almost entirely to the study of music, and I particularly wanted 'Dormstock.' Do you think there is any chance of its early return, and will you reserve it for me?"

"Reserve it!" said Mr. Tolman. "Most certainly I will." And then he reflected a second or two. "If you will come here the day after to-morrow, I will be able to tell you something definite."

She said she would come.

Mr. Tolman was out a long time at lunch-time the next day. He went to all the leading bookstores to see if he could buy a copy of Dormstock's great work. But he was unsuccessful. The booksellers told him that there was no probability that he could get a copy in the country, unless, indeed, he found it in the stock of some second-hand dealer. There was no demand at all for it, and that if he even sent for it to England, where it was published, it was not likely he could get it, for it had been long out of print. The next day he went to several second-hand stores, but no "Dormstock" could he find.

When he came back he spoke to Glascow on the subject. He was sorry to do so, but thought that simple justice compelled him to mention the matter. The night druggist was thrown into a perturbed state of mind by the information that some one wanted his beloved book.

"A woman!" he exclaimed. "Why, she would not understand two pages out of the whole of it. It is too bad. I didn't suppose any one would want this book."

"Do not disturb yourself too much," said Mr. Tolman. "I am not sure that you ought to give it up."

"I am very glad to hear you say so," said Glascow. "I have no doubt it is only a passing fancy with her. I dare say she would really rather have a good new novel"; and then, having heard that the lady was expected that afternoon, he went out to walk, with the "Dormstock" under his arm.

When the young lady arrived, an hour or so later, she was not at all satisfied to take out a new novel, and was very sorry indeed not to find the *Logarithms of the Diapason* waiting for her. Mr. Tolman told her that he had tried to buy another copy of the work, and for this she expressed herself gratefully. He also found himself compelled to say that the book was in the possession of a gentleman who had had it for some time—all the time it had been out, in fact—and had not yet finished it.

At this the young lady seemed somewhat nettled.

"Is it not against the rules for any person to keep one book out so long?" she asked.

"No," said Mr. Tolman. "I have looked into that. Our rules are very simple, and merely say that a book may be renewed by the payment of a certain sum."

"Then I am never to have it?" remarked the young lady.

"Oh, I wouldn't despair about it," said Mr. Tolman. "He has not had time to reflect upon the matter. He is a reasonable young man, and I believe that he will be willing to give up his study of the book for a time, and let you take it."

"No," said she, "I don't wish that. If he is studying, as you say he is, day and night, I do not wish to interrupt him. I should want the book at least a month, and that, I suppose, would upset his course of study entirely. But I do not think any one should begin in a circulating library to study a book that will take him a year to finish; for, from what you say, it will take this gentleman at least that time to finish Dormstock's book." And so she went her way.

When P. Glascow heard all this in the evening, he was very grave. He had evidently been reflecting.

"It is not fair," said he. "I ought not to keep the book so long. I now give it up for a while. You may let her have it when she comes." And he put the "Dormstock" on the counter, and went and sat down by the stove.

Mr. Tolman was grieved. He knew the night druggist had done right, but still he was sorry for him. "What will you do?" he asked. "Will you stop your studies?"

"Oh no!" said Glascow, gazing solemnly into the stove. "I will take up some other books on the diapason which I have, and will so keep my ideas fresh on the subject until this lady is done with the book. I do not really believe she will study it very long." And then he added: "If it is all the same to you, I will come around here and read, as I have been doing, until you shall get a regular assistant."

Mr. Tolman would be delighted to have him come, he said. He had entirely given up the idea of getting an assistant; but this he did not say.

It was some time before the lady came back, and Mr. Tolman was afraid she was not coming at all. But she did come, and asked for Miss Burney's *Evelina*. She smiled when she named the book, and said that she believed she would have to take a novel after all, and she had always wanted to read that one.

"I wouldn't take a novel if I were you," said Mr. Tolman; and he triumphantly took down the "Dormstock" and laid it before her.

She was evidently much pleased, but when he told her of Mr. Glascow's gentlemanly conduct in the matter, her countenance instantly changed.

"Not at all," said she, laying down the book; "I will not break up his study. I will take the *Evelina*, if you please."

And as no persuasion from Mr. Tolman had any effect upon her, she went away with Miss Burney's novel in her muff.

"Now, then," said Mr. Tolman to Glascow, in the evening, "you may as well take the book along with you. She won't have it."

But Glascow would do nothing of the kind. "No," he remarked, as he sat looking into the stove; "when I said I would let her have it, I meant it. She'll take it when she sees that it continues to remain in the library."

Glascow was mistaken: she did not take it, having the idea that he would soon conclude that it would be wiser for him to read it than to let it stand idly on the shelf.

"It would serve them both right," said Mr. Tolman to himself, "if somebody else would come and take it." But there was no one else among his subscribers who would even think of such a thing.

One day, however, the young lady came in and asked to look at the book. "Don't think that I am going to take it out," she said, noticing Mr. Tolman's look of pleasure as he handed her the volume. "I only wish to see what he says on a certain subject which I am studying now"; and so she sat down by the stove, on the chair which Mr. Tolman placed for her, and opened "Dormstock."

She sat earnestly poring over the book for half an hour or more, and then she looked up and said, "I really cannot make out what this part means. Excuse my troubling you, but I would be very glad if you would explain the latter part of this passage."

"Me!" exclaimed Mr. Tolman; "why, my good madam—miss, I mean—I couldn't explain it to you if it were to save my life. But what page is it?" said he, looking at his watch.

"Page twenty-four," answered the young lady.

"Oh, well, then," said he, "if you can wait ten or fifteen minutes, the gentleman who has had the book will be here, and I think he can explain anything in the first part of the work."

The young lady seemed to hesitate whether to wait or not; but as she had a certain curiosity to see what sort of a person he was who had been so absorbed in the book, she concluded to sit a little longer and look into some other parts of the book. The night druggist soon came in; and when Mr. Tolman introduced him to the lady, he readily agreed to explain the passage to her if he could. So Mr. Tolman got him a chair from the inner room, and he also sat down by the stove.

The explanation was difficult, but it was achieved at last; and then the young lady broached the subject of leaving the book unused. This was discussed for some time, but came to nothing, although Mr. Tolman put down his afternoon paper and joined in the argument, urging, among other points, that as the matter now stood he was deprived by the dead-lock of all income from the book. But even this strong argument proved of no avail.

"Then I'll tell you what I wish you would do," said Mr. Tolman, as the young lady rose to go; "come here and look at the book whenever you wish to do so. I'd like to make this more of a reading-room anyway. It would give me more company."

After this the young lady looked into "Dormstock" when she came in; and as her holidays had been extended by the continued absence of the family in which she taught, she had plenty of time for study, and came quite frequently. She often met with Glascow in the shop; and on such occasions they generally consulted "Dormstock," and sometimes had quite lengthy talks on musical matters. One afternoon they came in together, having met on their way to the library, and entered into a conversation on diapasonic logarithms, which continued during the lady's stay in the shop.

"The proper thing," thought Mr. Tolman, "would be for these two people to get married. Then they could take the book and study it to their hearts' content. And they would certainly suit each other, for they are both greatly attached to musical mathematics and philosophy, and neither of them either plays or sings, as they have told me. It would be an admirable match."

Mr. Tolman thought over this matter a good deal, and at last determined to mention it to Glascow. When he did so, the young man coloured, and expressed the opinion that it would be of no use to think of such a thing. But it was evident from his manner and subsequent discourse that he had thought of it.

Mr. Tolman gradually became quite anxious on the subject, especially as the night druggist did not seem inclined to take any steps in the matter. The weather was now beginning to be warmer, and Mr. Tolman reflected that the little house and the little shop were probably much more cosy and comfortable in winter than in summer. There were higher buildings all about the house, and even now he began to feel that the circulation of air would be quite as agreeable as the circulation of books. He thought a good deal about his airy rooms in the neighbouring city. "Mr. Glascow," said he, one afternoon, "I have made up my mind to shortly sell out this business."

"What!" exclaimed the other. "Do you mean you will give it up and go away—leave the place altogether?"

"Yes," replied Mr. Tolman, "I shall give up the place entirely, and leave the city." The night druggist was shocked. He had spent many happy hours in that shop, and his hours there were now becoming pleasanter than ever. If Mr. Tolman went away, all this must end. Nothing of the kind could be expected of any new proprietor.

"And considering this," continued Mr. Tolman, "I think it would be well for you to bring your love matters to a conclusion while I am here to help you."

"My love matters!" exclaimed Mr. Glascow, with a flush.

"Yes, certainly," said Mr. Tolman. "I have eyes, and I know all about it. Now let me tell you what I think. When a thing is to be done, it ought to be done the first time there is a good chance. That's the way I do business. Now you might as well come around here to-morrow afternoon, prepared to propose to Miss Edwards. She is due to-morrow, for she has been two days away. If she don't come, we'll postpone the matter until the next day. But you should be ready to-morrow. I don't believe you can see her much when you don't meet her here; for that family is expected back very soon, and from what I infer from her account of her employers, you won't care to visit her at their house."

The night druggist wanted to think about it.

"There is nothing to think," said Mr. Tolman. "We know all about the lady." (He spoke truly, for he had informed himself about both parties to the affair.) "Take my advice, and be here to-morrow afternoon—and come rather early."

The next morning Mr. Tolman went up to his parlour on the second floor, and brought down two blue stuffed chairs, the best he had, and put them in the little room back of the shop. He also brought down one or two knick-knacks and put them on the mantelpiece, and he dusted and brightened up the room as well as he could. He even covered the table with a red cloth from the parlour.

When the young lady arrived, he invited her to walk into the back room to look over some new books he had just got in. If she had known he proposed to give up the business, she would have thought it rather strange that he should be buying new books. But she knew nothing of his intentions. When she was seated at the table whereon the new books were spread, Mr. Tolman stepped outside of the shop door to watch for Glascow's approach. He soon appeared.

"Walk right in," said Mr. Tolman. "She's in the back room looking over books. I'll wait here, and keep out customers as far as possible. It's pleasant, and I want a little fresh air. I'll give you twenty minutes."

Glascow was pale, but he went in without a word; and Mr. Tolman, with his hands under his coat-tail, and his feet rather far apart, established a blockade on the door-step. He stood there for some time looking at the people outside, and wondering what the people inside were doing. The little girl who had borrowed the milk of him, and who had never returned it, was about to pass the door; but seeing him standing there, she crossed over to the other side of the street. But he did not notice her. He was wondering if it was time to go in. A boy came up to the door, and wanted to know if he kept Easter-eggs. Mr. Tolman was happy to say he did not. When he had allowed the night druggist a very liberal twenty minutes, he went in. As he entered the shop door, giving the bell a very decided ring as he did so, P. Glascow came down the two steps that led from the inner room. His face showed that it was all right with him.

A few days after this, Mr. Tolman sold out his stock, good-will, and fixtures, together with the furniture and lease of the house. And who should he sell out to but to Mr. Glascow! This piece of business was one of the happiest points of the whole affair. There was no reason why the happy couple should not be married very soon, and the young lady was charmed to give up her position as teacher and governess in a family, and come and take charge of that delightful little store and that cunning little house, with almost everything in it that they wanted. One thing in the establishment Mr. Tolman refused to sell. That was Dormstock's great work. He made the couple a present of the volume, and between two of the earlier pages he placed a bank-note, which in value was very much more than that of the ordinary wedding-gift.

"And what are *you* going to do?" they asked of him, when all these things were settled. And then he told them how he was going back to his business in the neighbouring city, and he told them what it was, and how he had come to manage a circulating library. They did not think him crazy. People who studied the logarithms of the diapason would not be apt to think a man crazy for such a little thing as that. When Mr. Tolman returned to the establishment of Pusey & Co., he found everything going on very satisfactorily.

"You look ten years younger, sir," said Mr. Canterfield. "You must have had a very pleasant time. I did not think there was enough to interest you in —— for so long a time."

"Interest me!" exclaimed Mr. Tolman. "Why, objects of interest crowded on me. I never had a more enjoyable holiday in my life."

When he went home that evening (and he found himself quite willing to go), he tore up the will he had made. He now felt that there was no necessity for proving his sanity.

# THE TRANSFERRED GHOST

### Frank R. Stockton

The country residence of Mr. John Hinckman was a delightful place to me, for many reasons. It was the abode of a genial, though somewhat impulsive, hospitality. It had broad, smooth-shaven lawns and towering oaks and elms; there were bosky shades at several points, and not far from the house there was a little rill spanned by a rustic bridge with the bark on; there were fruits and flowers, pleasant people, chess, billiards, rides, walks, and fishing. These were great attractions, but none of them, nor all of them together, would have been sufficient to hold me to the place very long. I had been invited for the trout season, but should, probably, have finished my visit early in the summer had it not been that upon fair days, when the grass was dry, and the sun not too hot, and there was but little wind, there strolled beneath the lofty elms, or passed lightly through the bosky shades, the form of my Madeline.

This lady was not, in very truth, my Madeline. She had never given herself to me, nor had I, in any way, acquired possession of her. But as I considered her possession the only sufficient reason for the continuance of my existence, I called her, in my reveries, mine. It may have been that I would not have been obliged to confine the use of this possessive pronoun to my reveries had I confessed the state of my feelings to the lady.

But this was an unusually difficult thing to do. Not only did I dread, as almost all lovers dread, taking the step which would in an instant put an end to that delightful season which may be termed the ante-interrogatory period of love, and which might at the same time terminate all intercourse or connection with the object of my passion; but I was, also, dreadfully afraid of John Hinckman. This gentleman was a good friend of mine, but it would have required a bolder man than I was at that time to ask him for the gift of his niece, who was the head of his household, and, according to his own frequent statement, the main prop of his declining years. Had Madeline acquiesced in my general views on the subject, I might have felt encouraged to open the matter to Mr. Hinckman, but, as I said before, I had never asked her whether or not she would be mine. I thought of these things at all hours of the day and night, particularly the latter.

I was lying awake one night, in the great bed in my spacious chamber, when, by the dim light of the new moon, which partially filled the room, I saw John Hinckman standing by a large chair near the door. I was very much surprised at this for two reasons. In the first place, my host had never before come into my room, and, in the second place, he had gone from home that morning, and had not expected to return for several days. It was for this reason that I had been able that evening to sit much later than usual with Madeline on the moonlit porch. The figure was certainly that of John Hinckman in his ordinary dress, but there was a vagueness and indistinctness about it which presently assured me that it was a ghost. Had the good old man been murdered? and had his spirit come to tell me of the deed, and to confide to me the protection of his dear —— ? My heart fluttered at what I was about to think, but at this instant the figure spoke.

"Do you know," he said, with a countenance that indicated anxiety, "if Mr. Hinckman will return to-night?"

I thought it well to maintain a calm exterior, and I answered:

"We do not expect him."

"I am glad of that," said he, sinking into the chair by which he stood. "During the two years and a half that I have inhabited this house, that man has never before been away for a single night. You can't imagine the relief it gives me."

And as he spoke he stretched out his legs and leaned back in the chair. His form became less vague, and the colours of his garments more distinct and evident, while an expression of gratified relief succeeded to the anxiety of his countenance.

"Two years and a half!" I exclaimed. "I don't understand you."

"It is fully that length of time," said the ghost, "since I first came here. Mine is not an ordinary case. But before I say anything more about it, let me ask you again if you are sure Mr. Hinckman will not return to-night?"

"I am as sure of it as I can be of anything," I answered. "He left to-day for Bristol, two hundred miles away."

"Then I will go on," said the ghost, "for I am glad to have the opportunity of talking to some one who will listen to me; but if John Hinckman should come in and catch me here, I should be frightened out of my wits."

"This is all very strange," I said, greatly puzzled by what I had heard. "Are you the ghost of Mr. Hinckman?"

This was a bold question, but my mind was so full of other emotions that there seemed to be no room for that of fear.

"Yes, I am his ghost," my companion replied, "and yet I have no right to be. And this is what makes me so uneasy and so much afraid of him. It is a strange story, and, I truly believe, without precedent. Two years and a half ago, John Hinckman was dangerously ill in this very room. At one time he was so far gone that he was really believed to be dead. It was in consequence of too precipitate a report in regard to this matter that I was, at that time, appointed to be his ghost. Imagine my surprise and horror, sir, when, after I had accepted the position and assumed its responsibilities, that old man revived, became convalescent, and eventually regained his usual health. My situation was now one of extreme delicacy and embarrassment. I had no power to return to my original unembodiment, and I had no right to be the ghost of a man who was not dead. I was advised by my friends to quietly maintain my position, and was assured that, as John Hinckman was an elderly man, it could not be long before I could rightfully assume the position for which I had been selected. But I tell you sir," he continued, with animation, "the old fellow seems as vigorous as ever, and I have no idea how much longer this annoying state of things will continue. I spend my time trying to get out of that old man's way. I must not leave this house, and he seems to follow me everywhere. I tell you, sir, he haunts me."

"That is truly a queer state of things," I remarked. "But why are you afraid of him? He couldn't hurt you."

"Of course he couldn't," said the ghost. "But his very presence is a shock and terror to me. Imagine, sir, how you would feel if my case were yours."

I could not imagine such a thing at all. I simply shuddered.

"And if one must be a wrongful ghost at all," the apparition continued, "it would be much pleasanter to be the ghost of some man other than John Hinckman. There is in him an irascibility of temper, accompanied by a facility of invective, which is seldom met with. And what would happen if he were to see me, and find out, as I am sure he would, how long and why I had inhabited his house, I can scarcely conceive. I have seen him in his bursts of passion, and although he did not hurt the people he stormed at any more than he would hurt me, they seemed to shrink before him."

All this I knew to be very true. Had it not been for this peculiarity of Mr. Hinckman, I might have been more willing to talk to him about his niece.

"I feel sorry for you," I said, for I really began to have a sympathetic feeling toward this unfortunate apparition. "Your case is indeed a hard one. It reminds me of those persons who have had doubles, and I suppose a man would often be very angry indeed when he found that there was another being who was personating himself."

"Oh, the cases are not similar at all," said the ghost. "A double or *doppleganger* lives on the earth with a man, and, being exactly like him, he makes all sorts of trouble, of course. It is very different with me. I am not here to live with Mr. Hinckman. I am here to take his place. Now, it would make John Hinckman very angry if he knew that. Don't you know it would?"

I assented promptly.

"Now that he is away I can be easy for a little while," continued the ghost, " and I am so glad to have an opportunity of talking to you. I have frequently come into your room, and watched you while you slept, but did not dare to speak to you for fear that if you talked with me Mr. Hinckman would hear you, and come into the room to know why you were talking to yourself."

"But would he not hear you?" I asked.

"Oh no," said the other, "there are times when any one may see me, but no one hears me except the person to whom I address myself."

"But why did you wish to speak to me?" I asked.

"Because," replied the ghost, "I like occasionally to talk to people, and especially to some one like yourself, whose mind is so troubled and perturbed that you are not likely to be frightened by a visit from one of us. But I particularly wanted to ask you to do me a favour. There is every probability, so far as I can see, that John Hinckman will live a long time, and my situation is becoming insupportable. My great object at present is to get myself transferred, and I think that you may, perhaps, be of use to me."

"Transferred!" I exclaimed. "What do you mean by that?"

"What I mean," said the other, "is this: Now that I have started on my career I have got to be the ghost of somebody; and I want to be the ghost of a man who is really dead."

"I should think that would be easy enough," I said. "Opportunities must continually occur."

"Not at all! not at all!" said my companion quickly. "You have no idea what a rush and pressure there is for situations of this kind. Whenever a vacancy occurs, if I may express myself in that way, there are crowds of applications for the ghostship."

"I had no idea that such a state of things existed," I said, becoming quite interested in the matter. "There ought to be some regular system, or order of precedence, by which you could all take your turns like customers in a barber's shop."

"Oh dear, that would never do at all!" said the other. "Some of us would have to wait for ever. There is always a great rush whenever a good ghostship offers itself—while, as you know, there are some positions that no one would care for. And it was in consequence of my being in too great a hurry on an occasion of the kind that I got myself into my present disagreeable predicament, and I have thought that it might be possible that you would help me out of it. You might know of a case where an opportunity for a ghost-ship was not generally expected, but which might present itself at any moment. If you would give me a short notice, I know I could arrange for a transfer."

"What do you mean?" I exclaimed. "Do you want me to commit suicide? Or to undertake a murder for your benefit?"

"Oh no, no, no!" said the other, with a vapoury smile. "I mean nothing of that kind. To be sure, there are lovers who are watched with considerable interest, such persons have been known, in moments of depression, to offer very desirable ghostships, but I did not think of anything of that kind in connection with you. You were the only person I cared to speak to, and I hoped that you might give me some information that would be of use; and, in return, I shall be very glad to help you in your love affair."

"You seem to know that I have such an affair," I said.

"Oh yes," replied the other, with a little yawn. "I could not be here so much as I have been without knowing all about that."

There was something horrible in the idea of Madeline and myself having been watched by a ghost, even, perhaps, when we wandered together in the most delightful and bosky places. But, then, this was quite an exceptional ghost, and I could not have the objections to him which would ordinarily arise in regard to beings of his class.

"I must go now," said the ghost, rising, "but I will see you somewhere to-morrow night. And remember—you help me, and I'll help you."

I had doubts the next morning as to the propriety of telling Madeline anything about this interview, and soon convinced myself that I must keep silent on the subject. If she knew there was a ghost about the house she would probably leave the place instantly. I did not mention the matter, and so regulated my demeanour that I am quite sure Madeline never suspected what had taken place. For some time I had wished that Mr. Hinckman would absent himself, for a day at least, from the premises. In such case I thought I might more easily nerve myself up to the point of speaking to Madeline on the subject of our future collateral existence, and now that the opportunity for such speech had really occurred, I did not feel ready to avail myself of it. What would become of me if she refused me?

I had an idea, however, that the lady thought that, if I were going to speak at all, this was the time. She must have known that certain sentiments were afloat within me, and she was not unreasonable in her wish to see the matter settled one way or the other. But I did not feel like taking a bold step in the dark. If she wished me to ask her to give herself to me, she ought to offer me some reason to suppose that she would make the gift. If I saw no probability of such generosity, I would prefer that things should remain as they were.

That evening I was sitting with Madeline in the moonlit porch. It was nearly ten o'clock, and ever since supper-time I had been working myself up to the point of making an avowal of my sentiments. I had not positively determined to do this, but wished gradually to reach the proper point when, if the prospect looked bright, I might speak. My companion appeared to understand the situation—at least, I imagined that the nearer I came to a proposal the more she seemed to expect it. It was certainly a very critical and important epoch in my life. If I spoke, I should make myself happy or miserable for ever, and if I did not speak I had every reason to believe that the lady would not give me another chance to do so.

Sitting thus with Madeline, talking a little, and thinking very hard over these momentous matters, I looked up and saw the ghost, not a dozen feet away from us. He was sitting on the railing of the porch, one leg thrown up before him, the other dangling down as he leaned against a post. He was behind Madeline, but almost in front of me, as I sat facing the lady. It was fortunate that Madeline was looking out over the landscape, for I must have appeared very much startled. The ghost had told me that he would see me some time this night, but I did not think he would make his appearance when I was in the company of Madeline. If she should see the spirit of her uncle, I could not answer for the consequences. I made no exclamation, but the ghost evidently saw that I was troubled.

" Don't be afraid," he said—" I shall not let her see me ; and she cannot hear me speak unless I address myself to her, which I do not intend to do."

I suppose I looked grateful.

" So you need not trouble yourself about that," the ghost continued ; " but it seems to me that you are not getting along very well with your affair. If I were you, I should speak out without waiting any longer. You will never have a better chance. You are not likely to be interrupted ; and, so far as I can judge, the lady seems disposed to listen to you favourably ; that is, if she ever intends to do so. There is no knowing when John Hinckman will go away again ; certainly not this summer. If I were in your place, I should never dare to make love to Hinckman's niece if he were anywhere about the place. If he should catch any one offering himself to Miss Madeline, he would then be a terrible man to encounter."

I agreed perfectly to all this.

" I cannot bear to think of him ! " I ejaculated aloud.

" Think of whom ? " asked Madeline, turning quickly toward me.

Here was an awkward situation. The long speech of the ghost, to which Madeline paid no attention, but which I heard with perfect distinctness, had made me forget myself.

It was necessary to explain quickly. Of course, it would not do to admit that it was of her dear uncle that I was speaking; and so I mentioned hastily the first name I thought of.

"Mr. Vilars," I said.

This statement was entirely correct, for I never could bear to think of Mr. Vilars, who was a gentleman who had, at various times, paid much attention to Madeline.

"It is wrong for you to speak in that way of Mr. Vilars," she said. "He is a remarkably well-educated and sensible young man, and has very pleasant manners. He expects to be elected to the legislature this fall, and I should not be surprised if he made his mark. He will do well in a legislative body, for whenever Mr. Vilars has anything to say he knows just how and when to say it."

This was spoken very quietly, and without any show of resentment, which was all very natural, for if Madeline thought at all favourably of me she could not feel displeased that I should have disagreeable emotions in regard to a possible rival. The concluding words contained a hint which I was not slow to understand. I felt very sure that if Mr. Vilars were in my present position he would speak quickly enough.

"I know it is wrong to have such ideas about a person," I said, "but I cannot help it."

The lady did not chide me, and after this she seemed even in a softer mood. As for me, I felt considerably annoyed, for I had not wished to admit that any thought of Mr. Vilars had ever occupied my mind.

"You should not speak aloud that way," said the ghost, "or you may get yourself into trouble. I want to see everything go well with you, because then you may be disposed to help me, especially if I should chance to be of any assistance to you, which I hope I shall be."

I longed to tell him that there was no way in which he could help me so much as by taking his instant departure. To make love to a young lady with a ghost sitting on the railing near by, and that ghost the apparition of a much-dreaded uncle, the very idea of whom in such a position and at such a time made me tremble, was a difficult, if not an impossible, thing to do; but I forbore to speak, although I may have looked my mind.

"I suppose," continued the ghost, "that you have not heard anything that might be of advantage to me. Of course I am very anxious to hear, but if you have anything to tell me, I can wait until you are alone. I will come to you to-night in your room, or I will stay here until the lady goes away."

"You need not wait here," I said; "I have nothing at all to say to you."

Madeline sprang to her feet, her face flushed and her eyes ablaze.
"Wait here!" she cried. "What do you suppose I am waiting for? Nothing to say to me indeed!—I should think so! What should you have to say to me?"

"Madeline," I exclaimed, stepping toward her, "let me explain." But she had gone.

Here was the end of the world for me! I turned fiercely to the ghost.

"Wretched existence!" I cried. "You have ruined everything. You have blackened my whole life. Had it not been for you——"

But here my voice faltered. I could say no more.

"You wrong me," said the ghost. "I have not injured you. I have tried only to encourage and assist you, and it is your own folly that has done this mischief. But do not despair. Such mistakes as these can be explained. Keep up a brave heart. Good-bye."

And he vanished from the railing like a bursting soap-bubble.

I went gloomily to bed, but I saw no apparitions that night except those of despair and misery which my wretched thoughts called up. The words I had uttered had sounded to Madeline like the basest insult. Of course there was only one interpretation she could put upon them.

As to explaining my ejaculations, that was impossible. I thought the matter over and over again as I lay awake that night, and I determined that I would never tell Madeline the facts of the case. It would be better for me to suffer all my life than for her to know that the ghost of her uncle haunted the house. Mr. Hinckman was away, and if she knew of his ghost she could not be made to believe that he was not dead. She might not survive the shock! No, my heart could bleed but I would never tell her.

The next day was fine, neither too cool nor too warm; the breezes were gentle, and Nature smiled. But there were no walks or rides with Madeline. She seemed to be much engaged during the day, and I saw but little of her. When we met at meals she was polite, but very quiet and reserved. She had evidently determined on a course of conduct, and had resolved to assume that, although I had been very rude to her, she did not understand the import of my words. It would be quite proper, of course, for her not to know what I meant by my expressions of the night before.

I was downcast and wretched, and said but little, and the only bright streak across the black horizon of my woe was the fact that she did not appear to be happy, although she affected an air of unconcern. The moonlit porch was deserted that evening, but wandering about the house I found Madeline in the library alone. She was reading, but I went in and sat down near her. I felt that, although I could not do so fully, I must in a measure explain my conduct of the night before. She listened quietly to a somewhat laboured apology I made for the words I had used.

"I have not the slightest idea what you meant," she said, "but you were very rude."

I earnestly disclaimed any intention of rudeness, and assured her, with a warmth of speech that must have made some impression upon her, that rudeness to her would be an action impossible to me. I said a great deal upon the subject, and implored her to believe that if it were not for a certain obstacle I could speak to her so plainly that she would understand everything.

She was silent for a time, and then she said, rather more kindly, I thought, than she had spoken before:

"Is that obstacle in any way connected with my uncle?"

"Yes," I answered, after a little hesitation, "it is, in a measure, connected with him."

She made no answer to this, and sat looking at her book, but not reading. From the expression of her face, I thought she was somewhat softened toward me. She knew her uncle as well as I did, and she may have been thinking that, if he were the obstacle that prevented my speaking (and there were many ways in which he might be that obstacle), my position would be such a hard one that it would excuse some wildness of speech and eccentricity of manner. I saw, too, that the warmth of my partial explanations had had some effect on her, and I began to believe that it might be a good thing for me to speak my mind without delay. No matter how she should receive my proposition, my relations with her could not be worse than they had been the previous night and day, and there was something in her face which encouraged me to hope that she might forget my foolish exclamations of the evening before if I began to tell her my tale of love.

I drew my chair a little nearer to her, and as I did so the ghost burst into the room from the doorway behind her. I say burst, although no door flew open and he made no noise. He was wildly excited, and waved his arms above his head. The moment I saw him, my heart fell within me. With the entrance of that impertinent apparition, every hope fled from me. I could not speak while he was in the room.

I must have turned pale, and I gazed steadfastly at the ghost, almost without seeing Madeline, who sat between us.

"Do you know," he cried, "that John Hinckman is coming up the hill? He will be here in fifteen minutes, and if you are doing anything in the way of love-making, you had better hurry it up. But this is not what I came to tell you. I have glorious news! At last I am transferred! Not forty minutes ago a Russian nobleman was murdered by the Nihilists. Nobody ever thought of him in connection with an immediate ghostship. My friends instantly applied for the situation for me, and obtained my transfer. I am off before that horrid Hinckman comes up the hill. The moment I reach my new position, I shall put off this hated semblance. Good-bye.

You can't imagine how glad I am to be, at last, the real ghost of somebody."

"Oh!" I cried, rising to my feet and stretching out my arms in utter wretchedness, "I would to heaven you were mine!"

"I *am* yours," said Madeline, raising to me her tearful eyes.

# THE LADY, OR THE TIGER?

### Frank R. Stockton

In the very olden time there lived a semi-barbaric king whose ideas, though somewhat polished and sharpened by the progressiveness of distant Latin neighbours, were still large, florid, and untrammelled, as became the half of him which was barbaric. He was a man of exuberant fancy, and, withal, of an authority so irresistible that, at his will, he turned his varied fancies into facts. He was greatly given to self-communing; and, when he and himself agreed upon anything, the thing was done. When every member of his domestic and political systems moved smoothly in its appointed course, his nature was bland and genial; but whenever there was a little hitch, and some of his orbs got out of their orbits, he was blander and more genial still, for nothing pleased him so much as to make the crooked straight, and crush down uneven places.

Among the borrowed notions by which his barbarism had become semified was that of the public arena, in which, by exhibitions of manly and beastly valour, the minds of his subjects were refined and cultured.

But even here the exuberant and barbaric fancy asserted itself. The arena of the king was built, not to give the people an opportunity of hearing the rhapsodies of dying gladiators, nor to enable them to view the inevitable conclusion of a conflict between religious opinions and hungry jaws, but for purposes far better adapted to widen and develop the mental energies of the people. This vast amphitheatre, with its encircling galleries, its mysterious vaults, and its unseen passages, was an agent of poetic justice, in which crime was punished, or virtue rewarded, by the decrees of an impartial and incorruptible chance.

When a subject was accused of a crime of sufficient importance to interest the king, public notice was given that on an appointed day the fate of the accused person would be decided in the king's arena,—a structure which well deserved its name; for, although its form and plan were borrowed from afar, its purpose emanated solely from the brain of this man, who, every barleycorn a king, knew no tradition to which he owed more allegiance than pleased his fancy, and who ingrafted on every adopted form of human thought and action the rich growth of his barbaric idealism.

When all the people had assembled in the galleries, and the king, surrounded by his court, sat high up on his throne of royal state on one side of the arena, he gave a signal, a door beneath him opened, and the accused subject stepped out into the amphitheatre. Directly opposite him, on the other side of the enclosed space, were two doors, exactly alike and side by side. It was the duty and the privilege of the person on trial to walk directly to these doors and open one of them. He could open either door he pleased: he was subject to no guidance or influence but that of the aforementioned impartial and incorruptible chance. If he opened the one, there came out of it a hungry tiger, the fiercest and most cruel that could be procured, which immediately sprang upon him, and tore him to pieces, as a punishment for his guilt. The moment that the case of the criminal was thus decided, doleful iron bells were clanged, great wails went up from the hired mourners posted on the outer rim of the arena, and the vast audience, with bowed heads and downcast hearts, wended slowly their homeward way, mourning greatly that one so young and fair, or so old and respected, should have merited so dire a fate.

But, if the accused person opened the other door, there came forth from it a lady, the most suitable to his years and station that his majesty could select among his fair subjects; and to this lady he was immediately married, as a reward of his innocence. It mattered not that he might already possess a wife and family, or that his affections might be engaged upon an object of his own selection; the king allowed no such subordinate arrangements to interfere with his great scheme of retribution and reward. The exercises, as in the other instance, took place immediately, and in the arena. Another door opened beneath the king, and a priest, followed by a band of choristers, and dancing maidens blowing joyous airs on golden horns and treading an epithalamic measure, advanced to where the pair stood, side by side; and the wedding was promptly and cheerily solemnised. Then the gay brass bells rang forth their merry peals, the people shouted glad hurrahs, and the innocent man, preceded by children strewing flowers on his path, led his bride to his home.

This was the king's semi-barbaric method of administering justice. Its perfect fairness is obvious. The criminal could not know out of which door would come the lady: he opened either he pleased, without having the slightest idea whether, in the next instant, he was to be devoured or married. On some occasions the tiger came out of one door, and on some out of the other. The decisions of this tribunal were not only fair, they were positively determinate: the accused person was instantly punished if he found himself guilty; and, if innocent, he was rewarded on the spot, whether he liked it or not. There was no escape from the judgments of the king's arena.

The institution was a very popular one. When the people gathered together on one of the great trial days, they never knew whether they were to witness a bloody slaughter or a hilarious wedding. This element of uncertainty lent an interest to the occasion which it could not otherwise have attained. Thus the masses were entertained and pleased, and the thinking part of the community could bring no charge of unfairness against this plan; for did not the accused person have the whole matter in his own hands?

This semi-barbaric king had a daughter as blooming as his most florid fancies, and with a soul as fervent and imperious as his own. As is usual in such cases, she was the apple of his eye, and was loved by him above all humanity. Among his courtiers was a young man of that fineness of blood and lowness of station common to the conventional heroes of romance who love royal maidens. This royal maiden was well satisfied with her lover, for he was handsome and brave to a degree unsurpassed in all this kingdom; and she loved him with an ardour that had enough of barbarism in it to make it exceedingly warm and strong. This love affair moved on happily for many months, until one day the king happened to discover its existence. He did not hesitate nor waver in regard to his duty in the premises. The youth was immediately cast into prison, and a day was appointed for his trial in the king's arena. This, of course, was an especially important occasion; and his majesty, as well as all the people, was greatly interested in the workings and development of this trial. Never before had such a case occurred; never before had a subject dared to love the daughter of a king. In after years such things became commonplace enough; but then they were, in no slight degree, novel and startling.

The tiger-cages of the kingdom were searched for the most savage and relentless beasts, from which the fiercest monster might be selected for the arena; and the ranks of maiden youth and beauty throughout the land were carefully surveyed by competent judges, in order that the young man might have a fitting bride in case fate did not determine for him a different destiny. Of course, everybody knew that the deed with which the accused was charged had been done. He had loved the princess, and neither he, she, nor any one else thought of denying the fact; but the king would not think of allowing any fact of this kind to interfere with the workings of the tribunal, in which he took such great delight and satisfaction. No matter how the affair turned out, the youth would be disposed of; and the king would take an aesthetic pleasure in watching the course of events, which would determine whether or not the young man had done wrong in allowing himself to love the princess.

The appointed day arrived. From far and near the people gathered, and thronged the great galleries of the arena; and crowds, unable to gain admittance, massed themselves against its outside walls. The king and his court were in their places, opposite the twin doors—those fateful portals, so terrible in their similarity.

All was ready. The signal was given. A door beneath the royal party opened, and the lover of the princess walked into the arena. Tall, beautiful, fair, his appearance was greeted with a low hum of admiration and anxiety. Half the audience had not known so grand a youth had lived among them. No wonder the princess loved him! What a terrible thing for him to be there!

As the youth advanced into the arena, he turned, as the custom was, to bow to the king: but he did not think at all of that royal personage; his eyes were fixed upon the princess, who sat to the right of her father. Had it not been for the moiety of barbarism in her nature, it is probable that lady would not have been there; but her intense and fervid soul would not allow her to be absent on an occasion in which she was so terribly interested. From the moment that the decree had gone forth, that her lover should decide his fate in the king's arena, she had thought of nothing, night or day, but this great event and the various subjects connected with it. Possessed of more power, influence, and force of character than any one who had ever before been interested in such a case, she had done what no other person had done—she had possessed herself of the secret of the doors. She knew in which of the two rooms, that lay behind those doors, stood the cage of the tiger, with its open front, and in which waited the lady. Through these thick doors, heavily curtained with skins on the inside, it was impossible that any noise or suggestion should come from within to the person who should approach to raise the latch of one of them; but gold, and the power of a woman's will, had brought the secret to the princess.

And not only did she know in which room stood the lady ready to emerge, all blushing and radiant, should her door be opened, but she knew who the lady was. It was one of the fairest and lovelist of the damsels of the court who had been selected as the reward of the accused youth, should he be proved innocent of the crime of aspiring to one so far above him; and the princess hated her. Often had she seen, or imagined that she had seen, this fair creature throwing glances of admiration upon the person of her lover, and sometimes she thought these glances were perceived and even returned. Now and then she had seen them talking together; it was but for a moment or two, but much can be said in a brief space; it may have been on most unimportant topics, but how could she know that? The girl was lovely, but she had dared to raise her eyes to the loved one of the princess; and, with all the intensity of the savage blood transmitted to her through long lines of wholly barbaric ancestors, she hated the woman who blushed and trembled behind that silent door.

When her lover turned and looked at her, and his eye met hers as she sat there paler and whiter than any one in the vast ocean of anxious faces about her, he saw, by that power of quick perception which is given to those whose souls are one, that she knew behind which door crouched the tiger, and behind which stood the lady. He had expected her to know it. He understood her nature, and his soul was assured that she would never rest until she had made plain to herself this thing, hidden to all other lookers-on, even to the king. The only hope for the youth in which there was any element of certainty was based upon the success of the princess in discovering this mystery; and the moment he looked upon her, he saw she had succeeded, as in his soul he knew she would succeed.

Then it was that his quick and anxious glance asked the question: "Which?" It was as plain to her as if he shouted it from where he stood. There was not an instant to be lost. The question was asked in a flash; it must be answered in another.

Her right arm lay on the cushioned parapet before her. She raised her hand, and made a slight, quick movement toward the right. No one but her lover saw her. Every eye but his was fixed on the man in the arena. He turned, and with a firm and rapid step he walked across the empty space. Every heart stopped beating, every breath was held, every eye was fixed immovably upon that man. Without the slightest hesitation he went to the door on the right and opened it.

Now, the point of the story is this: Did the tiger come out of that door, or did the lady? The more we reflect upon this question, the harder it is to answer. It involves a study of the human heart which leads us through devious mazes of passion, out of which it is difficult to find our way. Think of it, fair reader, not as if the decision of the question depended upon yourself, but upon that hot-blooded, semi-barbaric princess, her soul at a white heat beneath the combined fires of despair and jealousy. She had lost him, but who should have him?

How often, in her waking hours and in her dreams, had she started in wild horror, and covered her face with her hands as she thought of her lover opening the door on the other side of which waited the cruel fangs of the tiger!

But how much oftener had she seen him at the other door! How in her grievous reveries had she gnashed her teeth, and torn her hair, when she saw his start of rapturous delight as he opened the door of the lady? How her soul had burned in agony when she had seen him rush to meet that woman, with her flushing cheek and sparkling eye of triumph; when she had seen him lead her forth, his whole frame kindled with the joy of recovered life; when she had heard the glad shouts from the multitude, and the wild ringing of the happy bells; when she had seen the priest, with his joyous followers, advance to the couple, and make them man and wife before her very eyes; and when she had seen them walk away together upon their path of flowers, followed by the tremendous shouts of the hilarious multitude, in which her one despairing shriek was lost and drowned!

Would it not be better for him to die at once, and go to wait for her in the blessed regions of semi-barbaric futurity?

And yet, that awful tiger, those shrieks, that blood!

Her decision had been indicated in an instant, but it had been made after days and nights of anguished deliberation. She had known she would be asked, she had decided what she would answer, and, without the slightest hesitation, she had moved her hand to the right.

The question of her decision is one not to be lightly considered, and it is not for me to presume to set myself up as the one person able to answer it. And so I leave it with all of you: Which came out of the opened door—the lady, or the tiger?

# HARRIET PRESCOTT SPOFFORD
1835-1921

## THE MOUNT OF SORROW

NEVER did anything seem fresher and sweeter than the plateau on which we emerged in the early sunset, after defiling all day through the dark deep mountain-sides in the rain.

We had promised Rhoda to assault her winter fastness whenever she should summon us ; and now, in obedience to her message, a gay party of us had left the railway, and had driven, sometimes in slushy snow and sometimes on bare ground, up the old mountain-road, laughing and singing, and jangling our bells, till at length the great bare woods, lifting their line for ever before us and above us, gave place to bald black mountain-sides, whose oppressive gloom and silence stifled everything but a longing to escape from between them, and from the possible dangers in crossing bridges, and fording streams swollen by the fortnight's thaws and rains. Now and then the stillness resolved itself into the murmuring of bare sprays, the rustling of rain, the dancing of innumerable unfettered brooks glittering with motion, but without light, from the dusky depths ; now and then a ghastly lustre shot from the ice still hanging like a glacier upon some upper steep, or a strange gleam from the sodden snow on their floors lightened the roofs of the leafless forests that overlapped the chasms, and trailed their twisted roots like shapes of living horror. What was there, I wondered, so darkly familiar in it all ? in what nightmare had I dreamed it all before ? Long ere the journey's end our spirits became dead as last night's wine ; we shared the depression of all nature, and felt as if we had come out of chaos and the end of all things when the huge mountain gates closed behind us, and we dashed out on the plateau where the grass, from which the wintry wrapping had been washed, had not lost all its greenness, and in the sudden lifting of the raincloud a red sparkle of sunset lighted the windows, as if a hundred flambeaux had been kindled to greet us.

A huge fire burned in the fireplace of the drawing-room when we had mounted the stairs and crossed the great hall, where other fires were blazing and sending ruddy flames to skim among the cedar rafters ; and all that part of the house sacred to Colonel Vorse, and opened now the first time in many winters, was thoroughly warm and cheerful with lights and flowers and rugs and easy-chairs and books. We might easily have fancied ourselves, that night, in those spacious rooms, when, toilets made and dinner over, we reassembled around the solid glow of the chimney logs, a modern party in some old mediæval chamber, all the more for the spirit of the scene outside, where the storm was telling its rede again, rain changing to snow, and a cruel blast keening round the many gables and screaming down the chimneys. After all, Rhoda's and Merivale's plan of having us in the hills before late-lingering winter should be quite gone, and doing a little Sintram business with skates and wolves and hill visions, should have been carried out earlier. To them it was all but little less novel than it was to me, and Rhoda, who, although a year or two my junior, had been my intimate, so far as I ever had an intimate, would not rest till she had devised this party, without which she knew she could not have me, even persuading our good old Dr. Devens to leave his pulpit and people, and stamp the proceeding with his immaculate respectability. As it was, however, it looked as though we were simply to be shut in by a week of storm following the thaw. Well, there are compensations in all things : perhaps two people in whom I had some interest would know each other a trifle better before the week ended then.

The place was really the home of Rhoda and Merivale, or was now to become so. Colonel Vorse, their father, who had married so young that he felt but little older than they, and was quite their companion, was still the owner of the vast summer hostelry, although no longer its manager. After accumulating his fortune he had taken his children about the world, educating them and himself at the same time, with now an object lesson in Germany and now another in Peru, and finally returning to this place, which, so far as we could see, was absolute desolation, without a neighbour, but which to him was bristling with memories and associations and old friends across the intervale and over the mountain and round the spur. There was something weird to me, as I looked out at the flying whiteness of the moonlit storm, in those acquaintances of his among the hollows of these pallid hills ; it seemed as though they must partake of the coldness and whiteness, and as if they were only dead people, when all was said. Perhaps Dr. Devens, who half the way up had been quoting,

> Pavilioned high, he sits
> In darkness from excessive splendour born,

had another phase of the same feeling. I heard him saying, as I passed him five minutes before, where he sat astride a chair in front of the long oriel casement : " There is a path which no fowl knoweth, and which the vulture's eye hath not seen : the lion's whelps have not trodden it, nor the fierce lion passed by it. He putteth forth his hand upon the rock ; he overturneth the mountains by the roots. He cutteth out rivers among the rocks ; and his eye seeth every precious thing. He bindeth the floods from overflowing ; and the thing that is hid bringeth he forth to light." He is expecting a convulsion of nature, I remember thinking, as I went by and paused at another window myself. A convulsion of nature! I fancy that he found it.

" There is something eerie here," I said, as I still gazed at the scene ; for the dim gigantic shapes of the hills rose round us like sheeted ghosts, while the flying scud of the storm, filled with the white diffusion of unseen light, every now and then opened to let the glimpses out. " And see the witch-fires," as the rosy reflections of our burning logs and lights danced on the whirling snow without. " Is there anything wanting to make us feel as if we had been caught here by some spell, and were to be held by some charm ? "

" I wish I knew the charm," said Colonel Vorse, by my side, and half under his breath. And then I felt a little angrier with myself for coming than I had felt before.

" I often hear you talking of your belief in certain telluric forces that must have most power among the mountains where they first had play, and where earth is not only beneath, but is above you and around you. Well, we are here in the stronghold of these telluric forces. I am their old friend and ally : let me see what they will do for me."

It was true. And I half shivered with an indefinite fear that I might be compelled, in spite of all wish and prejudice, and birth-right—I, the child of proud old colonial grandees of the South ; he, the son of a mountain farmer, who had married a mate of his own degree, and had kept a mountain inn till fortune found him and death took her. My father at least was the child of those proud old colonials, and I had lived with his people and been reared on their traditions. Who my mother was I never knew ; for my father had married her in some romantic fashion—a runaway match—and she had died at my birth, and he had shortly followed her. I had nothing that belonged to her but the half of a broken miniature my father had once painted of her, as I understood. I always wore it, with I know not what secret sentiment, but I showed it to nobody. I had sometimes wondered about the other half, but my life had not left me much time for sentiment or wonder—full of gaiety till my grandfather's death left me homeless ; full of gaiety since his friend Mrs. Montresor had adopted me for child and companion, subject to her kind whims and tyrannies. But if she took me here and took me there, and clad me like a princess, I was none the less aware of the fact that I was without a penny—morbidly aware of it without doubt. But it disposed me to look with favour on no rich man's suit, and the lover as penniless as I and as fine as my ideal lover had not yet appeared. It made me almost hate the face and form, the colour, the hair, that they dared to call Titianesque, speak of as if it were the free booty of pigment and canvas, and wish to drag captive in the golden chains of their wealth. When I had met Colonel Vorse, a year ago, twice my age though he was, he was the first one I had wished as poor as I—he the plebeian newly rich. Yet not so newly rich was he that he had not had time to become used to his riches, to see the kingdoms of the earth and weigh them in his balance, to serve his country on the battlefield, and his State in the council chamber; and, for the rest, contact with the world is sadly educating.

"I often look at Colonel Vorse among the men born in the purple," said Mrs. Montresor once—she thought people born in the purple were simply those who had never earned their living—" and he is the superior of them all. What a country it is where a man keeping a common tavern in the first half of his life may make himself the equal of sovereigns in the other half! I don't understand it; he is the finest gentleman of them all. And he looks it. Don't you think so, Helena?"

But I never told Mrs. Montresor what I thought. It is all very well to generalise and to be glad that certain institutions produce certain effects; but of course you are superior to the institutions, or you wouldn't be generalising so, and all the more, of course, superior to the effects, and so I don't see how it signifies to you personally.

"You ought to have your head carried on a pike," said Mrs. Montresor again. "You will, if we ever have any *bonnets rouges* in America. You are the aristocrat pure and simple. The Princess Lamballe was nothing to you. You think humanity exists so that *nous autres*, by standing on it, may get the light and air. You are sure that you are made of different clay—the *canaille* of street mud, for instance, and you of the fine white stuff from which they mould Dresden china. You are quite a study to me, my love. I expect to see you marry a pavior yet, either one who lays down or one who tears up paving-stones." But I had only laughed again. She plumed herself on being cosmopolitan even to her principles.

"You give me credit for too much thinking on the subject." I said, "if it is credit. Indeed, I don't concern myself about such people; and as for marrying one of them, I could as soon marry into a different race, African or Mongolian. They *are* a different race."

And I remembered all this as Colonel Vorse stood leaning his hand above me on the jamb of the window-frame—for although I was tall, he was a son of Anak—with that air which, never vaunting strength, always made you aware of its repression. I could fancy hearing Mrs. Montresor say, "That air of his! it always fetches women!" for she loved a little slang, by some antipodal attraction of her refinement, and I instinctively stiffened myself, determined it should never fetch *me*. And here he was calling his allies, the spirits and powers of the dark and terrible mountain heights and depths, and openly giving battle. I don't know why it depressed me; I felt as if the very fact that it did was a half-surrender; I looked up at him a moment; I forgot who he was; I wished he was as poor as I. But to become the mother of Rhoda, my friend, and of Merivale, that laughing young giant—what absurdity, if all the rest were equal! And that other, the dead woman, the first wife—should one not always be jealous of that sweet early love? Could one endure it? Here among these hills with all their ghostliness she would haunt me. And then I turned and swept away to the fireside, holding out my hands to the flame, and glad to sink into the chair that some one had left empty there.

I hardly knew what world I was living in when, perhaps a half-hour later, I heard Colonel Vorse's voice. "The trouble is that men are *not* born free and equal," he was saying. "Free? They are hampered by inheritance and circumstance from the moment of birth. Equal? It is a self-evident lie. And the world has rhapsodised for a hundred years over so clumsy a statement. All men are born with equal rights. That is the precise statement. My rights—rights to life, liberty, and the pursuit of happiness—are equal to the rights of all the princelings of the earth; their rights equal only to mine. So far as they interfere with my rights they are public enemies, and are to be dealt with; and so far as I interfere with their rights, I am a trespasser to be punished. Otherwise, prince or peasant, each is a man, whether he wears a blouse or a star and garter; and if man was made in the image of God, let us do no indignity to that image in one or in another."

Did I understand him? Was Colonel Vorse proclaiming himself the equal of Prince San Sorcererino who had entertained us in his palaces last year? Well. And was he not? All at once something seemed to sift away from before my eyes—a veil that had hidden my kind from me. Was there no longer even that natural aristocracy in which Shakespeare or Homer or Dante was king? Was the world a brotherhood, and they the public enemy, the enemy of the great perfect race to come, who helped one brother take advantage of another? Were those ribbons in the buttonhole, the gifts of kings, of no more worth than the ribbons of cigars?

Mrs. Montresor was toying with her fan beside me, and talking in an undertone behind it. "What prince of all that you have seen or read of," said she, "if born on a meagre mountain farm, would have made his fortune and have educated himself as this man has done? I think the kings who founded races of kings were like him. And what prince of them all alike looks so much the prince as he? This one as fat as Falstaff and as low, that one with a hump on his back, the other without brains, the next with brains awry, and none of them made as becomes a man. Tell me, Helena?"

"I think you are in love yourself," I said.

She laughed. "As tall as Saul, as dark, as lordly in all proportions, as gentle as Jonathan, and with a soul like David's—why shouldn't I be?" she said. "And he not the equal of the grand-daughter of a South Carolina planter! Tell me again, Helena, what has she ever done to prove herself his equal?"

She had had a fancy—Heaven knows why—that her young mother, who had run away with her father, was the daughter of a noble foreign family; or else why should the match have been clandestine? She had had a fancy that she was therefore noble, as her mother was—the mother even whose name her child did not know other than as the slaves had told her the young bridegroom called her Pansy because of a pair of purple-dark eyes. That was about all. That was all the answer I could have made, had I spoken, to her gentle raillery, half mockery, in which she did not quite believe herself. But even were it so, and the daughter noble as the mother, could blood that had filtered through generations of oppressors lounging in laps of luxury be pure as this blood that had informed none but simple and innocent lives, and seemed just now as if it had come fresh from the hands of the Maker? I surveyed him from behind the hand-screen that failed to keep the ruddy flames from my face, and I felt him in that glance to be one of the sons of God, and I but one of the daughters of men. Again I did not tell Mrs. Montresor.

But the witch could always read my thoughts. "Still," she said, "he has kept a tavern. There is no getting round that fact by all the poetry in the world. Then why try to get round it? He has furnished food and shelter to the tired and roofless—as noble a way to make money, surely, as working the bones and muscles of slaves, and accepting the gold they earn."

"That is the last I have of such gold," I cried, in a stifled way; and I unclasped the old bracelet on my wrist and tossed it behind the back-log—people were too gaily engaged to observe us at the moment. "I think," I said then, turning upon her, "that you are employed as an advocate, unless—you are really weary of me."

"Weary of you!" she exclaimed, half under her breath though it was—"weary of you, when you are such unceasing variety to me that if you married ten thousand tavern-keepers I should always have a room in the inn!"

"Thank Heaven," I answered her gaily, "it is an impossibility that I should ever marry *one*." And then there was a lull in the laughter and the snatches of song and conversation on the other side of the room; and while I was still gazing after my bracelet and into the chimney-place, where the flames wallowed about unhewn forest logs that took two men to cast to them, Colonel Vorse came over to us.

"You will turn into salamanders," he said.

"It is bad enough to be in hot water," said Mrs. Montresort lightly. "I will leave the fire to you and Helena."

"Where you sit," said Colonel Vorse then to me, "if you turn your head slightly to the left, and shade your eyes, you can see the side of the darkest and sternest of our mountains. You know we do not call our hills by the names they have in maps and Government surveys; the old settlers who first came here called this one, for unknown reasons of their own, the Mount of Sorrow. It has always been the Mount of Sorrow."

"An ominous name for so near a neighbour," I said.

"Ah! you think this region is oppressive, or perhaps dull and tame, without life or stir—desolate, in fact. What if I should tell you that it bubbles, like a caldron over the bottomless pit, with griefs and sins!—that in lives condemned to perpetual imprisonment on these bare rocks, feeding on themselves, traits intensifying the loneliness, the labour, the negation, slowly extract the juices of humanity, and make crime a matter to be whispered of among them? If they feel they are forgotten by God, what matters the murder or the suicide more or less that gives release? It is hell here or hell there: they are sure of this—they have it; the other may not come to pass."

"What do you mean?" I said, with white lips; for as he spoke it seemed as if I had come into a land of lepers. "Here in this white solitude, among lives fed from the primitive sources of nature and the dew of the morning——"

"I mean," he said, "that I refuse to accept the factitious aid your thoughts have lately been bringing to me. You see I have preternatural senses. Because I was born in the snows of the mountains I am no whit whiter than those born in the purlieus of the police stations of the cities. We are simply of the same human nature. When I win regard, it must be for no idle fancy, but for my own identity."

"Well," I said, "I do not believe you."

"Ah!" he replied, "have I gained a point, and found an advocate in an ideal of me? That would be as romantic as any of the romance of the hills. And there *is* romance here, whether it is born of crime, or of joy or of sorrow. There is romance enough on that old Mount of Sorrow that you see when the storm opens and strips it in that sudden white glory. Keep your eye, if you please, on a spot halfway up the sky, and when the apparition comes again you will find the dark outline of a dwelling there. It was a dwelling once; now it is only a ruin, hut and barn and byre. Why do you shudder? Do you see it? It is only a shadow. But a shadow with outlines black enough to defy the whitest blast that ever blew. Sometimes it seems to me as though that old ruin were itself a ghostly thing, a spectre of tragedies that will not down; for the avalanches divide and leave it, and the storms whistle over and beat against it, and it is always there when the sun rises. I don't know what it has to do with my fortunes; I don't know why it is a blotch upon the face of nature to me; but if ever I grow sad or sick at heart I feel as though I should be made whole again could that evil thing be removed."

"Why not remove it?"

"It does not belong to me. I can do nothing with it. I am not sure that it belongs to any one—which adds to the spectral, you see—although I suppose there is somewhere a nameless heir. How restless you are!" he said gently. "Will you come out in the long hall where the great window gives an unobstructed view of the thing, and walk off this nervousness? The storm is lifting, I think; the moon is going to overcome. One may see by the way the fire burns that the temperature is mounting. Perhaps we shall have a snow-slide as we walk."

Rhoda and Merivale were singing some of the songs they had learned since they came into the hill country, Mrs. Montresor was nodding behind her fan an accompaniment to Dr. Devens' remarks, Adèle was deep in her novel, and a flirtation and some portfolios of prints occupied the rest. To refuse was only to attract attention; besides, I should like to walk. I rose and went out with him into the hall that shut off the wing from the great empty caravansary:

"And the long carpets rose along the gusty floor,"

I quoted as we walked; and despite the fire burning on either side, he had brought me a fur for my shoulders.

"Yes," he said, "there comes the moon at last. Now you shall see the black and white of it."

"Oh!" I cried, clasping my hands as all the silvery lights and immense shadows burst out in a terrible sort of radiance. "The world began to be made here! Poets should be born here!"

"Instead of tavern-keepers," said he, "which brings me to my story. I am forty-three years old. Of course I was younger twenty-three years ago. That must have been not long before you came into the world yourself. Do you insist upon thinking twenty years' difference in age makes any disparity, except in the case of him who has lost just that twenty years' sweetness out of his life?"

"I hardly see what that has to do with the story of the Mount of Sorrow," I said, as we turned from the window to measure the length of the hall again.

"I hope," said he, "that the suffrage reform, which is to admit women to the ballot, will never let them sit on the judicial bench, for mercy is foreign to the heart of a woman."

"Is it not a strange way of telling a story?" I exclaimed.

"Patience!" he laughed. "The story is so short it needs a little preface. As I was saying then, when I was twenty years old or so, the name of old Raynier, of the Mount of Sorrow, was a byword of terror through the region round, as the name of his father was, and his father before him. He had no other property than the sterile farm half-way up the mountain, and almost inaccessible—in winter entirely inaccessible—where he raised not half a support on the slips of earth among the ledges; his few starved sheep and goats did what they could for him, and his rifle did the rest. The first Raynier of them all was possibly an escaped convict, who fortified his retreat by these mountain-sides. He had no money; the women spun and wove all that was worn. He had no education; no Raynier had ever had; no Raynier had ever had occasion to sign his mark, let alone his name. There had been one son in each generation; neither church nor school ever saw him; his existence was scarcely known till he was ready to marry, and then he came down, and by no one knows what other magic than a savage force of nature, took the prettiest girl of the valley to his eyrie—sometimes his wife sometimes not. When she died, and she always died, the Raynier of the day replaced her. He did not always wait for her to die before replacing her. But sudden deaths were no uncommon thing in that house; there was a burial-ground scooped in the hill-side. And who was there to interfere? Perhaps no one knew there had been a death till the year was out. What if a woman went mad? That happened anywhere. People below might prate of murder, or suicide, or slow poison; there was nobody to whom it was vital enough to open the question seriously; and then they feared the Raynier with an uncanny fear, as people fear a catamount in the woods, or the goblin of old wives' tales after dark. There were horrible stories of bouts and brawls, of tortures, gags, whips, and—oh, no matter! Nor was all the crime on the shoulders of the Raynier men. It was understood that more than one woman of the name found life too intolerable to endure its conditions when the fumes of a charcoal fire after a drunken feast, or a quick thrust over the edge of a precipice, or a bit of weed in the broth, made life easier, till remorse brought madness. And finally, if any Raynier died what may be called a natural death, it was either from starvation or from delirium tremens. You see they were a precious lot."

"A precious lot!" I said, trembling. "Ah, what is heaven made of? Poor wretches, they could not help it. From generation to generation the children of such people must needs be criminal."

"I don't know. If removed from such influence. To my mind environment is strong as heredity, quite as strong. It destroys the old and creates the new. However, environment and heredity worked together up there. In my day—to continue—the Raynier family was larger than usual. The last wife still lived, a miserable cowed creature, white as ashes, face and hair and bleached scared eyes, eyes that looked as if they saw phantoms rather than people. Her mind was partially gone. I was a famous mountaineer then, and climbing wherever foot of man had been before, I once in a while came upon some or other of that family, and sometimes paused at the door, where I had first to teach the bloodhounds a

lesson. I never entered the filthy place but once. There were two
sons and a daughter. Oh, how immortally beautiful that girl was!
Such velvet darkness in the eye, such statuesque lines, such rose-
leaf colour, such hair—'hair like the thistledown tinted with gold,'
as John Mills, the Scotch poet-player, sang. The old man Raynier
worshipped her, perhaps as a wild beast loves its whelp. But he
had all sorts of fanciful names for her, Heart's-ease and Heart's
Delight, and Violet and Rose and Lily. He grew almost gentle
when he spoke to her; and he never knew that she was feeble-
minded. She just missed being an imbecile. Perhaps you would
not have known that all at once; you might not have found it out
at all only meeting her casually. The old man Raynier sent her
down to school—the first that had ever been there: she could
never learn to read. She could not always tell her name. Still,
her mind was innocent—perhaps because it was a blank. I have
sometimes thought that blank mind of hers may have been a
dead-wall through which the vices of her forebears could not pass,
and so her children, if she had them, may have escaped the inheritance, and found a chance for good again, as if crime should at last
estop itself. That may be."

"Oh, I think this is terrible!" I said, as we turned again in our
walk. "Make haste, please, and be through."

"Yes it is. But I would show you that life can be anything but
commonplace in this wilderness. Well, blank or not, she had a lover,
who had found her out in his sketching rambles, a young painter
from some distant parts, and the first boarder I ever had, by the
way. And all the Rayniers swore they would have his life sooner
than he should have her. One day I had been hunting on old
Mount Sorrow, as it happened; there had been a sudden frost
following rain that had frozen the water in the cracks of the cliffs,
and made the way not only slippery, but dangerous; for in the
heat of the noon sun the ice was melting, and every now and then
its expansion was rending some fragment of rock so that your
footing might vanish from beneath, or some shower of stones come
rattling down from above; and I was tired when I reached the
Raynier place, led by a blaze of maple boughs that started out like
torches to show the way, and stopped to rest. I looked up at an
enormous shelf of rock, half clad with reddened vines that fluttered
like pestilence flags—a shelf that, although some hundred feet or so
away from it, yet overhung the place and cast a perpetual shadow
there. I wondered then why Nature had no secret springs of feeling
to thrill her and cause her to rend the rocks and cover such a den of
iniquity as we all held the spot to be. But Nature was just as fair
that ambrosial September day as if there was not a dissonance.
Perhaps she knew the right of the Rayniers to life, liberty, and the
pursuit of happiness. A delicious scent of the balsam from the
pines filled the air, the sunshine swept over the hills below in waves

of light, and the hills themselves were like waves of a golden green
and purple sea where now and then a rainbow swam and broke.
Peace and perfectness, I said, peace and perfectness. These people
live and are happy. On the other side one looked into the dreary
defile of the mountain gate, with its black depths hung with cloud,
and remembered that if there was not a hell, there ought to be.
I was thinking this as I sat there, when I heard a wild cry, an
agonized shriek, blood-curdling, repeated and repeated from within.
It was the girl's voice. I was on my feet, and, in spite of the bloodhounds, making for the spot and among the crew. The old woman
cowered in the corner, the two brothers held the girl, the old man
towered over her, his great eyes blazing in his ashen face. I can't
tell you what they were doing. Sometimes I have thought old
Raynier was burning her with a hot iron he held——"

"Oh, horrible! horrible!"

"Burning her with a hot iron to make her give up her lover!
Sometimes I have thought he was only demolishing the little like-
nesses of him and of herself, which that lover had painted, and
which she cherished, perhaps as his work, perhaps for the unwonted
gewgaw of the slender golden frame, for the one picture was already
in fragments, and although she clutched half of the other, the broken
half had fallen and rolled away. I have it somewhere. I will show
it to you. I had no time, indeed, to see what it was they were
doing, for behind me bounded that lover like a whirlwind, thrust
one brother and the other aside, seized the girl, darted over the
door-sill with her, and down the crags of the mountain path. He
should have what help I could give. I was after him, stooping to
catch up the fragment of painting as I turned, down the cliff's
edge, they following. And all at once I stopped as if paralysed to
the marrow by a clap of thunder, and turned my head to see the
old man with his white hair streaming, and his arms uplifted in
his cursing, as he came leaping on, and the next moment the shelf
of overhanging rock had fallen, had cleft the house in twain, and
mother and father and sons and hounds were dust with the dust
flying over the precipices. I saw it."

"Oh!" I cried, with my hands over my eyes. "Why did it not
strike you blind?"

"And here," said Colonel Vorse, leading my steps to an old
cabinet in an alcove, "ought to be the half of that little likeness I
picked up as I ran. I wonder what became of the other half—
what became of the girl—if the lover married her—if she knew
enough to know he didn't marry her—if she lived long enough for
him to find out she was a fool—if she was the last of the Rayniers?"
As he ceased, he put the half of the little miniature into my hands.

It was a broken bit of ivory, and on it the upper part of a face,
sketchily done, with pansy-dark eyes and blush-rose skin—without
a frame. I had the frame.

A heart-beat, a fluttering breath, a reeling sense of the world staggering away from me, and then my bewildered senses were at work again, and an agony like death was cutting me to the heart as we resumed our walking.

Should I tell him? Should I go on with my secret, my inheritance, my curse, and let no man know? If it ate out my heart, the sooner to end; my heart was broken now. Never, never now could fireside shine for me, could lover's lips be mine, could little faces sun themselves in my smile.

We paused before the great window, with those vague white shapes before us, for my feet would not obey me, and the light behind us shone on the bit of ivory. If I told him, it would be easier for him to bear; he would see the impossibility, he would desire my love no longer. My fearful inheritance would yawn like a gulf between us with its impassable darkness.

"And the ruin on the hill-side is an eyesore," I said. "But it is easy to remove it. I suppose it belongs to me. For—look here— it is I who must be the last of the Rayniers." And I drew from my breast the broken thing, the halved miniature, that in my mock sentiment I had worn so long.

"You!" cried he. "You!" And his feet tottered, and he leaned against the casement for support—he who an hour or so ago had seemed so full of repressed strength that he could have pulled his house down about his ears. Well, had he not done so?

I moved to his side, and held the thing that he might see where the pieces matched, the line of the cheek flowing into the lovely curve of the chin, the flickering sweetness of the lovely mouth, the lambent glance of the lovely eye. "It is my mother, you see," I said. "And it needs no words to say it."

"It needs no words to say it," he repeated hoarsely. "It is your image. Oh, my God! What have I done! what have I done! My darling, my darling, you must let me repair it by a lifetime of devotion." And he had his arms about me, and was drawing me to his heaving breast, his throbbing heart.

"No! no! no!" I sobbed. "It is impossible. I am wrecked; I am ruined; I can be no man's wife. You see yourself—I will never——" But his lips were silencing mine, and I lay there with those arms about me a moment; I lay there like one in heaven suspended over hell.

"What do I care," he whispered, "for all the Rayniers in Christendom or out of it, but you? I have learned in this moment that you love me! I will never give you up."

"You must," I groaned.

"I tell you I never will," he said, his voice husky and low and trembling, but his eye and his grasp firm. "I have assured you that environment, education, art, can supplement nature and heredity. They have done so with you. You are your father's child. You received from your mother only the vital spark, only this beauty, this fatal beauty. If you inherited all that the Rayniers ever had, then I love, I love, I love all that the Rayniers ever were, for I love you. I have your love, Helena, and I will never let you go." While speaking he had touched the bell at his hand, and now he sent the answering servant for Dr. Devens, who came at once, supposing some sight of the snow was in store.

"Bid them all out here, Doctor," cried Colonel Vorse. "Ah, here they come! In this part of the country we need no licence for marriage. Here are a bride and groom awaiting your blessing. Perform your office, sir." And before I could summon heart or voice, making no response, bewildered and faint, I was the wife of Colonel Vorse, and my husband's arms were supporting me as the words of the prayer and benediction rolled over us.

"There is no time like the present," he cried gaily, his tones no longer broken, "as I have always found." And suddenly, before he ceased, and while they all thronged round me, there came a sharp strange sigh singing through the air, that grew into the wild discordant music of multitudinous echoes, and we all turned and sprang intuitively to see, rent in the moonlight and sheathed in the glorious spray of a thousand ice-falls, the Mount of Sorrow bow its head and come down, and, while the whole earth shook and smoked back in hoar vapours, the great snow-slide, in its swift sheeting splendour, flash and wipe out before our eyes the last timber of the hut and barn and byre of the Rayniers.

# MARK TWAIN
(Samuel Langhorne Clemens)
1835–1910

# THE CELEBRATED JUMPING FROG OF CALAVERAS COUNTY

In compliance with the request of a friend of mine, who wrote me from the East, I called on good-natured, garrulous old Simon Wheeler, and inquired after my friend's friend, *Leonidas W*. Smiley, as requested to do, and I hereunto append the result. I have a lurking suspicion that *Leonidas W*. Smiley is a myth; that my friend never knew such a personage; and that he only conjectured that, if I asked old Wheeler about him, it would remind him of his infamous *Jim* Smiley, and he would go to work and bore me nearly to death with some infernal reminiscence of him as long and tedious as it should be useless for me. If that was the design, it certainly succeeded.

I found Simon Wheeler dozing comfortably by the bar-room stove of the old, dilapidated tavern in the ancient mining camp of Angel's, and I noticed that he was fat and bald-headed, and had an expression of winning gentleness and simplicity upon his tranquil countenance. He roused up and gave me good-day. I told him a friend of mine had commissioned me to make some inquiries about a cherished companion of his boyhood named *Leonidas W*. Smiley—*Rev. Leonidas W*. Smiley—a young minister of the Gospel, who he had heard was at one time a resident of Angel's Camp. I added that, if Mr. Wheeler could tell me anything about this Rev. Leonidas W. Smiley, I would feel under many obligations to him.

Simon Wheeler backed me into a corner and blockaded me there with his chair, and then sat me down and reeled off the monotonous narrative which follows this paragraph. He never smiled, he never frowned, he never changed his voice from the gentle-flowing key to which he tuned the initial sentence, he never betrayed the slightest suspicion of enthusiasm; but all through the interminable narrative there ran a vein of impressive earnestness and sincerity, which showed me plainly that, so far from his imagining that there was anything ridiculous or funny about his story, he regarded it as a really important matter, and admired its two heroes as men of transcendent genius in *finesse*. To me the spectacle of a man drifting serenely along through such a queer yarn without ever smiling was exquisitely absurd. As I said before, I asked him to tell me what he knew of Rev. Leonidas W. Smiley, and he replied as follows. I let him go on in his own way, and never interrupted him once :

There was a feller here once by the name of *Jim* Smiley, in the winter of '49—or may be it was the spring of '50—I don't recollect exactly, somehow, though what makes me think it was one or the other is because I remember the big flume wasn't finished when he first came to the camp ; but any way he was the curiosest man about, always betting on anything that turned up you ever see, if he could get anybody to bet on the other side ; and if he couldn't, he'd change sides. Any way that suited the other man would suit him—any way just so's he got a bet, *he* was satisfied. But still he was lucky, uncommon lucky ; he most always come out winner. He was always ready and laying for a chance ; there couldn't be no solitry thing mentioned but that feller'd offer to bet on it, and take any side you please, as I was just telling you. If there was a horse-race, you'd find him flush, or you'd find him busted at the end of it ; if there was a dog-fight, he'd bet on it ; if there was a cat-fight, he'd bet on it ; if there was a chicken-fight, he'd bet on it ; why, if there was two birds sitting on a fence, he would bet you which one would fly first ; or if there was a camp-meeting, he would be there reg'lar, to bet on Parson Walker, which he judged to be the best exhorter about here, and so he was, too, and a good man. If he even seen a straddle-bug start to go anywheres, he would bet you how long it would take him to get wherever he was going to, and if you took him up, he would foller that straddle-bug to Mexico but what he would find out where he was bound for and how long he was on the road. Lots of the boys here has seen that Smiley, and can tell you about him. Why, it never made no difference to *him*—he would bet on *any* thing—the dangdest feller. Parson Walker's wife laid very sick once, for a good while, and it seemed as if they warn't going to save her ; but one morning he come in, and Smiley asked how she was, and he said she was considerable better—thank the Lord for His inf'nit mercy—and coming on so smart that, with the blessing of Prov'dence, she'd get well yet ; and Smiley, before he thought, says, " Well, I'll risk two-and-a-half that she don't, anyway."

This-yer Smiley had a mare—the boys called her the fifteen-minute nag, but that was only in fun, you know, because, of course, she was faster than that—and he used to win money on that horse, for all she was so slow and always had the asthma, or the distemper, or the consumption, or something of that kind. They used to give her two or three hundred yards' start, and then pass her under way; but always at the fag-end of the race she'd get excited and desperate-like, and come cavorting and straddling up, and scattering her legs around limber, sometimes in the air, and sometimes out to one side amongst the fences, and kicking up m-o-r-e dust, and raising m-o-r-e racket with her coughing and sneezing and blowing her nose—and always fetch up at the stand just about a neck ahead, as near as you could cipher it down.

And he had a little small bull pup, that to look at him you'd think he wan't worth a cent, but to set around and look ornery, and lay for a chance to steal something. But as soon as the money was up on him, he was a different dog; his under-jaw'd begin to stick out like the fo'castle of a steamboat, and his teeth would uncover, and shine savage like the furnaces. And a dog might tackle him, and bully-rag him, and bite him, and throw him over his shoulder two or three times, and Andrew Jackson—which was the name of the pup—Andrew Jackson would never let on but what *he* was satisfied, and hadn't expected nothing else—and the bets being doubled and doubled on the other side all the time, till the money was all up; and then all of a sudden he would grab that other dog jest by the j'int of his hind leg and freeze to it—not chaw, you understand, but only jest grip and hang on till they throwed up the sponge, if it was a year. Smiley always come out winner on that pup, till he harnessed a dog once that didn't have no hind legs, because they'd been sawed off by a circular saw, and when the thing had gone along far enough, and the money was all up, and he come to make a snatch for his pet holt, he saw in a minute how he'd been imposed on, and how the other dog had him in the door, so to speak, and he 'peared surprised, and then he looked sorter discouraged-like, and didn't try no more to win the fight, and so he got shucked out bad. He give Smiley a look, as much as to say his heart was broke, and it was *his* fault, for putting up a dog that hadn't no hind legs for him to take holt of, which was his main dependence in a fight, and then he limped off a piece and laid down and died. It was a good pup, was that Andrew Jackson, and would have made a name for hisself if he'd lived, for the stuff was in him, and he had genius—I know it, because he hadn't had no opportunities to speak of, and it don't stand to reason that a dog could make such a fight as he could under them circumstances, if he hadn't no talent. It always makes me feel sorry when I think of that last fight of his'n, and the way it turned out.

Well, this-yer Smiley had rat-tarriers, and chicken cocks, and tom-cats, and all them kind of things, till you couldn't rest, and you couldn't fetch nothing for him to bet on but he'd match you. He ketched a frog one day, and took him home, and said he cal'klated to edercate him; and so he never done nothing for three months but set in his back yard and learn that frog to jump. And you bet you he *did* learn him, too. He'd give him a little punch behind, and the next minute you'd see that frog whirling in the air like a doughnut—see him turn one somerset, or may be a couple, if he got a good start, and come down flat-footed and all right, like a cat. He got him up so in the matter of catching flies, and kept him in practice so constant, that he'd nail a fly every time as far as he could see him. Smiley said all a frog wanted was education, and he could do most anything—and I believe him. Why, I've seen him set Dan'l Webster down here on this floor—Dan'l Webster was the name of the frog—and sing out, " Flies, Dan'l, flies ! " and quicker'n you could wink, he's spring straight up, and snake a fly off'n the counter there, and flop down on the floor again as solid as a gob of mud, and fall to scratching the side of his head with his hind foot as indifferent as if he hadn't no idea he'd been doin' any more'n any frog might do. You never see a frog so modest and straight for'ard as he was, for all he was so gifted. And when it come to fair and square jumping on a dead level, he could get over more ground at one straddle than any animal of his breed you ever see. Jumping on a dead level was his strong suit, you understand ; and when it come to that, Smiley would ante up money on him as long as he had a red. Smiley was monstrous proud of his frog, and well he might be, for fellers that had travelled and been everywheres, all said he laid over any frog that ever *they* see.

Well, Smiley kept the beast in a little lattice box, and he used to fetch him down town sometimes and lay for a bet. One day a feller—a stranger in the camp, he was—come across him with his box, and says :

" What might it be that you've got in the box ? "

And Smiley says, sorter indifferent like, " It might be a parrot, or it might be a canary, may be, but it ain't—it's only just a frog."

And the feller took it, and looked at it careful, and turned it round this way and that, and says, " H'm, so 'tis. Well, what's *he* good for ? "

" Well," Smiley says, easy and careless, " he's good enough for *one* thing, I should judge—he can out-jump ary frog in Calaveras county."

The feller took the box again, and took another long, particular look, and give it back to Smiley, and says, very deliberate, " Well, I don't see no p'ints about that frog that's any better'n any other frog."

" May be you don't," Smiley says. " May be you understand frogs, and may be you don't understand 'em ; may be you've had experience, and may be you ain't, only a amature, as it were. Any ways, I've got *my* opinion, and I'll risk forty dollars that he can outjump any frog in Calaveras county."

And the feller studied a minute, and then says, kinder sad like, " Well, I'm only a stranger here, and I ain't got no frog ; but if I had a frog, I'd bet you."

And then Smiley says, "That's all right—that's all right—if you'll hold my box a minute, I'll go and get you a frog." And so the feller took the box, and put up his forty dollars along with Smiley's and set down to wait.

So he set there a good while thinking and thinking to hisself, and then he got the frog out and prized his mouth open and took a teaspoon and filled him full of quail shot—filled him pretty near up to his chin—and set him on the floor. Smiley he went to the swamp and slopped around in the mud for a long time, and finally be ketched a frog, and fetched him in, and give him to this feller, and says :

"Now, if you're ready, set him alongside of Dan'l, with his forepaws just even with Dan'l, and I'll give the word." Then he says, "One—two—three—jump!" and him and the feller touched up the frogs from behind, and the new frog hopped off, but Dan'l give a heave, and hysted up his shoulders—so—like a Frenchman, but it wan't no use—he couldn't budge ; he was planted as solid as an anvil, and he couldn't no more stir than if he was anchored out. Smiley was a good deal surprised, and he was disgusted too, but he didn't have no idea what the matter was, of course.

The feller took the money and started away ; and when he was going out at the door, he sorter jerked his thumb over his shoulders—this way—at Dan'l, and says again, very deliberate, "Well, I don't see no p'ints about that frog that's any better'n any other frog."

Smiley he stood scratching his head and looking down at Dan'l a long time, and at last he says, "I do wonder what in the nation that frog throw'd off for—I wonder if there ain't something the matter with him—he 'pears to look mightly baggy, somehow." And he ketched Dan'l by the nap of the neck, and lifted him up and says, "Why, blame my cats, if he don't weigh five pound!" and turned him upside down, and he belched out a double handful of shot. And then he see how it was, and he was the maddest man—he set the frog down and took out after that feller, but he never ketched him. And——

(Here Simon Wheeler heard his name called from the front yard, and got up to see what was wanted.) And turning to me as he moved away, he said : "Just set where you are, stranger, and rest easy—I an't going to be gone a second."

But, by your leave, I did not think that a continuation of the history of the enterprising vagabond *Jim* Smiley would be likely to afford me much information concerning the Rev. *Leonidas W.* Smiley, and so I started away.

At the door I met the sociable Wheeler returning, and he buttonholed me and recommenced :

"Well, this-yer Smiley had a yaller one-eyed cow that didn't have no tail, only just a short stump like a bannanner, and——"

"Oh, hang Smiley and his afflicted cow!" I muttered goodnaturedly, and bidding the old gentleman good-day, I departed.

# THE MAN WHO PUT UP AT GADSBY'S

MARK TWAIN

WHEN my old friend Riley and I were newspaper correspondents in Washington, in the winter of '67, we were coming down Pennsylvania Avenue one night, near midnight, in a driving storm of snow, when the flash of a street-lamp fell upon a man who was eagerly tearing along in the opposite direction. This man instantly stopped, and exclaimed:

"This is lucky! You are Mr. Riley, ain't you?"

Riley was the most self-possessed and solemnly deliberative person in the republic. He stopped, looked his man over from head to foot, and finally said:

"I am Mr. Riley. Did you happen to be looking for me?"

"That's just what I was doing," replied the man joyously, "and it's the biggest luck in the world that I've found you. My name is Lykins. I'm one of the teachers of the high school, San Francisco. As soon as I heard the San Francisco postmastership was vacant, I made up my mind to get it; and here I am."

"Yes," said Riley slowly, "as you have remarked, . . . Mr. Lykins, . . . here you are. And have you got it?"

"Well, not exactly *got* it, but the next thing to it. I've brought a petition, signed by the Superintendent of Public Instruction, and all the teachers, and by more than two hundred other people. Now I want you, if you'll be so good, to go around with me to the Pacific delegation, for I want to rush this thing through and get along home."

"If the matter is so pressing, you will prefer that we visit the delegation to-night," said Riley, in a voice that had nothing mocking in it—to an unaccustomed ear.

"Oh, to-night, by all means! I haven't got any time to fool around. I want their promise before I go to bed: I ain't the talking kind, I'm the *doing* kind."

"Yes, . . . you've come to the right place for that. When did you arrive?"

"Just an hour ago."

"When are you intending to leave?"

"For New York to-morrow evening—for San Francisco next morning."

"Just so. . . . What are you going to do to-morrow?"

"*Do!* Why, I've got to go to the President with the petition and the delegation, and get the appointment, haven't I?"

"Yes, . . . very true; . . . that is correct. And then what?"

"Executive session of the Senate at two P.M.,—got to get the appointment confirmed,—I reckon you'll grant that?"

"Yes, . . . yes," said Riley meditatively, "you are right again. Then you take the train for New York in the evening, and the steamer for San Francisco next morning?"

"That's it,—that's the way I map it out."

Riley considered awhile, and then said:

"You couldn't stay . . . a day . . . well, say two days longer?"

"Bless your soul, no! It's not my style. I ain't a man to go fooling around;—I'm a man that *does* things, I'll tell you."

The storm was raging, the thick snow blowing in gusts. Riley stood silent, apparently deep in a reverie, during a minute or more, then he looked up and said: "Have you ever heard about that man who put up at Gadsby's once? . . . But I see you haven't."

He backed Mr. Lykins against an iron fence, button-holed him, fastened him with his eye, like the Ancient Mariner, and proceeded to unfold his narrative as placidly and peacefully as if we were all stretched comfortably in a blossomy summer meadow instead of being persecuted by a wintry midnight tempest.

"I will tell you about that man. It was in Jackson's time. Gadsby's was the principal hotel, then. Well, this man arrived from Tennessee about nine o'clock, one morning, with a black coachman and a splendid four-horse carriage, and an elegant dog, which he was evidently fond and proud of; he drove up before Gadsby's and the clerk and the landlord and everybody rushed out to take charge of him, but he said, 'Never mind,' and jumped out and told the coachman to wait—said he hadn't time to take anything to eat, he only had a little claim against the Government to collect, would run across the way, to the Treasury, and fetch the money, and then get right along back to Tennessee, for he was in considerable of a hurry.

"Well, about eleven o'clock that night he came back and ordered a bed and told them to put the horses up—said he would collect the claim in the morning. This was in January, you understand—January, 1834—the 3rd of January—Wednesday.

"Well, on the 5th of February he sold the fine carriage and bought a cheap second-hand one—said it would answer just as well to take the money home in, and he didn't care for style.

"On the 11th of August he sold a pair of the fine horses—said he'd often thought a pair was better than four, to go over the rough mountain-roads with, where a body had to be careful about his driving—and there wasn't so much of his claim but he could lug the money home with a pair easy enough.

"On the 13th of December he sold another horse—said two weren't necessary to drag that old light vehicle with—in fact, one could snatch it along faster than was absolutely necessary, now that it was good solid winter weather, and the roads in splendid condition.

"On the 17th of February, 1835, he sold the old carriage and bought a cheap second-hand buggy—said a buggy was just the trick to skim along mushy, slushy early-spring roads with, and he had always wanted to try a buggy on those mountain-roads, anyway.

"On the 1st of August he sold the buggy and bought the remains of an old sulky—said he just wanted to see those green Tennesseans stare when they saw him come a-ripping along in a sulky; didn't believe they'd ever heard of a sulky in their lives.

"Well, on the 29th of August he sold his coloured coachman—said he didn't need a coachman for a sulky—wouldn't be room enough for two in it, anyway—and said it wasn't every day that Providence sent a man a fool who was willing to pay nine hundred dollars for such a third-rate negro as that—been wanting to get rid of the creature for years, but didn't like to *throw* him away.

"Eighteen months later—that is to say, on the 15th of February, 1837—he sold the sulky and bought a saddle—said horseback-riding was what the doctor had always recommended *him* to take, and dog'd if he wanted to risk *his* neck going over those mountain-roads on wheels in the dead of winter, not if he knew himself.

"On the 9th of April he sold the saddle—said he wasn't going to risk *his* life with any perishable saddle-girth that ever was made, over a rainy, miry April road, while he could ride bareback and know and feel he was safe; always *had* despised to ride on a saddle, anyway.

"On the 24th of April he sold his horse—said 'I'm just fifty-seven to-day, hale and hearty—it would be a *pretty* howdy-do for me to be wasting such a trip as that, and such weather as this, on a horse, when there ain't anything in the world so splendid as a tramp on foot through the fresh spring woods and over the cheery mountains, to a man that *is* a man; and I can make my dog carry my claim in a little bundle anyway, when it's collected. So to-morrow I'll be up bright and early, make my little old collection, and mosey off to Tennessee, on my own hind legs, with a rousing good-bye to Gadsby's.'

"On the 22nd of June he sold his dog, said, 'Dern a dog, anyway, where you're just starting off on a rattling bully pleasure-tramp through the summer woods and hills—perfect nuisance—chases the squirrels, barks at everything, goes a-capering and splattering around in the fords—man can't get any chance to reflect and enjoy nature—and I'd a blamed sight rather carry the claim myself, it's a mighty sight safer; a dog's mighty uncertain in a financial way—always noticed it—well, good-bye, boys—last call—I'm off for Tennessee with a good leg and a gay heart, early in the morning.'"

There was a pause and a silence—except the noise of the wind and the pelting snow. Mr. Lykins said impatiently: " Well? "

Riley said: " Well, that was thirty years ago."

" Very well, very well: what of it ? "

" I'm great friends with that old patriarch. He comes every evening to tell me good-bye. I saw him an hour ago: he's off for Tennessee early to-morrow morning—as usual ; said he calculated to get his claim through and be off before night-owls like me have turned out of bed. The tears were in his eyes, he was so glad he was going to see his old Tennessee and his friends once more."

Another silent pause. The stranger broke it: " Is that all ? "

" That is all."

" Well, for the *time* of night, and the *kind* of night, it seems to me the story was full long enough. But what's it all for ? "

" Oh, nothing in particular."

" Well, where's the point of it ? "

" Oh, there isn't any particular point to it. Only, if you are not in *too* much of a hurry to rush off to San Francisco with that post-office appointment, Mr. Lykins, I'd advise you to ' *put up at Gadsby's* ' for a spell, and take it easy. Good-bye. *God* bless you ! "

So saying, Riley blandly turned on his heel and left the astonished school-teacher standing there, a musing and motionless snow image shining in the broad glow of the street-lamp.

He never got that post-office.

# THOMAS BAILEY ALDRICH
1836-1907

## MARJORIE DAW

I

*Dr. Dillon to Edward Delaney, Esq., at The Pines, near Rye, N.H.*

*August 8, 187-.*

My dear Sir—I am happy to assure you that your anxiety is without reason. Flemming will be confined to the sofa for three or four weeks, and will have to be careful at first how he uses his leg. A fracture of this kind is always a tedious affair. Fortunately the bone was very skilfully set by the surgeon who chanced to be in the drug-store where Flemming was brought after his fall, and I apprehend no permanent inconvenience from the accident *Flemming is doing perfectly well physically;* but I must confess that the irritable and morbid state of mind into which he has fallen causes me a great deal of uneasiness. He is the last man in the world who ought to break his leg. You know how impetuous our friend is ordinarily, what a soul of restlessness and energy, never content unless he is rushing at some object, like a sportive bull at a red shawl; but amiable withal. He is no longer amiable. His temper has become something frightful. Miss Fanny Flemming came up from Newport, where the family are staying for the summer, to nurse him; but he packed her off the next morning in tears. He has a complete set of Balzac's works, twenty-seven volumes, piled up by his sofa, to throw at Watkins whenever that exemplary serving-man appears with his meals. Yesterday I very innocently brought Flemming a small basket of lemons. You know it was a strip of lemon-peel on the kerbstone that caused our friend's mischance. Well, he no sooner set his eyes upon these lemons than he fell into such a rage as I cannot describe adequately. This is only one of his moods, and the least distressing. At other times he sits with bowed head regarding his splintered limb, silent, sullen, despairing. When this fit is on him—and it sometimes lasts all day—nothing can distract his melancholy. He refuses to eat; does not even read the newspapers; books—except as projectiles for Watkins—have no charms for him. His state is truly pitiable.

Now, if he were a poor man, with a family dependent on his daily

labour, this irritability and despondency would be natural enough.
But in a young fellow of twenty-four, with plenty of money, and
seemingly not a care in the world, the thing is monstrous. If he continues to give way to his vagaries in this manner, he will end by
bringing on an inflammation of the fibula. It was the fibula he
broke. I am at my wits' end to know what to prescribe for him. I
have anæsthetics and lotions to make people sleep and to soothe
pain; but I've no medicine that will make a man have a little
common-sense. That is beyond my skill, but maybe it is not beyond
yours. You are Flemming's intimate friend, his *fidus Achates*. Write
to him, write to him frequently, distract his mind, cheer him up,
and prevent him from becoming a confirmed case of melancholia.
Perhaps he has some important plans disarranged by his present
confinement. If he has you will know, and will know how to advise
him judiciously. I trust your father finds the change beneficial?
I am, my dear sir, with great respect, &c.

II

*Edward Delaney to John Flemming, West 38th Street, New York.*
*August 9,—.*

MY DEAR JACK—I had a line from Dillon this morning, and was
rejoiced to learn that your hurt is not so bad as reported. Like a
certain personage you are not so black and blue as you are painted.
Dillon will put you on your pins again in two or three weeks, if you
will only have patience and follow his counsels. Did you get my
note of last Wednesday? I was greatly troubled when I heard of
the accident.

I can imagine how tranquil and saintly you are with your leg in a
trough! It's deuced awkward, to be sure, just as we had promised
ourselves a glorious month together at the seaside; but we must
make the best of it. It is unfortunate, too, that my father's health
renders it impossible for me to leave him. I think he has much improved; the sea air is his native element; but he still needs my arm
to lean upon in his walks, and requires some one more careful than a
servant to look after him. I cannot come to you, dear Jack, but I
have hours of unemployed time on hand, and I will write you a whole
post-office full of letters if that will divert you. Heaven knows, I
haven't anything to write about. It isn't as if we were living at one
of the beach houses; then I could do you some character studies,
and fill your imagination with hosts of sea-goddesses, with their
(or somebody else's) raven and blond manes hanging down their
shoulders. You should have Aphrodite in morning wrapper, in
evening costume, and in her prettiest bathing suit. But we are far
from all that here. We have rooms in a farm-house, on a cross-
road, two miles from the hotels, and lead the quietest of lives.

I wish I were a novelist. This old house, with its sanded floors and high wainscots, and its narrow windows looking out upon a cluster of pines that turn themselves into æolian-harps every time the wind blows, would be the place in which to write a summer romance. It should be a story with the odours of the forest and the breath of the sea in it. It should be a novel like one of that Russian fellow's—what's his name?—Tourguénieff, Tourguenef, Toorguniff, Turgénjew; nobody knows how to spell him. (I think his own mother must be in some doubt about him.) Yet I wonder if even a Liza or an Alexandra Paulovna could stir the heart of a man who has constant twinges in his leg. I wonder if one of our own Yankee girls of the best type, haughty and *spirituelle*, would be of any comfort to you in your present deplorable condition. If I thought so, I would rush down to the Surf House and catch one for you; or, better still, I would find you one over the way.

Picture to yourself a large white house just across the road, nearly opposite our cottage. It is not a house, but a mansion, built perhaps in the colonial period, with rambling extensions, and gambrel roof, and a wide piazza on three sides—a self-possessed, high-bred piece of architecture, with its nose in the air. It stands back from the road, and has an obsequious retinue of fringed elms and oaks and weeping willows. Sometimes in the morning, and oftener in the afternoon, when the sun has withdrawn from that part of the mansion, a young woman appears on the piazza, with some mysterious Penelope web of embroidery in her hand, or a book. There is a hammock over there —of pine-apple fibre, it looks from here. A hammock is very becoming when one is eighteen, and has gold hair, and dark eyes, and a blue illusion dress looped up after the fashion of a Dresden china shepherdess, and is *chaussée* like a belle of the time of Louis Quatorze. All this splendour goes into that hammock, and sways there like a pond-lily in the golden afternoon. The window of my bedroom looks down on that piazza, and so do I.

But enough of this nonsense, which ill becomes a sedate young attorney taking his vacation with an invalid father. Drop me a line, dear Jack, and tell me how you really are. State your case. Write me a long quiet letter. If you are violent or abusive I'll take the law to you.

### III
*John Flemming to Edward Delaney*

*August* 11—.

Your letter, dear Ned, was a god-send. Fancy what a fix I am in; I, who never had a day's sickness since I was born. My left leg weighs three tons. It is embalmed in spices, and smothered in layers of fine linen like a mummy. I can't move. I haven't moved for five thousand years. I'm of the time of Pharaoh.

I lie from morning till night on a lounge staring into the hot street. Everybody is out of town enjoying himself. The brown stone-front

houses across the street resemble a row of particularly ugly coffins
set up on end. A green mould is settling on the names of the
deceased, carved on the silver door-plates. Sardonic spiders have
sewed up the key-holes. All is silence and dust and desolation.—
I interrupt this a moment to take a shy at Watkins with the second
volume of *César Birotteau*. Missed him! I think I could bring
him down with a copy of *Sainte-Beuve*, or the *Dictionnaire Universel*,
if I had it. These small Balzac books somehow don't quite fit my
hand. But I shall fetch him yet. I've an idea Watkins is tapping
the old gentleman's Château Yquem. Duplicate key of the wine-
cellar. Hibernian swarries in the front basement. Young Cheops
upstairs, snug in his cerements. Watkins glides into my chamber
with that colourless, hypocritical face of his drawn out long like an
accordion; but I know he grins all the way downstairs, and is glad
I have broken my leg. Was not my evil star in the very zenith
when I ran up to town to attend that dinner at Delmonico's? I
didn't come up altogether for that. It was partly to buy Frank
Livingstone's roan mare Margot. And now I shall not be able to
sit in the saddle these two months. I'll send the mare down to
you at The Pines; is that the name of the place?

Old Dillon fancies that I have something on my mind. He drives
me wild with lemons. Lemons for a mind diseased. Nonsense. I
am only as restless as the devil under this confinement—a thing I'm
not used to. Take a man who has never had so much as a headache
or a toothache in his life, strap one of his legs in a section of water-
spout, keep him in a room in the city for weeks, with the hot weather
turned on, and then expect him to smile, and purr, and be happy!
It is preposterous. I can't be cheerful or calm.

Your letter is the first consoling thing I have had since my
disaster, a week ago. It really cheered me up for half an hour.
Send me a screed, Ned, as often as you can, if you love me. Anything will do. Write me more about that little girl in the hammock.
That was very pretty all that about the Dresden china shepherdess
and the pond-lily; the imagery a little mixed perhaps, but very
pretty. I didn't suppose you had so much sentimental furniture
in your upper storey. It shows how one may be familiar for years
with the reception-room of his neighbour, and never suspect what
is directly under his mansard. I supposed your loft stuffed with
dry legal parchments, mortgages, and affidavits; you take down a
package of manuscript, and lo! there are lyrics, and sonnets, and
canzonettas. You really have a graphic descriptive touch, Edward
Delaney, and I suspect you of short love-tales in the magazines.

I shall be a bear until I hear from you again. Tell me all about
your pretty *inconnue* across the road. What is her name? Who
is she? Who's her father? Where's her mother? Who's her
lover? You cannot imagine how this will occupy me. The more
trifling the better. My imprisonment has weakened me intellec-

tually to such a degree that I find your epistolary gifts quite considerable. I am passing into my second childhood. In a week or two I shall take to india-rubber rings and prongs of coral. A silver cup with an appropriate inscription would be a delicate attention on your part. In the meantime write!

## IV
### Edward Delaney to John Flemming
*August 12, —.*

The sick pasha shall be amused. *Bismillah!* he wills it so! If the story-teller becomes prolix and tedious—the bow-string and the sack, and two Nubians to drop him into the Piscataqua! But truly, Jack, I have a hard task. There is literally nothing here except the little girl over the way. She is swinging in the hammock at this moment. It is to me compensation for many of the ills of life to see her now and then put out a small kid boot, which fits like a glove, and set herself going. Who is she and what is her name? Her name is Daw. Only daughter of Mr. Richard W. Daw, ex-colonel and banker. Mother dead. One brother at Harvard; elder brother killed at the battle of Fair Oaks nine years ago. Old, rich family the Daws. This is the homestead where father and daughter pass eight months of the twelve; the rest of the year in Baltimore and Washington. The New England winter too many for the old gentleman. The daughter is called Marjorie—Marjorie Daw. Sounds odd at first, doesn't it? But after you say it over to yourself half a dozen times you like it. There's a pleasing quaintness to it, something prim and violet-like. Must be a nice sort of girl to be called Marjorie Daw.

I had mine host of The Pines in the witness-box last night, and drew the foregoing testimony from him. He has charge of Mr. Daw's vegetable-garden, and has known the family these thirty years. Of course I shall make the acquaintance of my neighbours before many days. It will be next to impossible for me not to meet Mr. Daw or Miss Daw in some of my walks. The young lady has a favourite path to the sea-beach. I shall intercept her some morning, and touch my hat to her. Then the princess will bend her fair head to me with courteous surprise, not unmixed with haughtiness. Will snub me, in fact. All this for thy sake, O Pasha of the Snapt Axle-tree! . . . How oddly things fall out! Ten minutes ago I was called down to the parlour—you know the kind of parlours in farm-houses on the coast; a sort of amphibious parlour, with sea-shells on the mantelpiece and spruce branches in the chimney-place —where I found my father and Mr. Daw doing the antique polite to each other. He had come to pay his respects to his new neighbours. Mr. Daw is a tall, slim gentleman of about fifty-five, with a florid face and snow-white moustache and side-whiskers. Looks like Mr. Dombey, or as Mr. Dombey would have looked if he had served a few years in the British army. Mr. Daw was a colonel in the late war, commanding the regiment in which his son was a lieutenant. Plucky old boy, backbone of New Hampshire granite. Before taking his leave the colonel delivered himself of an invitation, as if he were issuing a general order. Miss Daw has a few friends coming at 4 P.M., to play croquet on the lawn (parade-ground), and have tea (cold rations) on the piazza. Will we honour them with our company (or be sent to the guard-house)? My father declines on the plea of ill-health. My father's son bows with as much suavity as he knows, and accepts.

In my next I shall have something to tell you. I shall have seen the little beauty face to face. I have a presentiment, Jack, that this Daw is a *rara avis!* Keep up your spirits, my boy, until I write you another letter; and send me along word how's your leg.

V

*Edward Delaney to John Flemming*

August 13, —.

The party, my dear Jack, was as dreary as possible. A lieutenant of the navy, the rector of the Episcopal church at Stillwater, and a society swell from Nahant. The lieutenant looked as if he had swallowed a couple of his buttons and found the bullion rather indigestible; the rector was a pensive youth of the daffydowndilly sort; and the swell from Nahant was a very weak tidal wave indeed. The women were much better, as they always are; the two Miss Kingsburys of Philadelphia, staying at the Sea-shell House, two bright and engaging girls. But Majorie Daw!

The company broke up soon after tea, and I remained to smoke a cigar with the colonel on the piazza. It was like seeing a picture to see Miss Marjorie hovering around the old soldier and doing a hundred gracious little things for him. She brought the cigars and lighted the tapers with her own delicate fingers in the most enchanting fashion. As we sat there she came and went in the summer twilight, and seemed, with her white dress and pale gold hair, like some lovely phantom that had sprung into existence out of the smoke-wreaths. If she had melted into air, like the statue of the lady in the play, I should have been more sorry than surprised.

It was easy to perceive that the old colonel worshipped her, and she him. I think the relation between an elderly father and a daughter just blooming into womanhood the most beautiful possible. There is in it a subtle sentiment that cannot exist in the case of mother and daughter, or that of son and mother. But this is getting into deep water.

I sat with the Daws until half-past ten and saw the moon rise on the sea. The ocean, that had stretched motionless and black against the horizon, was changed by magic into a broken field of glittering ice. In the far distance the Isles of Shoals loomed up like a group of huge bergs drifting down on us. The polar regions in a June thaw! It was exceedingly fine. What did we talk about? We talked about the weather—and *you*! The weather has been disagreeable for several days past—and so have you. I glided from one topic to the other very naturally. I told my friends of your accident; how it had frustrated all our summer plans, and what our plans were. Then I described you; or, rather, I didn't. I spoke of your amiability; of your patience under this severe affliction; of your touching gratitude when Dillon brings you little presents of fruit; of your tenderness to your sister Fanny, whom you would not allow to stay in town to nurse you, and how you heroically sent her back to Newport, preferring to remain alone with Mary the cook and your man Watkins, to whom, by the way, you were devotedly attached. If you had been there, Jack, you wouldn't have known yourself. I should have excelled as a criminal lawyer if I had not turned my attention to a different branch of jurisprudence.

Miss Majorie asked all manner of leading questions concerning you. It did not occur to me then, but it struck me forcibly afterwards that she evinced a singular interest in the conversation. When I got back to my room I recalled how eagerly she leaned forward, with her full, snowy throat in strong moonlight, listening to what I said. Positively, I think I made her like you!

Miss Daw is a girl whom you would like immensely, I can tell you that. A beauty without affectation; a high and tender nature, if one can read the soul in the face. And the old colonel is a noble character too.

I am glad the Daws are such pleasant people. The Pines is an isolated place and my resources are few. I fear I should have found life here rather monotonous before long with no other society than that of my excellent sire. It is true I might have made a target of the defenceless invalid; but I haven't a taste for artillery, *moi*.

## VI

### *John Flemming to Edward Delaney*

*August 17, —.*

For a man who hasn't a taste for artillery it occurs to me, my friend, you are keeping up a pretty lively fire on my inner works. But go on. Cynicism is a small brass field-piece that eventually bursts and kills the artillery man.

You may abuse me as much as you like, and I'll not complain; for I don't know what I should do without your letters. They are curing me. I haven't hurled anything at Watkins since last Sunday, partly because I have grown more amiable under your teaching, and partly because Watkins captured my ammunition one night and carried it off to the library. He is rapidly losing the habit he had acquired of dodging whenever I rub my ear, or make any slight motion with my right arm. He is still suggestive of the wine cellar, however. You may break, you may shatter Watkins if you will, but the scent of the Roederer will hang round him still.

Ned, that Miss Daw must be a charming person. I should certainly like her. I like her already. When you spoke in your first letter of seeing a young girl swinging in a hammock under your chamber window I was somehow strangely drawn to her. I cannot account for it in the least. What you have subsequently written of Miss Daw has strengthened the impression. You seem to be describing a woman I have known in some previous state of existence, or dreamed of in this. Upon my word, if you were to send me her photograph I believe I should recognise her at a glance. Her manner, that listening attitude, her traits of character, as you indicate them, the light hair and the dark eyes, they are all familiar things to me. Asked a lot of questions, did she? Curious about me? That is strange.

You would laugh in your sleeve, you wretched old cynic, if you knew how I lie awake nights, with my gas turned down to a star, thinking of The Pines and the house across the road. How cool it must be down there! I long for the salt smell in the air. I picture the colonel smoking his cheroot on the piazza. I send you and Miss Daw off on afternoon rambles along the beach. Sometimes I let you stroll with her under the elms in the moonlight, for you are great friends by this time, I take it, and see each other every day. I know your ways and your manners! Then I fall into a truculent mood and would like to destroy somebody. Have you noticed anything in the shape of a lover hanging around the colonial Lares and Penates? Does that lieutenant of the horse-marines or that young Stillwater parson visit the house much? Not that I am pining for news of them, but any gossip of the kind would be in order. I wonder, Ned, you don't fall in love with Miss Daw. I am ripe to do it myself. Speaking of photographs, couldn't you manage to slip one of her *cartes-de-visite* from her album—she must have an album, you know—and send it to me? I will return it before it could be missed. That's a good fellow! Did the mare arrive safe and sound? It will be a capital animal this autumn for Central Park.

Oh—my leg? I forgot about my leg. It's better.

## VII

*Edward Delaney to John Flemming*

*August 20, —.*

You are correct in your surmises. I am on the most friendly terms with our neighbours. The colonel and my father smoke their afternoon cigar together in our sitting-room, or on the piazza opposite, and I pass an hour or two of the day or the evening with the daughter. I am more and more struck by the beauty, modesty, and intelligence of Miss Daw.

You ask me why I do not fall in love with her. I will be frank, Jack; I have thought of that. She is young, rich, accomplished, uniting in herself more attractions, mental and personal, than I can recall in any girl of my acquaintance; but she lacks the something that would be necessary to inspire in me that kind of interest. Possessing this unknown quantity, a woman neither beautiful, nor wealthy, nor very young could bring me to her feet. But not Miss Daw. If we were shipwrecked together on an uninhabited island—let me suggest a tropical island, for it costs no more to be picturesque—I would build her a bamboo hut, I would fetch her bread-fruit and cocoa-nuts, I would fry yams for her, I would lure the ingenuous turtle and make her nourishing soups; but I wouldn't make love to her—not under eighteen months. I would like to have her for a sister, that I might shield her and counsel her, and spend half my income on thread-laces and camel's-hair shawls. (We are off the island now.) If such were not my feeling there would still be an obstacle to my loving Miss Daw. A greater misfortune could scarcely befall me than to love her. Flemming, I am about to make a revelation that will astonish you. I may be all wrong in my premises, and consequently in my conclusions; but you shall judge.

That night when I returned to my room after the croquet party at the Daws', and was thinking over the trivial events of the evening, I was suddenly impressed by the air of eager attention with which Miss Daw had followed my account of your accident. I think I mentioned this to you. Well, the next morning as I went to mail my letter, I overtook Miss Daw on the road to Rye, where the post-office is, and accompanied her thither and back—an hour's walk. The conversation again turned on you, and again I remarked that inexplicable look of interest which had lighted up her face the previous evening. Since then I have seen Miss Daw perhaps ten times, perhaps oftener, and on each occasion I found that when I was not speaking of you, or your sister, or some person or place associated with you, I was not holding her attention. She would be absent-minded; her eyes would wander away from me to the sea, or to some distant object in the landscape; her fingers would play with the leaves of a book in a way that convinced me she was not listening. At these moments if I abruptly changed the theme—I did it several times as an experiment—and dropped some remark about my friend Flemming, then the sombre blue eyes would come back to me instantly.

Now, is not this the oddest thing in the world? No, not the oddest. The effect which, you tell me, was produced on you by my casual mention of an unknown girl swinging in a hammock, is certainly as strange. You can conjecture how that passage in your letter of Friday startled me. Is it possible then, that two people who have never met, and who are hundreds of miles apart, can exert a magnetic influence on each other? I have read of such psychological phenomena, but never credited them. I leave the solution of the problem to you. As for myself, all other things being favourable, it would be impossible for me to fall in love with a woman who listens to me only when I am talking of my friend!

I am not aware that any one is paying marked attention to my fair neighbour. The lieutenant of the navy—he is stationed at Rivermouth—sometimes drops in of an evening, and sometimes the rector from Stillwater; the lieutenant the oftener. He was there last night. I should not be surprised if he had an eye to the heiress; but he is not formidable. Mistress Daw carries a neat little spear of irony, and the honest lieutenant seems to have a particular facility for impaling himself on the point of it. He is not dangerous, I should say; though I have known a woman to satirise a man for years and marry him after all. Decidedly the lowly rector is not dangerous; yet, again, who has not seen cloth of frieze victorious in the lists where cloth of gold went down?

As to the photograph. There is an exquisite ivorytype of Marjorie in *passe-partout*, on the drawing-room mantelpiece. It would be missed at once if taken. I would do anything reasonable for you, Jack; but I've no burning desire to be hauled up before the local justice of the peace on a charge of petty larceny.

P.S.—Enclosed is a spray of mignonette, which I advise you to treat tenderly. Yes, we talked of you again last night as usual. It is becoming a little dreary for me.

## VIII
### Edward Delaney to John Flemming

*August 22, —.*

Your letter in reply to my last has occupied my thoughts all the morning. I do not know what to think. Do you mean to say that you are seriously half in love with a woman whom you have never seen—with a shadow, a chimera? for what else can Miss Daw be to you? I do not understand it at all. I understand neither you nor her. You are a couple of ethereal beings moving in finer air than I can breathe with my commonplace lungs. Such delicacy of sentiment is something I admire without comprehending. I am bewildered. I am of the earth earthy; and I find myself in the incongruous position of having to do with mere souls, with natures so finely tempered that I run some risk of shattering them in my awkwardness. I am as Caliban among the spirits!

Reflecting on your letter I am not sure it is wise in me to continue this correspondence. But no, Jack ; I do wrong to doubt the good sense that forms the basis of your character. You are deeply interested in Miss Daw ; you feel that she is a person whom you may perhaps greatly admire when you know her : at the same time you bear in mind that the chances are ten to five, that, when you do come to know her, she will fall far short of your ideal, and you will not care for her in the least. Look at it in this sensible light, and I will hold back nothing from you.

Yesterday afternoon my father and myself rode over to Rivermouth with the Daws. A heavy rain in the morning had cooled the atmosphere and laid the dust. To Rivermouth is a drive of eight miles, along a winding road lined all the way with wild barberry bushes. I never saw anything more brilliant than these bushes, the green of the foliage and the red of the coral berries intensified by the rain. The colonel drove, with my father in front, Miss Daw and I on the back seat. I resolved that for the first five miles your name should not pass my lips. I was amused by the artful attempts she made, at the start, to break through my reticence. Then a silence fell upon her ; and then she became suddenly gay. That keenness which I enjoyed so much when it was exercised on the lieutenant was not so satisfactory directed against myself. Miss Daw has great sweetness of disposition, but she can be disagreeable. She is like the young lady in the rhyme, with the curl on her forehead,

> When she is good,
> She is very, very good,
> And when she is bad, she is horrid !

I kept to my resolution, however ; but on the return home I relented, and talked of your mare ! Miss Daw is going to try a side-saddle on Margot some morning. The animal is a trifle too light for my weight. By the by, I nearly forgot to say Miss Daw sat for a picture yesterday to a Rivermouth artist. If the negative turns out well I am to have a copy. So our ends will be accomplished without crime. I wish, though, I could send you the ivorytype in the drawing-room ; it is cleverly coloured, and would give you an idea of her hair and eyes, which, of course, the other will not.

No, Jack, the spray of mignonette did not come from me. A man of twenty-eight doesn't enclose flowers in his letters—to another man. But don't attach too much significance to the circumstance. She gives sprays of mignonette to the rector, sprays to the lieutenant. She has even given a rose from her bosom to your slave. It is her jocund nature to scatter flowers, like spring.

If my letters sometimes read disjointedly you must understand that I never finish one at a sitting, but write at intervals, when the mood is on me.

The mood is not on me now.

## IX

*Edward Delaney to John Flemming*

*August 23, —.*

I have just returned from the strangest interview with Marjorie. She has all but confessed to me her interest in you. But with what modesty and dignity! Her words elude my pen as I attempt to put them on paper; and, indeed, it was not so much what she said as her manner; and that I cannot reproduce. Perhaps it was of a piece with the strangeness of this whole business that she should tacitly acknowledge to a third party the love she feels for a man she has never beheld! But I have lost, through your aid, the faculty of being surprised. I accept things as people do in dreams. Now that I am again in my room it all appears like an illusion—the black masses of shadow under the trees, the fire-flies whirling in Pyrrhic dances among the shrubbery, the sea over there, Marjorie sitting on the hammock!

It is past midnight, and I am too sleepy to write more.

*Tuesday Morning*—My father has suddenly taken it into his head to spend a few days at the Shoals. In the meanwhile you will not hear from me. I see Marjorie walking in the garden with the colonel. I wish I could speak to her alone, but shall probably not have an opportunity before we leave.

## X

*Edward Delaney to John Flemming*

*August 28, —.*

You were pssing into your second childhood, were you? Your intellect was so reduced that my epistolary gifts seemed quite considerable to you, did they? I rise superior to the sarcasm in your favour of the 11th instant, when I notice that five days' silence on my part is sufficient to throw you into the depths of despondency.

We returned only this morning from Appledore, that enchanted island—at four dollars per day. I find on my desk three letters from you! Evidently there is no lingering doubt in *your* mind as to the pleasure I derive from your correspondence. These letters are undated, but in what I take to be the latest are two passages that require my consideration. You will pardon my candour, dear Flemming, but the conviction forces itself upon me that as your leg grows stronger your head becomes weaker. You ask my advice on a certain point. I will give it. In my opinion you could do nothing more unwise than to address a note to Miss Daw, thanking her for the flower. It would, I am sure, offend her delicacy beyond pardon. She knows you only through me; you are to her an abstraction, a figure in a dream—a dream from which the slightest shock would awaken her. Of course, if you enclose a note to me and insist on its delivery, I shall deliver it; but I advise you not to do so.

You say you are able, with the aid of a cane, to walk about your chamber, and that you purpose to come to The Pines the instant Dillon thinks you strong enough to stand the journey. Again I advise you not to. Do you not see that, every hour you remain away, Marjorie's glamour deepens and your influence over her increases? You will ruin everything by precipitancy. Wait until you are entirely recovered; in any case do not come without giving we warning. I fear the effect of your abrupt advent here—in the circumstances.

Miss Daw was evidently glad to see us back again, and gave me both hands in the frankest way. She stopped at the door for a moment this afternoon in the carriage; she had been over to Rivermouth for her pictures. Unluckily the photographer had spilt some acid on the plate and she was obliged to give him another sitting. I have an impression that something is troubling Marjorie. She had an abstracted air not usual with her. However, it may be only my fancy.... I end this, leaving several things unsaid, to accompany my father on one of those long walks which are now his chief medicine—and mine!

## XI
### *Edward Delaney to John Flemming*
*August 29, —.*

I write in great haste to tell you what has taken place here since my letter of last night. I am in the utmost perplexity. Only one thing is plain—*you* must not dream of coming to The Pines. Marjorie has told her father everything! I saw her for a few minutes, an hour ago, in the garden; and, as near as I could gather from her confused statement, the facts are these: Lieutenant Bradly—that's the naval officer stationed at Rivermouth—has been paying court to Miss Daw for some time past, but not so much to her liking as to that of the colonel, who it seems is an old friend of the young gentleman's father. Yesterday (I knew she was in some trouble when she drove up to our gate) the colonel spoke to Marjorie of Bradly—urged his suit, I infer. Marjorie expressed her dislike for the lieutenant with characteristic frankness, and finally confessed to her father—well, I really do not know what she confessed. It must have been the vaguest of confessions, and must have sufficiently puzzled the colonel. At any rate, it exasperated him. I suppose I am implicated in the matter, and that the colonel feels bitterly towards me. I do not see why: I have carried no messages between you and Miss Daw; I have behaved with the greatest discretion. I can find no flaw anywhere in my proceeding. I do not see that anybody has done anything—except the colonel himself.

It is probable, nevertheless, that the friendly relations between the two houses will be broken off. " A plague o' both your houses," say you. I will keep you informed, as well as I can, of what occurs over the way. We shall remain here until the second week in September. Stay where you are, or at all events, do not dream of joining me. . . . Colonel Daw is sitting on the piazza looking rather ferocious. I have not seen Marjorie since I parted with her in the garden.

### XII

*Edward Delaney to Thomas Dillon, M.D., Madison Square, New York.*

*August* 30, —.

MY DEAR DOCTOR—If you have any influence over Flemming, I beg of you to exert it to prevent his coming to this place at present. There are circumstances, which I will explain to you before long, that make it of the first importance that he should not come into this neighbourhood. His appearance here, I speak advisedly, would be disastrous to him. In urging him to remain in New York, or to go to some inland resort, you will be doing him and me a real service. Of course you will not mention my name in this connection. You know me well enough, my dear doctor, to be assured that, in begging your secret co-operation, I have reasons that will meet your entire approval when they are made plain to you. My father, I am glad to state, has so greatly improved that he can no longer be regarded as an invalid. With great esteem, I am, &c. &c.

### XIII

*Edward Delaney to John Flemming*

*August* 30, —.

Your letter announcing your mad determination to come here has just reached me. I beg of you to reflect a moment. The step would be fatal to your interests and hers. You would furnish just cause for irritation to R. W. D.; and, though he loves Marjorie tenderly, he is capable of going to any lengths if opposed. You would not like, I am convinced, to be the means of causing him to treat *her* with severity. That would be the result of your presence at the Pines at this juncture. Wait and see what happens. Moreover, I understand from Dillon that you are in no condition to take so long a journey. He thinks the air of the coast would be the worst thing possible for you; that you ought to go inland, if anywhere. Be advised by me. Be advised by Dillon.

### XIV

TELEGRAMS.

*September* 1, —.

1. *To Edward Delaney*

Letter received. Dillon be hanged. I think I ought to be on the ground.

J. F.

#### 2. *To John Flemming*

Stay where you are. You would only complicate matters. Do not move until you hear from me.
E. D.

#### 3. *To Edward Delaney*

My being at The Pines could be kept secret. I must see her.
J. F.

#### 4. *To John Flemming*

Do not think of it. It would be useless. R. W. D. has locked M. in her room. You would not be able to effect an interview.
E. D.

#### 5. *To Edward Delaney*

Locked her in her room! That settles the question. I shall leave by the 12.15 express.
J. F.

On the 2nd of September 187–, as the down express due at 3.40 left the station at Hampton, a young man, leaning on the shoulder of a servant whom he addressed as Watkins, stepped from the platform into a hack, and requested to be driven to The Pines. On arriving at the gate of a modest farmhouse, a few miles from the station, the young man descended with difficulty from the carriage, and, casting a hasty glance across the road, seemed much impressed by some peculiarity in the landscape. Again leaning on the shoulder of the person Watkins, he walked to the door of the farmhouse and inquired for Mr. Edward Delaney. He was informed by the aged man who answered his knock that Mr. Edward Delaney had gone to Boston the day before, but that Mr. Jonas Delaney was within. This information did not appear satisfactory to the stranger, who inquired if Mr. Edward Delaney had left any message for Mr. John Flemming. There *was* a letter for Mr. Flemming, if he were that person. After a brief absence the aged man reappeared with a letter.

### XV

*Edward Delaney to John Flemming*
*September 1, —.*

I am horror-stricken at what I have done! When I began this correspondence I had no other purpose than to relieve the tedium of your sick-chamber. Dillon told me to cheer you up. I tried to. I thought you entered into the spirit of the thing. I had no idea, until within a few days, that you were taking matters *au sérieux*.

What can I say? I am in sackcloth and ashes. I am a Pariah, a dog of an outcast. I tried to make a little romance to interest you, something soothing and idyllic, and, by Jove! I have done it only too well! My father doesn't know a word of this, so don't jar the old gentleman any more than you can help. I fly from the wrath to come—when you arrive! For O, dear Jack, there isn't any colonial mansion on the other side of the road, there isn't any piazza, there isn't any hammock—there isn't any Marjorie Daw!!

# MADEMOISELLE OLYMPE ZABRISKI

### Thomas Bailey Aldrich

#### I

We are accustomed to speak with a certain light irony of the tendency which women have to gossip, as if the sin itself, if it is a sin, were of the gentler sex, and could by no chance be a masculine peccadillo. So far as my observation goes, men are as much given to small talk as women, and it is undeniable that we have produced the highest type of gossiper extant. Where will you find, in or out of literature, such another droll, delightful, chatty busybody as Samuel Pepys, Esq., Secretary to the Admiralty in the reigns of those fortunate gentlemen Charles II. and James II. of England? He is the king of tattlers, as Shakespeare is the king of poets.

If it came to a matter of pure gossip, I would back Our Club against the Sorosis or any women's club in existence. Whenever you see in your drawing-room four or five young fellows lounging in easy-chairs, cigar in hand, and now and then bringing their heads together over the small round Japanese table which is always the pivot of these social circles, you may be sure that they are discussing Tom's engagement, or Dick's extravagance, or Harry's hopeless passion for the younger Miss Fleurdelys. It is here old Tippleton gets execrated for that everlasting *bon mot* of his which was quite a success at dinner-parties forty years ago; it is here the belle of the season passes under the scalpels of merciless young surgeons; it is here B's financial condition is handled in a way that would make B's hair stand on end; it is here, in short, that everything is canvassed—everything that happens in our set, I mean—much that never happens, and a great deal that could not possibly happen. It was at Our Club that I learned the particulars of the Van Twiller affair.

It was great entertainment to Our Club, the Van Twiller affair, though it was rather a joyless thing, I fancy, for Van Twiller. To understand the case fully, it should be understood that Ralph Van Twiller is one of the proudest and most sensitive men living. He is a lineal descendant of Wouter Van Twiller, the famous old Dutch governor of New York—Nieuw Amsterdam, as it was then; his ancestors have always been burgomasters or admirals or generals, and his mother is the Mrs. Vanrensselaer Vanzandt Van Twiller whose magnificent place will be pointed out to you on the right bank of the Hudson as you pass up the historic river toward Idlewild. Ralph is about twenty-five years old. Birth made him a gentleman, and the rise of real estate—some of it in the family since the old governor's time—made him a millionaire. It was a kindly fairy that stepped in and made him a good fellow also. Fortune, I take it, was in her most jocund mood when she heaped her gifts in this fashion on Van Twiller, who was, and will be again, when this cloud blows over, the flower of Our Club.

About a year ago there came a whisper—if the word "whisper" is not too harsh a term to apply to what seemed a mere breath floating gently through the atmosphere of the billiard-room— imparting the intelligence that Van Twiller was in some kind of trouble. Just as everybody suddenly takes to wearing square-toed boots, or to drawing his neck-scarf through a ring, so it became all at once the fashion, without any preconcerted agreement, for everybody to speak of Van Twiller as a man in some way under a cloud. But what the cloud was, and how he got under it, and why he did not get away from it, were points that lifted themselves into the realm of pure conjecture. There was no man in the club with strong enough wing to his imagination to soar to the supposition that Van Twiller was embarrassed in money matters. Was he in love? That appeared nearly as improbable; for if he had been in love all the world—that is, perhaps a hundred first families—would have known all about it instantly.

"He has the symptoms," said Delaney, laughing. "I remember once when Jack Flemming——"

"Ned!" cried Flemming, "I protest against any allusion to that business."

This was one night when Van Twiller had wandered into the club, turned over the magazines absently in the reading-room, and wandered out again without speaking ten words. The most careless eye would have remarked the great change that had come over Van Twiller. Now and then he would play a game of billiards with De Peyster or Haseltine, or stop to chat a moment in the vestibule with old Duane; but he was an altered man. When at the club, he was usually to be found in the small smoking-room upstairs, seated on a fauteuil fast asleep, with the last number of *The Nation* in his hand. Once, if you went to two or three places of an evening, you were certain to meet Van Twiller at them all. You seldom met him in society now.

By and by came whisper number two—a whisper more emphatic than number one, but still untraceable to any tangible mouthpiece. This time the whisper said that Van Twiller *was* in love. But with whom? The list of possible Mrs. Van Twillers was carefully examined by experienced hands, and a check placed against a fine old Knickerbocker name here and there, but nothing satisfactory arrived at. Then that same still small voice of rumour, but now with an easily detected staccato sharpness to it, said that Van Twiller was in love—with an actress! Van Twiller, whom it had taken all these years and all this waste of raw material in the way of ancestors to bring to perfection—Ralph Van Twiller, the net result and flower of his race, the descendant of Wouter, the son of Mrs. Vanrensselaer Vanzandt Van Twiller—in love with an actress! That was too ridiculous to be believed—and so everybody believed it.

Six or seven members of the club abruptly discovered in themselves an unsuspected latent passion for the histrionic art. In squads of two or three they stormed successively all the theatres in town—Booth's, Wallack's, Daly's Fifth Avenue (not burned down then), and the Grand Opera House. Even the shabby homes of the drama over in the Bowery, where the Germanic Thespis has not taken out his naturalisation papers, underwent rigid exploration. But no clue was found to Van Twiller's mysterious attachment. The *opéra bouffe*, which promised the widest field for investigation, produced absolutely nothing, not even a crop of suspicions. One night, after several weeks of this, Delaney and I fancied that we caught sight of Van Twiller in the private box of an uptown theatre, where some thrilling trapeze performance was going on, which we did not care to sit through; but we concluded afterward that it was only somebody who looked like him. Delaney, by the way, was unusually active in this search. I daresay he never quite forgave Van Twiller for calling him Muslin Delaney. Ned is fond of ladies' society, and that's a fact.

The Cimmerian darkness which surrounded Van Twiller's inamorata left us free to indulge in the wildest conjectures. Whether she was black-tressed Melpomene, with bowl and dagger, or Thalia, with the fair hair and the laughing face, was only to be guessed at. It was popularly conceded, however, that Van Twiller was on the point of forming a dreadful *mésalliance*.

Up to this period he had visited the club regularly. Suddenly he ceased to appear. He was not to be seen on Fifth Avenue, or in the Central Park, or at the houses he generally frequented. His chambers—and mighty comfortable chambers they were—on Thirty-fourth Street were deserted. He had dropped out of the world, shot like a bright particular star from his orbit in the heaven of the best society.

The following conversation took place one night in the smoking-room:

"Where's Van Twiller?"
"Who's seen Van Twiller?"
"What has become of Van Twiller?"

Delaney picked up the *Evening Post*, and read—with a solemnity that betrayed young Firkins into exclaiming, "By Jove, now!——"

"Married, on the 10th instant, by the Rev. Friar Laurence, at the residence of the bride's uncle, Montague Capulet, Esq., Miss Adrienne Le Couvreur to Mr. Ralph Van Twiller, both of this city. No cards."

"Free List suspended," murmured De Peyster.

"It strikes me," said Frank Livingstone, who had been ruffling the leaves of a magazine at the other end of the table, "that you fellows are in a great fever about Van Twiller."

"So we are."

"Well, he has simply gone out of town."

"Where?"

"Up to the old homestead on the Hudson."

"It's an odd time of year for a fellow to go into the country."

"He has gone to visit his mother," said Livingstone.

"In February?"

"I didn't know, Delaney, that there was any statute in force prohibiting a man from visiting his mother in February if he wants to."

Delaney made some light remark about the pleasure of communing with Nature with a cold in her head, and the topic was dropped.

Livingstone was hand in glove with Van Twiller, and if any man shared his confidence it was Livingstone. He was aware of the gossip and speculation that had been rife in the club, but he either was not at liberty or did not think it worth while to relieve our curiosity. In the course of a week or two it was reported that Van Twiller was going to Europe; and go he did. A dozen of us went down to the "Scythia" to see him off. It was refreshing to have something as positive as the fact that Van Twiller had sailed.

II

Shortly after Van Twiller's departure the whole thing came out. Whether Livingstone found the secret too heavy a burden, or whether it transpired through some indiscretion on the part of Mrs. Vanrensselaer Vanzandt Van Twiller, I cannot say; but one evening the entire story was in the possession of the club.

Van Twiller had actually been very deeply interested—not in an actress, for the legitimate drama was not her humble walk in life, but—in Mademoiselle Olympe Zabriski, whose really perilous feats on the trapeze had astonished New York the year before, though they had failed to attract Delaney and me the night we wandered into the uptown theatre on the trail of Van Twiller's mystery.

That a man like Van Twiller should be fascinated even for an instant by a common circus-girl seems incredible; but it is always the incredible thing that happens. Besides, Mademoiselle Olympe was not a common circus-girl; she was a most daring and startling gymnast, with a beauty and a grace of movement that gave to her audacious performance almost an air of prudery. Watching her wondrous dexterity and pliant strength, both exercised without apparent effort, it seemed the most natural proceeding in the world that she should do those unpardonable things. She had a way of melting from one graceful posture into another like the dissolving figures thrown from a stereopticon. She was a lithe, radiant shape out of the Grecian mythology, now poised up there above the gas-lights, and now gleaming through the air like a slender gilt arrow.

I am describing Mademoiselle Olympe as she appeared to Van Twiller on the first occasion when he strolled into the theatre where she was performing. To me she was a girl of eighteen or twenty years of age (maybe she was much older, for pearl powder and distance keep these people perpetually young), slightly but exquisitely built, with sinews of silver wire; rather pretty, perhaps, after a manner, but showing plainly the effects of the exhaustive draughts she was making on her physical vitality. Now, Van Twiller was an enthusiast on the subject of calisthenics. "If I had a daughter," Van Twiller used to say, "I wouldn't send her to a boarding-school, or a nunnery; I'd send her to a gymnasium for the first five years. Our American women have no physique. They are lilies, pallid, pretty—and perishable. You marry an American woman, and what do you marry? A headache. Look at English girls. They are at least roses, and last the season through."

Walking home from the theatre that first night, it flitted through Van Twiller's mind that if he could give this girl's set of nerves and muscles to any one of the two hundred high-bred women he knew, he would marry her on the spot and worship her for ever.

The following evening he went to see Mademoiselle Olympe again. "Olympe Zabriski," he soliloquised as he sauntered through the lobby—"what a queer name! Olympe is French and Zabriski is Polish. It is her *nom de guerre*, of course; her real name is probably Sarah Jones. What kind of creature can she be in private life, I wonder? I wonder if she wears that costume all the time, and if she springs to her meals from a horizontal bar. Of course she rocks the baby to sleep on the trapeze." And Van Twiller went on making comical domestic tableaux of Mademoiselle Zabriski, like the clever, satirical dog he was, until the curtain rose.

This was on a Friday. There was a matinée the next day, and he attended that, though he had secured a seat for the usual evening entertainment. Then it became a habit of Van Twiller's to drop into the theatre for half an hour or so every night, to assist at the interlude, in which she appeared. He cared only for her part of the programme, and timed his visits accordingly. It was a surprise to himself when he reflected, one morning, that he had not missed a single performance of Mademoiselle Olympe for nearly two weeks.

"This will never do," said Van Twiller. " Olympe "— he called her Olympe, as if she were an old acquaintance, and so she might have been considered by that time—" is a wonderful creature ; but this will never do. Van, my boy, you must reform this altogether."

But half-past nine that night saw him in his accustomed orchestra chair, and so on for another week. A habit leads a man so gently in the beginning that he does not perceive he is led—with what silken threads and down what pleasant avenues it leads him ! By and by the soft silk threads become iron chains, and the pleasant avenues Avernus !

Quite a new element had lately entered into Van Twiller's enjoyment of Mademoiselle Olympe's ingenious feats—a vaguely born apprehension that she might slip from that swinging bar ; that one of the thin cords supporting it might snap, and let her go headlong from the dizzy height. Now and then, for a terrible instant, he would imagine her lying a glittering, palpitating heap at the footlights, with no colour in her lips ! Sometimes it seemed as if the girl were tempting this kind of fate. It was a hard, bitter life, and nothing but poverty and sordid misery at home could have driven her to it. What if she should end it all some night, by just unclasping that little hand ? It looked so small and white from where Van Twiller sat !

This frightful idea fascinated while it chilled him, and helped to make it nearly impossible for him to keep away from the theatre. In the beginning his attendance had not interfered with his social duties or pleasures ; but now he came to find it distasteful after dinner to do anything but read or walk the streets aimlessly until it was time to go to the play. When that was over, he was in no mood to go anywhere but to his rooms. So he dropped away by insensible degrees from his habitual haunts, was missed, and began to be talked about at the club. Catching some intimation of this he ventured no more in the orchestra stalls, but shrouded himself behind the draperies of the private box in which Delaney and I thought we saw him on one occasion.

Now, I find it very perplexing to explain what Van Twiller was wholly unable to explain to himself. He was not in love with Mademoiselle Olympe. He had no wish to speak to her, or to hear her speak. Nothing could have been easier, and nothing further from his desire, than to know her personally. A Van Twiller personally acquainted with a strolling female acrobat ! Good heavens ! That was something possible only with the discovery of perpetual motion. Taken from her theatrical setting, from her lofty perch, so to say, on the trapeze-bar, Olympe Zabriski would have shocked every aristocratic fibre in Van Twiller's body. He was simply fascinated by her marvellous grace and *élan*, and the magnetic recklessness of the girl. It was very young in him and very weak, and no member of the Sorosis, or all the Sorosisters together, could have been more severe on Van Twiller than he was on himself. To be weak, and to know it, is something of a punishment for a proud man. Van Twiller took his punishment, and went to the theatre regularly.

"When her engagement comes to an end," he meditated, "that will finish the business."

Mademoiselle Olympe's engagement finally did come to an end and she departed. But her engagement had been highly beneficial to the treasury-chest of the uptown theatre, and before Van Twiller could get over missing her she had returned from a short Western tour, and her immediate reappearance was underlined on the play-bills.

On a dead wall opposite the windows of Van Twiller's sleeping-room there appeared, as if by necromancy, an aggressive poster with MADEMOISELLE OLYMPE ZABRISKI on it in letters at least a foot high. This thing stared him in the face when he woke up one morning. It gave him a sensation as if she had called on him overnight and left her card.

From time to time through the day he regarded that poster with a sardonic eye. He had pitilessly resolved not to repeat the folly of the previous month. To say that this moral victory cost him nothing would be to deprive it of merit. It cost him many internal struggles. It is a fine thing to see a man seizing his temptation by the throat, and wrestling with it, and trampling it underfoot like St. Anthony. This was the spectacle Van Twiller was exhibiting to the angels.

The evening Mademoiselle Olympe was to make her reappearance, Van Twiller, having dined at the club, and feeling more like himself than he had felt for weeks, returned to his chamber, and, putting on dressing-gown and slippers, piled up the greater portion of his library about him, and fell to reading assiduously. There is nothing like a quiet evening at home with some slight intellectual occupation, after one's feathers have been stroked the wrong way.

When the lively French clock on the mantelpiece—a base of malachite surmounted by a flying bronze Mercury with its arms spread gracefully in the air, and not remotely suggestive of Mademoiselle Olympe in the act of executing her grand flight from the trapeze—when the clock, I repeat, struck nine, Van Twiller paid no attention to it. That was certainly a triumph. I am anxious to render Van Twiller all the justice I can, at this point of the narrative, inasmuch as when the half-hour sounded musically, like a crystal ball dropping into a silver bowl, he rose from the chair automatically, thrust his feet into his walking-shoes, threw his overcoat across his arm, and strode out of the room.

To be weak and to scorn your weakness, and not to be able to conquer it, is, as has been said, a hard thing; and I suspect it was not with unalloyed satisfaction that Van Twiller found himself taking his seat in the back part of the private box night after night during the second engagement of Mademoiselle Olympe. It was so easy not to stay away!

In this second edition of Van Twiller's fatuity, his case was even worse than before. He not only thought of Olympe quite a number of time between breakfast and dinner, he not only attended the interlude regularly, but he began, in spite of himself, to occupy his leisure hours at night by dreaming of her. This was too much of a good thing, and Van Twiller regarded it so. Besides, the dream was always the same—a harrowing dream, a dream singularly adapted to shattering the nerves of a man like Van Twiller. He would imagine himself seated at the theatre (with all the members of Our Club in the parquette), watching Mademoiselle Olympe as usual, when suddenly that young lady would launch herself desperately from the trapeze, and come flying through the air like a firebrand hurled at his private box. Then the unfortunate man would wake up with cold drops standing on his forehead.

There is one redeeming feature in this infatuation of Van Twiller's which the sober moralist will love to look upon—the serene unconsciousness of the person who caused it. She went through her *rôle* with admirable aplomb, drew her salary, it may be assumed, punctually, and appears from first to have been ignorant that there was a miserable slave wearing her chains nightly in the left-hand proscenium box.

That Van Twiller, haunting the theatre with the persistency of an ex-actor, conducted himself so discreetly as not to draw the fire of Mademoiselle Olympe's blue eyes shows that Van Twiller, however deeply under a spell, was not in love. I say this, though I think if Van Twiller had not been Van Twiller, if he had been a man of no family and no position and no money, if New York had been Paris and Thirty-fourth Street a street in the Latin Quarter—but it is useless to speculate on what might have happened. What did happen is sufficient.

It happened, then, in the second week of Queen Olympe's second unconscious reign, that an appalling Whisper floated up the Hudson, effected a landing at a point between Spuyten Duyvil Creek and Cold Spring, and sought out a stately mansion of Dutch architecture standing on the bank of the river. The Whisper straightway informed the lady dwelling in this mansion that all was not well with the last of the Van Twillers; that he was gradually estranging himself from his peers, and wasting his nights in a playhouse watching a misguided young woman turning unmaidenly somersaults on a piece of wood attached to two ropes.

Mrs. Vanrensselaer Vanzandt Van Twiller came down to town by the next train to look into this little matter.

She found the flower of the family taking an early breakfast at

11 A.M., in his cosy apartments on Thirty-fourth Street. With the least possible circumlocution she confronted him with what rumour had reported of his pursuits, and was pleased, but not too much pleased, when he gave her an exact account of his relations with Mademoiselle Zabriski, neither concealing nor qualifying anything. As a confession, it was unique, and might have been a great deal less entertaining. Two or three times in the course of the narrative, the matron had some difficulty in preserving the gravity of her countenance. After meditating a few minutes, she tapped Van Twiller softly on the arm with the tip of her parasol, and invited him to return with her the next day up the Hudson and make a brief visit at the home of his ancestors. He accepted the invitation with outward alacrity and inward disgust.

When this was settled, and the worthy lady had withdrawn, Van Twiller went directly to the establishment of Messrs. Ball, Black, and Company, and selected, with unerring taste, the finest diamond bracelet procurable. For his mother? Dear me, no! She had the family jewels.

I would not like to state the enormous sum Van Twiller paid for this bracelet. It was such a clasp of diamonds as would have hastened the pulsation of a patrician wrist. It was such a bracelet as Prince Camaralzaman might have sent to the Princess Badoura, and the Princess Badoura—might have been very glad to get.

In the fragrant Levant morocco case, where these happy jewels lived, when they were at home, Van Twiller thoughtfully placed his card, on the back of which he had written a line begging Mademoiselle Olympe Zabriski to accept the accompanying trifle from one who had witnessed her graceful performances with interest and pleasure. This was not done inconsiderately. " Of course, I must enclose my card, as I would to any lady," Van Twiller had said to himself. " A Van Twiller can neither write an anonymous letter nor make an anonymous present." Blood entails its duties as well as its privileges.

The casket despatched to its destination, Van Twiller felt easier in his mind. He was under obligations to the girl for many an agreeable hour that might otherwise have passed heavily. He had paid the debt, and he had paid it *en prince*, as became a Van Twiller. He spent the rest of the day in looking at some pictures at Goupil's, and at the club, and in making a few purchases for his trip up the Hudson. A consciousness that this trip up the Hudson was a disorderly retreat came over him unpleasantly at intervals.

When he returned to his rooms late at night, he found a note lying on the writing-table. He started as his eyes caught the words "—— Theatre " stamped in carmine letters on one corner of the envelope. Van Twiller broke the seal with trembling fingers.

Now, this note some time afterward fell into the hands of Livingstone, who showed it to Stuyvesant, who showed it to Delaney, who showed it to me, and I copied it as a literary curiosity. The note ran as follows:

Mr. Van Twiller Dear Sir—i am verry greatfull to you for that Bracelett. it come just in the nic of time for me. The Mademoiselle Zabriski dodg is about Plaid out. my beard is getting to much for me. i shall have to grow a mustash and take to some other line of busyness, i dont no what now, but will let you no. You wont feel bad if i sell that Bracelett. i have seen Abrahams Moss and he says he will do the square thing. Pleas accep my thanks for youre Beautifull and Unexpected present.—Youre respectfull servent,

Charles Montmorenci Walters.

The next day Van Twiller neither expressed nor felt any unwillingness to spend a few weeks with his mother at the old homestead.
And then he went abroad.

# OUR NEW NEIGHBOURS AT PONKAPOG

### Thomas Bailey Aldrich

When I saw the little house building, an eighth of a mile beyond my own, on the Old Bay Road, I wondered who were to be the tenants. The modest structure was set well back from the road, among the trees, as if the inmates were to care nothing whatever for a view of the stylish equipages which sweep by during the summer season. For my part, I like to see the passing, in town or country; but each has his own unaccountable taste. The proprietor, who seemed to be also the architect of the new house, superintended the various details of the work with an assiduity that gave me a high opinion of his intelligence and executive ability, and I congratulated myself on the prospect of having some very agreeable neighbours.

It was quite early in the spring, if I remember, when they moved into the cottage—a newly married couple, evidently: the wife very young, pretty, and with the air of a lady; the husband somewhat older, but still in the first flush of manhood. It was understood in the village that they came from Baltimore; but no one knew them personally, and they brought no letters of introduction. (For obvious reasons I refrain from mentioning names.) It was clear that, for the present at least, their own company was entirely sufficient for them. They made no advances toward the acquaintance of any of the families in the neighbourhood, and consequently were left to themselves. That, apparently, was what they desired, and why they came to Ponkapog. For after its black bass and wild duck and teal, solitude is the chief staple of Ponkapog. Perhaps its perfect rural loveliness should be included. Lying high up under the wing of the Blue Hills, and in the odorous breath of pines and cedars, it chances to be the most enchanting bit of unlaced dishevelled country within fifty miles of Boston, which, moreover, can be reached in half an hour's ride by railway. But the nearest railway station (Heaven be praised!) is two miles distant, and the seclusion is without a flaw. Ponkapog has one mail a day; two mails a day would render the place uninhabitable.

The village—it looks like a compact village at a distance, but unravels and disappears the moment you drive into it—has quite a large floating population. I do not allude to the perch and pickerel in Ponkapog Pond. Along the Old Bay Road, a highway even in the colonial days, there are a number of attractive villas and cottages straggling off towards Milton, which are occupied for the summer by people from the city. These birds of passage are a distinct class from the permanent inhabitants, and the two seldom closely assimilate unless there has been some previous connection. It seemed to me that our new neighbours were to come under the head of permanent inhabitants; they had built their own house, and had the air of intending to live in it all the year round.

"Are you not going to call on them?" I asked my wife one morning.

"When they call on *us*," she replied lightly.

"But it is our place to call first, they being strangers."

This was said as seriously as the circumstance demanded; but my wife turned it off with a laugh, and I said no more, always trusting to her intuitions in these matters.

She was right. She would not have been received, and a cool "Not at home" would have been a bitter social pill to us if we had gone out of our way to be courteous.

I saw a great deal of our neighbours, nevertheless. Their cottage lay between us and the post office—where *he* was never to be met with by any chance—and I caught frequent glimpses of the two working in the garden. Floriculture did not appear so much an object as exercise. Possibly it was neither; maybe they were engaged in digging for specimens of those arrowheads and flint hatchets which are continually coming to the surface hereabouts. There is scarcely an acre in which the ploughshare has not turned up some primitive stone weapon or domestic utensil, disdainfully left to us by the red men who once held this domain—an ancient tribe called the Punkypoags, a forlorn descendant of which, one

Polly Crowd, figures in the annual Blue Book, down to the close of the Southern war, as a State pensioner. At that period she appears to have struck a trail to the Happy Hunting Grounds. I quote from the local historiographer.

Whether they were developing a kitchen-garden, or emulating Professor Schliemann at Mycenæ, the new-comers were evidently persons of refined musical taste: the lady had a contralto voice of remarkable sweetness, although of no great compass, and I used often to linger of a morning by the high gate and listen to her executing an arietta, conjecturally at some window upstairs, for the house was not visible from the turnpike. The husband, somewhere about the grounds, would occasionally respond with two or three bars. It was all quite an ideal, Arcadian business. They seemed very happy together, these two persons, who asked no odds whatever of the community in which they had settled themselves.

There was a queerness, a sort of mystery, about this couple which I admit piqued my curiosity, though as a rule I have no morbid interest in the affairs of my neighbours. They behaved like a pair of lovers who had run off and got married clandestinely. I willingly acquitted them, however, of having done anything unlawful; for, to change a word in the lines of the poet.

> It is a joy to *think* the best
> We may of human kind.

Admitting the hypothesis of elopement, there was no mystery in their neither sending nor receiving letters. But where did they get their groceries? I do not mean the money to pay for them—that is an enigma apart—but the groceries themselves. No express waggon, no butcher's cart, no vehicle of any description was ever observed to stop at their domicile. Yet they did not order family stores at the sole establishment in the village—an inexhaustible little bottle of a shop which, I advertise it gratis, can turn out anything in the way of groceries from a hand-saw to a pocket-handkerchief. I confess that I allowed this unimportant detail of their *ménage* to occupy more of my speculation than was creditable to me.

In several respects our neighbours reminded me of those inexplicable persons we sometimes come across in great cities, though seldom or never in suburban places, where the field may be supposed too restricted for their operations—persons who have no perceptible means of subsistence, and manage to live royally on nothing a year. They hold no Government bonds, they possess no real estate (our neighbours did own their house), they toil not, neither do they spin; yet they reap all the numerous soft advantages that usually result from honest toil and skilful spinning. How do they do it? But this is a digression, and I am quite of the opinion of the old lady in *David Copperfield*, who says, "Let us have no meandering."

Though my wife had declined to risk a ceremonious call on our neighbours as a family, I saw no reason why I should not speak to the husband as an individual when I happened to encounter him by the wayside. I made several approaches to do so, when it occurred to my penetration that my neighbour had the air of trying to avoid me. I resolved to put the suspicion to the test, and one forenoon, when he was sauntering along on the opposite side of the road, in the vicinity of Fisher's sawmill, I deliberately crossed over to address him. The brusque manner in which he hurried away was not to be misunderstood. Of course I was not going to force myself upon him.

It was at this time that I began to formulate uncharitable suppositions touching our neighbours, and would have been as well pleased if some of my choicest fruit-trees had not overhung their wall. I determined to keep my eyes open later in the season, when the fruit should be ripe to pluck. In some folks a sense of the delicate shades of difference between *meum* and *tuum* does not seem to be very strongly developed in the Moon of Cherries, to use the old Indian phrase.

I was sufficiently magnanimous not to impart any of these sinister impressions to the families with whom we were on visiting terms; for I despise a gossip. I would say nothing against the persons up the road until I had something definite to say. My interest in them was—well, not exactly extinguished, but burning low. I met the gentleman at intervals, and passed him without recognition; at rarer intervals I saw the lady.

After a while I not only missed my occasional glimpses of her pretty, slim figure, always draped in some soft black stuff with a bit of scarlet at the throat, but I inferred that she did not go about the house singing in her light-hearted manner as formerly. What had happened? Had the honeymoon suffered eclipse already? Was she ill? I fancied she was ill, and that I detected a certain anxiety in the husband, who spent the mornings digging solitarily in the garden, and seemed to have relinquished those long jaunts to the brow of Blue Hill, where there is a superb view of all Norfolk County combined with sundry venerable rattlesnakes with twelve rattles.

As the days went by it became certain that the lady was confined to the house, perhaps seriously ill, possibly a confirmed invalid. Whether she was attended by a physician from Canton or from Milton, I was unable to say; but neither the gig with the large white allopathic horse, nor the gig with the homœopathic sorrel mare, was ever seen hitched at the gate during the day. If a physician had charge of the case, he visited his patient only at night. All this moved my sympathy, and I reproached myself with having had hard thoughts of our neighbours. Trouble had come to them early. I would have liked to offer them such small, friendly services as lay in my power; but the memory of the repulse I had sustained still rankled in me. So I hesitated.

One morning my two boys burst into the library with their eyes sparkling.
" You know the old elm down the road? " cried one.
" Yes."
" The elm with the hang-bird's nest? " shrieked the other.
" Yes, yes! "
" Well, we both just climbed up, and there's three young ones in it! "
Then I smiled to think that our new neighbours had got such a promising little family.

# FRANCIS BRET HARTE
### 1839–1902

# TENNESSEE'S PARTNER

I DO not think that we ever knew his real name. Our ignorance of it certainly never gave us any social inconvenience, for at Sandy Bar in 1854 most men were christened anew. Sometimes these appellatives were derived from some distinctiveness of dress, as in the case of "Dungaree Jack," or from some peculiarity of habit, as shown in "Saleratus Bill," so called from an undue proportion of that chemical in his daily bread; or from some unlucky slip, as exhibited in "The Iron Pirate," a mild, inoffensive man, who earned that baleful title by his unfortunate mispronunciation of the term "iron pyrites." Perhaps this may have been the beginning of a rude heraldry; but I am constrained to think that it was because a man's real name in that day rested solely upon his own unsupported statement.

"Call yourself Clifford, do you?" said Boston, addressing a timid new-comer with infinite scorn; "hell is full of such Cliffords!" He then introduced the unfortunate man, whose name happened to be really Clifford, as "Jay-bird Charley"—an unhallowed inspiration of the moment that clung to him ever after.

But to return to Tennessee's Partner, whom we never knew by any other than this relative title; that he had ever existed as a separate and distinct individuality we only learned later. It seems that in 1853 he left Poker Flat to go to San Francisco, ostensibly to procure a wife. He never got any farther than Stockton. At that place he was attracted by a young person who waited upon the table at the hotel where he took his meals. One morning he said something to her which caused her to smile not unkindly, somewhat coquettishly to break a plate of toast over his upturned, serious, simple face, and to retreat to the kitchen. He followed her and emerged a few moments later, covered with more toast and victory. That day week they were married by a Justice of the Peace and returned to Poker Flat. I am aware that something more might be made of this episode, but I prefer to tell it as it was current at Sandy Bar—in the gulches and bar-rooms—where all sentiment was modified by a strong sense of humour.

Of their married felicity but little is known, perhaps for the

reason that Tennessee, then living with his partner, one day took
occasion to say something to the bride on his own account, at which,
it is said, she smiled not unkindly and chastely retreated—this time
as far as Marysville, where Tennessee followed her, and where they
went to housekeeping without the aid of a Justice of the Peace.
Tennessee's Partner took the loss of his wife simply and seriously,
as was his fashion. But to everybody's surprise, when Tennessee
one day returned from Marysville, without his partner's wife—she
having smiled and retreated with somebody else—Tennessee's
Partner was the first man to shake his hand and greet him with
affection. The boys who had gathered in the cañon to see the shooting were naturally indignant. Their indignation might have found
vent in sarcasm, but for a certain look in Tennessee's Partner's eye
that indicated a lack of humerous appreciation. In fact, he was a
grave man, with a steady application to practical detail which was
unpleasant in a difficulty.

Meanwhile a popular feeling against Tennessee had grown up on
the Bar. He was known to be a gambler; he was suspected to be a
thief. In these suspicions Tennessee's Partner was equally compromised; his continued intimacy with Tennessee after the affair
above quoted could only be accounted for on the hypothesis of a
co-partnership of crime. At last Tennessee's guilt became flagrant.
One day he overtook a stranger on his way to Red Dog. The
stranger afterwards related that Tennessee beguiled the time with
interesting anecdote and reminiscence, but illogically concluded the
interview in the following words:

"And now, young man, I'll trouble you for your knife, your
pistols, and your money. You see, your wrappings might get you
into trouble at Red Dog, and your money's a temptation to the
evilly disposed. I think you said your address was San Francisco.
I shall endeavour to call." It may be stated here that Tennessee
had a fine flow of humour, which no business preoccupation could
wholly subdue.

This exploit was his last. Red Dog and Sandy Bar made common
cause against the highwayman. Tennessee was hunted in very
much the same fashion as his prototype, the grizzly. As the toils
closed around him he made a desperate dash through the Bar,
emptying his revolver at the crowd before the Arcade Saloon, and
so on up Grizzly Cañon; but at its farther extremity he was stopped
by a small man on a grey horse. The men looked at each other a
moment in silence. Both were fearless, both self-possessed and
independent; and both types of a civilisation that in the seventeenth
century would have been called heroic, but in the nineteenth simply
"reckless."

"What have you got there? I call," said Tennessee, quietly.

"Two bowers and an ace," said the stranger, as quietly, showing
two revolvers and a bowie-knife.

"That takes me," returned Tennessee; and with this gambler's epigram he threw away his useless pistol and rode back with his captor.

It was a warm night. The cool breeze which usually sprang up with the going down of the sun behind the *chaparral*-crested mountain was that evening withheld from Sandy Bar. The little cañon was stifling with heated resinous odours, and the decaying driftwood on the Bar sent forth faint, sickening exhalations. The feverishness of day, and its fierce passions, still filled the camp. Lights moved restlessly along the bank of the river, striking no answering reflection from its tawny current. Against the blackness of the pines the windows of the old loft above the express-office stood out staringly bright, and through their curtainless panes the loungers below could see the forms of those who were even then deciding the fate of Tennessee. And above all this, etched on the dark firmament, rose the Sierra, remote and passionless, crowned with remoter passionless stars.

The trial of Tennessee was conducted as fairly as was consistent with a judge and jury who felt themselves to some extent obliged to justify in their verdict the previous irregularities of arrest and indictment. The law of Sandy Bar was implacable, but not vengeful. The excitement and personal feeling of the chase were over; with Tennessee safe in their hands they were ready to listen patiently to any defence, which they were already satisfied was insufficient. There being no doubt in their own minds, they were willing to give the prisoner the benefit of any that might exist. Secure in the hypothesis that he ought to be hanged, on general principles, they indulged him with more latitude of defence than his reckless hardihood seemed to ask. The Judge appeared to be more anxious than the prisoner, who, otherwise unconcerned, evidently took a grim pleasure in the responsibility he had created. " I don't take any hand in this yer game," had been his invariable but good-humoured reply to all questions. The Judge—who was also his captor—for a moment vaguely regretted that he had not shot him " on sight " that morning, but presently dismissed this human weakness as unworthy of the judicial mind. Nevertheless, when there was a tap at the door, and it was said that Tennessee's Partner was there on behalf of the prisoner, he was admitted at once without question. Perhaps the younger members of the jury, to whom the proceedings were becoming irksomely thoughtful, hailed him as a relief.

For he was not, certainly, an imposing figure. Short and stout, with a square face, sunburned into a preternatural redness, clad in a loose duck " jumper," and trousers streaked and splashed with red soil, his aspect in any circumstances would have been quaint, and was now even ridiculous. As he stooped to deposit at his feet a heavy carpet bag he was carrying, it became obvious, from partially developed legends and inscriptions, that the material with which his trousers had been patched had been originally intended for a less ambitious covering. Yet he advanced with great gravity, and after having shaken the hand of each person in the room with laboured cordiality, he wiped his serious, perplexed face on a red bandanna handkerchief, a shade lighter than his complexion, laid his powerful hand upon the table to steady himself, and thus addressed the Judge :

"I was passin' by," he began, by way of apology, "and I thought I'd just step in and see how things was gittin' on with Tennessee thar—my pardner. It's a hot night. I disremember any sich weather before on the Bar."

He paused a moment, but nobody volunteering any other meteorological recollection, he again had recourse to his pocket-handkerchief, and for some moments mopped his face diligently.

"Have you anything to say in behalf of the prisoner ? " said the Judge, finally.

"Thet's it," said Tennessee's Partner, in a tone of relief. "I come yar as Tennessee's pardner—knowing him nigh on four year, off and on, wet and dry, in luck and out o'luck. His ways ain't allers my ways, but thar ain't any p'ints in that young man, thar ain't any liveliness as he's been up to, as I don't know. And you sez to me, sez you—confidential-like, and between man and man—sez you, ' Do you know anything in his behalf ? ' and I sez to you, sez I—confidential-like, as between man and man—' What should a man know of his pardner ? ' "

"Is this all you have to say ? " asked the Judge, impatiently, feeling, perhaps, that a dangerous sympathy of humour was beginning to humanise the Court.

"Thet's so," continued Tennessee's Partner. "It ain't for me to say anything agin him. And now, what's the case ? Here's Tennessee wants money, wants it bad, and doesn't like to ask it of his old pardner. Well, what does Tennessee do ? He lays for a stranger, and he fetches that stranger. And you lays for *him*, and you fetches *him*—and the honours is easy. And I put it to you, bein' a far-minded man, and to you, gentlemen, all, as far-minded men, ef this isn't so."

"Prisoner," said the Judge, interrupting, " have you any questions to ask this man ? "

"No ! no ! " continued Tennessee's Partner, hastily. "I play this yer hand alone. To come down to the bed-rock, it's just this : Tennessee, thar, has played it pretty rough and expensive-like on a stranger, and on this yer camp. And now, what's the fair thing ? Some would say more ; some would say less. Here's seventeen hundred dollars in coarse gold and a watch—it's about all my pile—and call it square ! " And before a hand could be raised to prevent him, he had emptied the contents of the carpet-bag upon the table.

For a moment his life was in jeopardy. One or two men sprang to their feet, several hands groped for hidden weapons, and a suggestion to "throw him from the window" was only overridden by a gesture from the Judge. Tennessee laughed. And apparently oblivious of the excitement, Tennessee's Partner improved the opportunity to mop his face again with his handkerchief.

When order was restored, and the man was made to understand, by the use of forcible figures and rhetoric, that Tennessee's offence could not be condoned by money, his face took a more serious and sanguinary hue, and those who were nearest to him noticed that his rough hand trembled slightly on the table. He hesitated a moment as he slowly returned the gold to the carpet-bag, as if he had not yet entirely caught the elevated sense of justice which swayed the tribunal, and was perplexed with the belief that he had not offered enough. Then he turned to the Judge, and saying, "This yer is a lone hand, played alone, and without my pardner," he bowed to the jury, and was about to withdraw, when the Judge called him back.

"If you have anything to say to Tennessee, you had better say it now."

For the first time that evening the eyes of the prisoner and his strange advocate met. Tennessee smiled, showed his white teeth, and, saying, "Euchred, old man!" held out his hand.

Tennesee's Partner took it in his own, and saying, "I just dropped in as I was passin' to see how things was gittin' on," let the hand passively fall, and adding that "it was a warm night," again mopped his face with his handkerchief, and without another word withdrew.

The two men never again met each other alive. For the unparalleled insult of a bribe offered to Judge Lynch—who, whether bigoted, weak, or narrow, was at least incorruptible—firmly fixed in the mind of that mythical personage any wavering determination of Tennessee's fate, and at the break of day he was marched, closely guarded, to meet it at the top of Marley's Hill.

How he met it, how cool he was, how he refused to say anything, how perfect were the arrangements of the committee, were all duly reported, with the addition of a warning moral and example to all future evil-doers, in the *Red Dog Clarion*, by its editor, who was present, and to whose vigorous English I cheerfully refer the reader. But the beauty of that midsummer morning, the blessed amity of earth and air and sky, the awakened life of the free woods and hills, the joyous renewal and promise of Nature, and above all, the infinite serenity that thrilled through each, were not reported, as not being a part of the social lesson. And yet, when the weak and foolish deed was done, and a life, with its possibilities and responsibilities, had passed out of the misshapen thing that dangled between earth and sky, the birds sang, the flowers bloomed, the sun shone, as cheerily as before; and possibly the *Red Dog Clarion* was right.

Tennessee's Partner was not in the group that surrounded the ominous tree. But as they turned to disperse, attention was drawn to the singular appearanceof a motionless donkey-cart halted at the side of the road. As they approached they at once recognised the venerable " Jenny " and the two-wheeled cart as the property of Tennessee's Partner—used by him in carrying dirt from his claim ; and a few paces distant the owner of the equipage himself, sitting under a buckeye-tree, wiping the perspiration from his glowing face. In answer to an inquiry, he said he had come for the body of the " diseased," if it was all the same to the committee. He didn't wish to " hurry anything " ; he could " wait." He was not working that day ; and when the gentlemen were done with the " diseased," he would take him. " Ef thar is any present," he added, in his simple, serious way, " as would care to jine in the fun'l, they kin come." Perhaps it was from a sense of humour, which I have already intimated was a feature of Sandy Bar—perhaps it was from something even better than that ; but two-thirds of the loungers accepted the invitation at once.

It was noon when the body of Tennessee was delivered into the hands of his partner. As the cart drew up to the fatal tree, we noticed that it contained a rough oblong box—apparently made from a section of sluicing—and half filled with bark and the tassels of pine. The cart was further decorated with slips of willow, and made fragrant with buckeye-blossoms. When the body was deposited in the box, Tennessee's Partner drew over it a piece of tarred canvas, and gravely mounting the narrow seat in front, with his feet upon the shafts, urged the little donkey forward. The equipage moved slowly on, at that decorous pace which was habitual with " Jenny " even under less solemn circumstances. The men—half curiously, half jestingly, but all good-humouredly—strolled along beside the cart : some in advance, some a little in the rear of the homely catafalque. But, whether from the narrowing of the road, or some present sense of decorum, as the cart passed on the company fell to the rear in couples, keeping step, and otherwise assuming the external show of a formal procession. Jack Folinsbee, who had at the outset played a funeral march in dumb-show upon an imaginary trombone, desisted, from a lack of sympathy and appreciation—not having, perhaps, your true humourist's capacity to be content with the enjoyment of his own fun.

The way led through Grizzly Cañon—by this time clothed in funeral drapery and shadows. The redwoods, burying their moccasined feet in the red soil, stood in Indian file along the track, trailing an uncouth benediction from their bending boughs upon the passing bier. A hare, surprised into helpless inactivity, sat upright and pulsating in the ferns by the roadside as the *cortège* went by. Squirrels hastened to gain a secure outlook from higher boughs, and the blue-jays, spreading their wings, fluttered before them like outriders, until the outskirts of Sandy Bar were reached, and the solitary cabin of Tennessee's Partner.

Viewed under more favourable circumstances, it would not have been a cheerful place. The unpicturesque site, the rude and unlovely outlines, the unsavoury details, which distinguish the nest-building of the California miner, were all here, with the dreariness of decay superadded. A few paces from the cabin there was a rough enclosure, which, in the brief days of Tennessee's Partner's matrimonial felicity, had been used as a garden, but was now overgrown with fern. As we approached it we were surprised to find that what we had taken for a recent attempt at cultivation was the broken soil about an open grave.

The cart was halted before the enclosure, and, rejecting the offers of assistance with the same air of simple self-reliance he had displayed throughout, Tennessee's Partner lifted the rough coffin on his back, and deposited it, unaided, within the shallow grave. He then nailed down the board which served as a lid, and, mounting the little mound of earth beside it, took off his hat, and slowly mopped his face with his handkerchief. This the crowd felt was a preliminary to speech, and they disposed themselves variously on stumps and boulders, and sat expectant.

"When a man," began Tennessee's Partner, slowly, "has been running free all day, what's the natural thing for him to do? Why, to come home! And if he ain't in a condition to go home, what can his best friend do? Why, bring him home! And here's Tennessee has been running free, and we brings him home from his wandering." He paused, and picked up a fragment of quartz, rubbed it thoughtfully on his sleeve, and went on: "It ain't the first time that I've packed him on my back, as you see'd me now. It ain't the first time that I brought him to this yer cabin when he couldn't help himself; it ain't the first time that I and 'Jinny' have waited for him on yon hill, and picked him up and so fetched him home, when he couldn't speak, and didn't know me. And now that it's the last time, why—" he paused, and rubbed the quartz gently on his sleeve—"you see, it's sort of rough on his pardner. And now, gentlemen," he added, abruptly, picking up his long-handled shovel, "the fun'l's over, and my thanks, and Tennessee's thanks, to you for your trouble."

Resisting any proffers of assistance he began to fill in the grave, turning his back upon the crowd, that after a few moments' hesitation gradually withdrew. As they crossed the little ridge that hid Sandy Bar from view, some, looking back, thought they could see Tennessee's Partner, his work done, sitting upon the grave, his shovel between his knees, and his face buried in his red bandanna handkerchief. But it was argued by others that you couldn't tell his face from his handkerchief at that distance, and this point remained undecided.

In the reaction that followed the feverish excitement of that day, Tennessee's Partner was not forgotten. A secret investigation had cleared him of any complicity in Tennessee's guilt, and left only a suspicion of his general sanity. Sandy Bar made a point of calling on him and proffering various uncouth but well-meant kindnesses. But from that day his rude health and great strength seemed visibly to decline, and when the rainy season fairly set in, and the tiny grass-blades were beginning to peep from the rocky mound above Tennessee's grave, he took to his bed.

One night, when the pines beside the cabin were swaying in the storm, and trailing their slender fingers over the roof, and the roar and rush of the swollen river were heard below, Tennessee's Partner lifted his head from the pillow, saying, " It is time to go for Tennessee ; I must put ' Jinny ' in the cart," and would have risen from his bed but for the restraint of his attendant. Struggling, he still pursued his singular fancy : "There, now, steady, ' Jinny '— steady, old girl. How dark it is ! Look out for the ruts—and look out for him, too, old gal ! Sometimes, you know, when he's blind drunk, he drops down right in the trail. Keep on straight up to the pine on the top of the hill. Thar—I told you so !—thar he is— coming this way, too—all by himself, sober, and his face a-shining. Tennessee ! Pardner ! "

And so they met.

# MIGGLES

### Francis Bret Harte

WE were eight, including the driver. We had not spoken during the passage of the last six miles, since the jolting of the heavy vehicle over the roughening road had spoiled the Judge's last poetical quotation. The tall man beside the Judge was asleep, his arm passed through the swaying strap and his head resting upon it— altogether a limp, helpless-looking object, as if he had hanged himself and been cut down too late. The French lady on the back seat was asleep too, yet in a half-conscious propriety of attitude, shown even in the disposition of the handkerchief which she held to her forehead, and which partially veiled her face. The lady from Virginia City, travelling with her husband, had long since lost all individuality in a wild confusion of ribbons, veils, furs, and shawls. There was no sound but the rattling of wheels and the dash of rain upon the roof. Suddenly the stage stopped, and we became dimly aware of voices.

The driver was evidently in the midst of an exciting colloquy with some one in the road—a colloquy of which such fragments as "bridge gone," "twenty feet of water," "can't pass," were occasionally distinguishable above the storm. Then came a lull, and a mysterious voice from the road shouted the parting adjuration:

"Try Miggles's."

We caught a glimpse of our leaders, as the vehicle slowly turned, of a horseman vanishing through the rain, and we were evidently on our way to Miggles's.

Who and where was Miggles? The Judge, our authority, did not remember the name, and he knew the country thoroughly. The Washoe traveller thought Miggles must keep an hotel. We only knew that we were stopped by high water in front and rear, and that Miggles was our rock of refuge. A ten minutes' splashing through a tangle bye-road, scarcely wide enough for the stage, and we drew up before a barred and boarded gate in a wide stone wall or fence about eight feet high. Evidently Miggles's, and evidently Miggles did not keep an hotel.

The driver got down and tried the gate. It was securely locked.

"Miggles! O Miggles!"

No answer.

"Migg-ells! You Miggles!" continued the driver, with rising wrath.

"Migglesy!" joined in the expressman, persuasively. "O Miggy! Mig!"

But no reply came from the apparently insensate Miggles. The Judge, who had finally got the window down, put his head out, and propounded a series of questions, which, if answered categorically, would have undoubtedly elucidated the whole mystery, but which the driver evaded by replying that "if we didn't want to sit in the coach all night, we had better rise up and sing out for Miggles."

So we rose up and called on Miggles in chorus; then separately. And when we had finished a Hibernian fellow-passenger from the roof called for "Maygells!" whereat we all laughed. While we were laughing the driver cried "Shoo!"

We listened. To our infinite amazement the chorus of "Miggles" was repeated from the other side of the wall, even to the final and supplemental "Maygells."

"Extraordinary echo," said the Judge.

"Extraordinary d——d skunk!" roared the driver, contemptuously. "Come out of that, Miggles, and show yourself! Be a man, Miggles! Don't hide in the dark; I wouldn't if I were you, Miggles," continued Yuba Bill, now dancing about in an excess of fury.

"Miggles!" continued the voice, "Oh Miggles!"

"My good man! Mr. Myghail!" said the Judge, softening the asperities of the name as much as possible. "Consider the inhospitality of refusing shelter from the inclemency of the weather to helpless females. Really, my dear sir——" But a succession of "Miggles," ending in a burst of laughter, drowned his voice.

Yuba Bill hesitated no longer. Taking a heavy stone from the road he battered down the gate, and, with the expressman, entered the enclosure. We followed. Nobody was to be seen. In the gathering darkness all that we could distinguish was that we were in a garden—from the rose-bushes that scattered over us a minute spray from their dripping leaves—and before a long, rambling wooden building.

"Do you know this Miggles?" asked the Judge of Yuba Bill.

"No; nor don't want to," said Bill, shortly, who felt the Pioneer Stage Company insulted in his person by the contumacious Miggles.

"But, my dear sir," expostulated the Judge, as he thought of the barred gate.

"Lookee here," said Yuba Bill, with fine irony, "hadn't you better go back and sit in the coach till yer introduced? I'm going in"; and he pushed open the door of the building.

A long room, lighted only by the embers of a fire that was dying on the large hearth at its further extremity; the walls curiously papered, and the flickering firelight bringing out its grotesque pattern; somebody sitting in a large arm-chair by the fireplace. All this we saw as we crowded together into the room, after the driver and expressman.

"Hello, be you Miggles?" said Yuba Bill to the solitary occupant.

The figure neither spoke nor stirred. Yuba Bill walked wrathfully towards it, and turned the eye of his coach-lantern upon its face. It was a man's face, prematurely old and wrinkled, with very large eyes, in which there was that expression of perfectly gratuitous solemnity which I had sometimes seen in an owl's. The large eyes wandered from Bill's face to the lantern, and finally fixed their gaze on that luminous object, without further recognition.

Bill restrained himself with an effort.

"Miggles! Be you deaf? You ain't dumb, anyhow, you know"; and Yuba Bill shook the insensate figure by the shoulder.

To our great dismay, as Bill removed his hand, the venerable stranger apparently collapsed, sinking into half his size and an undistinguishable heap of clothing.

"Well, dern my skin," said Bill, looking appealingly at us, and hopelessly retiring from the contest.

The Judge now stepped forward, and we lifted the mysterious invertebrate back into his original position. Bill was dismissed with the lantern to reconnoitre outside, for it was evident that from the helplessness of this solitary man there must be attendants near at hand, and we all drew around the fire. The Judge, who had regained his authority, and had never lost his conversational amiability—standing before us with his back to the hearth—charged us, as an imaginary jury, as follows:

"It is evident that either our distinguished friend here has reached that condition described by Shakespeare as 'the sere and yellow leaf,' or has suffered some premature abatement of his mental and physical faculties. Whether he is really the Miggles——"

Here he was interrupted by "Miggles! Oh Miggles! Migglesy! Mig!" and, in fact, the whole chorus of Miggles, in very much the same key as it had once before been delivered unto us.

We gazed at each other for a moment in some alarm. The Judge, in particular, vacated his position quickly, as the voice seemed to come directly over his shoulder. The cause, however, was soon discovered in a large magpie who was perched upon a shelf over the fireplace, and who immediately relapsed into a sepulchral silence, which contrasted singularly with his previous volubility. It was, undoubtedly, his voice which we had heard in the road, and our friend in the chair was not responsible for the discourtesy. Yuba Bill, who re-entered the room after an unsuccessful search, was loth to accept the explanation, and still eyed the helpless sitter with suspicion. He had found a shed in which he had put up his horses, but he came back dripping and sceptical. "Thar ain't nobody but him within ten miles of the shanty, and that 'ar d——d old skeesicks knows it."

But the faith of the majority proved to be securely based. Bill had scarcely ceased growling before we heard a quick step upon the porch, the trailing of a wet skirt, the door was flung open, and with a flash of white teeth, a sparkle of dark eyes, and an utter absence of ceremony or diffidence, a young woman entered, shut the door, and, panting, leaned back against it.

"Oh, if you please, I'm Miggles!"

And this was Miggles! This bright-eyed, full-throated, young woman, whose wet gown of coarse blue stuff could not hide the beauty of the feminine curves to which it clung; from the chestnut crown of whose head, topped by a man's oil-skin sou'wester, to the little feet and ankles, hidden somewhere in the recesses of her boy's brogans, all was grace—this was Miggles, laughing at us, too, in the most airy, frank, off-hand manner imaginable.

"You see, boys," said she, quite out of breath, and holding one little hand against her side, quite unheeding the speechless discomfiture of our party, or the complete demoralisation of Yuba Bill, whose features had relaxed into an expression of gratuitous and imbecile cheerfulness—"you see, boys, I was mor'n two miles away when you passed down the road. I thought you might pull up here, and so I ran the whole way, knowing nobody was home but Jim—and—and—I'm out of breath—and—that lets me out."

And here Miggles caught her dripping oil-skin hat from her head,

with a mischievous swirl that scattered a shower of rain-drops over
us ; attempted to put back her hair ; dropped two hair-pins in the
attempt ; laughed and sat down beside Yuba Bill, with her hands
crossed lightly on her lap. The Judge recovered himself first, and
essayed an extravagant compliment.

"I'll trouble you for that thar har-pin," said Miggles, gravely.
Half-a-dozen hands were eagerly stretched forward ; the missing
hair-pin was restored to its fair owner ; and Miggles, crossing the
room, looked keenly in the face of the invalid. The solemn eyes
looked back at hers with an expression we had never seen before.
Life and intelligence seemed to struggle back into the rugged face.
Miggles laughed again—it was a singularly eloquent laugh—
and turned her black eyes and white teeth once more towards
us.

" This afflicted person is——" hesitated the Judge.

" Jim," said Miggles.

" Your father ? "

" No."

" Brother ? "

" No."

" Husband ? " Miggles darted a quick, half-defiant glance at the
two lady passengers who I had noticed did not participate in the
general masculine admiration of Miggles, and said, gravely, " No :
it's Jim."

There was an awkward pause. The lady passengers moved closer
to each other ; the Washoe husband looked abstractedly at the fire ;
and the tall man apparently turned his eyes inward for self-support
at this emergency. But Miggles's laugh, which was very infectious,
broke the silence. " Come," she said briskly, " you must be hungry.
Who'll bear a hand to help me get tea ? "

She had no lack of volunteers. In a few moments Yuba Bill was
engaged like Caliban in bearing logs for this Miranda ; the expressman was grinding coffee on the verandah ; to myself, the arduous
duty of slicing bacon was assigned ; and the Judge lent each man
his good-humoured and voluble counsel. And when Miggles,
assisted by the Judge and our Hibernian " deck passenger," set the
table with all the available crockery, we had become quite joyous
in spite of the rain that beat against windows, the wind that
whirled down the chimney, the two ladies who whispered together
in the corner, or the magpie who uttered a satirical and croaking
commentary on their conversation from his perch above. In the
now bright, blazing fire we could see that the walls were papered
with illustrated journals, arranged with feminine taste and dis-
crimination. The furniture was extemporised and adapted from
candle-boxes and packing-cases, and covered with gay calico, or
the skin of some animal. The armchair of the helpless Jim was
an ingenious variation of a flour-barrel. There was neatness, and

even a taste for the picturesque, to be seen in the few details of the long low room.

The meal was a culinary success. But more, it was a social triumph—chiefly, I think, owing to the rare tact of Miggles in guiding the conversation, asking all the questions herself, yet bearing throughout a frankness that rejected the idea of any concealment on her own part, so that we talked of ourselves, of our prospects, of the journey, of the weather, of each other—of everything but our host and hostess. It must be confessed that Miggles's conversation was never elegant, rarely grammatical, and that at times she employed expletives, the use of which had generally been yielded to our sex. But they were delivered with such a lighting up of teeth and eyes, and were usually followed by a laugh—a laugh peculiar to Miggles—so frank and honest, that it seemed to clear the moral atmosphere.

Once during the meal we heard a noise like the rubbing of a heavy body against the outer walls of the house. This was shortly followed by a scratching and sniffing at the door. "That's Joaquin," said Miggles, in reply to our questioning glances; "would you like to see him?" Before we could answer she had opened the door and disclosed a half-grown grizzly, who instantly raised himself on his haunches, with his forepaws hanging down in the popular attitude of mendicancy, and looked admiringly at Miggles, with a very singular resemblance in his manner to Yuba Bill. "That's my watch-dog." said Miggles in explanation. "Oh, he don't bite," she added, as the two lady passengers fluttered into a corner. "Does he, old Tuppy?" (the latter remark being addressed directly to the sagacious Joaquin). "I tell you what, boys," continued Miggles, after she had fed and closed the door on *Ursa Minor*, "you were in big luck that Joaquin wasn't hanging round when you dropped in to-night."

"Where was he?" asked the Judge.

"With me," said Miggles.

"Lord love you! he trots round with me nights like as if he was a man."

We were silent for a few moments, and listened to the wind. Perhaps we all had the same picture before us—of Miggles walking through the rainy woods with her savage guardian at her side. The Judge, I remember, said something about Una and her lion; but Miggles received it, as she did other compliments, with quiet gravity. Whether she was altogether unconscious of the admiration she excited—she could hardly have been oblivious of Yuba Bill's adoration—I know not, but her very frankness suggested a perfect sexual equality that was cruelly humiliating to the younger members of our party.

The incident of the bear did not add anything in Miggle's favour to the opinions of those of her own sex who were present. In fact, the repast over, a chillness radiated from the two lady passengers that no pine-boughs brought in by Yuba Bill and cast as a sacrifice upon the hearth could wholly overcome. Miggles felt it; and, suddenly declaring that it was time " to turn in," offered to show the ladies to their bed in an adjoining room. " You, boys, will have to camp out here by the fire as well as you can," she added, " for thar ain't but the one room."

Our sex—by which, my dear sir, I allude of course to the stronger portion of humanity—has been generally relieved from the imputation of curiosity or a fondness for gossip. Yet I am constrained to say, that hardly had the door closed on Miggles than we crowded together, whispering, snickering, smiling, and exchanging suspicions, surmises, and a thousand speculations in regard to our pretty hostess and her singular companion. I fear that we even hustled that imbecile paralytic who sat like a voiceless Memnon in our midst, gazing with the serene indifference of the Past in his passionless eyes upon our wordy counsels. In the midst of an exciting discussion the door opened again and Miggles re-entered.

But not, apparently, the same Miggles who a few hours before had flashed upon us. Her eyes were downcast, and as she hesitated for a moment on the threshold, with a blanket on her arm, she seemed to have left behind her the frank fearlessness which had charmed us a moment before. Coming into the room, she drew a low stool beside the paralytic's chair, sat down, drew the blanket over her shoulders, and saying, " If it's all the same to you, boys, as we're rather crowded, I'll stop here to-night," took the invalid's withered hand in her own and turned her eyes upon the dying fire. An instinctive feeling that this was only premonitory to more confidential relations, and perhaps some shame at our previous curiosity, kept us silent. The rain still beat upon the roof, wandering gusts of wind stirred the embers into momentary brightness, until, in a lull of the elements, Miggles suddenly lifted up her head, and throwing her hair over her shoulder, turned her face upon the group and asked :

" Is there any of you that knows me ? " There was no reply.

" Think again. I lived at Marysville in '53. Everybody knew me there, and everybody had the right to know me. I kept the Polka Saloon until I came to live with Jim. That's six years ago. Perhaps I've changed some."

The absence of recognition may have disconcerted her. She turned her head to the fire again, and it was some seconds before she again spoke, and then more rapidly :

" Well, you see I thought some of you must have known me. There's no great harm done any way. What I was going to say was this : Jim here "—she took his hand in both of hers as she spoke— " used to know me, if you didn't, and spent a heap of money upon me. I reckon he spent all he had. And one day—it's six years ago this winter—Jim came into my back room, sat down on my sofy, like as you see him in that chair, and never moved again without help. He was struck all of a heap, and never seemed to know what ailed him. The doctors came, and said as how it was caused all along of his way of life—for Jim was mighty free and wild like—and that he would never get better, and couldn't last long any way. They advised me to send him to 'Frisco, to the hospital, for he was no good to any one and would be a baby all his life. Perhaps it was something in Jim's eye, perhaps it was that I never had a baby, but I said ' No.' I was rich then, for I was popular with everybody—gentlemen like yourself, sir, came to see me—and I sold out my business and bought this yer place because it was sort of out of the way of travel, you see, and I brought my baby here."

With a woman's intuitive tact and poetry she had, as she spoke, slowly shifted her position so as to bring the mute figure of the ruined man between her and her audience, hiding in the shadow behind it, as if she offered it as a tacit apology for her actions. Silent and expressionless, it yet spoke for her; helpless, crushed, and smitten with the Divine thunderbolt, it still stretched an invisible arm around her.

Hidden in the darkness, but still holding his hand, she went on:
" It was a long time before I could get the hang of things about yer, for I was used to company and excitement. I couldn't get any woman to help me, and a man I dursen't trust; but what with the Indians hereabout, who'd do odd jobs for me, and having everything sent from the North Fork, Jim and I managed to worry through. The doctor would run up from Sacramento once in a while. He'd ask to see ' Miggles's baby,' as he called Jim, and when he'd go away, he'd say, ' Miggles, you're a trump—God bless you '; and it didn't seem so lonely after that. But the last time he was here he said as he opened the door to go, ' Do you know, Miggles, your baby will grow up to be a man yet, and an honour to his mother! but not here, Miggles, not here! ' And I thought he went away sad—and—and——" and here Miggles's voice and head were somehow both lost completely in the shadow.

" The folks about here are very kind," said Miggles after a pause, coming a little into the light again. " The men from the Fork used to hang around here, until they found they wasn't wanted, and the women are kind—and don't call. I was pretty lonely until I picked up Joaquin in the woods yonder one day, when he wasn't so high, and taught him to beg for his dinner; and then thar's Polly—that's the magpie—she knows no end of tricks, and makes it quite sociable of evenings with her talk, and so I don't feel like as I was the only living being about the ranch. And Jim here," said Miggles, with her old laugh again, and coming out quite into the firelight, " Jim—why, boys, you would admire to see how much he knows for a man like him. Sometimes I bring him flowers, and he looks at 'em just as natural as if he knew 'em ; and times, when we're sitting alone, I read him those things on the wall. Why, Lord!" said Miggles, with her frank laugh, " I've read him that whole side of the house this winter. There never was such a man for reading as Jim."

"Why," asked the Judge, "do you not marry this man to whom you have devoted your youthful life?"

"Well, you see," said Miggles, "it would be playing it rather low down on Jim to take advantage of his being so helpless. And then, too, if we were man and wife, now, we'd both know that I was *bound* to do what I do now of my own accord."

"But you are young yet and attractive——"

"It's getting late," said Miggles gravely, "and you'd better all turn in. Good-night, boys"; and, throwing the blanket over her head, Miggles laid herself down beside Jim's chair, her head pillowed on the low stool that held his feet, and spoke no more. The fire slowly faded from the hearth ; we each sought our blankets in silence ; and presently here was no sound in the long room but the pattering of the rain upon the roof and the heavy breathing of the sleepers.

It was nearly morning when I awoke from a troubled dream. The storm had passed, the stars were shining, and through the shutterless window the full moon, lifting itself over the solemn pines without, looked into the room. It touched the lonely figure in the chair with an infinite compassion, and seemed to baptize with a shining flood the lowly head of the woman whose hair, as in the sweet old story, bathed the feet of Him she loved. It even lent a kindly poetry to the rugged outline of Yuba Bill, half reclining on his elbow between them and his passengers, with savagely patient eyes keeping watch and ward. And then I fell asleep, and only woke at broad day, with Yuba Bill standing over me, and "All aboard" ringing in my ears.

Coffee was waiting for us on the table, but Miggles was gone. We wandered about the house, and lingered long after the horses were harnessed, but she did not return. It was evident that she wished to avoid a formal leave-taking, and had so left us to depart as we had come. After we had helped the ladies into the coach we returned to the house, and solemnly shook hands with the paralytic Jim, as solemnly settling him back into position after each handshake. Then we looked for the last time around the long, low room, at the stool where Miggles had sat, and slowly took our seats in the waiting coach. The whip cracked and we were off!

But as we reached the high road Bill's dexterous hand laid the six horses back on their haunches, and the stage stopped with a jerk. For there, on a little eminence beside the road, stood Miggles, her hair flying, her eyes sparkling, her white handkerchief waving, and her white teeth flashing a last "good-bye." We waved our hats in return. And then Yuba Bill, as if fearful of further fascination, madly lashed his horses forward, and we sank back in our seats. We exchanged not a word until we reached the North Fork and the stage drew up at the Independence House. Then, the Judge leading, we walked into the bar-room and took our places gravely at the bar.

"Are your glasses charged, gentlemen?" said the Judge, solemnly taking off his white hat. They were.

"Well, then, here's to *Miggles*; GOD BLESS HER!"

Perhaps He had. Who knows?

# THE LUCK OF ROARING CAMP

### FRANCIS BRET HARTE

THERE was commotion in Roaring Camp. It could not have been a fight, for in 1850 that was not novel enough to have called together the entire settlement. The ditches and claims were not only deserted, but "Tuttle's Grocery" had contributed its gamblers, who, it will be remembered, calmly continued their game the day that French Pete and Kanaka Joe shot each other to death over the bar in the front room. The whole camp was collected before a rude cabin on the outer edge of the clearing. Conversation was carried on in a low tone, but the name of a woman was frequently repeated. It was a name familiar enough in the camp—"Cherokee Sal."

Perhaps the less said of her the better. She was a coarse, and, it is to be feared, a very sinful woman. But at that time she was the only woman in Roaring Camp, and was just then lying in sore extremity, when she most needed the ministration of her own sex. Dissolute, abandoned, and irreclaimable, she was yet suffering a martyrdom hard enough to bear even when veiled by sympathising womanhood, but now terrible in her loneliness. The primal curse had come to her in that original isolation which must have made the punishment of the first transgression so dreadful. It was, perhaps, part of the expiation of her sin that, at a moment when she most lacked her sex's intuitive tenderness and care, she met only the half-contemptuous faces of her masculine associates. Yet a few of the spectators were, I think, touched by her sufferings. Sandy Tipton thought it was "rough on Sal," and, in the contemplation of her condition, for a moment rose superior to the fact that he had an ace and two bowers in his sleeve.

It will be seen, also, that the situation was novel. Deaths were by no means uncommon in Roaring Camp, but a birth was a new thing. People had been dismissed the camp effectively, finally, and with no possibility of return; but this was the first time that anybody had been introduced *ab initio*. Hence the excitement.

"You go in there, Stumpy," said a prominent citizen known as "Kentuck," addressing one of the loungers. "Go in there, and see what you kin do. You've had experience in them things."

Perhaps there was a fitness in the selection. Stumpy, in other climes, had been the putative head of two families; in fact, it was owing to some legal informality in these proceedings that Roaring Camp—a city of refuge—was indebted for his company. The crowd approved the choice, and Stumpy was wise enough to bow to the majority. The door closed on the extempore surgeon and midwife, and Roaring Camp sat down outside, smoked its pipe, and awaited the issue.

The assemblage numbered about a hundred men. One or two of these were actual fugitives from justice, some were criminal, and all were reckless. Physically, they exhibited no indication of their past lives and character. The greatest scamp had a Raphael face, with a profusion of blond hair; Oakhurst, a gambler, had the melancholy air and intellectual abstraction of a Hamlet; the coolest and most courageous man was scarcely over five feet in height, with a soft voice and an embarrassed, timid manner. The term "roughs" applied to them was a distinction rather than a definition. Perhaps in the minor details of fingers, toes, ears, etc., the camp may have been deficient; but these slight omissions did not detract from their aggregate force. The strongest man had but three fingers on his right hand; the best shot had but one eye.

Such was the physical aspect of the men that were dispersed around the cabin. The camp lay in a triangular valley, between two hills and a river. The only outlet was a steep trail over the summit of a hill that faced the cabin, now illuminated by the rising moon. The suffering woman might have seen it from the rude bunk whereon she lay—seen it winding like a silver thread, until it was lost in the stars above.

A fire of withered pine-boughs added sociability to the gathering. By degrees the natural levity of Roaring Camp returned. Bets were freely offered and taken regarding the result. Three to five that "Sal would get through with it"; even that the child would survive; side bets as to the sex and complexion of the coming stranger. In the midst of an excited discussion an exclamation came from those nearest the door, and the camp stopped to listen. Above the swaying and moaning of the pines, the swift rush of the river, and the crackling of the fire, rose a sharp, querulous cry— a cry unlike anything heard before in the camp. The pines stopped moaning, the river ceased to rush, and the fire to crackle. It seemed as if nature had stopped to listen too.

The camp rose to its feet as one man ! It was proposed to explode a barrel of gunpowder, but, in consideration of the situation of the mother, better counsels prevailed, and only a few revolvers were discharged ; for, whether owing to the rude surgery of the camp, or some other reason, Cherokee Sal was sinking fast. Within an hour she had climbed, as it were, that rugged road that led to the stars, and so passed out of Roaring Camp, its sin and shame, for ever. I do not think that the announcement disturbed them much, except in speculation as to the fate of the child. " Can he live now ? " was asked of Stumpy. The answer was doubtful. The only other being of Cherokee Sal's sex and maternal condition in the settlement was an ass. There was some conjecture as to fitness, but the experiment was tried. It was less problematical than the ancient treatment of Romulus and Remus, and apparently as successful.

When these details were completed, which exhausted another hour, the door was opened, and the anxious crowd of men, who had already formed themselves into a queue, entered in single file. Beside the low bunk or shelf on which the figure of the mother was starkly outlined below the blankets, stood a pine table. On this a candle-box was placed, and within it, swathed in staring red flannel, lay the last arrival at Roaring Camp. Beside the candle-box was placed a hat. Its use was soon indicated. " Gentlemen," said Stumpy, with a singular mixture of authority and *ex officio* complacency—" Gentlemen will please pass in at the front door, round the table, and out at the back door. Them as wishes to contribute anything toward the orphan will find a hat handy." The first man entered with his hat on ; he uncovered, however, as he looked about him, and so, unconsciously, set an example to the next. In such communities good and bad actions are catching. As the procession filed in, comments were audible—criticism addressed, perhaps, rather to Stumpy, in the character of showman—" Is that him ? " " Mighty small specimen ! " " Hasn't mor'n got the colour " ? " Ain't bigger nor a derringer." The contributions were as characteristic : A silver tobacco-box ; a doubloon ; a navy revolver, silver mounted ; a gold specimen ; a very beautifully embroidered lady's handkerchief (from Oakhurst the gambler) ; a diamond breastpin ; a diamond ring (suggested by the pin with the remark from the giver that he " saw that pin and went two diamonds better ") ; a slung shot ; a Bible (contributor not detected) ; a golden spur ; a silver teaspoon (the initials, I regret to say, were not the giver's) ; a pair of surgeon's shears ; a lancet ; a Bank of England note for £5 ; and about 200 dols. in loose gold and silver coin. During these proceedings Stumpy maintained a silence as impassive as the dead on his left, a gravity as inscrutable as that of the newly born on his right. Only one incident occurred to break the monotony of the curious procession. As Kentuck bent over the candle-box, half curiously, the child turned, and, in a spasm of pain, caught at his groping finger, and held it fast for a moment. Kentuck looked foolish and embarrassed. Something like a blush tried to assert itself in his weather-beaten cheek. "The d—d little cuss!" he said, as he extricated his finger, with, perhaps, more tenderness and care than he might have been deemed capable of showing. He held that finger a little part from its fellows as he went out, and examined it curiously. The examination provoked the same original remark in regard to the child. In fact he seemed to enjoy repeating it. "He rastled with my finger," he remarked to Tipton, holding up the member; "the d—d little cuss!"

It was four o'clock before the camp sought repose. A light burnt in the cabin where the watchers sat, for Stumpy did not go to bed that night. Nor did Kentuck. He drank quite freely, and related with great gusto his experience, invariably ending with his characteristic condemnation of the newcomer. It seemed to relieve him of any unjust implication of sentiment, and Kentuck had the weaknesses of the nobler sex. When everybody else had gone to bed, he walked down to the river and whistled reflectingly. Then he walked up the gulch, past the cabin, still whistling with demonstrative unconcern. At a large redwood-tree he paused and retraced his steps, and again passed the cabin. Halfway down to the river's bank he again paused, and then returned and knocked at the door. It was opened by Stumpy. "How goes it?" said Kentuck looking past Stumpy towards the candle-box. "All serene," replied Stumpy. "Anything up?" "Nothing." There was a pause—an embarrassing one—Stumpy still holding the door. Then Kentuck had recourse to his finger, which he held up to Stumpy, "Rastled with it—the d—d little cuss!" he said, and retired.

The next day Cherokee Sal had such rude sepulture as Roaring Camp afforded. After her body had been committed to the hillside there was a formal meeting of the camp to discuss what should be done with her infant. A resolution to adopt it was unanimous and enthusiastic. But an animated discussion in regard to the manner and feasibility of providing for its wants at once sprung up. It was remarkable that the argument partook of none of those fierce personalities with which discussions were usually conducted at Roaring Camp. Tipton proposed that they should send the child to Red Dog—a distance of forty miles—where female attention could be procured. But the unlucky suggestion met with fierce and unanimous opposition. It was evident that no plan which entailed parting with their new acquisition would for a moment be entertained. "Besides," said Tom Ryder, "them fellows at Red Dog would swap it, and ring in somebody else on us." A disbelief in the honesty of other camps prevailed at Roaring Camp as in other places.

The introduction of a female nurse in the camp also met with objection. It was argued that no decent woman could be prevailed to accept Roaring Camp as her home, and the speaker urged that "they didn't want any more of the other kind." This unkind allusion to the defunct mother, harsh as it may seem, was the first spasm of propriety—the first symptom of the camp's regeneration. Stumpy advanced nothing. Perhaps he felt a certain delicacy in interfering with the selection of a possible successor in office. But when questioned he averred stoutly that he and "Jinny"—the mammal before alluded to—could manage to rear the child. There was something original, independent, and heroic about the plan that pleased the camp. Stumpy was retained. Certain articles were sent for to Sacramento. "Mind," said the treasurer, as he pressed a bag of gold-dust into the expressman's hand, "the best that can be got—lace, you know, and filigree-work and frills; d—the cost!"

Strange to say, the child thrived. Perhaps the invigorating climate of the mountain camp was compensation for material deficiencies. Nature took the foundling to her broader breast. In that rare atmosphere of the Sierra foothills—that air pungent with balsamic odour, that ethereal cordial at once bracing and exhilarating—he may have found food and nourishment, or a subtle chemistry that transmuted asses' milk to lime and phosphorus. Stumpy inclined to the belief that it was the latter and good nursing. "Me and that ass," he would say, "has been father and mother to him! Don't you," he would add, apostrophising the helpless bundle before him, "never go back on us."

By the time he was a month old the necessity of giving him a name became apparent. He had generally been known as "the Kid," "Stumpy's boy," "the Cayote" (an allusion to his vocal powers), and even by Kentuck's endearing diminutive of "the d—d little cuss." But these were felt to be vague and unsatisfactory, and were at last dismissed under another influence. Gamblers and adventurers are generally superstitious, and Oakhurst one day declared that the baby had brought "the luck" to Roaring Camp. It was certain that of late they had been successful. "Luck" was the name agreed upon, with the prefix of Tommy for greater convenience. No allusion was made to the mother, and the father was unknown. "It's better," said the philosophical Oakhurst, "to take a fresh deal all round. Call him luck, and start him fair." A day was accordingly set apart for the christening. What was meant by this ceremony the reader may imagine, who has already gathered some idea of the reckless irreverence of Roaring Camp. The master of ceremonies was one "Boston," a noted wag, and the occasion seemed to promise the greatest facetiousness. This ingenious satirist had spent two days in preparing a burlesque of the church service, with pointed local allusions. The choir was properly trained, and Sandy Tipton was to stand godfather. But after the procession had marched to the grove with music and banners, and the child had been deposited before a mock altar, Stumpy stepped before the expectant crowd. "It ain't my style to spoil fun, boys," said the little man stoutly, eyeing the faces around him, "but it strikes me that this thing ain't exactly on the squar. It's playing it pretty low down on this yer baby to ring in fun on him that he ain't going to understand. And ef there's going to be any godfathers round, I'd like to see who's got any better rights than me." A silence followed Stumpy's speech. To the credit of all humourists be it said that the first man to acknowledge its justice was the satirist, thus stopped of his fun. "But," said Stumpy quickly, following up his advantage, "we're here for a christening, and we'll have it. I proclaim you Thomas Luck, according to the laws of the United States and the State of California, so help me God." It was the first time that the name of the Deity had been uttered otherwise than profanely in the camp. The form of christening was perhaps even more ludicrous than the satirist had conceived ; but, strangely enough, nobody saw it and nobody laughed. "Tommy" was christened as seriously as he would have been under a Christian roof, and cried and was comforted in as orthodox fashion.

And so the work of regeneration began in Roaring Camp. Almost imperceptibly a change came over the settlement. The cabin assigned to "Tommy Luck"—or "The Luck," as he was more frequently called—first showed signs of improvement. It was kept scrupulously clean and whitewashed. Then it was boarded, clothed, and papered. The rosewood cradle—packed eighty miles by mule—had, in Stumpy's way of putting it, "sorter killed the rest of the furniture." So the rehabilitation of the cabin became a necessity. The men who were in the habit of lounging in at Stumpy's to see "how The Luck got on" seemed to appreciate the change, and, in self-defence, the rival establishment of "Tuttle's Grocery" bestirred itself and imported a carpet and mirrors. The reflections of the latter on the appearance of Roaring Camp tended to produce stricter habits of personal cleanliness. Again, Stumpy imposed a kind of quarantine upon those who aspired to the honour and privilege of holding "The Luck." It was a cruel mortification to Kentuck—who, in the carelessness of a large nature and the habits of frontier life, had begun to regard all garments as a second cuticle, which, like a snake's, only sloughed off through decay—to be debarred this privilege from certain prudential reasons. Yet such was the subtle influence of innovation that he thereafter appeared regularly every afternoon in a clean shirt, and face still shining from his ablutions. Nor were moral and social sanitary laws neglected. "Tommy," who was supposed to spend his whole existence in a persistent attempt to repose, must not be disturbed by noise. The

shouting and yelling which had gained the camp its infelicitous title
were not permitted within hearing distance of Stumpy's. The men
conversed in whispers, or smoked with Indian gravity. Profanity
was tacitly given up in these sacred precincts, and throughout the
camp a popular form of expletive, known as " D—n the luck ! "
and " Curse the luck ! " was abandoned as having a new personal
bearing. Vocal music was not interdicted, being supposed to have
a soothing, tranquillising quality, and one song, sung by " Man-o'-
War Jack," an English sailor, from Her Majesty's Australian
colonies, was quite popular as a lullaby. It was a lugubrious recital
of the exploits of " the *Arethusa*, Seventy-four," in a muffled minor,
ending with a prolonged dying fall at the burden of each verse,
" On b-o-o-o-ard of the *Arethusa*." It was a fine sight to see Jack
holding The Luck, rocking from side to side as if with the motion of
a ship, and crooning forth this naval ditty. Either through the
peculiar rocking of Jack or the length of his song—it contained
ninety stanzas and was continued with conscientious deliberation
to the bitter end—the lullaby generally had the desired effect.
At such times the men would lie at full length under the trees, in
the soft summer twilight, smoking their pipes and drinking in the
melodious utterances. An indistinct idea that this was pastoral
happiness pervaded the camp. " This 'ere kind o' think," said the
Cockney Simmons, meditatively reclining on his elbow, " is 'evingly."
It reminded him of Greenwich.

On the long summer days The Luck was usually carried to the
gulch, whence the golden store of Roaring Camp was taken. There
on a blanket spread over pine-boughs, he would lie while the men
were working in the ditches below. Latterly, there was a rude
attempt to decorate this bower with flowers and sweet-smelling
shrubs, and generally some one would bring him a cluster of wild
honeysuckle, azaleas, or the painted blossoms of Las Mariposas.
The men had suddenly awakened to the fact that there were beauty
and significance in these trifles which they had so long trodden
carelessly beneath their feet. A flake of glittering mica, a fragment
of variegated quartz, a bright pebble from the bed of the creek,
became beautiful to the eyes thus cleared and strengthened, and
were invariably put aside for " The Luck." It was wonderful
how many treasures the woods and hillsides yielded that " would do
for Tommy." Surrounded by playthings such as never child out
of fairyland had before, it is to be hoped that Tommy was content.
He appeared to be securely happy, albeit there was an infantine
gravity about him, a contemplative light in his round grey eyes
that sometimes worried Stumpy. He was always tractable and
quiet ; and it is recorded that once, having crept beyond his
" corral "—a hedge of tesselated pine-boughs which surrounded his
bed—he dropped over the bank on his head in the soft earth, and
remained with his mottled legs in the air in that position for at least

five minutes with unflinching gravity. He was extricated without a murmur. I hesitate to record the many other instances of his sagacity which rest, unfortunately, upon the statements of prejudiced friends. Some of them were not without a tinge of superstition.

"I crep' up the bank just now," said Kentuck one day in a breathless state of excitement, "and dern my skin if he wasn't a-talking to a jay-bird as was a-sitting on his lap. There they was just as free and sociable as anything you please, a-jawin' at each other just like two cherrybums."

Howbeit, whether creeping over the pine-boughs or lying lazily on his back blinking at the leaves above him, to him the birds sang, the squirrels chattered, and the flowers bloomed. Nature was his nurse and playfellow. For him she would let slip between the leaves golden shafts of sunlight that fell just within his grasp; she would send wandering breezes to visit him with the balm of bay and resinous gums; to him the tall redwoods nodded familiarly and sleepily, the bumble-bees buzzed, and the rooks cawed a slumberous accompaniment.

Such was the golden summer of Roaring Camp. They were "flush times"—and The Luck was with them. The claims had yielded enormously. The camp was jealous of its privileges and looked suspiciously on strangers. No encouragement was given to emigration, and, to make their seclusion more perfect, the land on either side of the mountain wall that surrounded the camp they duly pre-empted. This, and a reputation for singular proficiency with the revolver, kept the reserve of Roaring Camp inviolate. The expressman—their only connecting link with the surrounding world —sometimes told wonderful stories of the camp. He would say:

"They've a street up there in ' Roaring ' that would lay over any street in Red Dog. They've got vines and flowers round their houses and they wash themselves twice a day. But they're mighty rough on strangers and they worship an Ingin baby."

With the prosperity of the camp came a desire for further improvement. It was proposed to build an hotel in the following spring, and to invite one or two decent families to reside there for the sake of "The Luck," who might perhaps profit by female companionship. The sacrifice that this concession to sex cost these men, who were fiercely sceptical in regard to its general virtue and usefulness, can only be accounted for by their affection for Tommy. A few still held out. But the resolve could not be carried into effect for three months, and the minority meekly yielded in the hope that something might turn up to prevent it. And it did.

The winter of 1851 will long be remembered in the foothills. The snow lay deep on the Sierras, and every mountain creek became a river and every river a lake. Each gorge and gulch was transformed into a tumultuous watercourse, that descended the hillsides, tearing down giant trees and scattering its drift and *débris* along the plain.

Red Dog had been twice under water and Roaring Camp had been forewarned.

"Water put the gold into them gulches," said Stumpy. "It's been here once and will be here again!" And that night the North Fork suddenly leaped over its banks and swept up the triangular valley of Roaring Camp.

In the confusion of rushing water, crushing trees, and crackling timber, and the darkness which seemed to flow with the water and blot out the fair valley but little could be done to collect the scattered camp. When the morning broke, the cabin of Stumpy nearest the river-bank was gone. Higher up the gulch they found the body of its unlucky owner; but the pride, the hope, the joy, the Luck, of Roaring Camp had disappeared. They were returning with sad hearts when a shout from the bank recalled them.

It was a relief-boat from down the river. They had picked up, they said, a man and an infant, nearly exhausted, about two miles below. Did anybody know them? and did they belong here?

It needed but a glance to show them Kentuck lying there, cruelly crushed and bruised, but still holding The Luck of Roaring Camp in his arms. As they bent over the strangely assorted pair they saw that the child was cold and pulseless. "He is dead," said one. Kentuck opened his eyes. "Dead?" he repeated feebly. "Yes, my man; and you are dying too." A smile lit the eyes of the expiring Kentuck. "Dying," he repeated; "he's a-taking me with him—tell the boys I've got The Luck with me now"; and the strong man, clinging to the frail babe as a drowning man is said to cling to a straw drifted away into the shadowy river that flows for ever to the unknown sea.

# THE OUTCASTS OF POKER FLAT

### Francis Bret Harte

As Mr. John Oakhurst, gambler, stepped into the main street of Poker Flat on the morning of the twenty-third of November, 1850, he was conscious of a change in its moral atmosphere since the preceding night. Two or three men, conversing earnestly together, ceased as he approached, and exchanged significant glances. There was a Sabbath lull in the air, which, in a settlement unused to Sabbath influences, looked ominous.

Mr. Oakhurst's calm, handsome face betrayed small concern in these indications. Whether he was conscious of any predisposing cause was another question. "I reckon they're after somebody," he reflected; "likely it's me." He returned to his pocket the handkerchief with which he had been whipping away the red dust of Poker Flat from his neat boots and quietly discharged his mind of any further conjecture.

In point of fact, Poker Flat was "after somebody." It had lately suffered the loss of several thousand dollars, two valuable horses, and a prominent citizen. It was experiencing a spasm of virtuous reaction, quite as lawless and ungovernable as any of the acts that had provoked it. A secret committee had determined to rid the town of all improper persons. This was done permanently in regard to two men who were then hanging from the boughs of a sycamore in the gulch, and temporarily in the banishment of certain other objectionable characters. I regret to say that some of these were ladies. It is but due to the sex, however, to state that their impropriety was professional, and it was only in such easily established standards of evil that Poker Flat ventured to sit in judgment.

Mr. Oakhurst was right in supposing that he was included in this category. A few of the committee had urged hanging him as a possible example, and a sure method of reimbursing themselves from his pockets of the sums he had won from them. "It's agin justice," said Jim Wheeler, "to let this yer young man from Roaring Camp—an entire stranger—carry away our money." But a crude sentiment of equity residing in the breasts of those who had been fortunate enough to win from Mr. Oakhurst overruled this narrow local prejudice.

Mr. Oakhurst received his sentence with philosophic calmness, none the less cooly that he was aware of the hesitation of his judges. He was too much of a gambler not to accept Fate. With him, life was at best an uncertain game, and he recognised the usual percentage in favour of the dealer.

A body of armed men accompanied the deported wickedness of Poker Flat to the outskirts of the settlement. Besides Mr. Oakhurst, who was known to be a cooly desperate man, and for whose intimidation the armed escort was intended, the expatriated party consisted of a young woman, familiarly known as "The Duchess"; another, who had won the title of "Mother Shipton"; and "Uncle Billy," a suspected sluice-robber and confirmed drunkard. The cavalcade provoked no comments from the spectators, nor was any word uttered by the escort. Only when the gulch which marked the uttermost limit of Poker Flat was reached, the leader spoke briefly and to the point. The exiles were forbidden to return, at the peril of their lives.

As the escort disappeared, their pent-up feelings found vent in a few hysterical tears from the Duchess, some bad language from

Mother Shipton, and a Parthian volley of expletives from Uncle Billy. The philosophic Oakhurst alone remained silent. He listened calmly to Mother Shipton's desire to cut somebody's heart out, to the repeated statements of the Duchess that she would die in the road, and to the alarming oaths that seemed to be bumped out of Uncle Billy as he rode forward. With the easy good-humour characteristic of his class, he insisted upon exchanging his own riding-horse, "Five Spot," for the sorry mule which the Duchess rode. But even this act did not draw the party into any closer sympathy. The young woman readjusted her somewhat draggled plumes with a feeble, faded coquetry; Mother Shipton eyed the possessor of "Five Spot" with malevolence; and Uncle Billy included the whole party in one sweeping anathema.

The road to Sandy Bar—a camp that, not having as yet experienced the regenerating influences of Poker Flat, consequently seemed to offer some invitation to the emigrants—lay over a steep mountain range. It was distant a day's severe travel. In that advanced season, the party soon passed out of the moist, temperate regions of the foot-hills into the dry, cold, bracing air of the Sierras. The trail was narrow and difficult. At noon the Duchess, rolling out of her saddle upon the ground, declared her intention of going no farther, and the party halted.

The spot was singularly wild and impressive. A wooded amphitheatre, surrounded on three sides by precipitous cliffs of naked granite, sloped gently toward the crest of another precipice that overlooked the valley. It was, undoubtedly, the most suitable spot for a camp, had camping been advisable. But Mr. Oakhurst knew that scarcely half the journey to Sandy Bar was accomplished, and the party were not equipped or provisioned for delay. This fact he pointed out to his companions curtly, with a philosophic commentary on the folly of "throwing up their hand before the game was played out." But they were furnished with liquor, which in this emergency stood them in place of food, fuel, rest, and prescience. In spite of his remonstrances, it was not long before they were more or less under its influence. Uncle Billy passed rapidly from a bellicose state into one of stupor, the Duchess became maudlin, and Mother Shipton snored. Mr. Oakhurst alone remained erect, leaning against a rock, calmly surveying them.

Mr. Oakhurst did not drink. It interfered with a profession which required coolness, impassiveness, and presence of mind, and, in his own language, he " couldn't afford it." As he gazed at his recumbent fellow-exiles, the loneliness begotten of his pariah-trade, his habits of life, his very vices, for the first time seriously oppressed him. He bestirred himself in dusting his black clothes, washing his hands and face, and other acts characteristic of his studiously neat habits, and for a moment forgot his annoyance. The thought of deserting his weaker and more pitiable companions never perhaps occurred to him. Yet he could not help feeling the want of that excitement which, singularly enough, was most conducive to that calm equanimity for which he was notorious. He looked at the gloomy walls that rose a thousand feet sheer above the circling pines around him ; at the sky, ominously clouded ; at the valley below, already deepening into shadow. And, doing so, suddenly he heard his own name called.

A horseman slowly ascended the trail. In the fresh, open face of the new-comer Mr. Oakhurst recognised Tom Simson, otherwise known as " The Innocent " of Sandy Bar. He had met him some months before over a " little game," and had, with perfect equanimity, won the entire fortune—amounting to some forty dollars—of that guileless youth. After the game was finished, Mr. Oakhurst drew the youthful speculator behind the door, and thus addressed him : " Tommy, you're a good little man, but you can't gamble worth a cent. Don't try it over again." He then handed him his money back, pushed him gently from the room, and so made a devoted slave of Tom Simson.

There was a remembrance of this in his boyish and enthusiastic greeting of Mr. Oakhurst. He had started, he said, to go to Poker Flat to seek his fortune. " Alone ? " No, not exactly alone ; in fact (a giggle) he had run away with Piney Woods. Didn't Mr. Oakhurst remember Piney ? She that used to wait on the table at the Temperance House ? They had been engaged a long time, but old Jake Woods had objected ; and so they had run away, and were going to Poker Flat to be married, and here they were. And they were tired out, and how lucky it was they had found a place to camp and company. All this the Innocent delivered rapidly, while Piney, a stout, comely damsel of fifteen, emerged from behind the pine-tree where she had been blushing unseen, and rode to the side of her lover.

Mr. Oakhurst seldom troubled himself with sentiment, still less with propriety ; but he had a vague idea that the situation was not fortunate. He retained, however, his presence of mind sufficiently to kick Uncle Billy, who was about to say something, and Uncle Billy was sober enough to recognise in Mr. Oakhurst's kick a superior power that would not bear trifling. He then endeavoured to dissuade Tom Simson from delaying further, but in vain. He even pointed out the fact that there was no provision, nor means of making a camp. But, unluckily, the Innocent met this objection by assuring the party that he was provided with an extra mule loaded with provisions, and by the discovery of a rude attempt at a loghouse near the trail. " Piney can stay with Mrs. Oakhurst," said the Innocent, pointing to the Duchess, " and I can shift for myself."

Nothing but Mr. Oakhurst's admonishing foot saved Uncle Billy from bursting into a roar of laughter. As it was, he felt compelled to retire up the cañon until he could recover his gravity. There he confided the joke to the tall pine-trees, with many slaps of his leg, contortions of his face, and the usual profanity. But when he returned to the party, he found them seated by a fire—for the air had grown strangely chill and the sky overcast—in apparently amicable conversation. Piney was actually talking in an impulsive, girlish fashion to the Duchess, who was listening with an interest and animation she had not shown for many days. The Innocent was holding forth, apparently with equal effect, to Mr. Oakhurst and Mother Shipton, who was actually relaxing into amiability. "Is this yer a d——d picnic?" said Uncle Billy, with inward scorn, as he surveyed the sylvan group, the glancing firelight, and the tethered animals in the foreground. Suddenly an idea mingled with the alcoholic fumes that disturbed his brain. It was apparently of a jocular nature, for he felt impelled to slap his leg again and cram his fist into his mouth.

As the shadows crept slowly up the mountain, a slight breeze rocked the tops of the pine-trees, and moaned through their long and gloomy aisles. The ruined cabin, patched and covered with pine-boughs, was set apart for the ladies. As the lovers parted, they unaffectedly exchanged a kiss, so honest and sincere that it might have been heard above the swaying pines. The frail Duchess and the malevolent Mother Shipton were probably too stunned to remark upon this last evidence of simplicity, and so turned without a word to the hut. The fire was replenished, the men lay down before the door, and in a few minutes were asleep.

Mr. Oakhurst was a light sleeper. Toward morning he awoke, benumbed and cold. As he stirred the dying fire, the wind, which was now blowing strongly, brought to his cheek that which caused the blood to leave it—snow.

He started to his feet with the intention of awakening the sleepers, for there was no time to lose. But turning to where Uncle Billy had been lying, he found him gone. A suspicion leaped to his brain and a curse to his lips. He ran to the spot where the mules had been tethered; they were no longer there. The tracks were already rapidly disappearing in the snow.

The momentary excitement brought Mr. Oakhurst back to the fire with his usual calm. He did not waken the sleepers. The Innocent slumbered peacefully, with a smile on his good-humoured, freckled face; the virgin Piney slept beside her frailer sisters as sweetly as though attended by celestial guardians, and Mr. Oakhurst, drawing his blanket over his shoulders, stroked his moustaches and waited for the dawn. It came slowly in a whirling mist of snowflakes, that dazzled and confused the eye. What could be seen of the landscape appeared magically changed. He looked over the valley, and summed up the present and future in two words—"snowed in!"

A careful inventory of the provisions, which, fortunately for the party, had been stored within the hut, and so escaped the felonious fingers of Uncle Billy, disclosed the fact that with care and prudence they might last ten days longer. "That is," said Mr. Oakhurst, *sotto voce* to the Innocent, "if you're willing to board us. If you ain't— and perhaps you'd better not—you can wait till Uncle Billy gets back with provisions." For some occult reason, Mr. Oakhurst could not bring himself to disclose Uncle Billy's rascality, and so offered the hypothesis that he had wandered from the camp, and had accidentally stampeded the animals. He dropped a warning to the Duchess and Mother Shipton, who of course knew the facts of their associate's defection. "They'll find out the truth about us *all* when they find out anything," he added, significantly, "and there's no good frightening them now."

Tom Simson not only put all his worldly store at the disposal of Mr. Oakhurst, but seemed to enjoy the prospect of their enforced seclusion. "We'll have a good camp for a week, and then the snow'll melt, and we'll all go back together." The cheerful gaiety of the young man and Mr. Oakhurst's calm infected the others. The Innocent, with the aid of pine-boughs, extemporised a thatch for the roofless cabin, and the Duchess directed Piney in the rearrangement of the interior with a taste and tact that opened the blue eyes of that provincial maiden to their fullest extent. "I reckon now you're used to fine things at Poker Flat," said Piney. The Duchess turned away sharply to conceal something that reddened her cheek through its professional tint, and Mother Shipton requested Piney not to "chatter." But when Mr. Oakhurst returned from a weary search for the trail, he heard the sound of happy laughter echoed from the rocks. He stopped in some alarm, and his thoughts first naturally reverted to the whisky, which he had prudently *cachéd*. "And yet it don't somehow sound like whisky" said the gambler. It was not until he caught sight of the blazing fire through the still blinding storm, and the group around it, that he settled to the conviction that it was "square fun."

Whether Mr. Oakhurst had *cachéd* his cards with the whisky, as something debarred the free access of the community, I cannot say. It was certain that, in Mother Shipton's words he "didn't say cards once" during that evening. Happily, the time was bequiled by an accordion, produced somewhat ostentatiously by Tom Simson from his pack. Notwithstanding some difficulties attending the manipulation of this instrument, Piney Woods managed to pluck several reluctant melodies from its keys, to an accompaniment by the Innocent on a pair of bone castanets. But the crowning festivity of the evening was reached in a rude camp-meeting hymn, which the lovers, joining hands, sang with great earnestness and vociferation. I fear that a certain defiant tone and Covenanter's swing to its chorus, rather than any devotional quality, caused it speedily to infect the others, who at last joined in the refrain :

> " I'm proud to live in the service of the Lord,
> And I'm bound to die in His army."

The pines rocked, the storm eddied and whirled above the miserable group, and the flames of their altar leaped heavenward, as if in token of the vow.

At midnight the storm abated, the rolling clouds parted, and the stars glittered keenly above the sleeping camp. Mr. Oakhurst, whose professional habits had enabled him to live on the smallest possible amount of sleep, in dividing the watch with Tom Simson, somehow managed to take upon himself the greater part of that duty. He excused himself to the Innocent by saying that he had " often been a week without sleep."

" Doing what ? " asked Tom.

" Poker ! " replied Oakhurst, sententiously ; " when a man gets a streak of luck—nigger-luck—he don't get tired. The luck gives in first. Luck," continued the gambler, reflectively, " is a mighty queer thing. All you know about it for certain is that it's bound to change. And it's finding out when it's going to change that makes you. We've had a streak of bad luck since we left Poker Flat—you come along, and slap you get into it, too. If you can hold your cards right along, you're all right. For," added the gambler, with cheerful irrelevance :

> " I'm proud to live in the service of the Lord,
> And I'm bound to die in His army."

The third day came, and the sun, looking through the white-curtained valley, saw the outcasts divide their slowly decreasing store of provisions for the morning meal. It was one of the peculiarities of that mountain climate that its rays diffused a kindly warmth over the wintry landscape, as if in regretful commiseration of the past. But it revealed drift on drift of snow piled high around the hut—a hopeless, unchartered, trackless sea of white lying below the rocky shores to which the castaways still clung. Through the marvellously clear air the smoke of the pastoral village of Poker Flat rose miles away. Mother Shipton saw it, and from a remote pinnacle of her rocky fastness hurled in that direction a final malediction. It was her last vituperative attempt, and perhaps for that reason was invested with a certain degree of sublimity. It did her good, she privately informed the Duchess. " Just you go out there and cuss, and see." She then set herself to the task of amusing " the child," as she and the Duchess were pleased to call Piney. Piney was no chicken, but it was a soothing and original theory of the pair thus to account for the fact that she didn't swear and wasn't improper.

When night crept up again through the gorges, the reedy notes of the accordion rose and fell in fitful spasms and long-drawn gasps by the flickering camp-fire. But music failed to fill entirely the aching void left by insufficient food, and a new diversion was proposed by Piney—story-telling. Neither Mr. Oakhurst nor his female companions caring to relate their personal experiences, this plan would have failed too, but for the Innocent. Some months before he had chanced upon a stray copy of Mr. Pope's ingenious translation of the *Iliad*. He now proposed to narrate the principal incidents of that poem—having thoroughly mastered the argument and fairly forgotten the words—in the current vernacular of Sandy Bar. And so for the rest of that night the Homeric demi-gods again walked the earth. Trojan bully and wily Greek wrestled in the winds, and the great pines in the cañon seemed to bow to the wrath of the son of Peleus. Mr. Oakhurst listened with quiet satisfaction. Most especially was he interested in the fate of "Ash-heels," as the Innocent persisted in denominating the "swift-footed Achilles."

So with small food and much of Homer and the accordion, a week passed over the heads of the outcasts. The sun again forsook them, and again from leaden skies the snowflakes were sifted over the land. Day by day closer around them drew the snowy circle, until at last they looked from their prison over drifted walls of dazzling white that towered twenty feet above their heads. It became more and more difficult to replenish their fires, even from the fallen trees beside them, now half hidden in the drifts. And yet no one complained. The lovers turned from the dreary prospect, and looked into each other's eyes, and were happy. Mr. Oakhurst settled himself coolly to the losing game before him. The Duchess, more cheerful than she had been, assumed the care of Piney. Only Mother Shipton—once the strongest of the party—seemed to sicken and fade. At midnight on the tenth day she called Oakhurst to her side.

"I'm going," she said, in a voice of querulous weakness, "but don't say anything about it. Don't waken the kids. Take the bundle from under my head and open it."

Mr. Oakhurst did so. It contained Mother Shipton's rations for the last week, untouched.

"Give 'em to the child," she said, pointing to the sleeping Piney.

"You've starved yourself," said the gambler.

"That's what they call it," said the woman, querulously, as she lay down again, and, turning her face to the wall, passed quietly away.

The accordion and the bones were put aside that day, and Homer was forgotten. When the body of Mother Shipton had been committed to the snow, Mr. Oakhurst took the Innocent aside, and showed him a pair of snow-shoes, which he had fashioned from the old pack-saddle.

## THE OUTCASTS OF POKER FLAT

"There's one chance in a hundred to save her yet," he said, pointing to Piney; "but it's there," he added, pointing toward Poker Flat. "If you can reach there in two days, she's safe."

"And you?" asked Tom Simson.

"I'll stay here," was the curt reply.

The lovers parted with a long embrace.

"You are not going too?" said the Duchess, as she saw Mr. Oakhurst apparently waiting to accompany him.

"As far as the cañon," he replied. He turned suddenly, and kissed the Duchess, leaving her pallid face aflame, and her trembling limbs rigid with amazement.

Night came, but not Mr. Oakhurst. It brought the storm again and the whirling snow. Then the Duchess, feeding the fire, found that some one had quietly piled beside the hut enough fuel to last a few days longer. The tears rose to her eyes, but she hid them from Piney.

The women slept but little. In the morning, looking into each other's faces, they read their fate. Neither spoke; but Piney, accepting the position of the stronger, drew near and placed her arm around the Duchess's waist. They kept this attitude for the rest of the day. That night the storm reached its greatest fury, and, rending asunder the protecting pines, invaded the very hut.

Toward morning they found themselves unable to feed the fire, which gradually died away. As the embers slowly blackened, the Duchess crept closer to Piney, and broke the silence of many hours: "Piney, can you pray?"

"No, dear," said Piney, simply.

The Duchess, without knowing exactly why, felt relieved, and, putting her head upon Piney's shoulder, spoke no more. And so reclining, the younger and purer pillowing the head of her soiled sister upon her virgin breast, they fell asleep.

The wind lulled as if it feared to waken them. Feathery drifts of snow, shaken from the long pine-boughs, flew like white-winged birds, and settled about them as they slept. The moon through the rifted clouds looked down upon what had been the camp. But all human stain, all trace of earthly travail, was hidden beneath the spotless mantle mercifully flung from above.

They slept all that day and the next, nor did they waken when voices and footsteps broke the silence of the camp. And when pitying fingers brushed the snow from their wan faces, you could scarcely have told, from the equal peace that dwelt upon them, which was she that had sinned. Even the law of Poker Flat recognised this, and turned away, leaving them still locked in each other's arms.

But at the head of the gulch, on one of the largest pine-trees, they found the deuce of clubs pinned to the bark with a bowie-knife. It bore the following, written in pencil, in a firm hand:

†<br>
BENEATH THIS TREE<br>
LIES THE BODY<br>
OF<br>
JOHN OAKHURST<br>
WHO STRUCK A STREAK OF BAD LUCK<br>
ON THE 23RD OF NOVEMBER, 1850,<br>
AND<br>
HANDED IN HIS CHECKS<br>
ON THE 7TH DECEMBER, 1850.<br>
↧

And pulseless and cold, with a derringer by his side and a bullet in his heart, though still calm as in life, beneath the snow lay he who was at once the strongest and yet the weakest of the outcasts of Poker Flat.

# THE IDYL OF RED GULCH

## Francis Bret Harte

SANDY was very drunk. He was lying under an azalea-bush, in pretty much the same attitude in which he had fallen some hours before. How long he had been lying there he could not tell, and didn't care; how long he should lie there was a matter equally indefinite and unconsidered. A tranquil philosophy, born of his physical condition, suffused and saturated his moral being.

The spectacle of a drunken man, and of this drunken man in particular, was not, I grieve to say, of sufficient novelty in Red Gulch to attract attention. Earlier in the day some local satirist had erected a temporary tombstone at Sandy's head, bearing the inscription, " Effects of McCorkle's whisky—kills at forty rods," with a hand pointing to McCorkle's saloon. But this, I imagine, was, like most local satire, personal; and was a reflection upon the unfairness of the process rather than a commentary upon the impropriety of the result. With this facetious exception, Sandy had been undisturbed. A wandering mule, released from his pack, had cropped the scant herbage beside him, and sniffed curiously at the prostrate man; a vagabond dog, with that deep sympathy that the species have for drunken men, had licked his dusty boots and curled himself up at his feet, and lay there, blinking one eye in the sunlight, with a simulation of dissipation that was ingenious and dog-like in its implied flattery of the unconscious man beside him.

Meanwhile the shadows of the pine-trees had slowly swung around until they crossed the road, and their trunks barred the open meadow with gigantic parallels of black and yellow. Little puffs of red dust, lifted by the plunging hoofs of passing teams, dispersed in a grimy shower upon the recumbent man. The sun sank lower and lower, and still Sandy stirred not. And then the repose of this philosopher was disturbed, as other philosophers have been, by the intrusion of an unphilosophical sex.

"Miss Mary," as she was known to the little flock that she had just dismissed from the log schoolhouse beyond the pines, was taking her afternoon walk. Observing an unusually fine cluster of blossoms on the azalea-bush opposite, she crossed the road to pluck it, picking her way through the red dust, not without certain fierce little shivers of disgust and some feline circumlocution. And then she came suddenly upon Sandy!

Of course she uttered the little staccato cry of her sex. But when she had paid that tribute to her physical weakness she became over-bold and halted for a moment—at least six feet from this prostrate monster—with her white skirts gathered in her hand, ready for flight. But neither sound nor motion came from the bush. With one little foot she then overturned the satirical headboard, and muttered "Beasts!"—an epithet which probably, at that moment, conveniently classified in her mind the entire male population of Red Gulch. For Miss Mary, being possessed of certain rigid notions of her own, had not, perhaps, properly appreciated the demonstrative gallantry for which the Californian has been so justly celebrated by his brother Californians, and had, as a new-comer, perhaps fairly earned the reputation of being "stuck-up."

As she stood there she noticed, also, that the slant sunbeams were heating Sandy's head to what she judged to be an unhealthy temperature, and that his hat was lying uselessly at his side. To pick it up and to place it over his face was a work requiring some courage, particularly as his eyes were open. Yet she did it and made good her retreat. But she was somewhat concerned, on looking back, to see that the hat was removed, and that Sandy was sitting up and saying something.

The truth was, that in the calm depths of Sandy's mind he was satisfied that the rays of the sun were beneficial and healthful; that from childhood he had objected to lying down in a hat; that no people but condemned fools, past redemption, ever wore hats; and that his right to dispense with them when he pleased was inalienable. This was the statement of his inner consciousness. Unfortunately, its outward expression was vague, being limited to a repetition of the following formula: " Su'shine all ri'! Wasser maär, eh? Wass up, su'shine? "

Miss Mary stopped, and, taking fresh courage from her vantage of distance, asked him if there was anything that he wanted.

" Wass up? Wasser maär? " continued Sandy, in a very high key.

" Get up, you horrid man! " said Miss Mary, now thoroughly incensed; " get up and go home."

Sandy staggered to his feet. He was six feet high, and Miss Mary trembled. He started forward a few paces and then stopped.

" Wass I go home for? " he suddenly asked, with great gravity.

" Go and take a bath," replied Miss Mary, eyeing his grimy person with great disfavour.

To her infinite dismay, Sandy suddenly pulled off his coat and vest, threw them on the ground, kicked off his boots, and, plunging wildly forward, darted headlong over the hill in the direction of the river.

" Goodness heavens! the man will be drowned! " said Miss Mary; and then, with feminine inconsistency, she ran back to the schoolhouse and locked herself in.

That night, while seated at supper with her hostess, the blacksmith's wife, it came to Miss Mary to ask, demurely, if her husband ever got drunk. " Abner," responded Mrs. Stidger reflectively— " let's see! Abner hasn't been tight since last 'lection." Miss Mary would have liked to ask if he preferred lying in the sun on these occasions, and if a cold bath would have hurt him; but this would have involved an explanation, which she did not then care to give. So she contented herself with opening her grey eyes widely at the red-cheeked Mrs. Stidger—a fine specimen of South-western efflorescence—and then dismissed the subject altogether. The next day she wrote to her dearest friend in Boston: " I think I find the intoxicated portion of this community the least objectionable. I refer, my dear, to the men, of course. I do not know anything that could make the women tolerable."

In less than a week Miss Mary had forgotten this episode, except that her afternoon walks took thereafter, almost unconsciously, another direction. She noticed, however, that every morning a fresh cluster of azalea blossoms appeared among the flowers on her desk. This was not strange, as her little flock were aware of her fondness for flowers, and invariably kept her desk bright with anemones, syringas, and lupines; but, on questioning them, they one and all professed ignorance of the azaleas. A few days later, Master Johnny Stidger, whose desk was nearest to the window, was suddenly taken with spasms of apparently gratuitous laughter, that threatened the discipline of the school. All that Miss Mary could get from him was, that some one had been " looking in the winder." Irate and indignant, she sallied from her hive to do battle with the intruder. As she

turned the corner of the schoolhouse she came plump upon the
quondam drunkard, now perfectly sober, and inexpressibly sheepish
and guilty-looking.

These facts Miss Mary was not slow to take a feminine advantage
of, in her present humour. But it was somewhat confusing to
observe, also, that the beast, despite some faint signs of past dissipation, was amiable-looking—in fact, a kind of blond Samson, whose
corn-coloured silken beard apparently had never yet known the
touch of barber's razor or Delilah's shears. So that the cutting
speech which quivered on her ready tongue died upon her lips, and
she contented herself with receiving his stammering apology with
supercilious eyelids and the gathered skirts of uncontamination.
When she re-entered the schoolroom, her eyes fell upon the azaleas
with a new sense of revelation ; and then she laughed, and the little
people all laughed, and they were all unconsciously very happy.

It was a hot day, and not long after this, that two short-legged
boys came to grief on the threshold of the school with a pail of water,
which they had laboriously brought from the spring, and that Miss
Mary compassionately seized the pail and started for the spring herself. At the foot of the hill a shadow crossed her path, and a blue-
shirted arm dexterously but gently relieved her of her burden. Miss
Mary was both embarrassed and angry. "If you carried more of
that for yourself," she said spitefully to the blue arm, without
deigning to raise her lashes to its owner, "you'd do better." In the
submissive silence that followed she regretted the speech, and
thanked him so sweetly at the door that he stumbled. Which caused
the children to laugh again—a laugh in which Miss Mary joined,
until the colour came faintly into her pale cheek. The next day
a barrel was mysteriously placed beside the door, and as mysteriously
filled with fresh spring-water every morning.

Nor was this superior young person without other quiet attentions.
"Profane Bill," driver of the Slumgullion Stage, widely known in
the newspapers for his "gallantry" in invariably offering the box-
seat to the fair sex, had excepted Miss Mary from this attention, on
the ground that he had a habit of "cussin' on up grades," and gave
her half the coach to herself. Jack Hamlin, a gambler, having once
silently ridden with her in the same coach, afterward threw a
decanter at the head of a confederate for mentioning her name in
a bar-room. The over-dressed mother of a pupil whose paternity
was doubtful had often lingered near this astute Vestal's temple,
never daring to enter its sacred precincts, but content to worship the
priestess from afar.

With such unconscious intervals the monotonous procession of
blue skies, glittering sunshine, brief twilights, and starlit nights
passed over Red Gulch. Miss Mary grew fond of walking in the
sedate and proper woods. Perhaps she believed, with Mrs. Stidger,
that the balsamic odours of the firs "did her chest good," for

certainly her slight cough was less frequent and her step was firmer ; perhaps she had learned the unending lesson which the patient pines are never weary of repeating to heedful or listless ears. And so one day she planned a picnic on Buckeye Hill, and took the children with her. Away from the dusty road, the straggling shanties, the yellow ditches, the clamour of restless engines, the cheap finery of show-windows, the deeper glitter of paint and coloured glass, and the thin veneering which barbarism takes upon itself in such localities, what infinite relief was theirs ! The last heap of ragged rock and clay passed, the last unsightly chasm crossed—how the waiting woods opened their long files to receive them ! How the children—perhaps because they had not yet grown quite away from the breast of the bounteous Mother—threw themselves face downward on her brown bosom with uncouth caresses, filling the air with their laughter ; and how Miss Mary herself—felinely fastidious and intrenched as she was in the purity of spotless skirts, collar, and cuffs—forgot all, and ran like a crested quail at the head of her brood, until, romping, laughing, and panting, with a loosened braid of brown hair, a hat hanging by a knotted ribbon from her throat, she came suddenly and violently, in the heart of the forest, upon the luckless Sandy !

The explanations, apologies, and not overwise conversation that ensued need not be indicated here. It would seem, however, that Miss Mary had already established some acquaintance with this ex-drunkard. Enough that he was soon accepted as one of the party ; that the children, with that quick intelligence which Providence gives the helpless, recognised a friend, and played with his blond beard and long silken moustache, and took other liberties—as the helpless are apt to do. And when he had built a fire against a tree, and had shown them other mysteries of woodcraft, their admiration knew no bounds. At the close of two such foolish, idle, happy hours he found himself lying at the feet of the schoolmistress, gazing dreamily in her face as she sat upon the sloping hillside weaving wreaths of laurel and syringa, in very much the same attitude as he had lain when first they met. Nor was the similitude greatly forced. The weakness of an easy, sensuous nature, that had found a dreamy exaltation in liquor, it is to be feared was now finding an equal intoxication in love.

I think that Sandy was dimly conscious of this himself. I know that he longed to be doing something—slaying a grizzly, scalping a savage, or sacrificing himself in some way for the sake of this sallow-faced, grey-eyed schoolmistress. As I should like to present him in an heroic attitude, I stay my hand with great difficulty at this moment, being only withheld from introducing such an episode by a strong conviction that it does not usually occur at such times. And I trust that my fairest reader, who remembers that, in a real crisis, it is always some uninteresting stranger or unromantic policeman, and not Adolphus, who rescues, will forgive the omission.

So they sat there undisturbed—the woodpeckers chattering overhead and the voices of the children coming pleasantly from the hollow below. What they said matters little. What they thought—which might have been interesting—did not transpire. The woodpeckers only learned how Miss Mary was an orphan; how she left her uncle's house to come to California for the sake of health and independence; how Sandy was an orphan too; how he came to California for excitement; how he had lived a wild life, and how he was trying to reform; and other details, which, from a woodpecker's viewpoint, undoubtedly must have seemed stupid and a waste of time. But even in such trifles was the afternoon spent; and when the children were again gathered, and Sandy, with a delicacy which the schoolmistress well understood, took leave of them quietly at the outskirts of the settlement, it had seemed the shortest day of her weary life.

As the long, dry summer withered to its roots, the school term of Red Gulch—to use a local euphuism—"dried up" also. In another day Miss Mary would be free, and for a season, at least, Red Gulch would know her no more. She was seated alone in the schoolhouse, her cheek resting on her hand, her eyes half closed in one of those day-dreams in which Miss Mary, I fear, to the danger of school discipline, was lately in the habit of indulging. Her lap was full of mosses, ferns, and other woodland memories. She was so preoccupied with these and her own thoughts that a gentle tapping at the door passed unheard, or translated itself into the remembrance of far-off woodpeckers. When at last it asserted itself more distinctly, she started up with a flushed cheek and opened the door. On the threshold stood a woman, the self-assertion and audacity of whose dress were in singular contrast to her timid, irresolute bearing.

Miss Mary recognised at a glance the dubious mother of her anonymous pupil. Perhaps she was disappointed, perhaps she was only fastidious; but as she coldly invited her to enter, she half unconsciously settled her white cuffs and collar, and gathered closer her own chaste skirts. It was, perhaps, for this reason that the embarrassed stranger, after a moment's hesitation, left her gorgeous parasol open and sticking in the dust beside the door, and then sat down at the further end of a long bench. Her voice was husky as she began:

"I heerd tell that you were goin' down to the Bay to-morrow, and I couldn't let you go until I came to thank you for your kindness to my Tommy."

"Tommy," Miss Mary said, "was a good boy, and deserved more than the poor attention she could give him."

"Thank you, miss; thank ye!" cried the stranger, brightening even through the colour which Red Gulch knew facetiously as her "war paint," and striving, in her embarrassment, to drag the long bench nearer the schoolmistress. " I thank you, miss, for that ; and if I am his mother, there ain't a sweeter, dearer, better boy lives than him. And if I ain't much as says it, thar ain't a sweeter, dearer, angeler teacher lives than he's got."

Miss Mary, sitting primly behind her desk, with a ruler over her shoulder, opened her grey eyes widely at this, but said nothing.

" It ain't for you to be complimented by the like of me, I know," she went on hurriedly. " It ain't for me to be comin' here, in broad day, to do it, either ; but I come to ask a favour—not for me, miss—not for me, but for the darling boy."

Encouraged by a look in the young schoolmistress's eye, and putting her lilac-gloved hands together, the fingers downward, between her knees, she went on, in a low voice :

" You see, miss, there's no one the boy has any claim on but me, and I ain't the proper person to bring him up. I thought some, last year, of sending him away to 'Frisco to school, but when they talked of bringing a schoolma'am here, I waited till I saw you, and then I knew it was all right, and I could keep my boy a little longer. And, oh ! miss, he loves you so much ; and if you could hear him talk about you in his pretty way, and if he could ask you what I ask you now, you couldn't refuse him.

" It is natural," she went on rapidly, in a voice that trembled strangely between pride and humility—" it's natural that he should take to you miss, for his father, when I first knew him, was a gentleman—and the boy must forget me, sooner or later—and so I ain't a-goin' to cry about that. For I come to ask you to take my Tommy—God bless him for the bestest, sweetest boy that lives—to—to—take him with you."

She had risen and caught the young girl's hand in her own, and had fallen on her knees beside her.

" I've money plenty, and it's all yours and his. Put him in some good school, where you can go and see him, and help him to—to—to forget his mother. Do with him what you like. The worst you can do will be kindness to what he will learn with me. Only take him out of this wicked life, this cruel place, this home of shame and sorrow. You will ! I know you will—won't you ? You will—you must not, you cannot say no ! You will make him as pure, as gentle as yourself ; and when he has grown up, you will tell him his father's name—the name that hasn't passed my lips for years—the name of Alexander Morton, whom they call here Sandy ! Miss Mary !—do not take your hand away ! Miss Mary speak to me ! You will take my boy ? Do not put your face from me. I know it ought not to look on such as me. Miss Mary !—my God, be merciful !—she is leaving me ! "

Miss Mary had risen, and in the gathering twilight had felt her way to the open window. She stood there, leaning against the casement, her eyes fixed on the last rosy tints that were fading from the western sky. There was still some of its light on her pure young forehead, on her white collar, on her clasped white hands, but all fading slowly away. The suppliant had dragged herself, still on her knees, beside her.

"I know it takes time to consider. I will wait here all night; but I cannot go until you speak. Do not deny me now. You will!— I see it in your sweet face—such a face as I have seen in my dreams. I see it in your eyes, Miss Mary!—you will take my boy!"

The last red beam crept higher, suffused Miss Mary's eyes with something of its glory, flickered, and faded, and went out. The sun had set on Red Gulch. In the twilight and silence Miss Mary's voice sounded pleasantly.

"I will take the boy. Send him to me to-night."

The happy mother raised the hem of Miss Mary's skirts to her lips. She would have buried her hot face in its virgin folds, but she dared not. She rose to her feet.

"Does—this man—know of your intention?" asked Miss Mary suddenly.

"No, nor cares. He has never seen the child to know it."

"Go to him at once—to-night—now? Tell him what you have done. Tell him I have taken his child, and tell him—he must never see—see—the child again. Wherever it may be, he must not come; wherever I may take it, he must not follow! There, go now, please— I'm weary, and—have much yet to do!"

They walked together to the door. On the threshold the woman turned.

"Good-night!"

She would have fallen at Miss Mary's feet. But at the same moment the young girl reached out her arms, caught the sinful woman to her own pure breast for one brief moment, and then closed and locked the door.

It was with a sudden sense of great responsibility that Profane Bill took the reins of the Slumgullion stage the next morning, for the schoolmistress was one of his passengers. As he entered the high road, in obedience to a pleasant voice from the "inside," he suddenly reined up his horses and respectfully waited, as Tommy hopped out at the command of Miss Mary.

"Not that bush, Tommy—the next."

Tommy whipped out his new pocket-knife, and cutting a branch from a tall azalea-bush, returned with it to Miss Mary.

"All right now?"

"All right!"

And the stage-door closed on the Idyl of Red Gulch.

## GEORGE BROOKE
*circa* 1840

# HOW
# ANGELS GOT RELIGION

" NEVER heard how we got religion to Angels, stranger ? I thought, uv course, everybody'd heerd that yarn. Tell ye ? Why sure ; but let's licker again and I'll reminisce.

" Yer see, 'twas afore Angels got to be sech a big camp as 'twas later on, but it was a rich camp and a mighty wicked one. There were lots uv chaps there who'd jest as soon die in their boots as eat ; and every other house was a dance-house or a saloon or a gambling-hell. Pretty Pete and his pardner, Five-Ace Bob, was reckoned the wickedest men in the State ; and Old Bill Jones, what kept the Golden West Hotel, had a national reputation for cussin'. The idea of a parson striking the camp never was thought uv ; but one day I was playing bank into Pete's game when Five-Ace came a runnin' in 'n' sez :

" ' Boys, I'll be derned, but there's an ornery cuss of a parson jest rid up to Jones's. He's got a partner with him, and he 'lows he's goin' to convert the camp.'

" ' The hell he is ! ' sez Pete. ' I'll finish the deal and go down and see about that ! '

" So we all walked down to Jones's, and thar, sure 'nuff, in the bar, talking with Old Bill, wuz the parson, black coat and white tie 'n' all. He was a big, squar'-shouldered chap with a black beard, and keen grey eyes that looked right through yer. His pardner was only a boy of twenty or so, with yeller, curly ha'r, pink-and-white gal's face, and big blue eyes. We all walked in, 'n' Pete he stands to the bar 'n' shouts fer all hands ter drink ; 'n' to our surprise the parson 'n' the kid both stepped up and called fer red licker 'n' drank it. After the drink was finished, the parson sez :

" ' Gents, as yer see, I'm a minister of the Gospel, but I see no harm in any man drinking, ez long ez he ain't no drunkard. I drank just now because I want yer to see that I am not ashamed to do before yer face what I'd do behind yer back.'

" ' Right yer are, parson,' sez Pete ; ' put it thar ' ; 'n' they shook hands, 'n' then Pete he up and called off the hull gang—

Five-Ace 'n' Lucky Barnes 'n' Dirty Smith, 'n' one 'n' all the rest ub 'em.

"The parson shook hands with all uv us, and sed he was going to have a meetin' in Shifty Sal's dance-house that night, ez 'twas the biggest room in camp, 'n' ast us all to come, 'n' we sed we would. When we got outside, Pete sez : ' Boys, you mind me, that devil-dodger'll capture the camp ' ; 'n' he did. That night we all went along to Shifty's, and found the parson and the kid on the platform where the fiddlers used to sit ; and every man in camp wuz in the audience. The parson spoke first :

"' Gents, I want to tell yer first off I don't want any uv yer dust. I've got enough fer myself and my young friend, 'n' there won't be no rake-off in this yer meetin'-house, 'n' I'm not here to preach against any man's way o' makin' a livin'. I will preach ag'in drunkenness, and I shall speak privately with the gamblers ; but I want to keep you men in mind uv yer homes 'n' yer mothers 'n' yer wives 'n' yer sweethearts, and get yer to lead cleaner lives, so's when yer meet 'em ag'in yer'll not hev to be 'shamed.'

"And then he sed we'd hev a song, 'n' the youngster he started in 'n' played a concertina and sang ' Yes, we'll gather at the River ' ; 'n' there wuzn't one uv us that it didn't remind uv how our mothers used to dress us up Sundays 'n' send us to Sunday school, and stand at the door to watch us down street, and call us back to ast if we were sure we had our clean pocket handkerchur ; 'n' I tell yer, mister, thar wuzn't a man with dry eyes in the crowd when he'd finished. That young feller had a v'ice like a angel. Pete he sed it wuz a tenner v'ice, but Five-Ace offered to bet him a hundred to fifty it wuz more like a fifteener or a twenty. Pete told Five-Ace he wuz a derned old fool 'n' didn't know what he wuz talkin' about.

"Well, things run along for about a week, 'n' one day Pete come to me and sez :

"' Look here, Ralters, this yere camp ain't no jay camp, 'n' we've got to hev a church fer the parson. He's a jim-dandy, and won't ask for nothing. He'd jest natchelly go on prayin' and preachin', 'n' tryin' ter save a couple uv old whisky-soaked souls like yourn and Bill Jones's, which ain't wuth powder to blow 'em to hell, 'n' you'd let him go on doin' it in that old shack of Sal's 'n' never make a move. Now, I'm goin' to rustle round 'n' dig up dust enough from the boys, and we'll jest build him a meetin'-house as'll be a credit to the camp ' ; 'n' in a few days the boys hed a good log meetin'-house, built, floored, 'n' benches in it, 'n' everythin'.

"The parson was tickled 'most to death. Next they built him a house, 'n' he 'n' his pardner moved into it. Then Pete said the gals must go ; sed it wuz a dead, rank, snide game to work on the parson ter hev to go down street 'n' be guyed by them hussies ('n' they did guy him awful sometimes, too) ; so the gals they went. Then Pete sed the church had to be properly organised ; hed to

hev deacons 'n' churchwardens 'n' sextons 'n' things ; so Old Bill
Jones 'n' Alabam 'n' me wuz made deacons, 'n' Pete 'n' Five-Ace
was churchwardens.

"In a month every last man in camp wuz worryin' 'bout his future
state. Old Bill Jones came into meetin' one night with his face 'n'
hands washed 'n' an old black suit on, 'n' sot down on the anxious
bench and ast to be prayed fer. The parson knelt down 'n' put his
arm round him,'n' how he did pray! Before he got through, Lucky
Barnes, Alabam, 'n' me wuz on the bench too, 'n' Pete shoved his
Chinaman up the aisle by the collar 'n' sot him down 'longside o'
me. Pete sed he was high-toned Christian gentleman himself, hed
been born 'n' raised a Christian, 'n' wuz a senior churchwarden to
boot, and that he'd make a Christian of Ah Foo or spoil a Chinaman.

"That parson prayed most powerful that night. As a offhand,
rough 'n' tumble, free 'n' easy prayer, I never see his beat ; he hed
the whole aujience in tears, 'n' you might hev heard Pete's amens 'n'
glory-halleluyers off to Buller's Flat. Old Jones wuz a rolling
around on the floor 'n' hollering fer to be saved from the devil before
the parson were half finished, 'n' he made so much noise that Pete
hed to fire a bucket uv water over him to quiet him down. That
meetin' wuz so plum full uv the spirit (ez the parson called it) that
it never broke up till twelve o'clock, ez Jones's shift to deal faro
begun at twelve.

"There wuz over twenty perfesses that night, not countin' Pete's
Chinaman, 'n' next Sunday we hed a big baptism in the crick, 'n'
forty uv us wuz put through. Pete sed he reckoned Ah Foo hed
better be put through every day for a week or so, sence he'd always
bin a dodgasted heathen, but the parson 'lowed wunst wuz enuff;
but he giv' him an extra dip jest fer luck, 'n' I never see a more
ornery-lookin' cuss in my life than that Chinese were when he came
out.

"The Chinese laundrymen were ast to jine the church, but they
wouldn't savey, 'n' so Pete 'n' Five-Ace, Old Bill 'n' me 'n' Alabam
we waited on 'em 'n' told 'em to git, 'n' took 'em down to the crick
'n' baptized 'em jest fer luck. Pete sed if they stayed Ah Foo 'ud
git to backslidin' fust thing he knowed, 'n' then where'd *his* reputation be ?

"Waal, stranger, things run along nice 'n' smooth fer a couple uv
months er so till Chris'mus come nigh. The boys hed been a keepin'
mighty straight ; there wuzn't a man in camp that drinked more'n
wuz hullsome fer him ; there hedn't bin a shootin' scrape fer weeks.
Pete sed things wuz gittin' so all-fired ca'm 'n' peaceful that he
wouldn't be at all surprised to git up some fine day 'n' find Ah Foo
with wings, 'n' feathers on his legs like a Bramah hen. Nary a man
packed a gun, 'n' when a gent 'ud forgit 'n' drop a cuss word he'd
beg parding. The parson wuz thick with all the boys. He writ
letters for us, advised us about all out biznus, 'n' knew all about

everybody's affairs. Lots uv 'em gave him their dust-sack to keep fer 'em, 'n' he knowed where every man hed his cached.

"Along jest afore Chris'mus cum Pete called a meetin' uv the deacons 'n' churchwardens down to his place, 'n' after the sexton (Ah Foo) hed brought in a round of drinks, he sed:

"'Gents, ez chairman *ex-officer* in this yer layout, I move that we give the parson a little present fer Chris'mus. Yer know he won't take a dern cent from us, 'n' never has. Uv course, he has taken a few thousand from time to time to send to orfings 'n' things uv that kind, but not a red fer hisself or pard; 'n' I move that we make him a little present on Chris'mus Day, 'n' it needn't be so derned little, either. Gents in favour'll say so, and gents wot ain't kin keep mum. Carried, 'n' that settles it. Five-Ace 'n' me'll take in contributions, 'n' we won't take any less than fifty cases.'

"That wuz two days afore Chris'mus Day, 'n' when it cum Pete 'n' Five-Ace hed about five thousand in dust 'n' nuggets fer the parson's present. Pete assessed Ah Foo a month's pay, 'n' he kicked hard, but twer'n't no use.

"The day wuz bright 'n' clear, 'n' at 'leven o'clock every man in camp wuz at church. The little buildin' looked mighty tasty—all fixed off with pine-tassels 'n' red berries we'd got in the woods, 'n' every man wuz dressed out in his best duds. At 'leven exact the parson 'n' the kid, who hed bin standin' at the door shakin' hands 'n' wishin' everybody what cum in Merry Chris'mus, cum in 'n' took their seats on the platform. Pete 'n' Five-Ace 'n' Bill Jones 'n' Alabam 'n' me sot on a bench jest in front o' the platform. We wuz all togged out in our best fixin's, 'n' Pete 'n' Five-Ace they sported dimon's till yer couldn't rest. Waal, ez usual, the perceedin's opened up with er prayer from the parson; 'n' then we hed singin' 'n' it seemed ter me ez if I never hed heerd sich singin' in my life afore ez thet kid let out o' him thet day.

"Then the parson he started in ter jaw, 'n' I must ellow he giv' us a great discourse. I never see him so long-winded afore tho', 'n' Pete was beginnin' to get mighty restless 'n' oneasy, when all uv a suddint we heerd the door open 'n' shet quick 'n' sharp, 'n' every one turned round to find a great, big, black-bearded cuss at the door a coverin' the hull gang uv us with a double-bar'led shotgun, 'n' jest a standin' thar cool 'n' silent.

"'Face round here, ye derned fools!" yelled somebody in a sharp, quick, biznus-meanin' v'ice, 'n' all hands faced round to find the parson holding 'em up with another shotgun—own brother to the one the other cuss hed. 'I don't want a word out er yer,' he sed. 'Yer see my game now, don't yer? Thar ain't a gun in the house 'cept the ones you see, 'n' if any gent makes any row in this yer meetin' I'll fill his hide so plum full o' holes 'twon't hold his bones. The kid will now take up the collection, 'n' ez it's the first one we ever hev taken up, yer must make it a liber'l one, see?'

"The kid started out with a gunny-sack, 'n' went through the very last man in the crowd. He took everything, even to the rings on our fingers. The parson hed the drop, 'n' we knew it 'n' never kicked, but jest giv' up our stuff like lambs.

"After the kid hed finished he took the sack outside, 'n' thet's the last we ever seed o' him. Then the parson he sez:

"'Now, gents, I must say adoo, ez I must be a travellin', for I hev another meetin' to attend this eve. I want to say, tho', afore I go, thet you're the orneriest gang uv derned fools I ever played fer suckers. A few friends uv mine hev taken the liberty, while yer've been to meetin' this blessed Chris'mus Day, uv goin' through yer cabins 'n' diggin' up yer little caches uv dust 'n' uther val'ables. Yer stock hez all been stampeded, 'n' yer guns yer'll find somewhar at the bottom of the crick. My friend at the door will hold yer level while I walk out, 'n' we will then keep yer quiet fer a few minutes longer through ther winder jest so's we can git a nice, cumf'table start'; 'n' so they did. What c'u'd we do? The parson walked out, grinning all over himself, 'n' he 'n' his pals they nailed up the door 'n' winders (thar wuz only two), 'n' very soon after they had finished we heerd the clatter o' huffs 'n' knowed they wuz gone.

"I must draw a veil over the rest uv thet day's purceedin's, stranger. The langwidge used by ther boys wuz too awful to repeat; but t'was jest ez this parson sed, when we got out o' thet meetin'-house we found every animal on the location gone, 'n' the only arms left wuz knives 'n' clubs; yet we'd hev gone after 'em with nothin' but our hands, but we couldn't follow afoot.

"How much did they get? I don't rightly know, but not fur frum fifty thousand. The hull camp wuz stone-brook, all excep' Ah Foo, 'n' he wuz the only one uv us as hed sense enuff not to tell thet durned parson whar he cached his stuff. Pete 'n' Five-Ace wuz so everlastin' hurt at the hull biznus that they shut up the Bird o' Prey, borrowed Ah Foo's sack, 'n' left for the Bay to try 'n' find thet parson; but they never did find him, 'n' no one ever heard uv him again."

# W. H. H. MURRAY
1840–1904

## A RIDE WITH A MAD HORSE IN A FREIGHT CAR

It was at the battle of Malvern Hill—a battle where the carnage was more frightful, as it seems to me, than in any this side of the Alleghanies during the whole war—that my story must begin. I was then serving as Major in the —th Massachusetts Regiment—the old —th, as we used to call it—and a bloody time the boys had of it too. About 2 P.M. we had been sent out to skirmish along the edge of the wood in which, as our generals suspected, the Rebs lay massing for a charge across the slope, upon the crest of which our army was posted. We had barely entered the underbrush when we met the heavy formations of Magruder in the very act of charging. Of course, our thin line of skirmishers was no impediment to those on-rushing masses. They were on us and over us before we could get out of the way. I do not think that half of those running, screaming masses of men ever knew that they had passed over the remnants of as plucky a regiment as ever came out of the old Bay State. But many of the boys had good reason to remember that afternoon at the base of Malvern Hill, and I among the number; for when the last line of Rebs had passed over me, I was left among the bushes with the breath nearly trampled out of me and an ugly bayonet-gash through my thigh; and mighty little consolation was it for me at that moment to see the fellow who ran me through lying stark dead at my side, with a bullet-hole in his head, his shock of coarse black hair matted with blood, and his stony eyes looking into mine. Well, I bandaged up my limb the best I might, and started to crawl away, for our batteries had opened, and the grape and canister that came hurtling down the slope passed but a few feet over my head. It was slow and painful work, as you can imagine, but at last, by dint of perseverance, I had dragged myself away to the left of the direct range of the batteries, and, creeping to the verge of the wood, looked off over the green slope. I understood by the crash and roar of the guns, the yells and cheers of the men, and that hoarse murmur which those who have been in battle know, but which I cannot describe in words, that there was hot work going on

out there; but never have I seen, no, not in that three days'
desperate *mêlée* at the Wilderness, nor at that terrific repulse we had
at Cold Harbour, such absolute slaughter as I saw that afternoon on
the green slope of Malvern Hill. The guns of the entire army were
massed on the crest, and thirty thousand of our infantry lay, musket
in hand, in front. For eight hundred yards the hill sank in easy
declension to the wood, and across this smooth expanse the Rebs
must charge to reach our lines. It was nothing short of downright
insanity to order men to charge that hill; and so his generals told
Lee, but he would not listen to reason that day, and so he sent
regiment after regiment, and brigade after brigade, and division
after division, to certain death. Talk about Grant's disregard of
human life, his effort at Cold Harbour—and I ought to know, for
I got a minie in my shoulder that day—was hopeful and easy work
to what Lee laid on Hill's and Magruder's divisions at Malvern. It
was at the close of the second charge, when the yelling mass reeled
back from before the blaze of those sixty guns and thirty thousand
rifles, even as they began to break and fly backward toward the
wood, that I saw from the spot where I lay a riderless horse break
out of the confused and flying mass, and, with mane and tail erect
and spreading nostril, come dashing obliquely down the slope. Over
fallen steeds and heaps of the dead she leaped with a motion as airy
as that of the flying fox when, fresh and unjaded, he leads away from
the hounds, whose sudden cry has broken him off from hunting mice
amid the bogs of the meadow. So this riderless horse came vaulting
along. Now from my earliest boyhood I have had what horsemen
call a "weakness" for horses. Only give me a colt of wild irregular
temper and fierce blood to tame, and I am perfectly happy. Never
did lash of mine, singing with cruel sound through the air, fall on
such a colt's soft hide. Never did yell or kick send his hot blood
from heart to head deluging his sensitive brain with fiery currents,
driving him into frenzy or blinding him with fear; but touches,
soft and gentle as a woman's, caressing words, and oats given from
the open palm, and unfailing kindness, were the means I used to
"subjugate" him. Sweet subjugation, both to him who subdues
and to him who yields! The wild, unmannerly, and unmanageable
colt, the fear of horsemen the country round, finding in you not an
enemy, but a friend, receiving his daily food from you, and all those
little "nothings" which go as far with a horse as a woman, to win
and retain affection, grows to look upon you as his protector and
friend, and testifies in countless ways his fondness for you. So
when I saw this horse, with action so free and motion so graceful,
amid that storm of bullets, my heart involuntarily went out to her,
and my feelings rose higher and higher at every leap she took from
amid the whirlwind of fire and lead. And as she plunged at last over
a little hillock out of range and came careering toward me as only
a riderless horse might come, her head flung wildly from side to

side, her nostrils widely spread, her flank and shoulders flecked with foam, her eye dilating, I forgot my wound and all the wild roar of battle, and, lifting myself involuntarily to a sitting posture as she swept grandly by, gave her a ringing cheer.

Perhaps in the sound of a human voice of happy mood amid the awful din she recognised a resemblance to the voice of him whose blood moistened her shoulders and was even yet dripping from saddle and housings. Be that as it may, no sooner had my voice sounded than she flung her head with a proud upward movement into the air, swerved sharply to the left, neighed as she might to a master at morning from her stall, and came trotting directly up to where I lay, and, pausing, looked down upon me as it were in compassion. I spoke again, and stretched out my hand caressingly. She pricked her ears, took a step forward, and lowered her nose until it came in contact with my palm. Never did I fondle anything more tenderly, never did I see an animal which seemed to so court and appreciate human tenderness as that beautiful mare. I say "beautiful." No other word might describe her. Never will her image fade from my memory while memory lasts.

In weight she might have turned, when well conditioned, nine hundred and fifty pounds. In colour she was a dark chestnut, with a velvety depth and soft look about the hair indescribably rich and elegant. Many a time have I heard ladies dispute the shade and hue of her plush-like coat as they ran their white, jewelled fingers through her silken hair. Her body was round in the barrel and perfectly symmetrical. She was wide in the haunches, without projection of the hip-bones, upon which the shorter ribs seemed to lap. High in the withers as she was, the line of her back and neck perfectly curved, while her deep, oblique shoulders and long, thick forearm, ridgy with swelling sinews, suggested the perfection of stride and power. Her knees across the pan were wide, the cannon-bone below them short and thin ; the pasterns long and sloping ; her hoofs round, dark, shiny, and well set on. Her mane was a shade darker than her coat, fine and thin, as a thoroughbred's always is whose blood is without taint or cross. Her ear was thin, sharply pointed, delicately curved, nearly black around the borders, and as tremulous as the leaves of an aspen. Her neck rose from the withers to the head in perfect curvature, hard, devoid of fat, and well cut up under the chops. Her nostrils were full, very full, and thin almost as parchment. The eyes, from which tears might fall or fire flash, were well brought out, soft as a gazelle's, almost human in their intelligence, while over the small bony head, over neck and shoulders, yea, over the whole body and clean down to the hoofs, the veins stood out as if the skin were but tissue-paper against which the warm blood pressed, and which it might at any moment burst asunder. "A perfect animal," I said to myself as I lay looking her over—" an animal which might have been born from the wind and the sunshine, so cheerful and so swift she seems; an animal which a man would present as his choicest gift to the woman he loved, and yet one which that woman, wife or lady-love, would give him to ride when honour and life depended on bottom and speed."

All that afternoon the beautiful mare stood over me, while away to the right of us the hoarse tide of battle flowed and ebbed. What charm, what delusion of memory held her there? Was my face to her as the face of her dead master, sleeping a sleep from which not even the wildest roar of battle, no, nor her cheerful neigh at morning, would ever wake him? Or is there in animals some instinct, answering to our intuition, only more potent, which tells them whom to trust and whom to avoid? I know not, and yet some such sense they may have, they must have; or else why should this mare so fearlessly attach herself to me? By what process of reason or instinct I know not, but there she chose me for her master; for when some of my men at dusk came searching, and found me, and, laying me on a stretcher, started toward our lines, the mare, uncompelled, of her own free will, followed at my side; and all through that stormy night of wind and rain, as my men struggled along through the mud and mire toward Harrison's Landing, the mare followed, and ever after, until she died, was with me, and was mine, and I, so far as man might be, was hers. I named her Gulnare.

As quickly as my wound permitted, I was transported to Washington, whither I took the mare with me. Her fondness for me grew daily, and soon became so marked as to cause universal comment. I had her boarded while in Washington at the corner of —— Street and —— Avenue. The groom had instructions to lead her around to the window against which was my bed, at the hospital, twice every day, so that by opening the sash I might reach out my hand and pet her. But the second day, no sooner had she reached the street that she broke suddenly from the groom and dashed away at full speed. I was lying, bolstered up in bed, reading, when I heard the rush of flying feet, and in an instant, with a loud, joyful neigh, she checked herself in front of my window. And when the nurse lifted the sash, the beautiful creature thrust her head through the aperture, and rubbed her nose against my shoulder like a dog. I am not ashamed to say that I put both my arms around her neck, and, burying my face in her silken mane, kissed her again and again. Wounded, weak, and away from home, with only strangers to wait upon me, and scant service at that, the affection of this lovely creature for me, so tender and touching, seemed almost human, and my heart went out to her beyond any power of expression, as to the only being, of all the thousands around me, who thought of me and loved me. Shortly after her appearance at my window, the groom, who had divined where he should find her, came into the yard. But she would not allow him to come near her, much less touch her. If he tried to approach she would lash out at him with her heels most spitefully, and then, laying back her ears and opening her mouth savagely, would make a short dash at him, and, as the terrified African disappeared around the corner of the hospital, she would wheel, and, with a face bright as a happy child's, come trotting to the window for me to pet her. I shouted to the groom to go back to the stable, for I had no doubt but that she would return to her stall when I closed the window. Rejoiced at the permission, he departed. After some thirty minutes, the last ten of which she was standing with her slim, delicate head in my lap, while I braided her foretop and combed out her silken mane, I lifted her head, and, patting her softly on either cheek, told her that she must "go." I gently pushed her head out of the window and closed it, and then, holding up my hand, with the palm turned toward her, charged her, making the appropriate motion, to "go away right straight back to her stable." For a moment she stood looking steadily at me, with an indescribable expression of hesitation and surprise in her clear, liquid eyes, and then, turning lingeringly, walked slowly out of the yard.

Twice a day for nearly a month, while I lay in the hospital, did Gulnare visit me. At the appointed hour the groom would slip her headstall, and, without a word of command, she would dart out of the stable, and, with her long, leopard-like lope, go sweeping down the street and come dashing into the hospital yard, checking herself with the same glad neigh at my window; nor did she ever once fail, at the closing of the sash, to return directly to her stall. The groom informed me that every morning and evening, when the hour of her visit drew near, she would begin to chafe and worry, and, by pawing and pulling at the halter, advertise him that it was time for her to be released.

But of all exhibitions of happiness, either by beast or man, hers was the most positive on that afternoon when, racing into the yard, she found me leaning on a crutch outside the hospital building. The whole corps of nurses came to the doors, and all the poor fellows that could move themselves—for Gulnare had become a universal favourite, and the boys looked for her daily visits nearly, if not quite, as ardently as I did—crawled to the windows to see her. What gladness was expressed in every movement! She would come prancing toward me, head and tail erect, and, pausing, rub her head against my shoulder, while I patted her glossy neck; then suddenly, with a sidewise spring, she would break away, and with her long tail elevated until her magnificent brush, fine and silken as the golden hair of a blonde, fell in a great spray on either flank, and, her head curved to its proudest arch, pace around me with that high action and springing step peculiar to the thoroughbred. Then like a flash, dropping her brush and laying back her ears and stretching her nose straight out, she would speed away with that quick, nervous, low-lying action which marks the rush of racers, when side by side and nose to nose lapping each other, with the roar of cheers on either hand and along the seats above them, they come straining up the home stretch. Returning from one of these arrowy flights, she would come curvetting back, now pacing sidewise as on parade, now dashing her hind feet high into the air, and anon vaulting up and springing through the air, with legs well under her, as if in the act of taking a five-barred gate, and finally would approach and stand happy in her reward—my caress.

The war, at last, was over. Gulnare and I were in at the death with Sheridan at the Five Forks. Together we had shared the pageant at Richmond and Washington, and never had I seen her in better spirits than on that day at the capital. It was a sight indeed to see her as she came down Pennsylvania Avenue. If the triumphant procession had been all in her honour and mine, she could not have moved with greater grace and pride. With dilating eye and tremulous ear, ceaselessly champing her bit, her heated blood bringing out the magnificent lacework of veins over her entire body, now and then pausing, and with a snort gathering herself back upon her haunches as for a mighty leap, while she shook the froth from her bits, she moved with a high, prancing step down the magnificent street, the admired of all beholders. Cheer after cheer was given, huzza after huzza rang out over her head from roofs and balcony, bouquet after bouquet was launched by fair and enthusiastic admirers before her; and yet, amid the crash and swell of music, the cheering and tumult, so gentle and manageable was she, that, though I could feel her frame creep and tremble under me as she moved through that whirlwind of excitement, no check or curb was needed, and the bridle-lines—the same she wore when she came to me at Malvern Hill—lay unlifted on the pommel of the saddle. Never before had I seen her so grandly herself. Never before had the fire and energy, the grace and gentleness, of her blood so revealed themselves. This was the day and the event she needed. And all the royalty of her ancestral breed—a race of equine kings—flowing as without taint or cross from him that was the pride and wealth of the whole tribe of desert rangers, expressed itself in her. I need not say that I shared her mood. I sympathised in her every step. I entered into all her royal humours. I patted her neck and spoke loving and cheerful words to her. I called her my beauty, my pride, my pet. And did she not understand me? Every word! Else why that listening ear turned back to catch my softest whisper; why the responsive quiver through the frame, and the low, happy neigh? "Well," I exclaimed, as I leaped from her back at the close of the review—alas! that words spoken in lightest mood should portend so much!—" well, Gulnare, if you should die, your life has had its triumph. The nation itself, through its admiring capital, has paid tribute to your beauty, and death can never rob you of your fame." And I patted her moist neck and foam-flecked shoulders, while the grooms were busy with head and loins.

That night our brigade made its bivouac just over Long Bridge, almost on the identical spot where, four years before, I had camped my company of three months' volunteers. With what experiences of march and battle were those four years filled! For three of these years Gulnare had been my constant companion. With me she had shared my tent, and not rarely my rations, for in appetite she was truly human, and my steward always counted her as one of our "mess." Twice had she been wounded—once at Fredericksburg, through the thigh; and once at Cold Harbour, where a piece of shell tore away a part of her scalp. So completely did it stun her, that for some moments I thought her dead, but to my great joy she shortly recovered her senses. I had the wound carefully dressed by our brigade surgeon, from whose care she came in a month with the edges of the wound so nicely united that the eye could with difficulty detect the scar. This night, as usual, she lay at my side, her head almost touching mine. Never before, unless when on a raid and in face of the enemy, had I seen her so uneasy. Her movements during the night compelled wakefulness on my part. The sky was cloudless, and in the dim light I lay and watched her. Now she would stretch herself at full length, and rub her head on the ground. Then she would start up, and, sitting on her haunches, like a dog, lift one foreleg and paw her neck and ears. Anon she would rise to her feet and shake herself, walk off a few rods, return and lie down again by my side. I did not know what to make of it, unless the excitement of the day had been too much for her sensitive nerves. I spoke to her kindly and petted her. In response she would rub her nose against me, and lick my hand with her tongue—a peculiar habit of hers—like a dog. As I was passing my hand over her head, I discovered that it was hot, and the thought of the old wound flashed into my mind, with a momentary fear that something might be wrong about her brain, but after thinking it over I dismissed it as incredible. Still I was alarmed. I knew that something was amiss, and I rejoiced at the thought that I should soon be at home where she could have quiet, and, if need be, the best of nursing. At length the morning dawned, and the mare and I took our last meal together on Southern soil—the last we ever took together. The brigade was formed in line for the last time, and as I rode down the front to review the boys she moved with all her old battle grace and power. Only now and then, by a shake of the head, was I reminded of her actions during the night. I said a few words of farewell to the men whom I had led so often to battle, with whom I had shared perils not a few, and by whom, as I had reason to think, I was loved, and then gave, with a voice slightly unsteady, the last order they would ever receive from me: "Brigade, Attention, Ready to break ranks, *Break Ranks.*" The order was obeyed. But ere they scattered, moved by a common impulse, they gave first three cheers for me, and then, with the same heartiness and even more power, three cheers for Gulnare. And she, standing there, looking with her bright, cheerful countenance full at the men, pawing with her forefeet, alternately, the ground, seemed to understand the compliment; for no sooner had the cheering died away than she arched her neck to its proudest curve, lifted her thin, delicate head into the air, and gave a short, joyful neigh.

My arrangements for transporting her had been made by a friend the day before. A large, roomy car had been secured, its floor strewn with bright, clean straw, a bucket and a bag of oats provided, and everything done for her comfort. The car was to be attached to the through express, in consideration of fifty dollars extra, which I gladly paid, because of the greater rapidity with which it enabled me to make my journey. As the brigade broke up into groups, I glanced at my watch and saw that I had barely time to reach the cars before they started. I shook the reins upon her neck, and with a plunge, startled at the energy of my signal, away she flew. What a stride she had! What an elastic spring! She touched and left the earth as if her limbs were of spiral wire. When I reached the car my friend was standing in front of it, the gang-plank was ready, I leaped from the saddle and, running up the plank into the car, whistled to her; and she, timid and hesitating, yet unwilling to be separated from me, crept slowly and cautiously up the steep incline and stood beside me. Inside I found a complete suit of flannel clothes, with a blanket and, better than all, a lunch-basket. My friend explained that he had bought the clothes as he came down to the depot, thinking, as he said, " that they would be much better than your regimentals," and suggested that I doff the one and don the other. To this I assented the more readily as I reflected that I would have to pass one night at least in the car, with no better bed than the straw under my feet. I had barely time to undress before the cars were coupled and started. I tossed the clothes to my friend with the injunction to pack them in my trunk and express them on to me, and waved him my adieu. I arrayed myself in the nice, cool flannel and looked around. The thoughtfulness of my friend had anticipated every want. An old cane-seated chair stood in one corner. The lunch-basket was large and well supplied. Amid the oats I found a dozen oranges, some bananas, and a package of real Havana cigars. How I called down blessings on his thoughtful head as I took the chair and, lighting one of the fine-flavoured *figaros*, gazed out on the fields past which we were gliding, yet wet with morning dew. As I sat dreamily admiring the beauty before me, Gulnare came and, resting her head upon my shoulder, seemed to share my mood. As I stroked her fine-haired, satin-like nose, recollection quickened and memories of our companionship in perils thronged into my mind. I rode again that midnight ride to Knoxville, when Burnside lay intrenched, desperately holding his own, waiting for news from Chattanooga of which I was the bearer, chosen by Grant himself because of the reputation of my mare. What riding that was! We started, ten riders of us in all, each with the same message. I parted company the first hour out with all save one, an iron-grey stallion of Messenger blood. Jack Murdock rode him, who learned his horsemanship from buffalo and Indian hunting on the plains— not a bad school to graduate from. Ten miles out of Knoxville the grey, his flanks dripping with blood, plunged up abreast of the mare's shoulders and fell dead; and Gulnare and I passed through the lines alone. *I had ridden the terrible race without whip or spur.* With what scenes of blood and flight she would ever be associated!

And then I thought of home, unvisited for four long years—that home I left a stripling, but to which I was returning a bronzed and brawny man. I thought of mother and Bob—how they would admire her!—of old Ben, the family groom, and of that one who shall be nameless, whose picture I had so often shown to Gulnare as the likeness of her future mistress; had they not all heard of her, my beautiful mare, she who came to me from the smoke and whirlwind, my battle-gift? How they would pat her soft, smooth sides, and tie her mane with ribbons, and feed her with all sweet things from open and caressing palm! And then I thought of one who might come after her to bear her name and repeat at least some portion of her beauty—a horse honoured and renowned the country through, because of the transmission of the mother's fame.

About three o'clock in the afternoon a change came over Gulnare. I had fallen asleep upon the straw, and she had come and awakened me with a touch of her nose. The moment I started up I saw that something was the matter. Her eyes were dull and heavy. Never before had I seen the light go out of them. The rocking of the car as it went jumping and vibrating along seemed to irritate her. She began to rub her head against the side of the car. Touching it, I found that the skin over the brain was hot as fire. Her breathing grew rapidly louder and louder. Each breath was drawn with a kind of gasping effort. The lids with their silken fringe drooped wearily over the lustreless eyes. The head sank lower and lower, until the nose almost touched the floor. The ears, naturally so lively and erect, hung limp and widely apart. The body was cold and senseless. A pinch elicited no motion. Even my voice was at last unheeded. To word and touch there came, for the first time in all our intercourse, no response. I knew as the symptoms spread what was the matter. The signs bore all one way. She was in the first stages of phrenitis, or inflammation of the brain. In other words, *my beautiful mare was going mad.*

I was well versed in the anatomy of the horse. Loving horses from my very childhood, there was little in veterinary practice with which I was not familiar. Instinctively, as soon as the symptoms had developed themselves, and I saw under what frightful disorder Gulnare was labouring, I put my hand into my pocket for my knife, in order to open a vein. *There was no knife there.* Friends, I have met with many surprises. More than once in battle and scout have I been nigh death; but never did my blood desert my veins and settle so around the heart, never did such a sickening sensation possess me, as when, standing in that car with my beautiful mare before me marked with those horrible symptoms, I made that discovery. My knife, my sword, my pistols even, were with my suit in the care of my friend, two hundred miles away. Hastily, and with trembling fingers, I searched my clothes, the lunch-basket, my linen; not even a pin could I find. I shoved open the sliding door, and swung my hat and shouted, hoping to attract some brakesman's attention. The train was thundering along at full speed, and none saw or heard me. I knew her stupor would not last long. A slight quivering of the lip, an occasional spasm running through the frame, told me too plainly that the stage of frenzy would soon begin. "My God," I exclaimed in despair, as I shut the door and turned toward her, "must I see you die, Gulnare, when the opening of a vein would save you? Have you borne me, my pet, through all these years of peril, the icy chill of winter, the heat and torment of summer, and all the thronging dangers of a hundred bloody battles, only to die torn by fierce agonies, when so near a peaceful home?"

But little time was give me to mourn. My life was soon to be in peril, and I must summon up the utmost power of eye and limb to escape the violence of my frenzied mare. Did you ever see a mad horse when his madness is on him? Take your stand with me in that car, and you shall see what suffering a dumb creature can endure before it dies. In no malady does a horse suffer more than in phrenitis, or inflammation of the brain. Possibly in severe cases of colic, probably in rabies in its fiercest form, the pain is equally intense. These three are the most agonising of all the diseases to which the noblest of animals is exposed. Had my pistols been with me, I should then and there, with whatever strength Heaven granted, have taken my companion's life, that she might be spared the suffering which was so soon to rack and wring her sensitive frame. A horse labouring under an attack of phrenitis is as violent as a horse can be. He is not ferocious as is one in a fit of rabies. He may kill his master, but he does it without design. There is in him no desire of mischief for its own sake, no cruel cunning, no stratagem and malice. A rabid horse is conscious in every act and motion. He recognises the man he destroys. There is in him an insane *desire* to *kill*. Not so with the phrenetic horse. He is unconscious in his violence. He sees and recognises no one. There is no method or purpose in his madness. He kills without knowing it.

I knew what was coming. I could not jump out, that would be certain death. I must abide in the car, and take my chance of life. The car was fortunately high, long, and roomy. I took my position in front of my horse, watchful, and ready to spring. Suddenly her lids, which had been closed, came open with a snap, as if an electric shock had passed through her, and the eyes, wild in their brightness, stared directly at me. And what eyes they were! The membrane grew red and redder until it was of the colour of blood, standing out in frightful contrast with the transparency of the cornea. The pupil gradually dilated until it seemed about to burst out of the socket. The nostrils, which had been sunken and motionless, quivered, swelled, and glowed. The respiration became short, quick, and gasping. The limp and dripping ears stiffened and stood erect, pricked sharply forward, as if to catch the slightest sound. Spasms, as the car swerved and vibrated, ran along her frame. More horrid than all, the lips slowly contracted, and the white, sharp-edged teeth stood uncovered, giving an indescribable look of ferocity to the partially opened mouth. The car suddenly reeled as it dashed around a curve, swaying her almost off her feet, and, as a contortion shook her, she recovered herself, and rearing upward as high as the car permitted, plunged directly at me. I was expecting the movement, and dodged. Then followed exhibitions of pain which I pray God I may never see again. Time and again did she dash herself upon the floor, and roll over and over, lashing out with her feet in all directions. Pausing a moment, she would stretch her body to its extreme length, and, lying upon her side, pound the floor with her head as if it were a maul. Then like a flash she would leap to her feet, and whirl round and round until from very giddiness she would stagger and fall. She would lay hold of the straw with her teeth, and shake it as a dog shakes a struggling woodchuck; then dashing it from her mouth, she would seize hold of her own sides, and rend herself. Springing up, she would rush against the end of the car, falling all in a heap from the violence of the concussion. For some fifteen minutes without intermission the frenzy lasted. I was nearly exhausted. My efforts to avoid her mad rushes, the terrible tension of my nervous system, produced by the spectacle of such exquisite and prolonged suffering, were weaking me beyond what I should have thought it possible an hour before for anything to weaken me. In fact, I felt my strength leaving me. A terror such as I had never yet felt was taking possession of my mind. I sickened at the sight before me, and at the thought of agonies yet to come. "My God," I exclaimed, "must I be killed by my own horse in this miserable car!" Even as I spoke the end came. The mare raised herself until her shoulders touched the roof, then dashed her body upon the floor with a violence which threatened the stout frame beneath her. I leaned, panting and exhausted, against the side of the car. Gulnare did not stir. She lay motionless, her breath coming and going in lessening respirations. I tottered toward her, and, as I stood above her, my ear detected a low gurgling sound. I cannot describe the feeling that followed. Joy and grief contended within me. I knew the meaning of that sound. Gulnare, in her frenzied violence, had broken a blood-vessel, and was bleeding internally. Pain and life were passing away together. I knelt down by her side. I laid my head upon her shoulders and sobbed aloud. Her body moved a little beneath me. I crawled forward, and lifted her beautiful head into my lap. O, for one more sign of recognition before she died! I smoothed the tangled masses of her mane. I wiped, with a fragment of my coat, torn in the struggle, the blood which oozed from her nostril. I called her by name. My desire was granted. In a moment Gulnare opened her eyes. The redness of frenzy had passed out of them. She saw and recognised me. I spoke again. Her eye lighted a moment with the old and intelligent look of love. Her ear moved. Her nostril quivered slightly as she strove to neigh. The effort was in vain. Her love was greater than her strength. She moved her head a little, as if she would be nearer me, looked once more with her clear eyes into my face, breathed a long breath, straightened her shapely limbs, and died. And there, holding the head of my dead mare in my lap, while the great warm tears fell one after another down my cheeks, I sat until the sun went down, the shadows darkened in the car, and night drew her mantle, coloured like my grief, over the world.

## LOUISE STOCKTON
*circa* 1840

# KIRBY'S COALS OF FIRE

CONSIDERING it simply as an excursion, George Scott thought, leaning over the side of the canal-boat and looking at the shadow of the hills in the water, his plan for spending his summer vacation might be a success, but he was not so sure about his opportunities for studying human nature under the worst conditions. It was true that the conditions were bad enough, but so were the results, and George was not in search of logical sequences. He had been in the habit of saying that nothing interested him as much as the study of his fellows; and that he was in earnest was proved by the fact that even his college experiences had not yet disheartened him, although they had cost him not a few neckties and coats, and sometimes too many of his dollars. But George had higher aspirations, and was not disposed to be satisfied with the opportunities presented by crude collegians or even learned professors, and so meant to go out among men. When he was younger,—a year or two before—he had dreamed of a mission among the Indians, fancying that he would reach original principles among them; but the Modocs and Captain Jack had lowered his faith, while the Rev. Dr. Buck's story of how the younger savages had been taught to make beds and clean knives, until they preferred these civilised occupations to their old habit of scampering through the woods, had dispelled more of the glitter, and he had resolved to confine his labours to his white brethren. He did not mean to seek his opportunities among the rich, nor among the monotonously dreary poor of the city, but in a fresher field. Like most theological students, he was well read in current literature, and he had learned how often the noblest virtues are found among the roughest classes. It was true, they were sometimes so latent that like the jewel in a toad's head they had the added grace of unexpectedness, but that did not interfere with the fact of their existence. He had read of California gamblers who had rushed from tables where they had sat with bowie-knives between their teeth, to warn a coming train of broken rails, and, when picked up maimed and dying, had simply asked if the children were saved, and then, content, had turned aside and died. He knew the story of the Mississippi engineer who, going home with a long-sought fortune to claim his waiting bride, had saved his boat from wreck by supplying the want of fuel by hat, coat, boots, wedding-clothes, gloves, favours, and finally his bag of greenbacks and Northern Pacific bonds, then returning to his duty, sans money, sans wife, but plus honour and a rewarding conscience. When men are capable of such heroism, George would say, arguing from these and similar stories, they are open to true reformation, all that is necessary being some exercise of an influence that shall make such impulses constant instead of spasmodic.

About noon he had not been quite so sanguine regarding his mission, and had almost resolved that when they reached Springfield he would return East and join some of his class who were going to the Kaatskills. The sun was then pouring down directly on the boat, the cabin was stifling, the horses crept sluggishly along, the men were rude and brutal, and around him was an atmosphere of frying fish and boiling cabbage. The cabbage was perhaps the crowning evil; for while he found it possible to force his ear and eye to be deaf and blind to the disagreeable, he had no amount of will that could conquer the sense of smell. There seemed to be little, he thought, with some contempt for his expectations, to reward his quest or maintain his theory that every one had at least one story to tell. It was not necessarily one's own story, he had said, but lives the most barren in incident come into contact with those more vehement, and have the chance of looking into tragedies, into moral victories and fierce conflicts, through other men's eyes. He had hinted something of this to Joe Lakin early in the morning, when the mist was rising off the hills, when the air was fresh and keen, and the sun was making the long lines of oil upon the river glitter like so many brilliant snakes. Joe was the laziest and roughest of the men on the boat, but he sometimes had such a genial and even superior manner, that George had felt sure that he would comprehend his meaning. Thus when noon came, hot, close, and heavy with prophecy of dinner, George had sickened of human nature and of psychological studies; but now the sun had set, and a golden glory lit the sky; the fields on one side of the river rolled away green in clover and wavy in corn, the hills heavily wooded rose high and picturesquely on the other side, and the little island in the bend of the river seemed the home of quiet and of peace. The horses plodded patiently through the water, going out on the shallows and avoiding the deeper currents near the shore, and the boys, forgetting to shout and swear, rode along softly whistling. Over by the hills stood a cottage, and in the terraced garden a group of girls with bright ribbons in their hair were playing quoits with horseshoes. A rowboat was carrying passengers over the river to meet the evening train, and under the sweetness of the twilight George's spirits arose lightly to their level, his old faith returned to him, and he looked up with a new sense of fellowship to Joe, who was filling his pipe with his favourite " towhead."

It's a pity you don't smoke," said Joe, carefully striking a match and holding his cap before it, " for it seems a gift thrown away ; and this tobacco is uncommon good, though you might fancy it a notion too strong. I've noticed that most preachers smoke, although they don't take kindly to drinking. I suppose they think it wouldn't seem the proper thing, and perhaps it wouldn't ; but there's Parson Robinson—I should think that a good, solid drink would be a real comfort to him sometimes. He's got a hard pull of it with a half share of victuals and a double share of children, so the two ends hardly ever see each other, much less think of meeting."

George hesitated for reply. He thought Joe was unnecessarily rough at times, and alluded to the ministry much too frequently. He had fancied when he left home that his blue flannel and grey tweed, with rather a jovial manner, would divest him of all resemblance to a theological student, and enable him to meet his companions on the ground of a common humanity, especially as he had at present no missionary intentions excepting those that might flow indirectly from his personal influence. Still, while he wanted Joe to recognise his broad liberality, he owed it to himself not to be loose in his expression of opinion.

" Well, yes," he said slowly, " I suppose it would help a man to forget his troubles for a time, but the getting over the spree and coming back to the same old bothers, not a bit better for the forgetting, would hardly be much comfort, even if the thing were right."

" Maybe not," replied Joe ; " I s'pose it wouldn't be comfortable if those were your feelin's, but I reckon you don't know much about it unless from hearsay. But I tell you one thing, whisky's a friend to be trusted "—adding, slowly, with a glance at George's face—" to get you into trouble if you let it get the upper hand of you. It's like a woman in that ! It begins with the same letter too, and that's another likeness ! "

George made no answer to this joke, over which Joe chuckled enough for both, and then returned to the charge :

" I've seen a good deal of life, one way and another," Joe said, " but I don't know much of parsons. Somehow they haven't been in my line ; but if I had to choose between being a parson or a doctor, I'd take the doctor by long odds. You see the world's pretty much of a hospital as far as he's concerned, and when he can't tinker a man up, he lets him slide off and nobody minds ; but the parson's different. When a man takes sick he looks kind of friendly on the doctor, because, you see, he expects him to cure him ; but when the parson comes, he tells him what a miserable sinner he is and what he's coming to at last. Now, it ain't in nature to like that, and I don't blame the fellows who say they can stand a parson when they are well, but that he's worse than a break-bone fever and no water handy when they're sick. And I shouldn't think any man would like to go about making himself unpleasant to others! Leastways, I wouldn't. Kicking Kirby used to say that he'd rather be a woman than a parson, and the force of language couldn't go further than that! He knew what he was talking about, for some of his folks were preachers; and there was good in Kirby, too! People may say what they please, but I'll allers hold to *that*!"

"Who was he?" asked George, happy to change the subject, being a little uneasy in his hold upon it, and hopeful of a story at last.

Joe looked over the hills.

"Well, he was a friend of mine when I was prospecting for oil once. I allers liked Kicking Kirby."

George sat patiently waiting, while Jim refilled his pipe and then began:

"There ain't so much to tell, but men do curious things sometimes, and Kirby, I guess, was a man few folks would have expected very much of. There was hard things said of him, but he could allers strike a blow for a friend, or hold his own with the next man, let him be who might. You see, there were a good many of us in camp, and we had fair enough luck; for the men over at Digger's Run had struck a good vein, so money was plenty and changed hands fast enough. We'd all hung together in our camp until Clint Bowers got into trouble. None of the rest of us wanted to get mixed up in the fuss, but somehow we did, and the other camp fought shy of us and played mostly among themselves; and I've allers held that it is poor fun to take out of one pocket to put into the other. Our boys had different opinions about it, and some of them held that it wasn't Clint's awkward work that they'd got mad at, but that they meant to shut down on Kirby. You see, Kirby was a very lucky player, and although pretty rough things were said about it, nobody ever got a clear handle against him, and he wasn't the kind of fellow that was pleasant to affront. Kirby used to say it was all along of Clint; that he ought to have been kept from the cards, or sent down the river; that we'd have had a good run of luck all winter if it hadn't been for him. I don't know the rights properly, but I allers thought it was about six of one and a half dozen of the other. Anyhow, there was bad blood about it, and *that* don't run uphill, you know, and so there was trouble soon enough. The boys got into words one night, and Kirby threw a mug at Clint, who out with his knife and was at Kirby like a flash. Lucky for him Clint's eyes weren't in good seeing order, and the liquor hadn't made his arm any the more steady, so Kirby only got a scratch on his arm. It showed what Clint would like to do, though, and some of the boys made pretty heavy bets on the end of it. I stuck up for Kirby, for you see I knew him pretty well, and there was true grit in him; and then, too, he was oncommon pleasant about it, and even stopped saying much about Clint's blocking up our luck over at the Run.

"Well, just about then Jack White came over from Cambria and told Clint that he'd heard that his uncle was asking around where he was. You see, Clint's uncle had a store down there, and had made a tidy pile of money, and as he hadn't any children, he said he wouldn't mind leaving it to him if he was living respectable. Clint had lived with him when he was a boy, but they hadn't got along very well, so Clint ran off. The old man didn't mind this, though, and now he wanted to find him. Jack said he was sure that if Clint was to go over and play his cards right he'd get the money. You may be sure this was a stroke of luck for Clint just then, and he didn't like to lose it; but you see he didn't look very genteel, and he knew his uncle was sharp enough to find it out. He was fat enough, for whisky never made a living skeleton of him, but it was plain that it wasn't good health that had made his nose so red, nor fine manners that had given him the cut across his cheek and bruised up his eye. The boys all allowed that he was the hardest-looking chap in the camp, and if his uncle left him his money, it wouldn't be on the strength of his good countenance! But you know he had to do something right off, and so he wrote as pretty a letter to the old man as ever I want to see; but when the answer came it said his uncle was very sick, and as he had something particular to say to him, wouldn't Clint come over at once, and enclosed he'd find the money for his fare. I tell you this stumped Clint, for he'd had another fight, and was a picture to behold.

"But here's where the surprise to us all came in. Clint was pretty well puzzled what to do, and while all the boys were advising him, Kirby spoke up. I'd noticed he was pretty quiet, but nobody could have guessed what he was thinking about. He looked some like Clint, and once had been pitched into by a new Digger's Run boy for Clint. The fellow never made the second mistake about them. It wasn't as though they were twins, but they both had brown hair and long beards, blue eyes, and were about the same build, so you couldn't have made a descriptive list of the one that wouldn't have done for the other. What Kirby said was that Clint's uncle hadn't seen him since he was a boy, and he'd expect to find him changed; and although he—that's Kirby, you know—had had hard feelin's to Clint, he wasn't a man to hold a grudge, and he'd let bygones be bygones. So if Clint thought well of it, he'd go over to Cambria, and if he found the land lay right he'd pass off for him, and make things sure.

"This struck us all of a heap, for we knew Kirby could do it if he chose and if nobody interfered with him, and that he really could cajole the old man better than Clint could; for when that fellow got wound up to talk he was allers going you five better. Some of the boys thought it rather risky, and they wanted Clint to write and say he had the typhoid fever, and so stave it off until he looked fit to go; but he knew that if he crossed his uncle now he'd likely enough lose everything, and so he thought it best to make sure and let Kirby go and see, anyhow. One thing that helped Kirby along was that his first wife had come from Cambria, and he'd heard her talk so much about the people that he knew nearly as much of them as Clint did. To make the matter sure, Clint stuffed him with all he remembered, and one night we got up a-practising ; and we made out that we were the folks, and Kirby pow-wowed to the minister, and old Miss Cranby—that was me !—and the doctor, until he knew his lesson and we'd nearly split our sides laughing.

"Of course, seeing the interest we all took in it, we weren't going to do the thing half, so we clubbed together and got Kirby a suit of storeclothes and a shiny valise, and he went off as proper as a parson—begging your pardon !—and we settled down again. He wrote pretty prompt, and said everything was going on as smooth as oil. The old man had called out that it was Clint as soon as he saw him, before he'd said a word, and Kirby wrote it would have been kind of cruel to have told him better. So he didn't. He wrote several more letters, and once Jack White had a letter from his sister saying that Clint Bowers had come home, and it was said that the old man was tickled to death with his manners, and meant to leave him all he had. This clinched it sure enough, and Clint became tip-top among the boys, and his credit was good for all the drinks he chose to order, and I must say he was liberal enough, and nobody contradicted him. He wrote to Kirby—he was all the time writing to him—but this time he told how handsome he thought it was in him to do all this, considering everything. When the answer came, Kirby said he didn't profess much religion, and he thought that generally speakin' heaping coals of fire on any one's head was against the grain, but Clint was more than welcome to his services."

"He *was* a good fellow," exclaimed George. "I don't wonder you liked him ! "

"Yes, *I* allers stood up for Kirby when the boys were hardest on him. But to finish up, for I'm telling an oncommon long yarn, at last a letter came saying that the old man was dead, and the money fixed. How much it was Kirby couldn't say yet, but he meant to hurry matters up, he said. Of course he didn't put all he meant into plain words, for it wouldn't do to trust it, and he was allers more careful than Clint, who never knew when to hush. But now Kirby said he'd have everything straight inside of two weeks, and we weren't to look for another letter from him.

"Well, it *was* surprisin' how many birds Clint broiled for Kirby the next few weeks ! You see, Kirby allers was a gentleman in his tastes, and had a particular liking for birds on toast, and of course Clint wanted to give him a proper welcome home. We never knew just when the boats were likely to come, and Clint was allers ready for a surprise."

"And he came just when he was least expected," said George,

with a bright smile; "that is the way things always happen in this world. I am sure of that."

"Why no, bless your heart, *he* never came back! I allers knew he wouldn't. He bought a share in a circus with the money, and went down South. They said he married the girl who did the flying trapeze, but I'm not sure about that. Anyway it appears he's done a good business, and I'm sure he's kept Clint's letters to him. There was true grit in Kirby, I've allers stuck to *that*! Does the pipe seem too strong for you? The wind does blow it your way, that's a fact."

# MAX ADELER
(CHAS. HEBER CLARK)
1841-1915

## A DESPERATE ADVENTURE

WANTED, four persons who are bent upon commtting suicide, to engage in a hazardous adventure. Apply, etc., to Captain Cowgill, No.—, Blank Street, after nine o' clock in the morning.

CAPTAIN COWGILL inserted the above advertisement in three of the morning papers, with only a faint expectation that it would be responded to. But the result was that between nine o'clock and noon five men and two women called at his office to inquire respecting the nature of the proposed adventure, and to offer their services in the event that it should involve nothing of a criminal character. Of these seven, Captain Cowgill selected four, three men and one young woman ; and when he had dismissed the others, he shut the door and said to the four applicants :

"What I wanted you for was this : I have made up my mind that the North Pole can never be reached by an exploring party travelling upon ships and sledges. The only route that is possibly practicable is through the air, and the only available vehicle, of course, is a balloon. But an attempt to reach the Pole in a balloon must expose the explorers to desperate risks, and it occurred to me that those risks had better be taken by persons who do not value their lives, than by persons who do. It has always seemed to me that a part of the sin of suicide lies in the fact that the life wantonly sacrificed might have been expended in a cause which would have conferred benefits, directly or indirectly, upon the human race. I have a large and superbly equipped balloon, which will be thoroughly stocked for a voyage to the Arctic regions, and, among other things, it will contain apparatus for making fresh supplies of hydrogen gas. Are you four persons willing to make the required attempt in this balloon ? "

All four of the visitors answered, " Yes."

" Were you going to sacrifice your lives, at any rate ? "

An affirmative answer was given by the four.

" Permit me to take your names," said Captain Cowgill, and he wrote them down as follows :

## A DESPERATE ADVENTURE

WILLIAM P. CRUTTER,
DR. HENRY O'HAGAN,
EDMOND JARNVILLE,
MARY DERMOTT.

Mr. Crutter was a man apparently of about sixty years, handsomely dressed, manifestly a gentleman, but with a flushed face which indicated that he had perhaps indulged to some extent in dissipation.

Dr. O'Hagan was thin, pallid, and careworn. He looked as if he were ill, and as if all joy were dead in his heart.

Mr. Jarnville appeared to be a working-man, but his countenance, sad as it was, was full of intelligence, and his manner was that of a man who had occupied a social position much above the lowest.

Miss Dermott sat, with an air of dejection, her hands in her lap, a thin and faded shawl pinned about her, and with her pale cheeks suggestive of hunger and mental suffering.

"My hope," said Captain Cowgill, "is that you will safely reach your destination, and safely return. But you fully understand that the chances are against you. For my own protection I will ask you to certify in writing that you go with full knowledge of the risks. I will inflate the balloon to-morrow. Day after to-morrow come to this office at nine o'clock, and you shall then make the ascent at once."

On the appointed day the four volunteers appeared and Captain Cowgill drove with them, in a carriage, to a yard in the outskirts of the city, where the balloon, inflated and swaying to and fro in the wind, was held to the earth with stout ropes. The three men were supplied with warm clothing, but Miss Dermott had only her threadbare shawl, and so Captain Cowgill gave her his overcoat, and two blankets which he took from the carriage.

While the voyagers were taking their places in the commodious car attached to the balloon, a young man entered the yard and hurriedly approached Captain Cowgill.

"I am going with the balloon," he said, almost fiercely, and hardly deigning to look at the Captain.

"Impossible!" said the Captain. "The crew is made up. You don't comprehend our purpose."

"Yes, I do," said the young man. "These people are would-be suicides, and they are starting for the Pole. I am going along."

"But my dear sir——" began the Captain in a tone of expostulation.

"I will go, or I will slay myself right here before you! These people are not any more tired of life than I am,"

"Let him come," said Dr. O'Hagan, gloomily.

"But," returned Captain Cowgill, "I am afraid the balloon will be overloaded."

"I am going, anyhow," said the young man, as he leaped into the car.

Captain Cowgill sighed, and said, "Well, have your own way about it."

"My name is John Winden," remarked the intruder. "I tell you, so that you will know if any one inquires after me. But I don't imagine anybody will."

Then Captain Cowgill bade farewell to the party, the ropes were loosed, and the balloon went sailing swiftly towards the clouds. Dr. O'Hagan was the navigator in charge. Presently a northeasterly current of wind struck the air-ship, and it began to move with great rapidity upon a horizontal line.

For a long time nobody in the car spoke. Indeed, the voyagers scarcely looked at each other; and none had enough curiosity to peer over the side upon the glorious landscape that lay beneath. But, after awhile, Mr. Crutter, gazing at Miss Dermott, said:

"Are you fully resolved upon self-destruction?"

"Yes," she replied.

"So am I," said Mr. Crutter.

"So am I," remarked Mr. Winden.

"So am I," observed Mr. Jarnville.

"And I, also," added Dr. O'Hagan.

"Even if we reach the Pole safely, and return, I shall not want to live," said Mr. Crutter.

"Neither shall I," said Miss Dermott.

"Nor I," remarked Mr. Winden.

"Nor I," added Dr. O'Hagan and Mr. Jarnville in a breath.

Then there was silence for the space of half an hour or more.

Mr. Crutter then remarked: "Do you know, I find this to be rather a pleasant experience, sailing along here through the ether, calmly, far above the distractions of the world? If I were not so miserable I think I should really enjoy it!"

"I am too unhappy to enjoy anything," said Miss Dermott; but this, I confess, is not unpleasant."

"Pleasant enough," remarked Mr. Winden, "if a man had no anguish in his soul."

"I had no idea that there was so much exhilaration in the upper regions of the atmosphere," said Dr. O'Hagan, rather cheerily.

"I think I feel better, myself," said Mr. Jarnville.

"It is very strange," observed Mr. Crutter, addressing Miss Dermott, "that young people, like you and Mr. Winden here, should be weary of life. That an old man like me should long for death is comprehensible. But why do you wish to die?"

Neither Mr. Winden nor Miss Dermott made any response.

"I'll tell you," said Dr. O'Hagan, throwing a bag of ballast overboard, to check the descent of the balloon. "We are all going to destruction together; and why should we not, as companions in misery, unfold our griefs to each other ? "

"It would be very proper, I think," said Mr. Crutter; "and I will begin if the rest will consent to follow."

The other four travellers agreed to do so.

"Well, I haven't much to tell," said Mr. Crutter. "The fact is, I have always had plenty of money with which to live in idleness and luxury, and I have so lived. I have tried every kind of pleasure life can afford and money buy, and I have reached a condition of satiety. Moreover, I have ruined my digestion, and I am now a sufferer from chronic dyspepsia of a horrible kind. This makes existence a burden. I am eager to quit it. That is the whole story."

"How strange the difference between us!" said Dr. O'Hagan. "I have been deeply engaged in the practice of my profession for many years; and I am utterly worn-out and broken-down with overwork. I am nervous, exhausted, irritable, and wretched, but I have lost my savings in a speculative venture, and cannot rest. I must either work or die."

"That is partly my case," said Miss Dermott. "I am friendless and poor. I cannot earn enough by sewing to buy sufficient food, and I can no longer face the misery that I have endured for so many years. I prefer death a thousand times."

"And I," said Mr. Jarnville, "am a disappointed inventor. I have for years laboured upon the construction of a smoke-consumer, but now that it is done, I have not money enough to pay for a patent; and I am starving. After trying everywhere to obtain assistance, I have resolved to give up the struggle and to find refuge in the grave."

Mr. Winden cleared his throat once or twice before beginning his story. He seemed to labour under some embarrassment. "The truth is," he said, "I was rejected last night by a young lady whom I love, and I made up my mind that life without her would not be worth having."

Nobody spoke for some time, and then Dr. O'Hagan said: "The balloon is falling, and, instead of throwing out ballast, I think it might be better, perhaps, to let it come down and to tie it to a tree, and make a fresh start with additional gas in the morning."

The other aeronauts gave their approval to this plan, and Dr. O'Hagan threw out the grapnel. It caught upon a tree top, and after some difficulty the balloon was brought down and tied fast, while the whole party stepped out of the car.

It was a wild and desolate place, but the four men soon started a fire, and while Mr. Winden and Mr. Jarnville prepared supper, Dr. O'Hagan and Mr. Crutter went to work to arrange some kind of shelter for Miss Dermott for the night.

After supper the five people gathered about the fire, and there really seemed to be a growth of cheerfulness in the party.

"I've been thinking," said Mr. Crutter, "what an outrageous

shame it is that this poor child here," pointing to Miss Dermott, " should actually be in want of food, while I have more money than I know what to do with. I'll tell you what, Miss Dermott, if you will agree to go back you can have my whole fortune. I've left it to an asylum, but I'll write a new will now, and tell you where you can find the other one, so as to tear it up."

" I don't want to go back," said Miss Dermott.

" I would if I were you," said Mr. Winden. " It's a shame for you to go upon such an awful journey as this. And I've been thinking, Mr. Jarnville, since you spoke about your smoke-consumer, that my father, who is a wealthy iron-mill owner, has offered a large reward for a perfect contrivance of that sort. If yours is a good one, he will help you to a fortune."

" I wish I had known that yesterday," said Mr. Jarnville.

" Yes," said Dr. O'Hagan, " and if I had known that Mr. Crutter here was being driven to suicide by dyspepsia, I could have helped him, for I have been very successful in treating that complaint. Let me examine you, Mr. Crutter. Yes," said the doctor, after expending a few moments looking at and talking to Mr. Crutter, " I feel certain I can cure you."

" I would have given you half my fortune yesterday for such an assurance," said Mr. Crutter. " But it is now too late."

" If I had met you then," said the Doctor, " I should not have been here now."

" Can't we all go back again ? " asked Mr. Jarnville.

" Impossible ! " said Dr. O'Hagan.

" I've got nothing to go back for," said Mr. Winden. " There is no remedy for my trouble, that I an perceive."

" There are other young ladies who could make good wives," said Mr. Crutter.

" Oh, I know, but——" said Mr. Winden hesitating, and looking furtively at Miss Dermott. Miss Dermott blushed.

" Suppose we rest for the night and sleep on the matter," said Dr. O'Hagan. " There's no use being in a hurry."

Miss Dermott retired to sleep beneath a shelter of boughs, where were strewn some pine and hemlock branches. Dr. O'Hagan covered her carefully with the blankets, and then the four men stretched themselves by the fire and fell asleep.

The conversation between the travellers must inevitably have had a good effect. The surest remedy for a morbid propensity to brood over our own troubles is to have our sympathy excited for the troubles of other people. After breakfast in the morning Mr. Crutter said :

" I have solemnly considered all that was said last night, and I have a proposition to make. Dr. O'Hagan, if you will return with Miss Dermott and Mr. Jarnville, you three may divide my fortune between you, and Mr. Winden can give a letter to his father to

Mr. Jarnville, about the smoke-consumer; and dear Mr. Winden and I will continue this journey together. How will that do?"

"I am willing to drop off and return," said Mr. Jarnville.

"I will go only on condition you will go also," said Dr. O'Hagan. "I will make you a well man if you agree."

"But," said Mr. Crutter, "it would be a shame to leave Winden here alone with this balloon. No; I have had enough of life. I'll proceed on the voyage."

"There is a good deal of force in what the Doctor says, though," remarked Mr. Winden.

"Why, you are not thinking about backing out, too, are you?" inquired Mr. Crutter.

"Well, I don't know," said Mr. Winden, looking half ashamed. "It seemed to me last night, when I got to thinking about it, that a woman's scorn is hardly worth a man's life, and I——"

"You're right!" said Mr. Crutter. "It isn't. Suppose we put the matter in this way: If Dr. O'Hagan cures me, I will pay him fifty thousand dollars in cash, and I will go into partnership with Mr. Jarnville in his invention. We can see your father about it, and you can return to him while I adopt Miss Dermott as my daughter!"

"I had thought," said Mr. Winden, "of a slightly different plan, but possibly it could not be carried out."

"What was that?" asked Dr. O'Hagan.

"Why," said Mr. Winden, "I thought, perhaps—But, no! there is no use of mentioning it."

"Out with it," said Mr. Crutter. "We want the opinions of all hands."

"I did think," said Mr. Winden, "that possibly Miss Dermott instead of becoming your daughter would consent to become my wife. Would you entertain such a proposition, Miss Dermott?"

Miss Dermott hung her head, and seemed to be covered with confusion. "I will think about it," she said.

"That means she will give her consent," said Mr. Crutter, smiling. "Let her come with me while she is thinking the matter over. Are you all agreed to my plan?" Everybody expressed assent to it, and everybody seemed very happy.

"Why, what is that?" suddenly exclaimed Miss Dermott, pointing to a distant object above them.

"I verily believe that is our balloon," said Dr. O'Hagan. "Yes, it is gone! it must have broken loose while we were at breakfast."

"Oh, well," said Mr. Crutter, "let it go! Who cares! I'll pay Captain Cowgill for his losses. And now let us see about getting home."

Mr. Winden and Mr. Jarnville started to hunt for a conveyance, and in about two hours they returned with one. The nearest railway station was thirteen miles away, but in two more hours the party reached it, and while Mr. Crutter purchased tickets for the coming train, Dr. O'Hagan went into the telegraph office and sent the following despatch :—

"Captain W. A. Cowgill. Balloon escaped. Party all safe and perfectly happy. Will reach home to-morrow morning.

(*Signed*) HENRY O'HAGAN."

# GEORGE ALFRED TOWNSEND
## 1841-1914

# CRUTCH, THE PAGE

### I. CHIPS

THE Honourable Jeems Bee, of Texas, sitting in his committee-room half an hour before the convening of Congress, waiting for his negro familiar to compound a julep, was suddenly confronted by a small boy on crutches.

"A letter!" exclaimed Mr. Bee, "with the frank of Reybold on it—that Yankeest of Pennsylvania Whigs! Yer's familiarity! Wants me to appoint one U—U—U, what?"

"Uriel Basil," said the small boy on crutches, with a clear, bold, but rather sensitive voice.

"Uriel Basil, a page in the House of Representatives, bein' an infirm, deservin' boy, willin' to work to support his mother. Infirm boy wants to be a page, on the recommendation of a Whig, to a Dimmycratic committee. I say, gen'lemen, what do you think of that, heigh?"

This last addressed to some other members of the committee, who had meantime entered.

"Infum boy will make a spry page," said the Hon. Box Izard, of Arkansaw.

"Harder to get infum page than the Speaker's eye," said the orator, Pontotoc Bibb, of Georgia.

"Harder to get both than a 'pintment in these crowded times on a opposition recommendation when all ole Virginny is yaw to be tuk care of," said Hon. Fitzchew Smy, of the Old Dominion.

The small boy standing up on crutches, with large hazel eyes swimming and wistful, so far from being cut down by these criticisms, stood straighter, and only his narrow little chest showed feeling as it breathed quickly under his brown jacket.

"I can run as fast as anybody," he said impetuously. "My sister says so. You try me!"

"Who's yo' sister, bub?"

"Joyce."

"Who's Joyce?"

"Joyce Basil—*Miss* Joyce Basil to you, gentlemen. My mother keep boarders. Mr. Reybold boards there. I think it's hard, when a little boy from the South wants to work, that the only body to help him find it is a Northern man. Don't you?"

"Good hit!" cried Jeroboam Coffee, Esq., of Alabama. "That boy would run if he could!"

"Gentlemen," said another member of the committee, the youthful abstractionist from South Carolina, who was reputed to be a great poet on the stump, the Hon. Lowndes Cleburn—"gentlemen, that boy puts the thing on its igeel merits and brings it home to us. I'll ju my juty in this issue. Abe, wha's my julep?"

"Gentlemen," said the Chairman of the Committee, Jeems Bee, "it 'pears to me that there's a social p'int right here. Reybold, bein' the only Whig on the Lake and Bayou Committee, ought to have something if he sees fit to ask for it. That's courtesy! We, of all men, gentlemen, can't afford to forget it."

"No, by durn!" cried Fitzchew Smy.

"You're right, Bee!" cried Box Izard. "You give it a constitutional set."

"Reybold," continued Jeems Bee, thus encouraged, "Reybold is (to speak out) no genius! He never will rise to the summits of usefulness. He lacks the air, the swing, the *pose*, as the sculptors say; he won't treat, but he'll lend a little money, provided he knows where you goin' with it. If he ain't open-hearted, he ain't precisely mean!"

"You're right, Bee!" (General expression.)

"Further on, it may be said that the framers of the gov'ment never intended *all* the patronage to go to one side. Mr. Jeff'son put *that* on the steelyard principle: the long beam here, the big weight of being in the minority there. Mr. Jackson only threw it considabul more on one side, but even he, gentlemen, didn't take the whole patronage from the Outs; he always left 'em enough to keep up the courtesy of the thing, and we can't go behind *him*. Not and be true to our traditions. Do I put it right?"

"Bee," said the youthful Lowndes Cleburn, extending his hand, "you put it with the lucidity and spirituality of Kulhoon himself!"

"Thanks, Cleburn," said Bee; "this is a compliment not likely to be forgotten, coming from you. Then it is agreed, as the Chayman of yo' Committee, that I accede to the request of Mr. Reybold, of Pennsylvania?"

"Aye!" from everybody.

"And now," said Mr. Bee, "as we wair all up late at the club last night, I propose we take a second julep, and as Reybold is coming in he will jine us."

"I won't give you a farthing!" cried Reybold at the door, speaking to some one. "Chips, indeed! What shall I give you money to gamble away for? A gambling beggar is worse than an imposter! No, sir! Emphatically no!"

"A dollar for four chips for brave old Beau!" said the other voice. "I've struck 'em all but you. By the State Arms! I've got rights in this distreek! Everybody pays toll to brave old Beau! Come down!"

The Northern Congressman retreated before this pertinacious mendicant into his committee-room, and his pesterer followed him closely, nothing abashed, even into the privileged cloisters of the committee. The Southern members enjoyed the situation.

"Chips, Right Honourable! Chips for old Beau. Nobody this ten-year has run as long as you. I've laid for you, and now I've fell on you. Judge Bee, the fust business befo' yo' committee this mornin' is a assessment for old Beau, who's 'way down! Rheumatiz, bettin' on the black, failure of remittances from Fauqueeah, and other casualties by wind an' flood, have put ole Beau away down. He's a institution of his country and must be sustained!"

The laughter was general and cordial among the Southerners, while the intruder pressed hard upon Mr. Reybold. He was a singular object; tall, grim, half-comical, with a leer of low familiarity in his eyes, but his waxed moustache of military proportions, his patch of goatee just above the chin, his elaborately oiled hair and flaming necktie set off his faded face with an odd gear of finery and impressiveness. His skin was that of an old *roué's*, patched up and chalked, but the features were those of a once handsome man of style and carriage.

He wore what appeared to be a cast-off spring overcoat, out of season and colour on this blustering winter day, a rich buff waistcoat of an embossed pattern, such as few persons would care to assume, save, perhaps, a gambler, negro-buyer, or fine "buck" barber. The assumption of a large and flashy pin stood in his frilled shirt-bosom. He wore watch-seals without the accompanying watch, and his pantaloons, though faded and threadbare, were once of a fine material and cut in a style of extravagant elegance, and they covered his long, shrunken, but aristocratic limbs, and were strapped beneath his boots to keep them shapely. The boots themselves had been once of varnished kid or fine calf, but they were cracked and cut, partly by use, partly for comfort; for it was plain that their wearer had the gout, by his aristocratic hobble upon a gold-mounted cane, which was not the least inconsistent garniture of mendicancy.

"Boys," said Fitzchew Smy, "I s'pose we better come down early. There's a shillin', Beau. If I had one more such constituent as you, I should resign or die premachorely!"

"There's a piece o' tobacker," said Jeems Bee languidly, "all I can afford, Beau, this mornin'. I went to a chicken-fight yesterday and lost all my change."

"Mine," said Box Izard, "is a regulation pen-knife, contributed by the United States, with the regret, Beau, that I can't 'commodate you with a pine coffin for you to git into and git away down lower than you ever been."

"Yaw's a dollar," said Pontotoc Bibb; "it'll do for me an' Lowndes Cleburn, who's a poet and genius, and never has no money. This buys me off, Beau, for a month."

The gorgeous old mendicant took them all grimly and leering, and then pounced upon the Northern man, assured by their twinkles and winks that the rest expected some sport.

"And now, Right Honourable from the banks of the Susquehanna, Colonel Reybold—you see, I got your name; I ben a layin' for you!—come down handsome for the Uncle and ornament of this capital and country. What's yore's?"

"Nothing," said Reybold in a quiet way. "I cannot give a man like you anything, even to get rid of him."

"You're mean," said the stylish beggar, winking to the rest. "You hate to put your hands down in yer pocket, mightily. I'd rather be ole Beau, and live on suppers at the faro banks, than love a dollar like you!"

"I'll make it a V for Beau," said Pontotoc Bibb, "if he gives him a rub on the raw like that another lick. Durn a mean man, Cleburn!"

"Come down, Northerner," pressed the incorrigible loafer again; "it don't become a Right Honourable to be so mean with old Beau."

The little boy on crutches, who had been looking at this scene in a state of suspense and interest for some time, here cried hotly:

"If you say Mr. Reybold is a mean man, you tell a story, you nasty beggar! He often gives things to me and Joyce, my sister. He's just got me work, which is the best thing to give; don't you think so, gentlemen?"

"Work," said Lowndes Cleburn, "is the best thing to give away, and the most onhandy thing to keep. I like play the best—Beau's kind o' play!"

"Yes," said Jeroboam Coffee; "I think I prefer to make the chips fly out of a table more than out of a log."

"I like to work!" cried the little boy, his hazel eyes shining, and his poor, narrow body beating with unconscious fervour, half suspended on his crutches, as if he were of that good descent and natural spirit which could assert itself without bashfulness in the presence of older people. "I like to work for my mother. If I was strong, like other little boys, I would make money for her, so that she shouldn't keep any boarders—except Mr. Reybold. Oh! she has to work a lot; but she's proud and won't tell anybody. All the money I get I mean to give her; but I wouldn't have it if I had to beg for it like that man!"

"O Beau," said Colonel Jeems Bee, "you've cotched it now! Reybold's even with you. Little Crutch has cooked your goose! Crutch is right eloquent when his wind will permit."

The fine old loafer looked at the boy, whom he had not previously noticed, and it was observed that the last shaft had hurt his pride. The boy returned his wounded look with a straight, undaunted, spirited glance, out of a child's nature. Mr Reybold was impressed with something in the attitude of the two, which made him forget his own interest in the controversy.

Beau answered with a tone of nearly tender pacification :

" Now, my little man ; come, don't be hard on the old veteran ! He's down, old Beau is, sence the time he owned his blooded pacer and dined with the *Corps Diplomatique* ; Beau's down sence then ; but don't call the old feller hard names. We take it back, don't we ? we take *them* words back ? "

" There's a angel somewhere," said Lowndes Cleburn, " even in a Washington bummer, which responds to a little chap on crutches with a clear voice. Whether the angel takes the side of the bummer or the little chap, is a p'int out of our jurisdiction. Abe, give Beau a julep. He seems to have been demoralised by little Crutch's last."

" Take them hard words back, Bub," whined the licensed mendicant, with either real or affected pain ; " it's a p'int of honour I'm a-standin' on. Do, now, little Major ! "

" I shan't ! " cried the boy. " Go and work like me. You're big, and you called Mr. Reybold mean. Haven't you got a wife or little girl, or nobody to work for ? You ought to work for yourself, anyhow. Oughtn't he, gentlemen ? "

Reybold, who had slipped around by the little cripple and was holding him in a caressing way from behind, looked over to Beau and was even more impressed with that generally undaunted worthy's expression. It was that of acute and suffering sensibility, perhaps the effervescence of some little remaining pride, or it might have been a twinge of the gout. Beau looked at the little boy, suspended there with the weak back and the narrow chest, and that scintillant, sincere spirit beaming out with courage born in the stock he belonged to. Admiration, conciliation, and pain were in the ruined vagrants eyes. Reybold felt a sense of pity. He put his hand in his pocket and drew forth a dollar.

" Here, Beau," he said, " I'll make an exception. You seem to have some feeling. Don't mind the boy ! "

In an instant the coin was flying from his hand through the air. The beggar, with a livid face and clinched cane, confronted the Congressman like a maniac.

" You bilk ! " he cried. " You supper customer ! I'll brain you ! I had rather parted with my shoes at a dolly shop and gone gadding the hoof, without a doss to sleep on—a town pauper, done on the vag—than to have been made scurvy in the sight of that child and deserve his words of shame ! "

He threw his head upon the table and burst into tears.

## II. HASH

Mrs. Tryphonia Basil kept a boarding-house of the usual kind on Four-and-a-Half Street. Male clerks—there were no female clerks in the Government in 1854—to the number of half a dozen, two old bureau officers, an architect's assistant, Reybold, and certain temporary visitors made up the table. The landlady was the mistress ; the slave was Joyce.

Joyce Basil was a fine-looking girl, who did not know it—a fact so astounding as to be fitly related only in fiction. She did not know it, because she had to work so hard for the boarders and her mother. Loving her mother with the whole of her affection, she had suffered all the pains and penalties of love from that repository. She was to-day upbraided for her want of coquetry and neatness; to-morrow, for proposing to desert her mother and elope with a person she had never thought of. The mainstay of the establishment, she was not aware of her usefulness. Accepting every complaint and outbreak as if she deserved it, the poor girl lived at the capital a beautiful scullion, an unsalaried domestic, and daily forwarded the food to the table, led in the chamber work, rose from bed unrested and retired with all her bones aching. But she was of a natural grace that hard work could not make awkward ; work only gave her bodily power, brawn, and form. Though no more than seventeen years of age, she was a superb woman, her chest thrown forward, her back like the torso of a *Venus de Milo*, her head placed on the throat of a Minerva, and the nature of a child moulded in the form of a matron. Joyce Basil had black hair and eyes— very long, excessive hair, that in the mornings she tied up with haste so imperfectly that once Reybold had seen it drop like a cloud around her and nearly touched her feet. At that moment, seeing him, she blushed. He pleaded, for once, a Congressman's impudence, and without her objection wound that great crown of woman's glory around her head, and, as he did so, the perfection of her form and skin, and the overrunning health and height of the Virginia girl, struck him so thoroughly that he said :

"Miss Joyce, I don't wonder that Virginia is the mother of Presidents."

Between Reybold and Joyce there were already the delicate relations of a girl who did not know that she was a woman and a man who knew she was beautiful and worthy. He was a man vigilant over himself, and the poverty and menial estate of Joyce Basil were already insuperable obstacles to marrying her, but still he was attracted by her insensibility that he could ever have regarded her in the light of marriage. "Who was her father, the Judge?" he used to reflect. The Judge was a favourite topic with Mrs. Basil at the table.

"Mr. Reybold," she would say, "you commercial people of the Nawth can't hunt, I believe. Jedge Basil is now on the mountains of Fawquear hunting the plova. His grandfather's estate is full of plova."

If, by chance, Reybold saw a look of care on Mrs. Basil's face, he inquired for the Judge, her husband, and found he was still shooting on the Occequan.

"Does he never come to Washington, Mrs. Basil?" asked Reybold one day, when his mind was very full of Joyce, the daughter.

"Not while Congress is in session," said Mrs. Basil. "It's a little too much of the *oi polloi* for the Judge. His family, you may not know, Mr. Reybold, air of the Basils of King George. They married into the Tayloze of Mount Snaffle. The Tayloze of Mount Snaffle have Ingin blood in their veins—the blood of Pokyhuntus. They dropped the name of Taylor, which had got to be common through a want of Ingin blood, and spelled it with a E. It used to be Taylor, but now it's Tayloze."

On another occasion, at sight of Joyce Basil cooking over the fire, against whose flame her moulded arms took momentary roses upon their ivory, Reybold said to himself: "Surely there is something above the common in the race of this girl." And he asked the question of Mrs. Basil:

"Madame, how was the Judge, your husband, at the last advices?"

"Hunting the snipe, Mr. Reybold. I suppose you do not have the snipe in the Nawth. It is the aristocratic fowl of the Old Dominion. Its bill is only shorter than its legs, and it will not brown at the fire, to perfection, unless upon a silver spit. Ah! when the Jedge and myself were young, before his land troubles overtook us, we went to the springs with our own silver and carriages, Mr. Reybold."

Looking up at Mrs. Basil, Reybold noticed a pallor and flush alternately, and she evaded his eye.

Once Mrs. Basil borrowed a hundred dollars from Reybold in advance of board, and the table suffered in consequence.

"The Judge," she had explained, "is short of taxes on his Fawquear lands. It's a desperate moment with him." Yet in two days the Judge was shooting blue-winged teal at the mouth of the Accotink, and his entire indifference to his family set Reybold to thinking whether the Virginia husband and father was anything more than a forgetful savage. The boarders, however, made very merry over the absent unknown. If the beefsteak was tough, threats were made to send for "the Judge," and let him try a tooth on it; if scant, it was suggested that the Judge might have paid a gunning visit to the premises and inspected the larder. The daughter of the house kept such an even temper, and was so obliging within the limitations of the establishment, that many a boarder went to his department without complaint, though with an appetite only partly satisfied. The boy, Uriel, also was the guardsman of the household, old-faced as if with the responsibility of taking care

of two woman. Indeed, the children of the landlady were so well
behaved and prepossessing that, compared with Mrs. Basil's shabby
*hauteur* and garrulity, the legend of the Judge seemed to require
no other foundation than offspring of such good spirit and intonation.

Mrs. Tryphonia Basil was no respecter of persons. She kept
boarders, she said, as a matter of society, and to lighten the load
of the Judge. He had very little idea that she was making a mercantile matter of hospitality, but, as she feelingly remarked, " the
old families are misplaced in such times as these yer, when the
departments are filled with Dutch, Yankees, Crackers, Pore
Whites, and other foreigners." Her manner was, at periods, in-
solent to Mr. Reybold, who seldom protested, out of regard to the
daughter and the little Page; he was a man of quite ordinary
appearance, saying little, never making speeches or soliciting notice,
and he accepted his fare and quarters with little or no complaint.

" Crutch," he said one day to the little boy, " did you ever see
your father ? "

" No, I never saw him, Mr. Reybold, but I've had letters from
him."

" Don't he ever come to see you when you are sick ? "

" No. He wanted to come once when my back was very sick,
and I laid in bed weeks and weeks, sir, dreaming, oh ! such beautiful things. I thought mamma and sister and I were all with papa
in that old home we are going to some day. He carried me up and
down in his arms, and I felt such rest that I never knew anything
like it, when I woke up, and my back began to ache again. I
wouldn't let mamma send for him, though, because she said he
was working for us all to make our fortunes, and get doctors for
me, and clothes and school for dear Joyce. So I sent him my love,
and told papa to work, and he and I would bring the family out
all right."

" What did your papa seem like in that dream, my little boy ? "

" Oh ! sir, his forehead was bright as the sun. Sometimes I see
him now when I am tired at night after running all day through
Congress."

Reybold's eyes were full of tears as he listened to the boy, and,
turning aside, he saw Joyce Basil weeping also.

" My dear girl," he said to her, looking up significantly, " I fear
he will see his great Father very soon."

Reybold had few acquaintances, and he encouraged the landlady's
daughter to go about with him when she could get a leisure hour or
evening. Sometimes they took a seat at the theatre, more often
at the old Ascension Church, and once they attended a President's
reception. Joyce had the bearing of a well-bred lady, and the purity
of thought of a child. She was noticed as if she had been a new
and distinguished arrival in Washington.

" Ah ! Reybold," said Pontotoc Bibb, " I understand, ole feller, what keeps you so quiet now. You've got a wife unbeknown to the Kemittee! and a happy man I know you air."

It pleased Reybold to hear this, and deepened his interest in the landlady's family. His attention to her daughter stirred Mrs. Basil's pride and revolt together.

"My daughter, Colonel Reybold," she said, "is designed for the army. The Judge never writes to me but he says: 'Tryphonee, be careful that you impress upon my daughter the importance of the military profession. My mother, grandmother, and great-grandmother married into the army, and no girl of the Basil stock shall descend to civil life while I can keep the Fawquear estates.'"

"Madame," said the Congressman, "will you permit me to make the suggestion that your daughter is already a woman and needs a father's care if she is ever to receive it. I beseech you to impress this subject upon the Judge. His estates cannot be more precious to his heart if he is a man of honour; nay, what is better than honour, his duty requires him to come to the side of these children, though he be ever so constrained by business or pleasure to attend to more worldly concerns."

"The Judge," exclaimed Mrs. Basil, much miffed, "is a man of hereditary ijees, Colonel Reybold. He is now in pursuit of the—ahem!—the Kinvas-back on his ancestral waters. If he should hear that you suggests a pacific life and the grovelling associations of the capital for him, he might call you out, sir!"

Reybold said no more; but one evening when Mrs. Basil was absent, called across the Potomac, as happened frequently, at the summons of the Judge—and on such occasions she generally requested a temporary loan or a slight advance of board—Reybold found Joyce Basil in the little parlour of the dwelling. She was alone and in tears, but the little boy Uriel slept before the chimney-fire on a rug, and his pale thin face, catching the glow of the burning wood, looked beautiful as Reybold addressed the young woman.

"Miss Joyce," he said, "our little brother works too hard. Is there never to be relief for him? His poor, withered body, slung on those crutches for hours and hours, racing up the aisles of the House with stronger pages, is wearing him out. His ambition is very interesting to see, but his breath is growing shorter and his strength is frailer every week. Do you know what it will lead to?"

"O my Lord!" she said in the negrofied phrase natural to her latitude, "I wish it was no sin to wish him dead."

"Tell me, my friend," said Reybold, "can I do nothing to assist you both? Let me understand you. Accept my sympathy and confidence. Where is Uriel's father? What is this mystery?"

She did not answer.

"It is for no idle curiosity that I ask," he continued. "I will appeal to him for his family, even at the risk of his resentment. Where is he?"

"Oh, do not ask!" she exclaimed. "You want me to tell you only the truth. He is *there*.

She pointed to one of the old portraits in the room—a picture fairly painted by some provincial artist—and it revealed a handsome face, a little voluptuous, but aristocratic, the shoulders clad in a martial cloak, the neck in ruffles, and a diamond in the shirt bosom. Reybold studied it with all his mind.

"Then it is no fiction," he said, "that you have a living father, one answering to your mother's description. Where have I seen that face? Has some irreparable mistake, some miserable controversy, alienated him from his wife? Has he another family?"

She answered with spirit:

"No, sir. He is my father and my brother's only. But I can tell you no more."

"Joyce," he said, taking her hand, "this is not enough. I will not press you to betray any secret you may possess. Keep it. But of yourself I must know something more. You are almost a woman. You are beautiful."

At this he tightened his grasp, and it brought him closer to her side. She made a little struggle to draw away, but it pleased him to see that when the first modest opposition had been tried she sat quite happily, though trembling, with his arm around her.

"Joyce," he continued, "you have a double duty: one to your mother and this poor invalid, whose journey toward that Father's house not made with hands is swiftly hastening; another duty toward your nobler self—the future that is in you and your woman's heart. I tell you again that you are beautiful, and the slavery to which you are condemning yourself for ever is an offence against the Creator of such perfection. Do you know what it is to love?"

"I know what it is to feel kindness," she answered after a time of silence. "I ought to know no more. Your goodness is very dear to me. We never sleep, brother and I, but we say your name together, and ask God to bless you."

Reybold sought in vain to suppress a confession he had resisted. The contact of her form, her large dark eyes now fixed upon him in emotion, the birth of the conscious woman in the virgin and her affection still in the leashes of a slavish sacrifice, tempted him onward to the conquest.

"I am about to retire from Congress," he said. "It is no place for me in times so insubstantial. There is darkness and beggary ahead for all your Southern race. There is a crisis coming which will be followed by desolation. The generation to which your parents belong is doomed! I open my arms to you, dear girl, and offer you a home never yet gladdened by a wife. Accept it, and leave Washington with me and with your brother. I love you wholly."

A happy light shone in her face a moment. She was weary to the

bone with the day's work and had not the strength, if she had the
will, to prevent the Congressman drawing her to his heart. Sobbing
there, she spoke with bitter agony.

"Heaven bless you, dear Mr. Reybold, with a wife good enough
to deserve you! Blessings on your generous heart. But I cannot
leave Washington. I love another here!"

### III. DUST

The Lake and Bayou Committee reaped the reward of a good
action. Crutch, the page, as they all called Uriel Basil, affected the
sensibility of the whole committee to the extent that profanity
almost ceased there, and vulgarity became a crime in the presence
of a child. Gentle words and wishes became the rule; a glimmer
of reverence and a thought of piety were not unknown in that little
chamber.

"Dog my skin!" said Jeems Bee, "if I ever made a 'pintment
that give me sech satisfaction! I feel as if I had sot a nigger free!"

The youthful abstractionist, Lowndes Cleburn, expressed it even
better. "Crutch," he said, "is like a angel reduced to his bones.
Them air wings or pinions, that he might have flew off with, being
a pair of crutches, keeps him here to tarry awhile in our service.
But, gentlemen, he's not got long to stay. His crutches is growing
too heavy for that expanding sperit. Some day we'll look up and
miss him through our tears."

They gave him many a present; they put a silver watch in his
pocket and dressed him in a jacket with gilt buttons. He had a
bouquet of flowers to take home every day to that marvellous sister
of whom he spoke so often; and there were times when the whole
committee, seeing him drop off to sleep as he often did through frail
and weary nature, sat silently watching lest he might be wakened
before his rest was over. But no persuasion could take him off the
floor of Congress. In that solemn old Hall of Representatives, under
the semi-circle of grey columns, he darted with agility from noon to
dusk, keeping speed upon his crutches with the healthiest of the
pages, and racing into the document-room, and through the dark
and narrow corridors of the old Capitol loft, where the House library
was lost in twilight. Visitors looked with interest and sympathy
at the narrow back and body of this invalid child, whose eyes were
full of bright, beaming spirit. He sometimes nodded on the steps
by the Speaker's chair; and these spells of dreaminess and fatigue
increased as his disease advanced upon his wasting system. Once
he did not awaken at all until adjournment. The great Congress
and audience passed out, and the little fellow still slept, with his
head against the Clerk's desk, while all the other pages were grouped
around him, and they finally bore him off to the committee-room
in their arms, where, among the sympathetic watchers, was old

Beau. When Uriel opened his eyes the old mendicant was looking into them.

"Ah! little Major," he said, "poor Beau has been waiting for you to take those bad words back. Old Beau thought it was all bob with his little cove."

"Beau," said the boy, "I've had such a dream! I thought my dear father, who is working so hard to bring me home to him, had carried me out on the river in a boat. We sailed through the greenest marshes, among white lilies, where the wild ducks were tame as they can be. All the ducks were diving and diving, and they brought up long stalks of celery from the water and gave them to us. Father ate all his. But mine turned into lilies and grew up so high that I felt myself going with them, and the higher I went the more beautiful grew the birds. Oh! let me sleep and see if it will be so again."

The outcast raised his gold-headed cane and hobbled up and down the room with a laced handkerchief at his eyes.

"Great God!" he exclaimed, "another generation is going out, and here I stay without a stake, playing a lone hand for ever and for ever."

"Beau," said Reybold, "there's hope while one can feel. Don't go away until you have a good word from our little passenger."

The outstretched hand of the Northern Congressman was not refused by the vagrant, whose eccentric sorrow yet amused the Southern Committeemen.

"Ole Beau's jib-boom of a mustache 'll put his eye out," said Pontotoc Bibb, "ef he fetches another groan like that."

"Beau's very shaky around the hams an' knees," said Box Izard; "he's been a good figger, but even figgers can lie ef they stand up too long."

The little boy unclosed his eyes and looked around on all those kindly, watching faces.

"Did anybody fire a gun?" he said. "Oh! no. I was only dreaming that I was hunting with father, and he shot at the beautiful pheasants that were making such a whirring of wings for me. It was music. When can I hunt with father, dear gentlemen?"

They all felt the tread of the mighty hunter before the Lord very near at hand—the hunter whose name is Death.

"There are little tiny birds along the beach," muttered the boy. "They twitter and run into the surf and back again, and I am one of them! I must be, for I feel the water cold, and yet I see you all, so kind to me! Don't whistle for me now; for I don't get much play, gentlemen! Will the Speaker turn me out if I play with the beach birds just once? I'm only a little boy working for my mother."

"Dear Uriel," whispered Reybold, "here's Old Beau, to whom you once spoke angrily. Don't you see him?"

The little boy's eyes came back from far-land somewhere, and he saw the ruined gamester at his feet.

"Dear Beau," he said, "I can't get off to go home with you. They won't excuse me, and I give all my money to mother. But you go to the back gate. Ask for Joyce. She'll give you a nice warm meal every day. Go with him, Mr. Reybold! If you ask for him it will be all right: for Joyce—dear Joyce!—she loves you."

The beach birds played again along the strand; the boy ran into the foam with his companions and felt the spray once more. The Mighty Hunter shot his bird—a little cripple that twittered the sweetest of them all. Nothing moved in the solemn chamber of the committee but the voice of an old forsaken man, sobbing bitterly.

### IV. CAKE

The funeral was over, and Mr. Reybold marvelled much that the Judge had not put in an appearance. The whole committee had attended the obsequies of Crutch and acted as pall-bearers. Reybold had escorted the page's sister to the Congressional cemetry, and had observed even old Beau to come with a wreath of flowers and hobble to the grave and deposit them there. But the Judge, remorseless in death as frivolous in life, never came near his mourning wife and daughter in their severest sorrow. Mrs. Tryphonia Basil, seeing that this singular want of behaviour on the Judge's part was making some ado, raised her voice above the general din of meals.

"Jedge Basil," she exclaimed, "has been on his Tennessee purchase. These Christmas times there's no getting through the snow in the Cumberland Gap. He's stopped off thaw to shoot the—ahem!—the wild torkey—a great passion with the Jedge. His half-uncle, Gineral Johnson, of Awkinso, was a torkey-killer of high celebrity. He was a Deshay on his Maw's side. I s'pose you haven't the torkey in the Dutch country, Mr. Reybold?"

"Madame," said Reybold, in a quieter moment, "have you written to the Judge the fact of his son's death?"

"Oh yes—to Fawquear."

"Mrs. Basil," continued the Congressman, "I want you to be explicit with me. Where is the Judge, your husband, at this moment?"

"Excuse me, Colonel Reybold, this is a little of a assumption, sir. The Jedge might call you out, sir, for intruding upon his incog. He's very fine on his incog., you air awair."

"Madame," exclaimed Reybold straightforwardly, "there are reasons why I should communicate with your husband. My term in Congress is nearly expired. I might arouse your interest, if I chose, by recalling to your mind the memorandum of about seven hundred dollars in which you are my debtor. That would be a reason for seeing your husband anywhere north of the Potomac, but I do not intend to mention it. Is he aware—are you?—that Joyce Basil is in love with some one in this city?"

Mrs. Basil drew a long breath, raised both hands, and ejaculated: "Well, I declaw!"

"I have it from her own lips," continued Reybold. "She told me as a secret, but all my suspicions are awakened. If I can prevent it, madame, that girl shall not follow the example of hundreds of her class in Washington, and descend, through the boarding-house or the lodging quarter, to be the wife of some common and unambitious clerk, whose penury she must some day sustain by her labour. I love her myself, but I will never take her until I know her heart to be free. Who is this lover of your daughter?"

An expression of agitation and cunning passed over Mrs. Basil's face. "Colonel Reybold," she whined, "I pity your blasted hopes. If I was a widow, they should be comfoted. Alas! my daughter is in love with one of the Fitzchews of Fawqueeah. His parents is cousins of the Jedge, and attached to the military."

The Congressman looked disappointed, but not yet satisfied.

"Give me at once the address of your husband," he spoke. "If you do not, I shall ask your daughter for it, and she cannot refuse me."

The mistress of the boarding-house was not without alarm, but she dispelled it with an outbreak of anger. "If my daughter disobeys her mother," she cried, "and betrays the Jedge's incog., she is no Basil, Colonel Reybold. The Basils repudiate her, and she may jine the Dutch and other foreigners at her pleasure."

"That is her only safety," exclaimed Reybold. "I hope to break every string that holds her to yonder barren honour and exhausted soil." He pointed toward Virginia, and hastened away to the Capitol. All the way up the squalid and muddy avenue of that day he mused and wondered: "Who is Fitzhugh? Is there such a person any more than a Judge Basil? And yet there *is* a Judge, for Joyce has told me so. *She*, at least, cannot lie to me. At last," he thought, "the dream of my happiness is over. Invincible in her prejudice as all these Virginians, Joyce Basil has made her bed among the starveling First Families, and there she means to live and die. Five years hence she will have her brood around her. In ten years she will keep a boarding-house and borrow money. As her daughters grow up to the stature and grace of their mother, they will be proud and poor again and breed in and out, until the race will perish from the earth."

Slow to love, deeply interested, baffled but unsatisfied, Reybold made up his mind to cut his perplexity short by leaving the city for the county of Fauquier. As he passed down the avenue late that afternoon, he turned into E street, near the theatre, to engage a carriage for his expedition. It was a street of livery stables, gambling dens, drinking houses, and worse; murders had been

committed along its sidewalks. The more pretentious *canaille* of
the city harboured there to prey on the hotels close at hand and
aspire to the chance acquaintance of gentlemen. As Reybold stood
in an archway of this street, just as the evening shadows deepened
above the line of sunset, he saw something pass which made his
heart start to his throat and fastened him to the spot. Veiled and
walking fast, as if escaping detection or pursuit, the figure of Joyce
Basil flitted over the pavement and disappeared in a door about
the middle of this Alsatian quarter of the capital.

"What house is that?" he asked of a constable passing by,
pointing to the door she entered.

"Gambling den," answered the officer. "It used to be old Phil
Pendleton's."

Reybold knew the reputation of the house : a resort for the scions
of the old tidewater families, where hospitality thinly veiled the
paramount design of plunder. The connection established the
truth of Mrs. Basil's statement. Here, perhaps, already married
to the dissipated heir of some unproductive estate, Joyce Basil's
lot was cast for ever. It might even be that she had been tempted
here by some wretch whose villainy she knew not of. Reybold's
brain took fire at the thought, and he pursued the fugitive into the
doorway. A negro steward unfastened a slide and peeped at
Reybold knocking in the hall ; and, seeing him of respectable
appearance, bowed ceremoniously as he let down a chain and opened
the door.

"Short cards in the front saloon," he said ; "supper and faro
back. Chambers on the third floor. Walk up."

Reybold only tarried a moment at the gaming tables, where the
silent, monotonous deal from the tin box, the lazy stroke of the
markers, and the transfer of ivory "chips" from card to card of
the sweatcloth, impressed him as the dullest form of vice he had
ever found. Treading softly up the stairs, he was attracted by the
light of a door partly ajar, and a deep groan, as of a dying person.
He peeped through the crack of the door and beheld Joyce Vasil
leaning over an old man, whose brow she moistened with her handkerchief. "Dear father," he heard her say, and it brought consolation to more than the sick man. Reybold threw open the door
and entered into the presence of Mrs. Basil and her daughter. The
former arose with surprise and shame and cried :

"Jedge Basil, the Dutch have hunted you down. He's here—
the Yankee creditor."

Joyce Basil held up her hand in imploration, but Reybold did not
heed the woman's remark. He felt a weight rising from his heart,
and the blindness of many months lifted from his eyes. The dying
mortal upon the bed, over whose face the blue billow of death was
rolling rapidly, and whose eyes sought in his daughter's the promise of mercy from on high, was the mysterious parent who had

never arrived—the Judge from Fauquier. In that old man's long waxed moustache, crimped hair, and threadbare finery the Congressman recognised old Beau, the outcast gamester and mendicant, and the father of Joyce and Uriel Basil.

"Colonel Reybold," faltered that old wreck of manly beauty and of promise long departed, "old Beau's passing in his checks. The chant coves will be telling to-morrow what they know of his life in the papers, but I've dropped a cold deck on 'em these twenty years. Not one knows old Beau, the Bloke, to be Tom Basil, cadet at West Point in the last generation. I've kept nothing of my own but my children's good names. My little boy never knew me to be his father. I tried to keep the secret from my daughter, but her affection broke down my disguises. Thank God! the old rounder's deal has run out at last. For his wife he'll flash her diles no more, nor be taken on the vag."

"Basil," said Reybold, "what trust do you leave to me in your family?"

Mrs. Basil strove to interpose, but the dying man raised his voice: "Tryphonee can go home to Fauquier. She was always welcome there—without me. I was disinherited. But here, Colonel! My last drop of blood is in the girl. She loves you."

A rattle arose in the sinner's throat. He made an effort, and transferred his daughter's hand to the Congressman's. Not taking it away, she knelt with her future husband at the bedside and raised her voice:

"Lord, when Thou comest into Thy Kingdom, remember him!"

## AMBROSE BIERCE
1842–? 1914

# THE MAN AND THE SNAKE

It is of veritabyll report, and attested of so many that there be nowe of wyse and learned none to gaynsaye it, that ye serpente hys eye hath a magnetick propertie that whosoe falleth into its svasion is drawn forwards in despyte of his wille, and perisheth miserabyll by ye creature hys byte.

I

STRETCHED at ease upon a sofa, in gown and slippers, Harker Brayton smiled as he read the foregoing sentence in old Morryster's *Marvells of Science*. "The only marvel in the matter," he said to himself, "is that the wise and learned in Morryster's day should have believed such nonsense as is rejected by most of even the ignorant in ours."

A train of reflections followed—for Brayton was a man of thought—and he unconsciously lowered his book without altering the direction of his eyes. As soon as the volume had gone below the line of sight, something in an obscure corner of the room recalled his attention to his surroundings. What he saw, in the shadow under his bed, were two small points of light, apparently about an inch apart. They might have been reflections of the gas jet above him, in metal nail heads; he gave them but little thought and resumed his reading. A moment later something—some impulse which it did not occur to him to analyse—impelled him to lower the book again and seek for what he saw before. The points of light were still there. They seemed to have become brighter than before shining with a greenish lustre which he had not at first observed. He thought, too, that they might have moved a trifle—were somewhat nearer. They were still too much in shadow, however, to reveal their nature and origin to an indolent attention, and he resumed his reading. Suddenly something in the text suggested a thought which made him start and drop the book for the third time to the side of the sofa, whence, escaping from his hand, it fell sprawling to the floor, back upward. Brayton, half risen, was staring intently into the obscurity beneath the bed, where the points of light shone with, it seemed to him, an added fire. His attention was now fully aroused, his gaze eager and imperative. It disclosed, almost directly beneath the foot-rail of the bed, the coils of a large serpent—the points of light were its eyes! Its horrible head, thrust flatly forth from the innermost coil and resting upon the outermost, was directed straight toward him, the definition of the wide, brutal jaw and the idiot-like forehead serving to show the direction of its malevolent gaze. The eyes were no longer merely luminous points; they looked into his own with a meaning, a malign significance.

## II

A snake in a bedroom of a modern city dwelling of the better sort is, happily, not so common a phenomenon as to make explanation altogether needless. Harker Brayton, a bachelor of thirty-five, a scholar, idler, and something of an athlete, rich, popular, and of sound health, had returned to San Francisco from all manner of remote and unfamiliar countries. His tastes, always a trifle luxurious, had taken on an added exuberance from long privation; and the resources of even the Castle Hotel being inadequate to their perfect gratification, he had gladly accepted the hospitality of his friend, Dr. Druring, the distinguished scientist. Dr. Druring's house, a large, old-fashioned one in what was now an obscure quarter of the city, had an outer and visible aspect of proud reserve. It plainly would not associate with the contiguous elements of its altered environment, and appeared to have developed some of the eccentricities which come of isolation. One of these was a "wing," conspicuously irrelevant in point of architecture, and no less rebellious in the matter of purpose; for it was a combination of laboratory, menagerie, and museum. It was here that the doctor indulged the scientific side of his nature in the study of such forms of animal life as engaged his interest and comforted his taste—which, it must be confessed, ran rather to the lower forms. For one of the higher types nimbly and sweetly to recommend itself unto his gentle senses, it had at least to retain certain rudimentary characteristics allying it to such "dragons of the prime" as toads and snakes. His scientific sympathies were distinctly reptilian; he loved nature's vulgarians and described himself as the Zola of zoology. His wife and daughters, not having the advantage to share his enlightened curiosity regarding the works and ways of our ill-starred fellow-creatures, were, with needless austerity, excluded from what he called the Snakery, and doomed to companionship with their own kind, though, to soften the rigours of their lot, he had permitted them, out of his great wealth, to outdo the reptiles in the gorgeousness of their surroundings and to shine with a superior splendour.

Architecturally, and in point of "furnishing," the Snakery had a severe simplicity befitting the humble circumstances of its occupants, many of whom, indeed, could not safely have been intrusted with the liberty which is necessary to the full enjoyment of luxury, for they had the troublesome peculiarity of being alive. In their own apartments, however, they were under as little personal restraint as was compatible with their protection from the baneful habit, of swallowing one another; and, as Brayton had thoughtfully been apprised, it was more than a tradition that some of them had at divers times been found in parts of the premises where it would have embarrassed them to explain their presence. Despite the Snakery and its uncanny associations—to which, indeed, he gave little attention—Brayton found life at the Druring mansion very much to his mind.

### III

Beyond a smart shock of surprise and a shudder of mere loathing, Mr. Brayton was not greatly affected. His first thought was to ring the call-bell and bring a servant; but, although the bell-cord dangled within easy reach, he made no movement toward it; it had occurred to his mind that the act might subject him to the suspicion of fear, which he certainly did not feel. He was more keenly conscious of the incongruous nature of the situation than affected by its perils; it was revolting, but absurd.

The reptile was of a species with which Brayton was unfamiliar. Its length he could only conjecture; the body at the largest visible part seemed about as thick as his forearm. In what way was it dangerous, if in any way? Was it venomous? Was it a constrictor? His knowledge of nature's danger signals did not enable him to say; he had never deciphered the code.

If not dangerous, the creature was at least offensive. It was *de trop*—" matter out of place "—an impertinence. The gem was unworthy of the setting. Even the barbarous taste of our time and country, which had loaded the walls of the room with pictures, the floor with furniture, and the furniture with bric-à-brac, had not quite fitted the place for this bit of the savage life of the jungle. Besides—insupportable thought!—the exhalations of its breath mingled with the atmosphere which he himself was breathing!

These thoughts shaped themselves with greater or less definition in Brayton's mind and begot action. The process is what we call consideration and decision. It is thus that we are wise and unwise. it is thus that the withered leaf in an autumn breeze shows greater or less intelligence than its fellows, falling upon the land or upon the lake. The secret of human action is an open one: something contracts our muscles. Does it matter if we give to the preparatory molecular changes the name of will?

Brayton rose to his feet and prepared to back softly away from the snake, without disturbing it, if possible, and through the door People retire so from the presence of the great, for greatness is power, and power is a menace. He knew that he could walk backward without obstruction, and find the door without error. Should the monster follow, the taste which had plastered the walls with paintings had consistently supplied a rack of murderous Oriental weapons from which he could snatch one to suit the occasion. In the meantime the snake's eyes burned with a more pitiless malevolence than ever.

Brayton lifted his right foot free of the floor to step backward. That moment he felt a strong aversion to doing so.

"I am accounted brave," he murmured; " is bravery, then, no more than pride? Because there are none to witness the shame shall I retreat?" He was steadying himself with his right hand upon the back of the chair, his foot suspended.

"Nonsense!" he said aloud; "I am not so great a coward as to fear to seem to myself afraid."

He lifted the foot a little higher by slightly bending the knee, and thrust it sharply to the floor—an inch in front of the other! He could not think how that occurred. A trial with the left foot had the same result; it was again in advance of the right. The hand upon the chair back was grasping it; the arm was straight, reaching somewhat backward. One might have seen that he was reluctant to lose his hold. The snake's malignant head was still thrust forth from the inner coil as before, the neck level. It had not moved, but its eyes were now electric sparks, radiating an infinity of luminous needles.

The man had an ashy pallor. Again he took a step forward, and another, partly dragging the chair, which, when finally released, fell upon the floor with a crash. The man groaned; the snake made neither sound nor motion, but its eyes were two dazzling suns. The reptile itself was wholly concealed by them. They gave off enlarging rings of rich and vivid colours, which at their greatest expansion successively vanished like soap bubbles; they seemed to approach his very face, and anon were an immeasurable distance away. He heard, somewhere, the continuous throbbing of a great drum, with desultory bursts of far music, inconceivably sweet, like the tones of an æolian harp. He knew it for the sunrise melody of Memnon's statue, and thought he stood in the Nileside reeds, hearing, with exalted sense, that immortal anthem through the silence of the centuries.

The music ceased; rather, it became by insensible degrees the distant roll of a retreating thunderstorm. A landscape, glittering with sun and rain, stretched before him, arched with a vivid rainbow, framing in its giant curve a hundred visible cities. In the middle distance a vast serpent, wearing a crown, reared its head out of its voluminous convolutions and looked at him with his dead mother's eyes. Suddenly this enchanting landscape seemed to rise swiftly upward like the drop-scene at a theatre, and vanished in a blank. Something struck him a hard blow upon the face and breast. He had fallen to the floor; the blood ran from his broken nose and his bruised lips. For a moment he was dazed and stunned, and lay with closed eyes, his face against the floor. In a few moments he had recovered, and then realised that his fall, by withdrawing his eyes, had broken the spell which held him. He felt that now, by keeping his gaze averted, he would be able to retreat. But the thought of the serpent within a few feet of his head, yet unseen—perhaps in the very act of springing upon him and throwing its coils about his throat—was too horrible. He lifted his head, stared again into those baleful eyes, and was again in bondage.

The snake had not moved, and appeared somewhat to have lost its power upon the imagination; the gorgeous illusions of a few moments before were not repeated. Beneath that flat and brainless brow its black, beady eyes simply glittered, as at first, with an expression unspeakably malignant. It was as if the creature, knowing its triumph assured, had determined to practise no more alluring wiles.

Now ensued a fearful scene. The man, prone upon the floor, within a yard of his enemy raised the upper part of his body upon his elbows, his head thrown back, his legs extended to their full length. His face was white between its gouts of blood; his eyes were strained open to their uttermost expansion. There was froth upon his lips; it dropped off in flakes. Strong convulsions ran through his body, making almost serpentine undulations. He bent himself at the waist, shifting his legs from side to side. And every movement left him a little nearer to the snake. He thrust his hands forward to brace himself back, yet constantly advanced upon his elbows.

IV

Dr. Druring and his wife sat in the library. The scientist was in rare good humour. " I have just obtained, by exchange with another collector," he said, " a splendid specimen of the *ophiophagus*."

" And what may that be ? " the lady inquired with a somewhat languid interest.

" Why, bless my soul, what profound ignorance ! My dear, a man who ascertains after marriage that his wife does not know Greek, is entitled to a divorce. The *ophiophagus* is a snake which eats other snakes."

" I hope it will eat all yours," she said, absently shifting the lamp. " But how does it get the other snakes ? By charming them, I suppose."

" That is just like you, dear," said the doctor, with an affection of petulance. " You know how irritating to me is any allusion to that vulgar supersititon about the snake's power of fascination."

The conversation was interrupted by a mighty cry, which rang through the silent house like the voice of a demon shouting in a tomb ! Again and yet again it sounded, with terrible distinctness. They sprang to their feet, the man confused, the lady pale and speechless with fright. Almost before the echoes of the last cry had died away, the doctor was out of the room, springing up the staircase two steps at a time. In the corridor, in front of Brayton's chamber, he met some servants who had come from the upper floor. Together they rushed at the door without knocking. It was unfastened and gave way. Brayton lay upon his stomach on the floor dead. His head and arms were partly concealed under the foot-rail of the bed. They pulled the body away, turning it upon the back. The face was daubed with blood and froth, the eyes were wide open, staring—a dreadful sight !

"Died in a fit," said the scientist, bending his knee and placing his hand upon the heart. While in that position, he happened to glance under the bed. "Good God!" he added, "how did this thing get in here?" He reached under the bed, pulled out the snake, and flung it, still coiled, to the centre of the room, whence, with a harsh, shuffling sound, it slid across the polished floor till stopped by the wall, where it lay without motion. It was a stuffed snake; its eyes were two shoe buttons.

# THE DAMNED THING

## Ambrose Bierce

### I

By the light of a tallow candle, which had been placed on one end of a rough table, a man was reading something written in a book. It was an old account book, greatly worn; and the writing was not, apparently, very legible, for the man sometimes held the page close to the flame of the candle to get a stronger light upon it. The shadow of the book would then throw into obscurity a half of the room, darkening a number of faces and figures; for besides the reader, eight other men were present. Seven of them sat against the rough log walls, silent and motionless, and, the room being small, not very far from the table. By extending an arm any one of them could have touched the eighth man, who lay on the table, face upward, partly covered by a sheet, his arms at his sides. He was dead.

The man with the book was not reading aloud, and no one spoke; all seemed to be waiting for something to occur; the dead man only was without expectation. From the blank darkness outside came in, through the aperture that served for a window, all the ever unfamiliar noises of night in the wilderness—the long, nameless note of a distant coyote ; the stilly pulsing thrill of tireless insects in the trees ; strange cries of night birds, so different from those of the birds of day ; the drone of great blundering beetles and all that mysterious chorus of small sounds that seemed always to have been but half heard when they have suddenly ceased, as if conscious of an indiscretion. But nothing of all this was noted in that company ; its members were not overmuch addicted to idle interest in matters of no practical importance ; that was obvious in every line of their rugged faces—obvious even in the dim light of the single candle. They were evidently men of the vicinity—farmers and woodmen.

The person reading was a trifle different ; one would have said of him that he was of the world, worldly, albeit there was that in his attire which attested a certain fellowship with the organisms of his environment. His coat would hardly have passed muster in San Francisco : his footgear was not of urban origin, and the hat that lay by him on the floor (he was the only one uncovered) was such that if one had considered it as an article of mere personal adornment he would have missed its meaning. In countenance the man was rather prepossessing, with just a hint of sternness ; though that he may have assumed or cultivated, as appropriate to one in authority. For he was a coroner. It was by virtue of his office that he had possession of the book in which he was reading ; it had been found among the dead man's effects—in his cabin, where the inquest was now taking place.

When the coroner had finished reading he put the book into his breast pocket. At that moment the door was pushed open and a young man entered. He, clearly, was not of mountain birth and breeding : he was clad as those who dwell in cities. His clothing was dusty, however, as from travel. He had, in fact, been riding hard to attend the inquest.

The coroner nodded ; no one else greeted him.

"We have waited for you," said the coroner. "It is necessary to have done with this business to-night."

The young man smiled. "I am sorry to have kept you," he said, "I went away, not to evade your summons, but to post to my newspaper an account of what I suppose I am called back to relate."

The coroner smiled.

"The account that you posted to your newspaper," he said, "differs probably from that which you will give here under oath."

"That," replied the other, rather hotly and with a visible flush, "is as you choose. I used manifold paper and have a copy of what I sent. It was not written as news, for it is incredible, but as fiction. It may go as a part of my testimony under oath."

"But you say it is incredible."

"That is nothing to you, sir, if I also swear that it is true."

The coroner was apparently not greatly affected by the young man's manifest resentment. He was silent for some moments, his eyes upon the floor. The men about the sides of the cabin talked in whispers, but seldom withdrew their gaze from the face of the corpse. Presently the coroner lifted his eyes and said: " We will resume the inquest."

The men removed their hats. The witness was sworn.

" What is your name ? " the coroner asked.

" William Harker."

" Age ? "

" Twenty-seven."

" You knew the deceased, Hugh Morgan ? "

" Yes."

" You were with him when he died ? "

" Near him."

" How did that happen—your presence, I mean ? "

" I was visiting him at his place to shoot and fish. A part of my purpose, however, was to study him, and his odd, solitary way of life. He seemed a good model for a character in fiction. I sometimes write stories."

" I sometimes read them."

" Thank you."

" Stories in general—not yours."

Some of the jurors laughed. Against a sombre background humour shows high lights. Soldiers in the intervals of battle laugh easily, and a jest in the death chamber conquers by surprise.

" Relate the circumstances of this man's death," said the coroner. " You may use any notes or memoranda that you please."

The witness understood. Pulling a manuscript from his breast pocket he held it near the candle, and turning the leaves until he found the passage that he wanted, began to read.

II

" . . . The sun had hardly risen when we left the house. We were looking for quail, each with a shot-gun, but we had only one dog. Morgan said that our best ground was beyond a certain ridge that he pointed out, and we crossed it by trail through the *chaparral*. On the other side was comparatively level ground, thickly covered with wild oats. As we emerged from the *chaparral*, Morgan was but a few yards in advance. Suddenly, we heard, at a little distance to our right, and partly in front, a noise as of some animal thrashing about in the bushes, which we could see were violently agitated.

" ' We've started a deer,' I said. ' I wish we had brought a rifle.'

" Morgan, who had stopped and was intently watching the agitated *chaparral*, said nothing, but had cocked both barrels of his gun, and was holding it in readiness to aim. I thought him a trifle excited, which surprised me, for he had a reputation for exceptional coolness, even in moments of sudden and imminent peril.

"'O, come!' I said. 'You are not going to fill up a deer with quail-shot, are you?'"

"Still he did not reply; but, catching a sight of his face as he turned it slightly toward me, I was struck by the pallor of it. Then I understood that we had serious business on hand, and my first conjecture was that we had 'jumped' a grizzly. I advanced to Morgan's side, cocking my piece as I moved.

"The bushes were now quiet, and the sounds had ceased, but Morgan was as attentive to the place as before.

"'What is it? What the devil is it?' I asked.

"'That Damned Thing!' he replied, without turning his head. His voice was husky and unnatural. He trembled visibly.

"I was about to speak further, when I observed the wild oats near the place of the disturbance moving in the most inexplicable way. I can hardly describe it. It seemed as if stirred by a streak of wind, which not only bent it, but pressed it down—crushed it so that it did not rise, and this movement was slowly prolonging itself directly toward us.

"Nothing that I had ever seen had affected me so strangely as this unfamiliar and unaccountable phenomenon, yet I am unable to recall any sense of fear. I remember—and tell it here because, singularly enough, I recollected it then—that once, in looking carelessly out of an open window, I momentarily mistook a small tree close at hand for one of a group of larger trees at a little distance away. It looked the same size as the others, but, being more distinctly and sharply defined in mass and details, seemed out of harmony with them. It was a mere falsification of the law of aerial perspective, but it startled, almost terrified me. We so rely upon the orderly operation of familar natural laws that any seeming suspension of them is noted as a menace to our safety, a warning of unthinkable calamity. So now the apparently causeless movement of the herbage, and the slow, undeviating approach of the line of disturbance were distinctly disquieting. My companion appeared actually frightened, and I could hardly credit my senses when I saw him suddenly throw his gun to his shoulders and fire both barrels at the agitated grass! Before the smoke of the discharge had cleared away I heard a loud savage cry—a scream like that of a wild animal—and, flinging his gun upon the ground, Morgan sprang away and ran swiftly from the spot. At the same instant I was thrown violently to the ground by the impact of something unseen in the smoke—some soft, heavy substance that seemed thrown against me with great force.

"Before I could get upon my feet and recover my gun, which seemed to have been struck from my hands, I heard Morgan crying out as if in mortal agony, and mingling with his cries were such hoarse, savage sounds as one hears from fighting dogs. Inexpressibly terrified, I struggled to my feet and looked in the direction of Morgan's retreat; and may heaven in mercy spare me from another sight like that! At a distance of less than thirty yards was my friend, down upon one knee, his head thrown back at a frightful angle, hatless, his long hair in disorder and his whole body in violent movement from side to side, backward and forward. His right arm was lifted and seemed to lack the hand—at least, I could see none. The other arm was invisible. At times, as my memory now reports this extraordinary scene, I could discern but a part of his body; it was as if he had been partly blotted out—I can not otherwise express it—then a shifting of his position would bring it all into view again.

"All this must have occurred within a few seconds, yet in that time Morgan assumed all the postures of a determined wrestler vanquished by superior weight and strength. I saw nothing but him, and him not always distinctly. During the entire incident his shouts and curses were heard, as if through an enveloping uproar of such sounds of rage and fury as I had never heard from the throat of man or brute!

"For a moment only I stood irresolute, then throwing down my gun, I ran forward to my friend's assistance. I had a vague belief that he was suffering from a fit or some form of convulsion. Before I could reach his side he was down and quiet. All sounds had ceased, but, with a feeling of such terror as even these awful events had not inspired, I now saw the same mysterious movement of the wild oats prolonging itself from the trampled area about the prostrate man toward the edge of a wood. It was only when it had reached the wood that I was able to withdraw my eyes and look at my companion. He was dead."

### III

The coroner rose from his seat and stood beside the dead man. Lifting an edge of the sheet he pulled it away, exposing the entire body, altogether naked and showing in the candle-light a clay-like yellow. It had, however, broad maculations of bluish-black, obviously caused by extravasated blood from contusions. The chest and sides looked as if they had been beaten with a bludgeon. There were dreadful lacerations; the skin was torn in strips and shreds.

The coroner moved round to the end of the table and undid a silk handkerchief, which had been passed under the chin and knotted on the top of the head. When the handkerchief was drawn away it exposed what had been the throat. Some of the jurors who had risen to get a better view repented their curiosity, and turned away their faces. Witness Harker went to the open window and leaned out across the sill, faint and sick. Dropping the handkerchief upon the dead man's neck, the coroner stepped to an angle of the room, and from a pile of clothing produced one garment after another, each of which he held up a moment for inspection. All were torn, and stiff with blood. The jurors did not make a closer inspection. They seemed rather uninterested. They had, in truth, seen all this before; the only thing that was new to them being Harker's testimony.

"Gentlemen," the coroner said, "we have no more evidence, I think. Your duty has been already explained to you; if there is nothing you wish to ask you may go outside and consider your verdict."

The foreman rose—a tall, bearded man of sixty, coarsely clad.

"I should like to ask one question, Mr. Coroner," he said. "What asylum did this yer last witness escape from?"

"Mr. Harker," said the coroner, gravely and tranquilly, "from what asylum did you last escape?"

Harker flushed crimson again, but said nothing, and the seven jurors rose and solemnly filed out of the cabin.

"If you have done insulting me, sir," said Harker, as soon as he and the officer were left alone with the dead man, "I suppose I am at liberty to go?"

"Yes."

Harker started to leave, but paused, with his hand on the door latch. The habit of his profession was strong in him—stronger than his sense of personal dignity. He turned about and said:

"The book that you have there—I recognise it as Morgan's diary. You seemed greatly interested in it; you read in it while I was testifying. May I see it? The public would like——"

"The book will cut no figure in this matter," replied the official, slipping it into his coat pocket; "all the entries in it were made before the writer's death."

As Harker passed out of the house the jury re-entered and stood about the table, on which the now covered corpse showed under the sheet with sharp definition. The foreman seated himself near the candle, produced from his breast pocket a pencil and scrap of paper, and wrote rather laboriously the following verdict, which with various degrees of effort all signed:

"We, the jury, do find that the remains come to their death at the hands of a mountain lion, but some of us thinks, all the same, they had fits."

IV

In the dairy of the late Hugh Morgan are certain interesting entries having, possibly, a scientific value as suggestions. At the inquest upon his body the book was not put in evidence; possibly the coroner thought it not worth while to confuse the jury. The date of the first of the entries mentioned cannot be ascertained; the upper part of the leaf is torn away; the part of the entry remaining is as follows:

" . . . would run in a half circle, keeping his head turned

always toward the centre and again he would stand still, barking furiously. At last he ran away into the brush as fast as he could go. I thought at first that he had gone mad, but on returning to the house found no other alteration in his manner than what was obviously due to fear of punishment.

"Can a dog see with his nose? Do odours impress some olfactory centre with images of the thing emitting them? . . .

"Sept. 2.—Looking at the stars last night as they rose above the crest of the ridge east of the house, I observed them successively disappear—from left to right. Each was eclipsed but an instant, and only a few at the same time, but along the entire length of the ridge all that were within a degree or two of the crest were blotted out. It was as if something had passed along between me and them; but I could not see it, and the stars were not thick enough to define its outline. Ugh! I don't like this. . . ."

Several weeks' entries are missing, three leaves being torn from the book.

"Sept. 27.—It has been about here again—I find evidences of its presence every day. I watched again all of last night in the same cover, gun in hand, double-charged with buckshot. In the morning the fresh footprints were there, as before. Yet I would have sworn that I did not sleep—indeed, I hardly sleep at all. It is terrible, insupportable! If these amazing experiences are real I shall go mad; if they are fanciful I am mad already.

"Oct. 3.—I shall not go—it shall not drive me away. No, this is *my* house, *my* land. God hates a coward. . . .

"Oct. 5.—I can stand it no longer; I have invited Harker to pass a few weeks with me—he has a level head. I can judge from his manner if he thinks me mad.

"Oct. 7.—I have the solution of the problem; it came to me last night—suddenly, as by revelation. How simple—how terribly simple!

"There are sounds that we cannot hear. At either end of the scale are notes that stir no chord of that imperfect instrument, the human ear. They are too high or too grave. I have observed a flock of blackbirds occupying an entire tree-top—the tops of several trees —and all in full song. Suddenly—in a moment—at absolutely the same instant—all spring into the air and fly away. How? They could not all see one another—whole tree-tops intervened. At no point could a leader have been visible to all. There must have been a signal of warning or command, high and shrill above the din, but by me unheard. I have observed, too, the same simultaneous flight when all were silent, among not only blackbirds, but other birds— quail, for example, widely separated by bushes—even on opposite sides of a hill.

"It is known to seamen that a school of whales basking or sporting on the surface of the ocean, miles apart, with the convexity of the earth between them, will sometimes dive at the same instant—all gone out of sight in a moment. The signal has been sounded—too grave for the ear of the sailor at the masthead and his comrades on the deck—who nevertheless feel its vibrations in the ship as the stones of a cathedral are stirred by the bass of the organ.

"As with sounds, so with colours. At each end of the solar spectrum the chemist can detect the presence of what are known as 'actinic' rays. They represent colours—integral colours in the composition of light—which we are unable to discern. The human eye is an imperfect instrument; its range is but a few octaves of the real 'chromatic scale.' I am not mad; there are colours that we cannot see.

"And, God help me! the Damned Thing is of such a colour!"

# MY FAVOURITE MURDER

## Ambrose Bierce

Having murdered my mother under circumstances of singular atrocity, I was arrested and put upon trial, which lasted seven years. In summing up, the judge of the Court of Acquittal remarked that it was one of the most ghastly crimes that he had ever been called upon to explain away.

At this my counsel rose and said:

"May it please your honour, crimes are ghastly or agreeable only by comparison. If you were familiar with the details of my client's previous murder of his uncle, you would discern in his later offence something in the nature of tender forbearance and filial consideration for the feelings of the victim. The appalling ferocity of the former assassination was indeed inconsistent with any hypothesis but that of guilt; and had it not been for the fact that the honourable judge before whom he was tried was the president of a life insurance company which took risks on hanging, and in which my client held a policy, it is impossible to see how he could have been decently acquitted. If your honour would like to hear about it for the instruction and guidance of your honour's mind, this unfortunate man, my client, will consent to give himself the pain of relating it under oath."

The district attorney said: "Your honour, I object. Such a statement would be in the nature of evidence, and the testimony in this case is closed. The prisoner's statement should have been introduced three years ago, in the spring of 1881."

"In a statutory sense," said the judge, "you are right, and in the Court of Objections and Technicalities you would get a ruling in your favour. But not in a Court of Acquittal. The objection is overruled."

"I except," said the district attorney.

"You cannot do that," the judge said. "I must remind you that in order to take an exception you must first get this case transferred for a time to the Court of Exceptions upon a formal motion duly supported by affidavits. A motion to that effect by your predecessor in office was denied by me during the first year of this trial."

"Mr. Clerk, swear the prisoner."

The customary oath having been administered, I made the following statement, which impressed the judge with so strong a sense of the comparative triviality of the offence for which I was on trial that he made no further search for mitigating circumstances, but simply instructed the jury to acquit, and I left the court without a stain upon my reputation :

"I was born in 1856 in Kalamakee, Mich., of honest and reputable parents, one of whom Heaven has mercifully spared to comfort me in my later years. In 1867 the family came to California and settled near Nigger Head, where my father opened a road agency and prospered beyond the dreams of avarice. He was a silent, saturnine man then, though his increasing years have now somewhat relaxed the austerity of his disposition, and I believe that nothing but his memory of the sad event for which I am now on trial prevents him from manifesting a genuine hilarity.

"Four years after we had set up the road agency an itinerant preacher came along, and having no other way to pay for the night's lodging which we gave him, favoured us with an exhortation of such power that, praise God, we were all converted to religion. My father at once sent for his brother, the Hon. William Ridley of Stockton, and on his arrival turned over the agency to him, charging him nothing for the franchise or plant—the latter consisting of a Winchester rifle, a sawn-off shot gun and an assortment of masks made out of flour sacks. The family then moved to Ghost Rock and opened a dance house. It was called 'The Saints' Rest Hurdy-Gurdy,' and the proceedings each night began with a prayer. It was there that my now sainted mother, by her grace in the dance, acquired the sobriquet of 'The Bucking Walrus.'

"In the fall of '75 I had occasion to visit Coyote, on the road to Mahala, and took the stage at Ghost Rock. There were four other passengers. About three miles beyond Nigger Head, persons whom I identified as my Uncle William and his two sons, held up the stage. Finding nothing in the express box, they went through the passengers. I acted a most honourable part in the affair, placing myself in line with the others, holding up my hands and permitting myself to be deprived of forty dollars and a gold watch. From my behaviour no one could have suspected that I knew the gentlemen who gave the entertainment. A few days later, when I went to Nigger Head and asked for the return of my money and watch, my uncle and cousins swore they knew nothing of the matter, and they affected a belief that my father and I had done the job ourselves in dishonest violation of commercial good faith. Uncle William even threatened to retaliate by starting an opposition dance house at Ghost Rock. As 'The Saints' Rest' had become rather unpopular, I saw that this would assuredly ruin it and prove a paying enterprise, so I told my uncle that I was willing to overlook the past if he would take me into the scheme and keep the partnership a secret from my father. This fair offer he rejected, and I then perceived that it would be better and more satisfactory if he were dead.

"My plans to that end were soon perfected, and communicating them to my dear parents, I had the gratification of receiving their approval. My father said he was proud of me, and my mother promised that, although her religion forbade her to assist in taking human life, I should have the advantage of her prayers for my success. As a preliminary measure, looking to my security in case of detection, I made an application for membership in that powerful order, the Knights of Murder, and in due course was received as a member of the Ghost Rock Commandery. On the day that my probation ended I was for the first time permitted to inspect the records of the order and learn who belonged to it—all the rites of initiation having been conducted in masks. Fancy my delight, when, in looking over the roll of membership, I found the third name to be that of my uncle, who indeed was junior vice-chancellor of the order! Here was an opportunity exceeding my wildest dreams—to murder I could add insubordination and treachery. It was what my good mother would have called 'a special Providence.'

"At about this time something occurred which caused my cup of joy, already full, to overflow on all sides, a circular cataract of bliss. Three men, strangers in that locality, were arrested for the stage robbery in which I had lost my money and watch. They were brought to trial and, despite my efforts to clear them and fasten the guilt upon three of the most respectable and worthy citizens of Ghost Rock, convicted on the clearest proof. The murder would now be as wanton and reasonless as I could wish.

"One morning I shouldered my Winchester rifle and, going over to my uncle's house, near Nigger Head, asked my Aunt Mary, his wife, if he were at home, adding that I had come to kill him. My aunt replied with a peculiar smile that so many gentlemen called on the same errand and were afterward carried away without having performed it that I must excuse her for doubting my good faith in the matter. She said it did not look as if I would kill anybody, so, as a guarantee of good faith, I levelled my rifle and wounded a Chinaman who happened to be passing the house. She said she knew whole families who could do a thing of that kind, but Bill Ridley was a horse of another colour. She said, however, that I would find him over on the other side of the creek in the sheep lot; and she added that she hoped the best man would win.

"My Aunt Mary was one of the most fair-minded women whom I have ever met.

"I found my uncle down on his knees engaged in skinning a sheep. Seeing that he had neither gun nor pistol handy, I had not the heart to shoot him, so I approached him, greeted him pleasantly, and struck him a powerful blow on the head with the butt of my rifle. I have a very good delivery, and Uncle William lay down on his side, then rolled over on his back, spread out his fingers, and shivered. Before he could recover the use of his limbs I seized the knife that he had been using and cut his ham strings. You know, doubtless, that when you sever the tendon Achillis the patient has no further use of his leg; it is just the same as if he had no leg. Well, I parted them both, and when he revived he was at my service. As soon as he comprehended the situation, he said:

"'Samuel, you have got the drop on me, and can afford to be liberal about this thing. I have only one thing to ask of you, and that is that you carry me to the house and finish me in the bosom of my family.'

"I told him I thought that a pretty reasonable request, and I would do so if he would let me put him in a wheat sack; he would be easier to carry that way, and if we were seen by the neighbours en route it would cause less remark. He agreed to that, and, going to the barn, I got a sack. This, however, did not fit him; it was too short and much wider than he was; so I bent his legs, forced his knees up against his breast, and got him into it that way, tying the sack above his head. He was a heavy man, and I had all I could do to get him on my back, but I staggered along for some distance until I came to a swing which some of the children had suspended to the branch of an oak. Here I had laid him down and sat upon him to rest, and the sight of the rope gave me a happy inspiration. In twenty minutes my uncle, still in the sack, swung free to the sport of the wind. I had taken down the rope, tied one end tightly about the mouth of the bag, thrown the other across the limb, and hauled him up about five feet from the ground. Fastening the other end of the rope also to the mouth of the sack, I had the satisfaction to see my uncle converted into a huge pendulum. I must add that he was not himself entirely aware of the nature of the change which he had undergone in his relation to the exterior world, though in justice to a brave man's memory I ought to say that I do not think he would in any case have wasted much of my time in vain remonstrance.

"Uncle William had a ram which was famous in all that region as a fighter. It was in a state of chronic constitutional indignation.

Some deep disappointment in early life had soured its disposition, and it had declared war upon the whole world. To say that it would butt anything accessible is but faintly to express the nature and scope of its military activity ; the universe was its antagonist ; its method was that of a projectile. It fought, like the angels and devils, in mid-air, cleaving the atmosphere like a bird, describing a parabolic curve and descending upon its victim at just the exact angle of incidence to make the most of its velocity and weight. Its momentum, calculated in foot-tons, was something incredible. It had been seen to destroy a four-year-old bull by a single impact upon that animal's gnarly forehead. No stone wall had ever been known to resist its downward swoop ; there were no trees tough enough to stay it ; it would splinter them into matchwood and defile their leafy honours in the dust. This irascible and implacable brute—this incarnate thunderbolt—this monster of the upper deep, I had seen reposing in the shade of an adjacent tree, dreaming dreams of conquest and glory. It was with a view of summoning it forth to the field of honour that I suspended its master in the manner described.

" Having completed my preparations, I imparted to the avuncular pendulum a gentle oscillation, and retiring to cover behind a contiguous rock, lifted up my voice in a long, rasping cry, whose diminishing final note was drowned in a noise like that of a swearing cat, which emanated from the sack. Instantly that formidable sheep was upon its feet and had taken in the military situation at a glance. In a few moments it had approached, stamping, to within fifty yards of the swinging foeman who, now retreating and anon advancing, seemed to invite the fray. Suddenly I saw the beast's head drop earthward as if depressed by the weight of its enormous horns ; then a dim, white, wavy streak of sheep prolonged itself from that spot in a generally horizontal direction to within about four yards of a point immediately beneath the enemy. There it struck sharply upward, and before it had faded from my gaze at the place whence it had set out I heard a horrible thump and a piercing scream, and my poor uncle shot forward with a slack rope, higher than the limb to which he was attached. Here the rope tautened with a jerk, arresting his flight, and back he swung in a breathless curve to the other end of his arc. The ram had fallen, a head of indistinguishable legs, wool, and horns, but, pulling itself together and dodging as its antagonist swept downward, it retired at random, alternately shaking its head and stamping its fore-feet. When it had backed about the same distance as that from which it had delivered the assault, it paused again, bowed its head as if in prayer for victory, and again shot forward dimly visibly as before— a prolonging white streak with monstrous undulations, ending with a sharp ascension. Its course this time was at a right angle to its former one, and its impatience so great that it struck the enemy before he had nearly reached the lowest point of his arc. In consequence he went flying around and around in a horizontal circle, whose radius was about equal to half the length of the rope, which I forgot to say was nearly twenty feet long. His shrieks, crescendo in approach and diminuendo in recession, made the rapidity of his revolution more obvious to the ear than to the eye. He had evidently not yet been struck in a vital spot. His posture in the sack and the distance from the ground at which he hung compelled the ram to operate upon his lower extremities and the end of his back. Like a plant that has struck its root into some poisonous mineral, my poor uncle was dying slowly upward.

"After delivering its second blow the ram had not again retired. The fever of battle burned hot in its heart; its brain was intoxicated with the wine of strife. Like a pugilist who in his rage forgets his skill and fights ineffectively at half-arm's length, the angry beast endeavoured to reach its fleeting foe by awkward vertical leaps as he passed overhead, sometimes, indeed, succeeding in striking him feebly, but more frequently overthrown by its own misguided eagerness. But as the impetus was exhausted and the man's circles narrowed in scope and diminished in speed, bringing him nearer to the ground, these tactics produced better results and elicited a superior quality of screams, which I greatly enjoyed.

"Suddenly, as if the bugles had sung truce, the ram suspended hostilities and walked away, thoughtfully wrinkling and smoothing its great aquiline nose, and occasionally cropping a bunch of grass and slowly munching it. It seems to have tired of war's alarms and resolved to beat the sword into a ploughshare and cultivate the arts of peace. Steadily it held its course away from the field of fame until it had gained a distance of nearly a quarter of a mile. There it stopped and stood with its rear to the foe, chewing its cud and apparently half asleep. I observed, however, an occasional slight turn of its head, as if its apathy were more affected than real.

"Meanwhile, Uncle William's shrieks had abated with his emotion, and nothing was heard from him but long, low moans, and at long intervals my name, uttered in pleading tones exceedingly grateful to my ear. Evidently the man had not the faintest notion of what was being done to him, and was inexpressibly terrified. When Death comes cloaked in mystery he is terrible indeed. Little by little my uncle's oscillations diminished, and finally he hung motionless. I went to him and was about to give him the *coup de grâce*, when I heard and felt a succession of smart shocks which shook the ground like a series of light earthquakes, and turning in the direction of the ram, saw a cloud of dust approaching me with inconceivable rapidity and alarming effect. At a distance of some thirty yards away it stopped short, and from the near end of it rose into the air what I at first thought a great white bird. Its ascent was so smooth and easy and regular that I could not realise its extraordinary celerity, and was lost in admiration of its grace. To this day the impression remains that it was a slow, deliberate movement, the ram—for it was that animal—being upborne by some power other than its own impetus, and supported through the successive stages of its flight with infinite tenderness and care. My eyes followed its progress through the air with unspeakable pleasure, all the greater by contrast with my former terror of its approach by land. Onward and upward the noble animal sailed, its head bent down almost between its knees, its fore-feet thrown back, its hinder legs trailing to rear like the legs of a soaring heron. At a height of forty or fifty feet, as near as I could judge, it attained its zenith and appeared to remain an instant stationary; then, tilting suddenly forward without altering the relative position of its parts, it shot downward on a steeper and steeper course with augmenting velocity, passed immediately above me with a noise like the rush of a cannon shot, and struck my poor uncle almost squarely on top of the head! So frightful was the impact that not only the neck was broken, but the rope, too; and the body of the deceased, forced against the earth, was crushed to pulp beneath the awful front of that meteoric sheep. The concussion stopped all the clocks between Lone Hand and Dutch Dan's, and professor Davidson, who happened to be in the vicinity, promptly explained that the vibrations were from the north to south."

Altogether, I cannot help thinking that in point of atrocity my murder of Uncle William has seldom been excelled.

# AN OCCURRENCE AT OWL CREEK BRIDGE

### Ambrose Bierce

#### I

A MAN stood upon a railroad bridge in Northern Alabama, looking down into the swift waters twenty feet below. The man's hands were behind his back, the wrists bound with a cord. A rope loosely encircled his neck. It was attached to a stout cross-timber above his head, and the slack fell to the level of his knees. Some loose boards laid upon the sleepers supporting the metals of the railway supplied a footing for him and his executioners—two private soldiers of the Federal army, directed by a sergeant, who in civil life may have been a deputy sheriff. At a short remove upon the same temporary platform was an officer in the uniform of his rank, armed.

He was a captain. A sentinel at each end of the bridge stood with his rifle in the position known as " support," that is to say, vertical in front of the left shoulder, the hammer resting on the forearm thrown straight across the chest—a formal and unnatural position, enforcing an erect carriage of the body. It did not appear to be the duty of these two men to know what was occurring at the centre of the bridge ; they merely blockaded the two ends of the foot plank which traversed it.

Beyond one of the sentinels nobody was in sight ; the railroad ran straight away into a forest for a hundred yards, then, curving, was lost to view. Doubtless there was an outpost farther along. The other bank of the stream was open ground—a gentle acclivity crowned with a stockade of vertical tree trunks, loop-holed for rifles, with a single embrasure through which protruded the muzzle of a brass cannon commanding the bridge. Midway of the slope between bridge and fort were the spectators—a single company of infantry in line, at " parade rest," the butts of the rifles on the ground, the barrels inclining slightly backward against the right shoulder, the hands crossed upon the stock. A lieutenant stood at the right of the line, the point of his sword upon the ground, his left hand resting upon his right. Excepting the group of four at the centre of the bridge not a man moved. The company faced the bridge, staring stonily, motionless. The sentinels, facing the banks of the stream, might have been statues to adorn the bridge. The captain stood with folded arms, silent, observing the work of his subordinates but making no sign. Death is a dignitary who, when he comes announced is to be received with formal manifestations of respect, even by those most familiar with him. In the code of military etiquette silence and fixity are forms of deference.

The man who was engaged in being hanged was apparently about thirty-five years of age. He was a civilian, if one might judge from his dress, which was that of a planter. His features were good—a straight nose, firm mouth, broad forehead, from which his long, dark hair was combed straight back, falling behind his ears to the collar of his well-fitting frock-coat. He wore a moustache and pointed beard, but no whiskers ; his eyes were large and dark grey and had a kindly expression which one would hardly have expected in one whose neck was in the hemp. Evidently this was no vulgar assassin. The liberal military code makes provision for hanging many kinds of people, and gentlemen are not excluded.

The preparations being complete, the two private soldiers stepped aside and each drew away the plank upon which he had been standing. The sergeant turned to the captain, saluted and placed himself immediately behind that officer, who in turn moved apart one pace. These movements left the condemned man and the sergeant standing on the two ends of the same plank, which spanned three of the cross-ties of the bridge. The end upon which the civilian stood almost, but not quite, reached a fourth. This plank had been held in place by the weight of the captain; it was now held by that of the sergeant. At a signal from the former, the latter would step aside, the plank would tilt and the condemned man go down between two ties. The arrangement commended itself to his judgement as simple and effective. His face had not been covered nor his eyes bandaged. He looked a moment at his "unsteadfast footing," then let his gaze wander to the swirling water of the stream racing madly beneath his feet. A piece of dancing driftwood caught his attention and his eyes followed it down the current. How slowly it appeared to move! What a sluggish stream!

He closed his eyes in order to fix his last thoughts upon his wife and children. The water, touched to gold by the early sun, the brooding mists under the banks at some distance down the stream, the fort, the soldiers, the piece of drift—all had distracted him. And now he became conscious of a new disturbance. Striking through the thought of his dear ones was a sound which he could neither ignore nor understand, a sharp, distinct, metallic percussion like the stroke of a blacksmith's hammer upon the anvil; it had the same ringing quality. He wondered what it was, and whether immeasurably distant or near by—it seemed both. Its recurrence was regular, but as slow as the tolling of a death knell. He awaited each stroke with impatience and—he knew not why—apprehension. The intervals of silence grew progressively longer; the delays became maddening. With their greater infrequency the sounds increased in strength and sharpness. They hurt his ear like the thrust of a knife; he feared he would shriek. What he heard was the ticking of his watch.

He unclosed his eyes and saw again the water below him. "If I could free my hands," he thought, "I might throw off the noose and spring into the stream. By diving I could evade the bullets and, swimming vigorously, reach the bank, take to the woods, and get away home. My home, thank God, is as yet outside their lines; my wife and little ones are still beyond the invader's farthest advance."

As these thoughts, which have here to be set down in words, were flashed into the doomed man's brain rather than evolved from it, the captain nodded to the sergeant. The sergeant stepped aside.

## II

Peyton Farquhar was a well-to-do planter, of an old and highly-respected Alabama family. Being a slave owner, and, like other slave owners, a politician, he was naturally an original secessionist and ardently devoted to the Southern cause. Circumstances of an imperious nature, which it is unnecessary to relate here, had prevented him from taking service with the gallant army which had

fought the disastrous campaigns ending with the fall of Corinth, and
he chafed under the inglorious restraint, longing for the release of
his energies, the larger life of the soldier, the opportunity for distinction. That opportunity, he felt, would come, as it comes to all
in war-time. Meanwhile he did what he could. No service was
too humble for him to perform in aid of the South, no adventure
too perilous for him to undertake if consistent with the character
of a civilian who was at heart a soldier, and who in good faith and
without too much qualification assented to at least a part of the
frankly villainous dictum that all is fair in love and war.

One evening, while Farquhar and his wife were sitting on a rustic
bench near the entrance to his grounds, a grey-clad soldier rode up
to the gate and asked for a drink of water. Mrs. Farquhar was only
too happy to serve him with her own white hands. While she was
gone to fetch the water, her husband approached the dusty horseman and inquired eagerly for news from the front.

" The Yanks are repairing the railroads," said the man, " and are
getting ready for another advance. They have reached the Owl
Creek bridge, put it in order, and built a stockade on the other bank.
The commandant has issued an order, which is posted everywhere,
declaring that any civilian caught interfering with the railroad, its
bridges, tunnels, or trains, will be summarily hanged. I saw the
order."

" How far is it to the Owl Creek bridge ? " Farquhar asked.

" About thirty miles."

" Is there no force on this side the creek ? "

" Only a picket post half a mile out, on the railroad, and a single
sentinel at this end of the bridge."

" Suppose a man—a civilian and student of hanging—should elude
the picket post and perhaps get the better of the sentinel," said
Farquhar, smiling, " what could he accomplish ? "

The soldier reflected. " I was there a month ago," he replied.
" I observed that the flood of last winter had lodged a great quantity
of driftwood against the wooden pier at this end of the bridge. It
it now dry and would burn like tow."

The lady had now brought the water, which the soldier drank. He
thanked her ceremoniously, bowed to her husband, and rode away.
An hour later, after nightfall, he repassed the plantation, going
northward in the direction from which he had come. He was a
Federal scout.

III

As Peyton Farquhar fell straight downward through the bridge,
he lost consciousness and was as one already dead. From this state
he was awakened—ages later, it seemed to him—by the pain of a
sharp pressure upon his throat, followed by a sense of suffocation.
Keen, poignant agonies seemed to shoot from his neck downward

through every fibre of his body and limbs. These pains appeared to flash along well-defined lines of ramification, and to beat with an inconceivably rapid periodicity. They seemed like streams of pulsating fire heating him to an intolerable temperature. As to his head, he was conscious of nothing but a feeling of fullness—of congestion. These sensations were unaccompanied by thought. The intellectual part of his nature was already effaced; he had power only to feel, and feeling was torment. He was conscious of motion. Encompassed in a luminous cloud, of which he was now merely the fiery heart, without material substance, he swung through unthinkable arcs of oscillation, like a vast pendulum. Then all at once, with terrible suddenness, the light about him shot upward with the noise of a loud plash; a frightful roaring was in his ears, and all was cold and dark. The power of thought was restored; he knew that the rope had broken and he had fallen into the stream. There was no additional strangulation; the noose about his neck was already suffocating him, and kept the water from his lungs. To die of hanging at the bottom of a river!—the idea seemed to him ludicrous. He opened his eyes in the blackness and saw above him a gleam of light, but how distant, how inaccessible! He was still sinking, for the light became fainter and fainter until it was a mere glimmer. Then it began to grow and brighten, and he knew that he was rising toward the surface—knew it with reluctance, for he was now very comfortable. "To be hanged and drowned," he thought, "that is not so bad; but I do not wish to be shot. No; I will not be shot; that is not fair."

He was not conscious of an effort, but a sharp pain in his wrists apprised him that he was trying to free his hands. He gave the struggle his attention, as an idler might observe the feat of a juggler, without interest in the outcome. What splendid effort!—what magnificent, what superhuman strength! Ah, that was a fine endeavour! Bravo! The cord fell away; his arms parted and floated upward, the hands dimly seen on each side in the growing light. He watched them with a new interest as first one and then the other pounced upon the noose at his neck. They tore it away and thrust it fiercely aside, its undulations resembling those of a water-snake. "Put it back, put it back!" He thought he shouted these words to his hands, for the undoing of the noose had been succeeded by the direst pang which he had yet experienced. His neck ached horribly; his brain was on fire; his heart, which had been fluttering faintly, gave a great leap, trying to force itself out at his mouth. His whole body was racked and wrenched with an insupportable anguish! But his disobedient hands gave no heed to the command. They beat the water vigorously with quick, downward strokes, forcing him to the surface. He felt his head emerge; his eyes were blinded by the sunlight; his chest expanded convulsively, and with a supreme and crowning agony his lungs engulfed a great draught of air, which instantly he expelled in a shriek !

He was now in full possession of his physical senses. They were, indeed, preternaturally keen and alert. Something in the awful disturbance of his organic system had so exalted and refined them that they made record of things never before perceived. He felt the ripples upon his face and heard their separate sounds as they struck. He looked at the forest on the bank of the stream, saw the individual trees, the leaves and the veining of each leaf—saw the very insects upon them, the locusts, the brilliant-bodied flies, the grey spiders stretching their webs from twig to twig. He noted the prismatic colours in all the dewdrops upon a million blades of grass. The humming of the gnats that danced above the eddies of the stream, the beating of the dragon flies' wings, the strokes of the water spiders' legs, like oars which had lifted their boat—all these made audible music. A fish slid along beneath his eyes and he heard the rush of its body parting the water.

He had come to the surface facing down the stream ; in a moment the visible world seemed to wheel slowly round, himself the pivotal point, and he saw the bridge, the fort, the soldiers upon the bridge, the captain, the sergeant, the two privates, his executioners. They were in silhouette against the blue sky. They shouted and gesticulated, pointing at him ; the captain had drawn his pistol, but did not fire ; the others were unarmed. Their movements were grotesque and horrible, their forms gigantic.

Suddenly he heard a sharp report and something struck the water smartly within a few inches of his head, spattering his face with spray. He heard a second report, and saw one of the sentinels with his rifle at his shoulder, a light cloud of blue smoke rising from the muzzle. The man in the water saw the eye of the man on the bridge gazing into his own through the sights of the rifle. He observed that it was a grey eye, and remembered having read that grey eyes were keenest and that all famous marksmen had them. Nevertheless, this one had missed.

A counter swirl had caught Farquhar and turned him half round ; he was again looking into the forest on the bank opposite the fort. The sound of a clear, high voice in a monotonous singsong now rang out behind him and came across the water with a distinctness that pierced and subdued all other sounds, even the beating of the ripples in his ears. Although no soldier, he had frequented camps enough to know the dread significance of that deliberate, drawling, aspirated chant ; the lieutenant on shore was taking a part in the morning's work. How coldly and pitilessly—with what an even, calm intonation, presaging and enforcing tranquillity in the men—with what accurately measured intervals fell those cruel words :

" Attention, company. . . . Shoulder arms. . . . Ready. . . . Aim. . . . Fire."

Farquhar dived—dived as deeply as he could. The water roared in his ears like the voice of Niagara, yet he heard the dulled thunder of the volley, and rising again toward the surface, met shining bits of metal, singularly flattened, oscillating slowly downward. Some of them touched him on the face and hands, then fell away, continuing their descent. One lodged between his collar and neck; it was uncomfortably warm, and he snatched it out.

As he rose to the surface, gasping for breath, he saw that he had been a long time under water; he was perceptibly farther down stream—nearer to safety. The soldiers had almost finished reloading; the metal ramrods flashed all at once in the sunshine as they were drawn from the barrels, turned in the air, and thrust into their sockets. The two sentinels fired again, independently and ineffectually.

The hunted man saw all this over his shoulder; he was now swimming vigorously with the current. His brain was as energetic as his arms and legs; he thought with the rapidity of lightning.

"The officer," he reasoned, "will not make that martinet's error a second time. It is as easy to dodge a volley as a single shot. He has probably already given the command to fire at will. God help me, I cannot dodge them all!"

An appalling plash within two yards of him, followed by a loud rushing sound, *diminuendo*, which seemed to travel back through the air to the fort and died in an explosion which stirred the very river to its deeps! A rising sheet of water, which curved over him, fell down upon him, blinded him, strangled him! The cannon had taken a hand in the game. As he shook his head free from the commotion of the smitten water, he heard the deflected shot humming through the air ahead, and in an instant it was cracking and smashing the branches in the forest beyond.

"They will not do that again," he thought; "the next time they will use a charge of grape. I must keep my eye upon the gun; the smoke will apprise me—the report arrives too late; it lags behind the missile. It is a good gun."

Suddenly he felt himself whirled round and round—spinning like a top. The water, the banks, the forest, the now distant bridge, fort, and men—all were commingled and blurred. Objects were represented by their colours only; circular horizontal streaks of colour—that was all he saw. He had been caught in a vortex and was being whirled on with a velocity of advance and gyration which made him giddy and sick. In a few moments he was flung upon the gravel at the foot of the left bank of the stream—the southern bank—and behind a projecting point which concealed him from his enemies. The sudden arrest of his motion, the abrasion of one of his hands on the gravel, restored him and he wept with delight. He dug his fingers into the sand, threw it over himself in handfuls, and audibly blessed it. It looked like gold, like diamonds, rubies, emeralds; he could think of nothing beautiful which it did not resemble. The trees upon the bank were giant garden plants; he noted a definite order in their arrangement, inhaled the fragrance of their blooms. A strange, roseate light shone through the spaces among their trunks, and the wind made in their branches the music of æolian harps. He had no wish to perfect his escape, was content to remain in that enchanting spot until retaken.

A whizz and rattle of grapeshot among the branches high above his head roused him from his dream. The baffled cannoneer had fired him a random farewell. He sprang to his feet, rushed up the sloping bank, and plunged into the forest.

All that day he travelled, laying his course by the rounding sun. The forest seemed interminable; nowhere did he discover a break in it, not even a woodman's road. He had not known that he lived in so wild a region. There was something uncanny in the revelation.

By nightfall he was fatigued, footsore, famishing. The thought of his wife and children urged him on. At last he found a road which led him in what he knew to be the right direction. It was as wide and straight as a city street, yet it seemed untravelled. No fields bordered it, no dwelling anywhere. Not so much as the barking of a dog suggested human habitation. The black bodies of the great trees formed a straight wall on both sides, terminating on the horizon in a point, like a diagram in a lesson in perspective. Overhead, as he looked up through this rift in the wood, shone great golden stars looking unfamiliar and grouped in strange constellations. He was sure they were arranged in some order which had a secret and malign significance. The wood on either side was full of singular noises, among which—once, twice, and again—he distinctly heard whispers in an unknown tongue.

His neck was in pain, and, lifting his hand to it, he found it horribly swollen. He knew that it had a circle of black where the rope had bruised it. His eyes felt congested; he could no longer close them. His tongue was swollen with thirst; he relieved its fever by thrusting it forward from between his teeth into the cool air. How softly the turf had carpeted the untravelled avenue! He could no longer feel the roadway beneath his feet!

Doubtless, despite his suffering, he fell asleep while walking, for now he sees another scene—perhaps he has merely recovered from a delirium. He stands at the gate of his own home. All is as he left it, and all bright and beautiful in the morning sunshine. He must have travelled the entire night. As he pushes open the gate and passes up the wide white walk, he sees a flutter of female garments; his wife, looking fresh and cool and sweet, steps down from the verandah to meet him. At the bottom of the steps she stands waiting, with a smile of ineffable joy, an attitude of matchless grace and dignity. Ah, how beautiful she is! He springs forward with extended arms. As he is about to clasp her, he feels a stunning blow upon the back of the neck; a blinding white light blazes all about him with a sound like the shock of a cannon—then all is darkness and silence!

Peyton Farquhar was dead; his body, with a broken neck, swung gently from side to side beneath the timbers of the Owl Creek bridge.

# THE AFFAIR AT COULTER'S NOTCH

AMBROSE BIERCE

"Do you think, colonel, that your brave Coulter would like to put one of his guns in here!" the general asked.

He was apparently not altogether serious; it certainly did not seem a place where any artillerist, however brave, would like to put a gun. The colonel thought that possibly his division commander meant good-humouredly to intimate that Captain Coulter's courage had been too highly extolled in a recent conversation between them.

"General," he replied warmly, "Coulter would like to put a gun anywhere within reach of those people," with a motion of his hand in the direction of the enemy.

"It is the only place," said the general. He was serious, then.

The place was a depression, a "notch," in the sharp crest of a hill. It was a pass, and through it ran a turnpike, which, reaching this highest point in its course by a sinuous ascent through a thin forest, made a similar, though less steep, descent toward the enemy. For a mile to the left and a mile to the right the ridge, though occupied by Federal infantry lying close behind the sharp crest, and appearing as if held in place by atmospheric pressure, was inaccessible to artillery. There was no place but the bottom of the notch, and that was barely wide enough for the roadbed. From the Confederate side this point was commanded by two batteries posted on a slightly lower elevation beyond a creek, and a half-mile away. All the guns but one were masked by the trees of an orchard; that one—it seemed a bit of impudence—was directly in front of a rather grandiose building, the planter's dwelling. The gun was safe enough in its exposure—but only because the Federal infantry had been forbidden to fire. Coulter's Notch—it came to be called so—was not, that pleasant summer afternoon, a place where one would "like to put a gun."

Three or four dead horses lay there, sprawling in the road, three or four dead men in a trim row at one side of it, and a little back, down the hill. All but one were cavalrymen belonging to the Federal advance. One was a quartermaster. The general commanding the division and the colonel commanding the brigade, with their staffs and escorts, had ridden into the notch to have a look at the enemy's guns—which had straightway obscured themselves in towering clouds of smoke. It was hardly profitable to be curious about guns which had the trick of the cuttlefish, and the season of observation was brief. At its conclusion—a short remove backward from where it began—occurred the conversation already partly reported. "It is the only place," the general repeated thoughtfully, " to get at them."

The colonel looked at him gravely. " There is room for but one gun, General—one against twelve."

"That is true—for only one at a time," said the commander with something like, yet not altogether like, a smile. " But then, your brave Coulter—a whole battery in himself."

The tone of irony was now unmistakable. It angered the colonel, but he did not know what to say. The spirit of military subordination is not favourable to retort, nor even deprecation. At this moment a young officer of artillery came riding slowly up the road attended by his bugler. It was Captain Coulter. He could not have been more than twenty-three years of age. He was of medium height, but very slender and lithe, sitting his horse with something of the air of a civilian. In face he was of a type singularly unlike the men about him; thin, high-nosed, grey-eyed, with a slight blonde moustache, and long, rather straggling hair of the same colour. There was an apparent negligence in his attire. His cap was worn with the visor a trifle askew; his coat was buttoned only at the sword belt, showing a considerable expanse of white shirt, tolerably clean for that stage of the campaign. But the negligence was all in his dress and bearing; in his face was a look of intense interest in his surroundings. His grey eyes, which seemed occasionally to strike right and left across the landscape, like searchlights, were for the most part fixed upon the sky beyond the Notch; until he should arrive at the summit of the road, there was nothing else in that direction to see. As he came opposite his division and brigade commanders at the roadside he saluted mechanically and was about to pass on. Moved by a sudden impulse, the colonel signed him to halt.

" Captain Coulter," he said, " the enemy has twelve pieces over there on the next ridge. If I rightly understand the general, he directs that you bring up a gun and engage them."

There was a blank silence; the general looked stolidly at a distant regiment swarming slowly up the hill through rough undergrowth, like a torn and draggled cloud of blue smoke; the captain appeared not to have observed him. Presently the captain spoke, slowly and with apparent effort :—

"On the next ridge, did you say, sir? Are the guns near the house?"

"Ah, you have been over this road before! Directly at the house."

"And it is—necessary—to engage them? The order is imperative?"

His voice was husky and broken. He was visibly paler. The colonel was astonished and mortified. He stole a glance at the commander. In that set, immobile face was no sign; it was as hard as bronze. A moment later the general rode away, followed by his staff and escort. The colonel, humiliated and indignant, was about to order Captain Coulter into arrest, when the latter spoke a few words in a low tone to his bugler, saluted, and rode straight forward into the Notch, where, presently, at the summit of the road, his field-glass at his eyes, he showed against the sky, he and his horse, sharply defined and motionless as an equestrian statue. The bugler had dashed down the road in the opposite direction at headlong speed and disappeared behind a wood. Presently his bugle was heard singing in the cedars, and in an incredibly short time a single gun with its caisson, each drawn by six horses and manned by its full complement of gunners, came bounding and banging up the grade in a storm of dust, unlimbered under cover, and was run forward by hand to the fatal crest among the dead horses. A gesture of the captain's arm, some strangely agile movements of the men in loading, and almost before the troops along the way had ceased to hear the rattle of the wheels, a great white cloud sprang forward down the slope, and with a deafening report the affair at Coulter's Notch had begun.

It is not intended to relate in detail the progress and incidents of that ghastly contest—a contest without vicissitudes, its alternations only different degrees of despair. Almost at the instant when Captain Coulter's gun blew its challenging cloud twelve answering clouds rolled upward from among the trees about the plantation house, a deep multiple report roared back like a broken echo, and thenceforth to the end the Federal cannoneers fought their hopeless battle in an atmosphere of living iron whose thoughts were lightnings and whose deeds were death.

Unwilling to see the efforts which he could not aid and the slaughter which he could not stay, the colonel had ascended the ridge at a point a quarter of a mile to the left, whence the Notch, itself invisible but pushing up successive masses of smoke, seemed the crater of a volcano in thundering eruption. With his glass he watched the enemy's guns, noting as he could the effects of Coulter's fire—if Coulter still lived to direct it. He saw that the Federal gunners, ignoring the enemy's pieces, whose position could be determined by their smoke only, gave their whole attention to the one which maintained its place in the open—the lawn in front of the house, with which it was accurately in line. Over and about that hardy piece the shells exploded at intervals of a few seconds. Some exploded in the house, as could be seen by thin ascensions of smoke from the breached roof. Figures of prostrate men and horses were plainly visible.

"If our fellows are doing such good work with a single gun," said the colonel to an aide who happened to be nearest, "they must be suffering like the devil from twelve. Go down and present the commander of that piece with my congratulations on the accuracy of his fire."

Turning to his adjutant-general he said, "Did you observe Coulter's damned reluctance to obey orders?"

"Yes, sir, I did."

"Well say nothing about it, please. I don't think the general will care to make any accusations. He will probably have enough to do in explaining his own connection with this uncommon way of amusing the rearguard of a retreating enemy."

A young officer approached from below, climbing breathless up the acclivity. Almost before he had saluted he gasped out:—

"Colonel, I am directed by Colonel Harmon to say that the enemy's guns are within easy reach of our rifles, and most of them visible from various points along the ridge."

The brigade commander looked at him without a trace of interest in his expression. "I know it," he said quietly.

The young adjutant was visibly embarrassed. "Colonel Harmon would like to have permission to silence those guns," he stammered.

"So should I," the colonel said in the same tone. "Present my compliments to Colonel Harmon and say to him that the general's orders not to fire are still in force."

The adjutant saluted and retired. The colonel ground his heel into the earth and turned to look again at the enemy's guns.

"Colonel," said the adjutant-general, "I don't know that I ought to say anything, but there is something wrong in all this. Do you happen to know that Captain Coulter is from the South?"

"No; *was* he, indeed?"

"I heard that last summer the division which the general then commanded was in the vicinity of Coulter's home—camped there for weeks, and——"

"Listen!" said the colonel, interrupting with an upward gesture. "Do you hear *that*?"

"That" was the silence of the Federal gun. The staff, the orderlies, the lines of infantry behind the crest—all had "heard," and were looking curiously in the direction of the crater, whence no smoke now ascended except desultory cloudlets from the enemy's shells. Then came the blare of a bugle, a faint rattle of wheels; a minute later the sharp reports recommenced with double activity. The demolished gun had been replaced with a sound one.

## THE AFFAIR AT COULTER'S NOTCH

"Yes," said the adjutant-general, resuming his narrative, "the general made the acquaintance of Coulter's family. There was trouble—I don't know the exact nature of it—something about Coulter's wife. She is a red-hot Secessionist, as they all are, except Coulter himself, but she is a good wife and high-bred lady. There was a complaint to army headquarters. The general was transferred to this division. It is odd that Coulter's battery should afterward have been assigned to it."

The colonel had risen from the rock upon which they had been sitting. His eyes were blazing with a generous indignation.

"See here, Morrison," said he, looking his gossiping staff officer straight in the face, "did you get that story from a gentleman or a liar?"

"I don't want to say how I got it, Colonel, unless it is necessary"—he was blushing a trifle—"but I'll stake my life upon its truth in the main."

The colonel turned toward a small knot of officers some distance away. "Lieutenant Williams!" he shouted.

One of the officers detached himself from the group, and, coming forward, saluted, saying: "Pardon me, Colonel, I thought you had been informed. Williams is dead down there by the gun. What can I do, sir?"

Lieutenant Williams was the aide who had had the pleasure of conveying to the officer in charge of the gun his brigade commander's congratulations.

"Go," said the colonel, "and direct the withdrawal of that gun instantly. Hold! I'll go myself."

He strode down the declivity toward the rear of the Notch at a break-neck pace, over rocks and through brambles, followed by his little retinue in tumultuous disorder. At the foot of the declivity they mounted their waiting animals and took to the road at a lively trot, round a bend and into the Notch. The spectacle which they encountered there was appalling.

Within that defile, barely broad enough for a single gun, were piled the wrecks of no fewer than four. They had noted the silencing of only the last one disabled—there had been a lack of men to replace it quickly. The *debris* lay on both sides of the road; the men had managed to keep an open way between, through which the fifth piece was now firing. The men?—they looked like demons of the pit! All were hatless, all stripped to the waist, their reeking skins black with blotches of powder and spattered with gouts of blood. They worked like madmen, with rammer and cartridge, lever and lanyard. They set their swollen shoulders and bleeding hands against the wheels at each recoil and heaved the heavy gun back to its place. There were no commands; in that awful environment of whooping shot, exploding shells, shrieking fragments of iron, and flying splinters of wood, none could have been heard.

Officers, if officers there were, were indistinguishable; all worked together—each while he lasted—governed by the eye. When the gun was sponged, it was loaded; when loaded, aimed and fired. The colonel observed something new to his military experience— something horrible and unnatural: the gun was bleeding at the mouth! In temporary default of water, the man sponging had dipped his sponge in a pool of his comrades' blood. In all this work there was no clashing; the duty of the instant was obvious. When one fell, another, looking a trifle cleaner, seemed to rise from the earth in the dead man's tracks, to fall in his turn.

With the ruined guns lay the ruined men—alongside the wreckage, under it and atop of it; and back down the road—a ghastly procession!—crept on hands and knees such of the wounded as were able to move. The colonel—he had compassionately sent his cavalcade to the right about—had to ride over those who were entirely dead in order not to crush those who were partly alive. Into that hell he tranquilly held his way, rode up alongside the gun, and, in the obscurity of the last discharge, tapped upon the cheek the man holding the rammer, who straightway fell, thinking himself killed. A fiend seven times damned sprang out of the smoke to take his place, but paused and gazed up at the mounted officer with an unearthly regard, his teeth flashing between his black lips, his eyes, fierce and expanded, burning like coals beneath his bloody brow. The colonel made an authoritative gesture and pointed to the rear. The fiend bowed in token of obedience. It was Captain Coulter.

Simultaneously with the colonel's arresting sign silence fell upon the whole field of action. The procession of missiles no longer streamed into that defile of death; the enemy also had ceased firing. His army had been gone for hours, and the commander of his rearguard, who had held his position perilously long in hope to silence the Federal fire, at that strange moment had silenced his own. " I was not aware of the breadth of my authority," thought the colonel facetiously, riding forward to the crest to see what had really happened.

An hour later his brigade was in bivouac on the enemy's ground, and its idlers were examining, with something of awe, as the faithful inspect a saint's relics, a score of straddling dead horses and three disabled guns, all spiked. The fallen men had been carried away; their crushed and broken bodies would have given too great satisfaction.

Naturally, the colonel established himself and his military family in the plantation house. It was somewhat shattered, but it was better than the open air. The furniture was greatly deranged and broken. The walls and ceilings were knocked away here and there, and there was a lingering odour of powder smoke everywhere. The beds, the closets of women's clothing, the cupboards were not greatly damaged. The new tenants for a night made themselves comfortable, and the practical effacement of Coulter's battery supplied them with an interesting topic.

During supper that evening an orderly of the escort showed himself into the dining-room, and asked permission to speak to the colonel.

"What is it, Barbour?" said that officer pleasantly, having overheard the request.

"Colonel, there is something wrong in the cellar; I don't know what—somebody there. I was down there rummaging about."

"I will go down and see," said a staff officer, rising.

"So will I," the colonel said; "let the others remain. Lead on orderly."

They took a candle from the table and descended the cellar stairs, the orderly in visible trepidation. The candle made but a feeble light, but presently, as they advanced, its narrow circle of illumination revealed a human figure seated on the ground against the black stone wall which they were skirting, its knees elevated, its head bowed sharply forward. The face, which should have been seen in profile, was invisible, for the man was bent so far forward that his long hair concealed it; and, strange to relate, the beard, of a much darker hue, fell in a great tangled mass and lay along the ground at his feet. They involuntarily paused; then the colonel, taking the candle from the orderly's shaking hand, approached the man and attentively considered him. The long dark beard was the hair of a woman—dead. The dead woman clasped in her arms a dead babe. Both were clasped in the arms of the man, pressed against his breast, against his lips. There was blood in the hair of the woman; there was blood in the hair of the man. A yard away lay an infant's foot. It was near an irregular depression in the beaten earth which formed the cellar's floor—a fresh excavation with a convex bit of iron, having jagged edges, visible in one of the sides. The colonel held the light as high as he could. The floor of the room above was broken through, the splinters pointing at all angles downward. "This casemate is not bomb-proof," said the colonel gravely; it did not occur to him that his summing up of the matter had any levity in it.

They stood about the group awhile in silence; the staff officer was thinking of his unfinished supper, the orderly of what might possibly be in one of the casks on the other side of the cellar. Suddenly the man, whom they had thought dead, raised his head and gazed tranquilly into their faces. His complexion was coal black; the cheeks were apparently tattooed in irregular sinuous lines from the eyes downward. The lips, too, were white, like those of a stage negro. There was blood upon his forehead.

The staff officer drew back a pace, the orderly two paces.

"What are you doing here, my man?" said the colonel, unmoved.

"This house belongs to me, sir," was the reply, civilly delivered. "To you? Ah, I see! And these?" "My wife and child. I am Captain Coulter."

# A WATCHER BY THE DEAD

### Ambrose Bierce

#### I

In an upper room of an unoccupied dwelling in that part of San Francisco known as North Beach lay the body of a man under a sheet. The hour was near nine in the evening; the room was dimly lighted by a single candle. Although the weather was warm, the two windows, contrary to the custom which gives the dead plenty of air, were closed and the blinds drawn down. The furniture of the room consisted of but three pieces—an arm-chair, a small reading-stand, supporting the candle, and a long kitchen-table, supporting the body of the man. All these, as also the corpse, would seem to have been recently brought in, for an observer, had there been one, would have seen that all were free from dust, whereas everything else in the room was pretty thickly coated with it, and there were cobwebs in the angles of the walls.

Under the sheet the outlines of the body could be traced, even the features, these having that unnaturally sharp definition which seems to belong to faces of the dead, but is really characteristic of those only that have been wasted by disease. From the silence of the room one would rightly have inferred that it was not in the front of the house, facing a street. It really faced nothing but a high breast of rock, the rear of the building being set into a hill.

As a neighbouring church clock was striking nine with an indolence which seemed to imply such an indifference to the flight of time that one could hardly help wondering why it took the trouble to strike at all, the single door of the room was opened and a man entered, advancing toward the body. As he did so the door closed, apparently of its own volition; there was a grating, as of a key turned with difficulty and the snap of the lock bolt as it shot into its socket. A sound of retiring footsteps in the passage outside ensued, and the man was, to all appearance, a prisoner. Advancing to the table, he stood a moment looking down at the body; then, with a slight shrug of the shoulders, walked over to one of the windows and hoisted the blind. The darkness outside was absolute, the panes were covered with dust, but, by wiping this away, he could see that the window was fortified with strong iron bars crossing it within a few inches of the glass, and imbedded in the masonry on each side. He examined the other window. It was the same. He manifested no great curiosity in the matter, did not even so much as raise the sash. If he was a prisoner he was apparently a tractable one. Having completed his examination of the room, he seated himself in the arm-chair, took a book from his pocket, drew the stand with its candle alongside and began to read.

The man was young—not more than thirty—dark in complexion, smoothed-shaven, with brown hair. His face was thin and high-nosed, with a broad forehead and a " firmness " of the chin and jaw which is said by those having it to denote resolution. The eyes were grey and steadfast, not moving except with definitive purpose. They were now for the greater part of the time fixed upon his book, but he occasionally withdrew them and turned them to the body on the table, not, apparently, from any dismal fascination which, in such circumstances, it might be supposed to exercise upon even a courageous person, nor with a conscious rebellion against the opposite influence which might dominate a timid one. He looked at it as if in his reading he had come upon something recalling him to a sense of his surroundings. Clearly this watcher by the dead was discharging his trust with intelligence and composure, as became him.

After reading for perhaps a half-hour he seemed to come to the end of a chapter and quietly laid away the book. He then rose, and, taking the reading-stand from the floor, carried it into a corner of the room near one of the windows, lifted the candle from it, and returned to the empty fireplace before which he had been sitting.

A moment later he walked over to the body on the table, lifted the sheet, and turned it back from the head, exposing a mass of dark hair and a thin face-cloth, beneath which the features showed with even sharper definition than before. Shading his eyes by interposing his free hand between them and the candle, he stood looking at his motionless companion with a serious and tranquil regard. Satisfied with his inspection, he pulled the sheet over the face again, and, returning to his chair, took some matches off the candlestick, put them in the side-pocket of his sack coat and sat down. He then lifted the candle from its socket and looked at it critically, as if calculating how long it would last. It was barely two inches long ; in another hour he would be in darkness ! He replaced it in the candlestick and blew it out.

II

In a physician's office in Kearny Street three men sat about a table, drinking punch and smoking. It was late in the evening, almost midnight, indeed, and there had been no lack of punch.

The eldest of the three, Dr. Helberson, was the host; it was in his rooms they sat. He was about thirty years of age; the others were even younger; all were physicians.

"The superstitious awe with which the living regard the dead," said Dr. Helberson, "is hereditary and incurable. One need no more be ashamed of it than of the fact that he inherits, for example, an incapacity for mathematics, or a tendency to lie."

The others laughed. "Oughtn't a man to be ashamed to be a liar?" asked the youngest of the three, who was, in fact a medical student not yet graduated.

"My dear Harper, I said nothing about that. The tendency to lie is one thing; lying is another."

"But do you think," said the third man, "that this superstitious feeling, this fear of the dead, reasonless as we know it to be, is universal? I am myself not conscious of it."

"Oh, but it is 'in your system' for all that," replied Helberson: "it needs only the right conditions—what Shakespeare calls the 'confederate season'—to manifest itself in some very disagreeable way that will open your eyes. Physicians and soldiers are, of course, more nearly free from it than others."

"Physicians and soldiers;—why don't you add hangmen and headsmen? Let us have in all the assassin classes."

"No, my dear Mancher; the juries will not let the public executioners acquire sufficient familiarity with death to be altogether unmoved by it."

Young Harper, who had been helping himself to a fresh cigar at the sideboard, resumed his seat. "What would you consider conditions under which any man of woman born would become insupportably conscious of his share of our common weakness in this regard?" he asked rather verbosely.

"Well, I should say that if a man were locked up all night with a corpse—alone—in a dark room—of a vacant house—with no bed-covers to pull over his head—and lived through it without going altogether mad—he might justly boast himself not of woman born, nor yet, like Macduff, a product of Cæsarean section."

"I thought you never would finish piling up conditions," said Harper; "but I know a man who is neither a physician nor a soldier who will accept them all, for any stake you like to name."

"Who is he?"

"His name is Jarette—a stranger in California; comes from my town in New York. I haven't any money to back him, but he will back himself with dead loads of it."

"How do you know that?"

"He would rather bet than eat. As for fear—I dare say he thinks it some cutaneous disorder, or, possibly, a particular kind of religious heresy."

"What does he look like?" Helberson was evidently becoming interested.

"Like Mancher, here—might be his twin brother."

"I accept the challenge," said Helberson promptly.

"Awfully obliged to you for the compliment, I'm sure," drawled Mancher, who was growing sleepy. "Can't I get into this?"

"Not against me," Helberson said. "I don't want *your* money."

"All right," said Mancher; "I'll be the corpse."

The others laughed.

The outcome of this crazy conversation we have seen.

### III

In extinguishing his meagre allowance of candle Mr. Jarette's object was to preserve it against some unforseen need. He may have thought, too, or half-thought, that the darkness would be no worse at one time than another, and if the situation became insupportable, it would be better to have a means of relief, or even release. At any rate, it was wise to have a little reserve of light, even if only to enable him to look at his watch.

No sooner had he blown out the candle and set it on the floor at his side than he settled himself comfortably in the arm-chair, leaned back and closed his eyes, hoping and expecting to sleep. In this he was disappointed; he had never in his life felt less sleepy, and in a few minutes he gave up the attempt. But what could he do? He could not go groping about in the absolute darkness at the risk of bruising himself—at the risk, too, of blundering against the table and rudely disturbing the dead. We all recognise their right to lie at rest, with immunity from all that is harsh and violent. Jarette almost succeeded in making himself believe that considerations of that kind restrained him from risking the collision and fixed him to the chair.

While thinking of this matter he fancied that he heard a faint sound in the direction of the table—what kind of sound he could hardly have explained. He did not turn his head. Why should he—in the darkness? But he listened—why should he not? And listening he grew giddy and grasped the arms of the chair for support. There was a strange ringing in his ears; his head seemed bursting; his chest was oppressed by the constriction of his clothing. He wondered why it was so, and whether these were symptoms of fear. Suddenly, with a long and strong expiration, his chest appeared to collapse, and with the great gasp with which he refilled his exhausted lungs the vertigo left him, and he knew that so intently had he listened that he had held his breath almost to suffocation. The revelation was vexatious; he arose, pushed away the chair with his foot, and strode to the centre of the room. But one does not stride far in darkness; he began to grope, and, finding the wall, followed it to an angle, turned, followed it past the two windows, and there in another corner came into violent contact with the reading-stand, overturning it. It made a clatter which startled him. He was annoyed. "How the devil could I have forgotten where it was!" he muttered, and groped his way along the third wall to the fireplace. "I must put things to rights," said Mr. Jarette, feeling the floor for the candle.

Having recovered that, he lighted it and instantly turned his eyes to the table, where, naturally, nothing had undergone any change. The reading-stand lay unobserved upon the floor; he had forgotten to "put it to rights." He looked all about the room, dispersing the deeper shadows by movements of the candle in his hand, and, finally, crossing over to the door, tried it by turning and pulling the knob with all his strength. It did not yield, and this seemed to afford him a certain satisfaction; indeed, he secured it more firmly by a bolt which he had not before observed. Returning to his chair, he looked at his watch; it was half-past nine. With a start of surprise he held the watch at his ear. It had not stopped. The candle was now visibly shorter. He again extinguished it, placing it on the floor at his side as before.

Mr. Jarette was not at his ease; he was distinctly dissatisfied with his surroundings, and with himself for being so. "What have I to fear?" he thought. "This is ridiculous and disgraceful; I will not be so great a fool." But courage does not come of saying, "I will be courageous," nor of recognising its appropriateness to the occasion. The more Jarette condemned himself, the more reason he gave himself for condemnation; the greater the number of variations which he played upon the simple theme of the harmlessness of the dead, the more horrible grew the discord of his emotions. "What!" he cried aloud in the anguish of his spirit, "what! shall I, who have not a shade of superstition in my nature—I, who have no belief in immortality—I, who know (and never more clearly than now) that the after-life is the dream of a desire—shall I lose at once my bet, my honour, and my self-respect, perhaps my reason, because certain savage ancestors, dwelling in caves and burrows, conceived the monstrous notion that the dead walk by night; that——" distinctly, unmistakably, Mr. Jarette heard behind him a light, soft sound of footfalls, deliberate, regular, and successively nearer!

## IV

Just before daybreak the next morning Dr. Helberson and his young friend Harper were driving slowly through the streets of North Beach in the doctor's coupé.

"Have you still the confidence of youth in the courage or stolidity of your friend?" said the elder man. "Do you believe that I have lost this wager?"

"I *know* you have," replied the other, with enfeebling emphasis.

"Well, upon my soul, I hope so." It was spoken earnestly,

almost solemnly. There was a silence for a few moments.

"Harper," the doctor resumed, looking very serious in the shifting half-lights that entered the carriage as they passed the street-lamps, "I don't feel altogether comfortable about this business. If your friend had not irritated me by the contemptuous manner in which he treated my doubt of his endurance—a purely physical quality—and by the cool incivility of his suggestion that the corpse be that of a physician, I should not have gone on with it. If anything should happen, we are ruined, as I fear we deserve to be."

"What can happen? Even if the matter should be taking a serious turn—of which I am not at all afraid—Mancher has only to resurrect himself and explain matters. With a genuine 'subject' from the dissecting-room, or one of your late patients, it might be different."

Dr. Mancher, then, had been as good as his promise; he was the "corpse." Dr. Helberson was silent for a long time, as the carriage, at a snail's pace, crept along the same street it had travelled two or three times already. Presently he spoke: "Well, let us hope that Mancher, if he has had to rise from the dead, has been discreet about it. A mistake in that might make matters worse instead of better."

"Yes," said Harper, "Jarette would kill him. But, doctor"—looking at his watch as the carriage passed a gas-lamp—"it is nearly four o'clock at last."

A moment later the two had quitted the vehicle, and were walking briskly toward the long unoccupied house belonging to the doctor, in which they had immured Mr. Jarette, in accordance with the terms of the mad wager. As they neared it, they met a man running. "Can you tell me," he cried, suddenly checking his speed, "where I can find a physician?"

"What's the matter?" Helberson asked, non-committal.

"Go and see for yourself," said the man, resuming his running.

They hastened on. Arrived at the house, they saw several persons entering in haste and excitement. In some of the dwellings near by and across the way the chamber windows were thrown up, showing a protrusion of heads. All heads were asking questions, none heeding the questions of the others. A few of the windows with closed blinds were illuminated; the inmates of those rooms were dressing to come down. Exactly opposite the door of the house which they sought a street-lamp threw a yellow, insufficient light upon the scene, seeming to say that it could disclose a good deal more if it wished. Harper, who was now deathly pale, paused at the door and laid a hand upon his companion's arm. "It's all up with us, doctor," he said in extreme agitation, which contrasted strangely with his free and easy words; "the game has gone against us all. Let's not go in there; I'm for lying low."

"I'm a physician," said Dr. Helberson calmly; "there may be need of one."

They mounted the doorsteps and were about to enter. The door was open; the street lamp opposite lighted the passage into which it opened. It was full of people. Some had ascended the stairs at the farther end, and, denied admittance above, waited for better fortune. All were talking, none listening. Suddenly, on the upper landing there was a great commotion; a man had sprung out of a door and was breaking away from those endeavouring to detain him. Down through the mass of affrighted idlers he came, pushing them aside, flattening them against the wall on one side, or compelling them to cling by the rail on the other, clutching them by the throat, striking them savagely, thrusting them back down the stairs, and walking over the fallen. His clothing was in disorder, he was without a hat. His eyes, wild and restless, had in them something more terrifying than his apparently superhuman strength. His face, smooth-shaven, was bloodless, his hair snow white.

As the crowd at the foot of the stairs, having more freedom, fell away to let him pass, Harper sprang forward. "Jarette! Jarette!" he cried.

Dr. Helberson seized Harper by the collar and dragged him back. The man looked into their faces without seeming to see them, and sprang through the door, down the steps, into the street and away. A stout policeman, who had had inferior success in conquering his way down the stairway, followed a moment later and started in pursuit, all the heads in the windows—those of women and children now—screaming in guidance.

The stairway being now partly cleared, most of the crowd having rushed down to the street to observe the flight and pursuit, Dr. Helberson mounted to the landing, followed by Harper. At a door in the upper passage an officer denied them admittance. "We are physicians," said the doctor, and they passed in. The room was full of men, dimly seen, crowded about a table. The newcomers edged their way forward, and looked over the shoulders of those in the front rank. Upon the table, the lower limbs covered with a sheet, lay the body of a man, brilliantly illuminated by the beam of a bull's-eye lantern held by a policeman standing at the feet. The others, excepting those near the head—the officer himself—all were in darkness. The face of the body showed yellow, repulsive, horrible! The eyes were partly open and upturned, and the jaw fallen; traces of froth defiled the lips, the chin, the cheeks. A tall man, evidently a physician, bent over the body with his hand thrust under the shirt front. He withdrew it and placed two fingers in the open mouth. "This man has been about two hours dead," said he. "It is a case for the coroner."

He drew a card from his pocket, handed it to the officer, and made his way toward the door.

"Clear the room—out, all!" said the officer sharply, and the body disappeared as if it had been snatched away, as he shifted the lantern and flashed its beam of light here and there against the faces of the crowd. The effect was amazing! The men, blinded, confused, almost terrified, made a tumultuous rush for the door, pushing, crowding, and tumbling over one another as they fled, like the hosts of Night before the shafts of Apollo. Upon the struggling, trampling mass the officer poured his light without pity and without cessation. Caught in the current, Helberson and Harper were swept out of the room and cascaded down the stairs into the street.

"Good God, doctor! did I not tell you that Jarette would kill him?" said Harper, as soon as they were clear of the crowd.

"I believe you did," replied the other without apparent emotion.

They walked on in silence, block after block. Against the greying east the dwellings of our hill tribes showed in silhouette. The familiar milk-waggon was already astir in the streets; the baker's man would soon come upon the scene; the newspaper carrier was abroad in the land.

"It strikes me, youngster," said Helberson, "that you and I have been having too much of the morning air lately. It is unwholesome; we need a change. What do you say to a tour in Europe?"

"When?"

"I'm not particular. I should suppose that four o'clock this afternoon would be early enough."

"I'll meet you at the boat," said Harper.

V

Seven years afterward these two men sat upon a bench in Madison Square, New York, in familiar conversation. Another man, who had been observing them for some time, himself unobserved, approached and, courteously lifting his hat from locks as white as snow, said: "I beg your pardon, gentlemen, but when you have killed a man by coming to life, it is best to change clothes with him, and at the first opportunity make a break for liberty."

Helberson and Harper exchanged significant glances. They were apparently amused. The former then looked the stranger kindly in the eye, and replied:

"That has always been my plan. I entirely agree with you as to its advant——" He stopped suddenly and grew deathly pale. He stared at the man, open-mouthed; he trembled visibly.

"Ah!" said the stranger, "I see that you are indisposed, doctor. If you cannot treat yourself, Dr. Harper can do something for you, I am sure."

"Who the devil are you?" said Harper bluntly.

The stranger came nearer, and, bending toward them, said in a whisper: " I call myself Jarette sometimes, but I don't mind telling you, for old friendship, that I am Dr. William Mancher."

The revelation brought both men to their feet. " Mancher! " they cried in a breath; and Helberson added: " It is true, by God! "

" Yes," said the stranger, smiling vaguely, " it is true enough, no doubt."

He hesitated, and seemed to be trying to recall something, then began humming a popular air. He had apparently forgotten their presence.

" Look here, Mancher," said the elder of the two, " tell us just what occurred that night—to Jarette, you know."

" Oh yes, about Jarette," said the other. " It's odd I should have neglected to tell you—I tell it so often. You see I knew, by overhearing him talking to himself, that he was pretty badly frightened. So I couldn't resist the temptation to come to life and have a bit of fun out of him—I couldn't, really. That was all right, though certainly I did not think he would take it so seriously; I did not, truly. And afterward—well, it was a tough job changing places with him, and then—damn you! you didn't let me out! "

Nothing could exceed the ferocity with which these last words were delivered. Both men stepped back in alarm.

" We ?—why—why——" Helberson stammered, losing his self-possession utterly, " we had nothing to do with it."

" Didn't I say you were Doctors Hellborn and Sharper ? " inquired the lunatic, laughing.

" My name is Helberson, yes; and this gentleman is Mr. Harper." replied the former, reassured. " But we are not physicians now; we are—well, hang it, old man, we are gamblers."

And that was the truth.

" A very good profession—very good, indeed; and, by the way, I hope Sharper here paid over Jarette's money like an honest stakeholder. A very good and honourable profession," he repeated, thoughtfully, moving carelessly away; " but I stick to the old one. I am High Supreme Medical Officer of the Bloomingdale Asylum; it is my duty to cure the superintendent."

# HENRY JAMES
## 1843–1916

# THE TREE OF KNOWLEDGE

## I

It was one of the secret opinions, such as we all have, of Peter Brench that his main success in life would have consisted in his never having committed himself about the work, as it was called, of his friend, Morgan Mallow. This was a subject on which it was, to the best of his belief, impossible, with veracity, to quote him, and it was nowhere on record that he had, in the connection, on any occasion and in any embarrassment, either lied or spoken the truth. Such a triumph had its honour even for a man of other triumphs—a man who had reached fifty, who had escaped marriage, who had lived within his means, who had been in love with Mrs. Mallow for years without breathing it, and who, last not least, had judged himself once for all. He had so judged himself in fact that he felt an extreme and general humility to be his proper portion; yet there was nothing that made him think so well of his parts as the course he had steered so often through the shallows just mentioned. It became thus a real wonder that the friends in whom he had most confidence were just those with whom he had most reserves. He couldn't tell Mrs. Mallow—or at least he supposed, excellent man, he couldn't—that she was the one beautiful reason he had never married; any more than he could tell her husband that the sight of the multiplied marbles in that gentleman's studio was an affliction of which even time had never blunted the edge. His victory, however, as I have intimated, in regard to these productions, was not simply in his not having let it out that he deplored them; it was, remarkably, in his not having kept it in by anything else.

The whole situation, among these good people, was verily a marvel, and there was probably not such another for a long way from the spot that engages us—the point at which the soft declivity of Hampstead began at that time to confess in broken accents to St. John's Wood. He despised Mallow's statues and adored Mallow's wife, and yet was distinctly fond of Mallow, to whom, in turn, he was equally dear. Mrs. Mallow rejoiced in the statues—though she preferred, when pressed, the busts ; and if she was visibly attached to Peter Brench it was because of his affection for Morgan. Each loved the other, moreover, for the love borne in each case to Lancelot, whom the Mallows respectively cherished as their only child and whom the friend of their fireside identified as the third, but decidedly the handsomest, of his godsons. Already in the old years it had come to that—that no one, for such a relation, could possibly have occurred to any of them, even to the baby itself, but Peter. There was luckily a certain independence, of the pecuniary sort, all round ; the Master could never otherwise have spent his solemn *Wanderjahre* in Florence and Rome and continued, by the Thames as well as by the Arno and the Tiber, to add unpurchased group to group and model, for what was too apt to prove in the event mere love, fancy-heads of celebrities either too busy or too buried—too much of the age or too little of it—to sit. Neither could Peter, lounging in almost daily, have found time to keep the whole complicated tradition so alive by his presence. He was massive, but mild, the depositary of these mysteries—large and loose and ruddy and curly, with deep tones, deep eyes, deep pockets, to say nothing of the habit of long pipes, soft hats and brownish, greyish, weather-faded clothes, apparently always the same.

He had " written," it was known, but had never spoken—never spoken, in particular, of that ; and he had the air (since, as was believed, he continued to write) of keeping it up in order to have something more—as if he had not, at the worst, enough—to be silent about. Whatever his air, at any rate, Peter's occasional unmentioned prose and verse were quite truly the result of an impulse to maintain the purity of his taste by establishing still more firmly the right relation of fame to feebleness. The little green door of his domain was in a garden-wall on which the stucco was cracked and stained, and in the small detached villa behind it everything was old, the furniture, the servants, the books, the prints, the habits and the new improvements. The Mallows, at Carrara Lodge, were within ten minutes, and the studio there was on their little land, to which they had added, in their happy faith, to build it. This was the good fortune, if it was not the ill, of her having brought him, in marriage, a portion that put them in a manner at their ease and enabled them thus, on their side, to keep it up. And they did keep it up—they always had—the infatuated sculptor and his wife, for whom Nature had refined on the impossible by relieving them of the sense of the difficult. Morgan had, at all events, everything of the sculptor but the spirit of Phidias—the brown velvet, the becoming *beretto*, the " plastic " presence, the fine fingers, the beautiful accent in Italian, and the old Italian factotum. He seemed to make up for everything when he addressed Egidio with the " tu " and waved him to turn one of the rotary pedestals of which the place was full. They were tremendous

Italians at Carrara Lodge, and the secret of the part played by this fact in Peter's life was, in a large degree, that it gave him, sturdy Briton that he was, just the amount of " going abroad " he could bear. The Mallows were all his Italy, but it was in a measure for Italy he liked them. His one worry was that Lance—to which they had shortened his godson—was, in spite of a public school, perhaps a shade too Italian. Morgan, meanwhile, looked like somebody's flattering idea of somebody's own person as expressed in the great room provided at the Uffizzi Museum for Portraits of Artists by Themselves. The Master's sole regret that he had not been born rather to the brush than to the chisel sprang from his wish that he might have contributed to that collection.

It appeared, with time, at any rate, to be to the brush that Lance had been born ; for Mrs. Mallow, one day when the boy was turning twenty, broke it to their friend, who shared, to the last delicate morsel, their problems and pains, that it seemed as if nothing would really do but that he should embrace the career. It had been impossible longer to remain blind to the fact that he gained no glory at Cambridge, where Brench's own college had, for a year, tempered its tone to him as for Brench's own sake. Therefore why renew the vain form of preparing him for the impossible ? The impossible—it had become clear—was that he should be anything but an artist.

" Oh dear, dear ! " said poor Peter.

" Don't you believe in it ? " asked Mrs. Mallow, who still, at more than forty, had her violet velvet eyes, her creamy satin skin, and her silken chestnut hair.

" Believe in what ? "

" Why, in Lance's passion."

" I don't know what you mean by ' believing in it.' I've never been unaware, certainly, of his disposition, from his earliest time, to daub and draw ; but I confess I've hoped it would burn out."

" But why should it," she sweetly smiled, " with his wonderful heredity ? Passion is passion—though of course, indeed, you, dear Peter, know nothing of that. Has the Master's ever burned out ? "

Peter looked off a little and, in his familiar, formless way, kept up for a moment a sound between a smothered whistle and a subdued hum. " Do you think he's going to be another Master ? "

She seemed scarce prepared to go that length, yet she had, on the whole, a most marvellous trust. " I know what you mean by that. Will it be a career to incur jealousies and provoke the machinations that have been at times almost too much for his father ? Well—say it may be, since nothing but clap-trap, in these dreadful days, *can*, it would seem, make its way, and since, with the curse of refinement and distinction, one may easily find one's self begging one's bread. Put it at the worst—say he *has* the misfortune to wing his flight further than the vulgar taste of his stupid countrymen can follow. Think, all the same, of the happiness—the same that the Master has had. He'll *know*."

Peter looked rueful. " Ah, but *what* will he know ? "

" Quiet joy ! " cried Mrs. Mallow, quite impatient and turning away.

## II

He had, of course, before long, to meet the boy himself on it and hear that, practically, everything was settled. Lance was not to go up again, but to go instead to Paris, where, since the die was cast, he would find the best advantages. Peter had always felt that he must be taken as he was, but had never perhaps found him so much as he was on this occasion. " You chuck Cambridge then altogether ? Doesn't that seem rather a pity ? "

Lance would have been like his father, to his friend's sense, had he had less humour, and like his mother had he had more beauty. Yet it was a good middle way, for Peter, that, in the modern manner, he was, to the eye, rather the young stockbroker than the young artist. The youth reasoned that it was a question of time—there was such a mill to go through, such an awful lot to learn. He had talked with fellows and had judged. " One has got to-day," he said, " don't you see ? to know."

His interlocutor, at this, gave a groan. " Oh, hang it, *don't* know ! "

Lance wondered. " ' Don't ' ? Then what's the use——? "

" The use of what ? "

" Why, of anything. Don't you think I've talent ? "

Peter smoked away, for a little, in silence ; then went on : " It isn't knowledge, it's ignorance that—as we've been beautifully told—is bliss."

" Don't you think I have talent ? " Lance repeated.

Peter, with his trick of queer, kind demonstrations, passed his arm round his godson and held him a moment. " How do I know ? "

" Oh " said the boy, " if it's your own ignorance you're defending——! "

Again, for a pause, on the sofa, his godfather smoked. " It isn't. I've the misfortune to be omniscient."

" Oh well," Lance laughed again, " if you know *too* much——! "

" That's what I do, and why I'm so wretched."

Lance's gaiety grew. " Wretched ? Come, I say ! "

" But I forgot," his companion went on, " you're not to know about that. It would indeed, for you too, make the too much. Only I'll tell you what I'll do." And Peter got up from the sofa. " If you'll go up again, I'll pay your way at Cambridge."

Lance stared, a little rueful in spite of being still amused. " Oh, Peter ! You disapprove so of Paris ? "

" Well, I'm afraid of it."

"Ah, I see."

"No, you don't see—yet. But you will—that is, you would. And you mustn't."

The young man thought more gravely. "But one's innocence, already——"

"Is considerably damaged? Ah, that won't matter," Peter persisted—"we'll patch it up here."

"Here? Then you want me to stay at home?"

Peter almost confessed to it. "Well, we're so right—we four together—just as we are. We're so safe. Come don't spoil it."

The boy, who had turned to gravity, turned from this, on the real pressure of his friend's tone, to consternation. "Then what's a fellow to be?"

"My particular care. Come, old man "—and Peter now fairly pleaded—" *I'll* look out for you."

Lance, who had remained on the sofa with his legs out and his hands in his pockets, watched him with eyes that showed suspicion. Then he got up. "You think there's something the matter with me—that I can't make a success."

"Well, what do you call a success?"

Lance thought again. "Why, the best sort, I suppose, is to please one's self. Isn't that the sort that, in spite of cabals and things, is, in his own peculiar line, the Master's?"

There were so much too many things in this question to be answered at once that they practically checked the discussion, which became particularly difficult in the light of such renewed proof that, though the young man's innocence might, in the course of his studies, as he contended, somewhat have shrunken, the finer essence of it still remained. That was indeed exactly what Peter had assumed and what, above all, he desired; yet, perversely enough, it gave him a chill. The boy believed in the cabals and things believed in the peculiar line, believed, in short, in the Master. What happened a month or two later was not that he went up again at the expense of his godfather, but that a fortnight after he had got settled in Paris this personage sent him fifty pounds.

He had meanwhile, at home, this personage, made up his mind to the worst; and what it might be had never yet grown quite so vivid to him as when, on his presenting himself one Sunday night, as he never failed to do, for supper, the mistress of Carrara Lodge met him with an appeal as to—of all things in the world—the wealth of the Canadians. She was earnest, she was even excited. "Are many of them *really* rich?"

He had to confess that he knew nothing about them, but he often thought afterwards of that evening. The room in which they sat was adorned with sundry specimens of the Master's genius, which had the merit of being, as Mrs. Mallow herself frequently suggested, of an unusually convenient size. They were indeed of dimensions

not customary in the products of the chisel and had the singularity
that, if the objects and features intended to be small looked too
large, the objects and features intended to be large looked too small.
The Master's intention, whether in respect to this matter or to any
other, had, in almost any case, even after years, remained undis-
coverable to Peter Brench. The creations that so failed to reveal
it stood about on pedestals and brackets, on tables and shelves, a
little staring white population, heroic, idyllic, allegoric, mythic,
symbolic, in which " scale " has so strayed and lost itself that the
public square and the chimney-piece seemed to have changed places,
the monumental being all diminutive and the diminutive all monumental; branches, at any rate, markedly, of a family in which
stature was rather oddly irrespective of function, age, and sex.
They formed, like the Mallows themselves, poor Brench's own family
—having at least, to such a degree, the note of familiarity. The
occasion was one of those he had long ago learnt to know and to
name—short flickers of the faint flame, soft gusts of a kinder air.
Twice a year, regularly, the Master believed in his fortune, in
addition to believing all the year round in his genius. This time
it was to be made by a bereaved couple from Toronto, who had
given him the handsomest order for a tomb to three lost children,
each of whom they desired to be, in the composition, emblematically
and characteristically represented.

Such was naturally the moral of Mrs. Mallow's question: if their
wealth was to be assumed, it was clear, from the nature of their
admiration, as well as from mysterious hints thrown out (they were
a little odd!) as to other possibilities of the same mortuary sort,
that their further patronage might be; and not less evident that,
should the Master become at all known in those climes, nothing
would be more inevitable than a run of Canadian custom. Peter
had been present before at runs of custom, colonial and domestic—
present at each of those of which the aggregation had left so few
gaps in the marble company round him; but it was his habit never,
at these junctures, to prick the bubble in advance. The fond
illusion, while it lasted, eased the wound of elections never won,
the long ache of medals and diplomas carried off, on every chance,
by every one but the Master; it lighted the lamp, moreover, that
would glimmer through the next eclipse. They lived, however,
after all—as it was always beautiful to see—at a height scarce
susceptible of ups and downs. They strained a point, at times,
charmingly, to admit that the public was here and there, not too
bad to buy; but they would have been nowhere without their
attitude that the Master was always too good to sell. They were,
at all events, deliciously formed, Peter often said to himself, for
their fate; the Master had a vanity, his wife had loyalty, of which
success, depriving these things of innocence, would have diminished the merit and the grace. Any one could be charming under a

charm, and, as he looked about him at a world of prosperity more void of proportion even than the Master's museum, he wondered if he knew another pair that so completely escaped vulgarity.

"What a pity Lance isn't with us to rejoice!" Mrs. Mallow on this occasion sighed at supper.

"We'll drink to the health of the absent," her husband replied, filling his friend's glass and his own and giving a drop to their companion; "but we must hope that he's preparing himself for a happiness much less like this of ours this evening—excusable as I grant it to be—than like the comfort we have always—whatever has happened or has not happened—been able to trust ourselves to enjoy. The comfort," the Master explained, leaning back in the pleasant lamplight and firelight, holding up his glass and looking round at his marble family, quartered more or less, a monstrous brood, in every room—" the comfort of art in itself!"

Peter looked a little shyly at his wine. "Well—I don't care what you may call it, a fellow doesn't—but Lance must learn to *sell*, you know. I drink to his acquisition of the secret of a base popularity!"

"Oh, yes, *he* must sell," the boy's mother, who was still more, however, this seemed to give out, the Master's wife, rather artlessly conceded.

"Oh," the sculptor, after a moment, confidently pronounced, "Lance *will*. Don't be afraid. He will have learnt."

"Which is exactly what Peter," Mrs. Mallow gaily returned—"why in the world were you so perverse, Peter?—wouldn't, when he told him, hear of."

Peter, when this lady looked at him, with accusatory affection—a grace, on her part, not infrequent—could never find a word; but the Master, who was always all amenity and tact, helped him out now as he had often helped him before. "That's his old idea, you know—on which we've so often differed; his theory that the artist should be all impulse and instinct. *I* go in, of course, for a certain amount of school. Not too much, but a due proportion. There's where his protest came in," he continued to explain to his wife, "as against what *might*, don't you see? be in question for Lance."

"Ah, well"—and Mrs. Mallow turned the violet eyes across the table at the subject of this discourse—"he's sure to have meant, of course, nothing but good; but that wouldn't have prevented him, if Lance *had* taken his advice from being, in effect, horribly cruel."

They had a sociable way of talking of him to his face as if he had been in the clay or—at most—in the plaster, and the Master was unfailingly generous. He might have been waving Egidio to make him revolve. "Ah, but poor Peter was not so wrong as to what it may, after all, come to that he *will* learn."

"Oh, but nothing artistically bad," she urged—still, for poor Peter, arch and dewy.

"Why, just the little French tricks," said the Master: on which their friend had to pretend to admit, when pressed by Mrs. Mallow, that these aesthetic vices had been the objects of his dread.

### III

"I know now," Lance said to him the next year, "why you were so much against it." He had come back, supposedly for a mere interval, and was looking about him at Carrara Lodge, where indeed he had already, on two or three occasions, since his expatriation, briefly appeared. This had the air of a longer holiday. "Something rather awful has happened to me. It *isn't* so very good to know."

"I'm bound to say high spirits don't show in your face," Peter was rather ruefully forced to confess. "Still, are you very sure you do know?"

"Well, I at least know as much as I can bear." These remarks were exchanged in Peter's den, and the young man, smoking cigarettes, stood before the fire with his back against the mantel. Something of his bloom seemed really to have left him.

Poor Peter wondered. "You're clear then as to what in particular I wanted you not to go for?"

"In particular?" Lance thought. "It seems to me that, in particular, there can have been but one thing."

They stood for a little sounding each other. "Are you quite sure?"

"Quite sure I'm a beastly duffer? Quite—by this time."

"Oh!"—and Peter turned away as if almost with relief.

"It's *that* that isn't pleasant to find out."

"Oh, I don't care for 'that,'" said Peter, presently coming round again. "I mean I personally don't."

"Yet I hope you can understand a little that I myself should!"

"Well, what do you mean by it?" Peter sceptically asked.

And on this Lance had to explain—how the upshot of his studies in Paris had inexorably proved a mere deep doubt of his means. These studies had waked him up, and a new light was in his eyes; but what the new light did was really to show him too much. "Do you know what's the matter with me? I'm too horribly intelligent. Paris was really the last place for me. I've learnt what I can't do."

Poor Peter stared—it was a staggerer; but even after they had had, on the subject, a longish talk in which the boy brought out to the full the hard truth of his lesson, his friend betrayed less pleasure than usually breaks into a face to the happy tune of "I told you so!" Poor Peter himself made now indeed so little a point of having told him so that Lance broke ground in a different place a day or two after. "What was it then that—before I went—you were afraid I should find out?" This, however, Peter refused to tell him, on the ground that if he hadn't yet guessed perhaps he never would, and that nothing at all, for either of them, in any case, was to be gained by giving the thing a name. Lance eyed him, on this, an instant, with the bold curiosity of youth—with the air indeed of having in his mind two or three names, of which one or other would be right. Peter, nevertheless, turning his back again, offered no encouragement, and when they parted afresh it was with some show of impatience on the side of the boy. Accordingly, at their next encounter, Peter saw at a glance that he had now, in the interval, divined and that, to sound his note, he was only waiting till they should find themselves alone. This he had soon arranged, and he then broke straight out. "Do you know your conundrum has been keeping me awake? But in the watches of the night the answer came over me—so that, upon my honour, I quite laughed out. Had you been supposing I had to go to Paris to learn *that*?" Even now, to see him still so sublimely on his guard, Peter's young friend had to laugh afresh. "You won't give a sign till you're sure? Beautiful old Peter!" But Lance at last produced it. "Why, hang it, the truth about the Master."

It made between them, for some minutes, a lively passage, full of wonder, for each, at the wonder of the other. "Then how long have you understood—"

"The true value of his work? I understood it," Lance recalled, "as soon as I began to understand anything. But I didn't begin fully to do that, I admit, till I got *là-bas*."

"Dear, dear!"—Peter gasped with retrospective dread.

"But for what have you taken me? I'm a hopeless muff—that I *had* to have rubbed in. But I'm not such a muff as the Master!" Lance declared.

"Then why did you never tell me——?"

"That I hadn't, after all"—the boy took him up—"remained such an idiot? Just because I never dreamed *you* knew. But I beg your pardon. I only wanted to spare you. And what I don't now understand is how the deuce then, for so long, you've managed to keep bottled."

Peter produced his explanation, but only after some delay and with a gravity not void of embarrassment. "It was for your mother."

"Oh!" said Lance.

"And that's the great thing now—since the murder *is* out. I want a promise from you. I mean"—and Peter almost feverishly followed it up—"a vow from you, solemn and such as you owe me, here on the spot, that you'll sacrifice anything rather than let her ever guess——"

"That *I've* guessed?"—Lance took it in. "I see." He evidently, after a moment, had taken in much. "But what is it you have in mind that I may have a chance to sacrifice?"

"Oh, one has always something."

Lance looked at him hard. "Do you mean that *you've* ha ——?" The look he received back, however, so put the question by that he found soon enough another. "Are you really sure my mother doesn't know?"

Peter, after renewed reflection, was really sure. "If she does, she's too wonderful."

"But aren't we all too wonderful?"

"Yes," Peter granted—"but in different ways. The thing's so desperately important because your father's little public consists only, as you know then," Peter developed—"well, of how many?"

"First of all," the Master's son risked, "of himself. And last of all too. I don't quite see of whom else."

Peter had an approach to impatience. "Of your mother, I say—*always*."

Lance cast it all up. "You absolutely feel that?"

"Absolutely."

"Well, then, with yourself, that makes three."

"Oh, *me*!" and Peter, with a wag of his kind old head, modestly excused himself. "The number is, at any rate, small enough for any individual dropping out to be too dreadfully missed. Therefore, to put it in a nutshell, take care, my boy—that's all—that *you're* not!"

"I've got to keep on humbugging?" Lance sighed.

"It's just to warn you of the danger of your failing of that that I've seized this opportunity."

"And what do you regard in particular," the young man asked, "as the danger?"

"Why, this certainty; that the moment your mother, who feels so strongly, should suspect your secret—well," said Peter desperately, "the fat would be on the fire."

Lance, for a moment, seemed to stare at the blaze. "She'd throw me over?"

"She'd throw *him* over."

"And come round to us?"

Peter, before he answered, turned away. "Come round to *you*." But he had said enough to indicate—and, as he evidently trusted, to avert—the horrid contingency.

## IV

Within six months again, however, his fear was, on more occasions than one, all before him. Lance had returned to Paris, to another trial; then had reappeared at home and had had, with his father, for the first time in his life, one of the scenes that strike sparks. He described it with much expression to Peter, as to whom—since they had never done so before—it was a sign of a new reserve on the part of the pair at Carrara Lodge that they at present failed, on a matter of intimate interest, to open themselves—if not in joy, then in sorrow—to their good friend. This produced perhaps, practically, between the parties, a shade of alienation and a slight intermission of commerce—marked mainly indeed by the fact that, to talk at his ease with his old playmate, Lance had, in general, to come to see him. The closest, if not quite the gayest relation they had yet known together was thus ushered in.

The difficulty for poor Lance was a tension at home, begotten by the fact that his father wished him to be, at least the sort of success he himself had been. He hadn't "chucked" Paris—though nothing appeared more vivid to him than that Paris had chucked him; he would go back again because of the fascination in trying, in seeing, in sounding the depths—in learning one's lesson, in fine, even if the lesson were simply that of one's impotence in the presence of one's larger vision. But what did the Master, all aloft in his senseless fluency, know of impotence, and what vision—to be called such—had he, in all his blind life, ever had? Lance, heated and indignant, frankly appealed to his godparent on this score.

His father, it appeared, had come down on him for having, after so long, nothing to show, and hoped that, on his next return, this deficiency would be repaired. *The* thing the Master complacently set forth was—for any artist, however inferior to himself—at least to " do " something. " What can you do ? That's all I ask ! " *He* had certainly done enough, and there was no mistake about what he had to show. Lance had tears in his eyes when it came thus to letting his old friend know how great the strain might be on the " sacrifice " asked of him. It wasn't so easy to continue humbugging—as from son to parent—after feeling one's self despised for not grovelling in mediocrity. Yet a noble duplicity was what, as they intimately faced the situation, Peter went on requiring ; and it was still, for a time, what his young friend, bitter and sore, managed loyally to comfort him with. Fifty pounds more than once again, it was true, rewarded, both in London and in Paris, the young friend's loyalty ; none the less sensibly, doubtless, at the moment, that the money was a direct advance on a decent sum for which Peter had long since privately pre-arranged an ultimate function. Whether by these arts or others, at all events, Lance's just resentment was kept for a season—but only for a season—at bay. The day arrived when he warned his companion that he could hold out—or hold in—no longer. Carrara Lodge had had to listen to another lecture delivered from a great height—an infliction really heavier, at last, than, without striking back or in some way letting the Master have the truth, flesh and blood could bear.

" And what I don't see is," Lance observed with a certain

irritated eye for what was, after all, if it came to that, due to himself too—" What I don't see is, upon my honour, how *you*, as things are going, can keep the game up."

"Oh, the game for me is only to hold my tongue," said placid Peter. "And I have my reason."

"Still my mother?"

Peter showed, as he had often shown it before—that is by turning it straight away—a queer face. "What will you have? I haven't ceased to like her."

She's beautiful—she's a dear, of course," Lance granted; but what is she to you, after all, and what is it to you that, as to anything whatever, she should or she shouldn't?"

Peter, who had turned red, hung fire a little. Well—it's all, simply, what I make of it."

There was now, however, in his young friend, a strange, an adopted, insistence. "What are you, after all, to *her*?"

"Oh, nothing. But that's another matter."

"She cares only for my father," said Lance the Parisian.

"Naturally—and that's just why."

"Why you've wished to spare her?"

"Because she cares so tremendously much."

Lance took a turn about the room, but with his eyes still on his host. "How awfully—always—you must have liked her!"

"Awfully. Always," said Peter Brench.

The young man continued for a moment to muse—then stopped again in front of him. "Do you know how much she cares?" Their eyes met on it, but Peter, as if his own found something new in Lance's, appeared to hesitate, for the first time for so long, to say he did know. "*I've* only just found out," said Lance. "She came to my room last night, after being present, in silence and only with her eyes on me, at what I had had to take from him; she came—and she was with me an extraordinary hour."

He paused again, and they had again for a while sounded each other. Then something—and it made him suddenly turn pale—came to Peter. "She *does* know?"

"She does know. She let it all out to me—so as to demand of me no more than that, as she said, of which she herself had been capable. She has always, always known," said Lance without pity.

Peter was silent a long time; during which his companion might have heard him gently breathe and, on touching him, might have felt within him the vibration of a long, low sound suppressed. By the time he spoke, at last, he had taken everything in. "Then I do see how tremendously much."

"Isn't it wonderful?" Lance asked.

"Wonderful," Peter mused.

"So that if your original effort to keep me from Paris was to keep me from knowledge——!" Lance exclaimed as if with a sufficient indication of his futility.

It might have been at the futility that Peter appeared for a little to gaze. "I think it must have been—without my quite at the time knowing it—to keep *me*!" he replied at last as he turned away.